The Case of

the

Overheard

Remark

E. L. Murray

The Second Cotswold Mystery

The author, Ray Henderson, writes under the pseudonym, E.L. Murray. He moved from his home in Scotland to London to begin a career in the Civil Service. Several career moves later, he started The Private Investor, an investment magazine, with his business partner. Later, he trained as a hypnotherapist. He lives in East Sussex.

Also by E.L. Murray:

Moveable Assets

Re:Moveable Assets

Murder Lurks

I would like to thank all the friends who have been a constant source of support throughout the writing of this book.

Special mention for Matt Oxley and James Watson without whose help this book would only be available in longhand!

Published by Faraday Publications, Hove, England

This paperback edition published 2017

Prologue

The murderer gazed through the crenellated window. His concentration absolute.

A hurried glance at the annoyingly loud ticking clock on the wall made him realise he'd been watching and listening for the best part of an hour. Both senses, on high alert, were beginning to wane, but in the end, the ears won, they heard it first before the eyes saw it - the taxi approaching the main gate.

He watched as the passenger alighted into the light rain that had been falling for most of the morning. Struggling to open an umbrella, the passenger clung tightly to a package under his arm before paying the fare.

The murderer's eyes were drawn to that package. The knowledge of what was inside had, at times, driven him close to the borders of madness. Now it was within his grasp and soon it would be his...but not before certain things had been done. Then, it would be his.

As the taxi drew away, the passenger stood for a moment, umbrella overhead, admiring the mighty edifice standing on the slight incline beyond the rusting gates. The medieval building with its great pointed arches and huge flying buttresses was situated in its own grounds of about five or six acres. Originally built in the twelfth century, the stonework was still in remarkable condition considering what had happened to buildings of this type in the mid-sixteenth century.

This was the passenger's first visit to the place but he was familiar with its history - all of its history.

The last but one owner, Sir Fergus MacDorn-Smythe, whose forebears made the family fortune inventing a way of speeding up the dyeing process at the beginning of the Industrial Revolution, left it in his will to the present owners. That was over one hundred years ago.

Next to the gate and looking totally incongruous in this setting was a red telephone box.

'I wonder if that's been there since the place was built?' the exhausted passenger laughed softly to himself before pushing at the rusty gate which gave way reluctantly, creaking like the mast of an old sailing ship.

The sound of the passenger's shoes slipping on the wet gravel of the tree-lined driveway as he walked towards the porticoed front entrance galvanised this callous murderer; it was time.

He quickly took the few steps to the front door and opened it.

'Senor Tartaglia?' enquired the murderer obsequiously using the alias the passenger had travelled under.

'Er...er, si, yes' replied the man hesitantly, not used to answering to this name, while shaking his umbrella and placing it in the hallstand inside the door.

'Please, allow me to show you to your room and let you get out of those wet clothes. Then, perhaps, a nice hot drink, hm?'

'Si, si, that would be nice. Er...when will I meet...' began 'Senor Tartaglia' in heavily accented English.

'He's in a meeting at present otherwise he would have greeted you himself. But he will be free shortly' responded the murderer brusquely, halting any further enquiries.

'Bene, bene' the man replied, happy to have the opportunity to freshen up before performing his duty.

The murderer led the man up the main staircase to a comfortably furnished suite of rooms on the first floor. As an honoured guest, the man had been allocated their very best room.

'This is very nice' commented the man in an accent which the murderer was well- acquainted with. The guest removed his coat, hat and scarf to reveal his true identity. The murderer gave a slight bow as he clasped his hands together and smiled but said nothing.

Carefully placing his precious cargo on a small table situated between two tall windows overlooking the driveway, the honoured guest stood for a moment looking out over the scene before him. He was captivated by everything the wet English Spring day had to offer: trees, grass, flower heads, all glistened as the raindrops continued to fall. Despite the weather, the trees were full of birds chirping happily - the worms would be coming up for air soon.

He turned back into the room, feeling the urge to comment on the natural beauty of the place just as the heavy brass candlestick swung towards his head. He raised his arms defensively and let out a cry.

The full force of the candlestick came crashing down on his skull silencing the strangulated cry. He died instantly, his eyes wide in astonishment, as if to say 'Why?' A question the honoured guest would never know the answer to.

In less than a minute, panicked voices could be heard in the corridor. Doors were opened then slammed shut. Within moments, the owners of those voices would reach the room where the murderer still stood over the body.

'Damn!' thought the murderer frantically. Still holding the bloodied candlestick, he grabbed the package from the table and hurried over to the fireplace. He twisted the heavily-carved figure of a cherub on the left-hand side of the stone fireplace. The whole frame swung silently open. Inside, a dark passage with a staircase leading downwards was revealed. There were many such secret passages in this place: the murderer knew them all.

With no time to spare, he ducked into the passageway. Clasping the package underarm with the candlestick gripped firmly in his free hand, he pulled a hidden handle; the fireplace returned to its original position as the door to the room flew open.

Not really the sort of welcome a senior prelate from Rome would expect within the confines of an English Dominican monastery in the middle of the Gloucestershire countryside.

One

One week earlier

If anyone had told Miss Hilary B Lavender, Librarian of the County of Gloucestershire, that she would find herself embroiled in a scandal involving one of the oldest and most respected aristocratic families in the land, a Papal Delegate, an assortment of dead bodies and a 'mysterious package', she would have laughed loudly and thundered: 'Ridiculous!', accompanied by the most dismissive wave of the hand.

Indeed, if it were not for Miss Lavender's kind offer to retrieve an item which had been lodged at a jeweller's in Cheltenham one month earlier by one of her housebound readers, there would, most certainly, have been a lot more bodies to add to the list of the dead.

It all began one morning in early Spring. Tuesdays: Miss Lavender's favourite day of the week. Tuesdays meant half-days and the game of kings: bridge. The perfect day.

Within fifteen minutes of rising from her bed, Miss Lavender, known to her close friends as Boo, was taking her morning constitutional with her faithful companion, Hamish, a member of the West Highland Terrier fraternity. The field behind her cottage, on the outskirts of Cheltenham, was teeming with rabbits breakfasting assiduously on the local farmer's turnip crop in the early morning mist, that is, until they caught sight of Hamish charging up the hill at them. Breakfast interrupted, the rabbits returned to their burrows until the danger had passed.

'I don't know why you bother, Hamish, you never catch them. But I admire your tenacity; you never give up, do you, you rascal!" she called out as she watched him scurrying around after the long-eared creatures bouncing over the furrows at a rate of knots that Hamish could never hope to match.

This particular morning, Miss Lavender was preoccupied. After a few minutes of 'Should I or shouldn't I?' she decided to wait and ask Sextus what he thought when he came over that evening for the weekly bridge game.

Sextus Phipps MPS (retired), he, of the walrus moustache and more than ample girth, was Boo's closest friend and bridge partner of many years. Tonight, they would be joined by their opponents: Mildred Bennett, besuited, chain-smoking railway worker and demon card-counter and her own long-standing bridge partner, Kitty Wardrop, tall and willowy with a brain as sharp as a butcher's knife, who also happened to be the owner of the most sophisticated couturier shop in Cheltenham.

The crispness of the morning air caused Boo to shiver and brought her thoughts back to the evening's festivities.

She made up her mind as she reached the top of the field. 'It'll have to be meringues. Yes, that's it; salmon and cucumber sandwiches with meringues to follow. That should keep the starvation at bay for Sextus'. She tittered to herself at the thought of her friend's less than modest appetite.

After Miss Lavender and Hamish had broken their fast (Miss Lavender with a strong cup of tea and Hamish with his usual doggie biscuits) they set off in Miss Lavender's car along the lane to Dumpty's. As usual, she was waiting by the gate.

Known to one and all as 'Dumpty', Doris Wall, as her birth certificate stated, became 'Dumpty' forever when a childhood classmate decided that she was the 'Wall' which Humpty had fallen from. Hamish was like an only child to Dumpty, she doted on him.

'Morning, Dumpty' Miss Lavender called out as she opened the passenger door to let Hamish out.

'And good morning to you, Miss Lavender' replied Dumpty in her broad Gloucestershire drawl. 'Well, some bloomin' good news at last, Miss Lavender, the first buds have just appeared on my Glory-in-the-Snow this morning! Let's hope it mean this cold weather will be moving on. I, for one, have had my fill of that cold, North wind blowing all the way down from those Scotch Highlands. Brrr' the diminutive bow-legged horticulturist shivered, rubbing her hands together. Dressed in dungarees tucked into a pair of wellies, Dumpty was the quintessential Gloucestershire land girl. Although the war had finished over a decade earlier, she still dressed as if she was going out to tend the fields while the men were away at war.

Miss Lavender did not bother to point out to Dumpty that "Scotch" was a popular drink which may indeed have emanated from the Highlands of Scotland but did not refer to that country nor its mountainous terrain.

'I do know what you mean, Dumpty, it has been absolutely horrid this year. But isn't it amazing what a few days of warm sunshine can do for the plants?'

'Just what I was thinking this morning! Usual time, Miss Lavender?' asked Dumpty, getting back to business.

'Yes, please. See you later. And be a good boy for Dumpty, Hamish' Miss Lavender commanded as she drove off, all the time watching the two pals playing in her rear-view mirror.

Two

No more than twelve minutes later, Miss Lavender pulled up at the back of Cheltenham District Library where 'Old Blunder', the library bus she drove around the Cotswold villages, was parked. The bus had a rather annoying habit of backfiring when one least expected it and often frightened entire populations of the Cotswold villages it visited. "A twenty-one gun salute" was one of the more repeatable descriptions of the sound it made.

After checking that no-one had made off with her precious cargo during the night, Miss Lavender entered the Library building and spent the next hour catching up with paperwork. With that out of the way for another week, she started up Old Blunder and drove towards her first stop of the morning: Bibury, a pretty little village in the Cotswolds, described by William Morris, the artist, as "the most beautiful village in England".

Feeling particularly seasonal, she was humming the opening bars of "Spring" from Vivaldi's Four Seasons as she put her trusty bus through its paces.

Innocently or perhaps foolishly, she imagined, as she hummed away merrily to herself, that her sleuthing days were over. Just how wrong can one person be on a Spring morning driving around the Cotswolds? A bit like old King Priam thinking that there was no way the Greeks would get into Troy. And we all know how wrong he got that!

'Nothing's happened for ages' she sighed with just a hint of disappointment as she turned into the narrow lane, leading to her parking spot by the local church hall.

She turned off the engine to be greeted by a great cacophony of sound.

The whole of Nature seemed to be out in force.

'Goodness gracious, it sounds like a Bartok Symphony' she reckoned as she opened the folding doors of the bus and walked down the stairs. Mr Bartok was not her most favourite composer; she preferred her music a little more melodic.

Indeed, Nature's choir seemed to be in full swing in the fields just beyond the wall where Old Blunder was parked.

To the naked ear, the bass line was supplied by the mooing cows in the nearby field while several dozen assorted species of bird were merrily chirping out the melody from the branches of the surrounding trees, reminding Miss Lavender of the choir stalls of St Paul's Cathedral which she had once visited. The mid-section, was provided by the sheep in the field next to the cows.

Miss Lavender was tempted to add her own voice to it but then thought twice about it.

'It would be a shame to spoil it'

But spoilt it was.

'Morning, Miss Lavender' came a gruff voice from behind her.

Miss Lavender did not have to use her specially-manufactured mirrored spectacles to know who that was. Although the mirrors which she'd had specially inserted on the inside of her spectacles frame had, on more than one occasion, proved their usefulness, especially with the light-fingered variety of borrower, on this occasion, she instantly knew that the voice belonged to Colonel Charles Forbes. Strictly speaking, as he was retired, it should have been Mr Forbes, or, wondered Miss Lavender mischievously, 'How pleasing it would be if one could address him as "ex-Colonel Forbes"?' But the fact was he positively wallowed in the title.

'Good morning to you, Colonel Forbes. Beautiful day, don't you think?' replied Miss Lavender turning to face the oncoming military man who, much as Boo hated to admit it, did look very dapper in his green tweed suit with a rich brown paisley-patterned waistcoat, his fedora at a jaunty angle and moustache neatly trimmed. The colonel towered over the diminutive rotund figure of Miss Lavender or as the French would have described her, 'rondelette'. That day, she herself was wearing her favourite two-piece black and grey suit of Prince of Wales check. She'd once worn the pattern and been complimented on how it suited her complexion and since then, every day, at least one item of her clothing comprised of the wonderful Prince of Wales check which she discovered came in a surprising variety of colours and materials.

'What? What? Er...yes, quite' was the "I hadn't really bothered to notice, actually" reply. 'Must crack on. What!' declared the man who spoke to everyone around him as if they were under his command.

'I wonder if I could ask you to revel in the joys of Spring for just a few moments longer, Colonel, while I set things up?' requested Miss Lavender who, although not a clock-watcher, was aware that strictly speaking, it was only ten to ten and she had only just arrived. Apart from anything else, if the truth be known, Boo Lavender did not respond easily to petty, small-minded, nit-picking, overbearing, high-handed, bossy sorts of people. And the Colonel fell into not a few of those categories.

'If I must' was the frosty reply on the sort of day which had produced so much timeless, awe-inspiring poetry.

'Thank you so much' was the equally wintry response from Miss Lavender as she mounted the stairs of Old Blunder to prepare for the onslaught. Although, in the case of Bibury, this amounted to about twenty people over the course of the hour she would be there. So, perhaps "trickle" would best describe it.

She made a point of closing the folding doors.

'Now then,' she reflected, removing the Colonel from her consciousness as she moved along the corridor, patting some of the books back into place which had been jostled out of position during the bumpy ride 'I wonder what today has in store?'

As was her habit before the borrowers arrived, Boo moved slowly along the rows of books on automatic pilot removing 'The Life and Times of Lord Palmerston' from Gardening and returning it to the History section.

'If I was a gambler, which I am not, I would say that whoever perused this, saw the picture on the front cover of the formal gardens of Lord Palmerston's country house and without thinking, put it back in the Gardening section. Honestly, the brain can play some funny old tricks' she pondered, picking up another errant tome. 'A pretty picture of Marie Antoinette on the front cover and where do they file it? Romantic fiction. And the title? "The Reign of Terror". One wonders sometimes what gear their brains are in. Reverse, in the case of these ones, I shouldn't wonder!' she hooted to herself.

Some voices, deep in conversation, could be heard approaching the bus when one of them broke off and hollered:

'Are we open for business yet, Colonel?"

'Not yet, Miss Devonshire. I've been asked to "revel in the joys of Spring" for a few minutes. Bah!' the grumpy old ex-soldier exclaimed.

'Oh well,' answered Miss Devonshire, who knew how cantankerous the Colonel could be from his frequent visits to her ex-employers '...no doubt Miss Lavender will let us know when she's ready'

'Thank you for that, Maisy' Miss Lavender thought gratefully as she passed her gaze one final time along the rows of books making sure everything was...as it should be.

'I feel like a shop assistant at Wards of Cheltenham just before the doors open for the first day of the Christmas sale...waiting for the rush'

But, of course, this was Bibury and the rush didn't quite happen. In fact, when Miss Lavender folded back the doors for business, there were four people waiting: Maisy Devonshire, the two sisters, Elizabeth and Margery Whittam, owners of a large chunk of the County and not forgetting cheery Charlie himself, Colonel Forbes.

'Good morning, everybody. Isn't it a glorious day?' Miss Lavender boomed from the top of the stairs.

'It is indeed, Miss Lavender' responded Miss Margery, the less frostier of the two sisters, looking around, taking in the vista. 'Truly wonderful' she sighed.

'I can imagine Wordsworth writing "I wandered lonely as a cloud" on a day like today' offered Maisy, who had a very vivid imagination which she gave full rein to in her choice of reading: detective thrillers.

'Why so can I!' Miss Margery declared with gusto. A concurrence she would regret for the rest of the day.

'Can you?' her incredulous sister, Miss Elizabeth, the female equivalent of, and more than a match for the Colonel, asked.

'Well, I was only saying...' began Miss Margery backpedalling to her own defence.

'Yes, quite!' the old grump himself interjected exasperatedly. 'Now may we get on with choosing our books?'

'Why, of course, Colonel. Do come on up' Miss Lavender insisted, jumping in to avert another World War quite so soon after the last one.

The Colonel marched up the stairs at the head of the "troops" and had his books stamped in first.

He was followed by the warring factions, Miss Elizabeth and Miss Margery both of whom stood, purse-lipped, each looking out opposite sides of the bus with one of those 'this isn't over yet' silences during the whole process.

'If Miss Elizabeth holds that head of hers any higher, she won't be looking down her nose at the rest of humanity, she'll be permanently looking at cloud formations' determined Miss Lavender, her feathers ever so slightly ruffled.

'Thank you' was the dismissive riposte from Miss Elizabeth as she flounced off to her favourite section: historical novels.

Miss Margery was a little more communicative.

'How have you been keeping, Miss Lavender?' she asked in a kind-hearted sort of way.

'I'm very well, Margery. Thank you for asking. And yourself?"

'Can't complain' she replied, looking archedly at her sister's retreating back.

'We've got a couple of new biographies which came in yesterday and from memory, they haven't been taken out yet. I think you'll find they're right up your street'

'Sounds wonderful, Miss Lavender. I'll have a look' and off she toddled.

Maisy, who was at the back of the queue, walked up to the desk and Miss Lavender whispered:

'"The Busman's Honeymoon" has only just come in, Maisy. I know you've been waiting for such a long time for it but Lord Peter Wimsey stories are so popular. Anyway, it's here now'

'I am so excited!' declared Maisy cheerily. She paused and then dropping her voice in consideration for the other browsers, she asked:

'I'll bet you won't be able to guess where I'll be this afternoon, Boo?'

'Oh, I couldn't possibly' the Librarian responded, feigning innocence. 'But let me try. Could it be at the kitchen table of a rather pretty little cottage not a million miles from this spot with a large pot of strong tea and a particular book?' ventured the woman who knew her borrowers so well.

'I am not prepared to say' giggled Maisy 'but...you could be right'

'Well, Lord Peter won't last you long, will he? You'd better go and find some others to keep you going'

'I shall' Maisy responded with gusto floating down towards the crime fiction shelves.

'If only we could all be content with such small pleasures. Nowadays, people seem to be less and less content with what they have and want more and more of what they don't have'

With thoughts like that going around in her head, Miss Lavender sat pondering the state of the world and the people in it while she waited for her browsers to make their choices.

'I still find it hard to believe what Mrs Holloway of Shurdington Road told me the other day. I mean, can it possibly be true? A schoolboy sat in his seat and didn't get up to offer it to an adult who was left to stand? What is this world we live in, coming to?'

As she tried to get her head around this particularly strange, unheard of, situation, the Colonel approached with his six book allowance.

'I'd like to take these, please' he said, using the minimum number of words required for politeness.

'Certainly' enthused Miss Lavender, who was determined not to let the Colonel leave feeling peeved. 'I'm so sorry I kept you waiting, Colonel, it really was very remiss of me not to have everything ready. So, do please accept my apologies'

A very smart cookie is Miss Hilary B Lavender. On a personal level, she found the Colonel's behaviour unacceptable. However, 'he is a borrower' and it was her duty to keep all of her borrowers happy.

A rather flummoxed Colonel huffed and puffed and in the end produced the most raffish smile saying:

'Really, there's no need, Miss Lavender. It was my fault, I was early. And do you know, it is a delightful morning. The sort of day where one could take a stroll and...'

Fortunately for Miss Lavender, she was rescued by Maisy who dropped one of her books as she approached the 'stamping in and out' desk.

'Allow me to retrieve that for you, dear lady' the Colonel offered, reaching down for the delinquent volume.

'Why, thank you so much, Colonel' Maisy replied graciously with the slightest of blushes.

'In fact, would you allow me to carry them home for you?' ventured the Colonel.

'That would be most kind. Thank you again' a suddenly demure Maisy Devonshire accepted.

Miss Lavender dutifully stamped their books out and watched as the two of them strolled along the lane together with the Colonel actually listening to Maisy.

'Well, I never!' she reflected: it was her turn to be flummoxed. 'It never ceases to amaze me how people's moods can change so quickly. From hot to cold and sometimes back again, quicker than you can turn over the page of the book you're reading'

For the next hour or so, Boo had the opportunity to ponder more than once on the chameleonic Colonel.

'And he's not alone' was the conclusion she came to, thinking about the motley collection of borrowers who frequented Old Blunder.

About five minutes after the Colonel and Maisy had departed, Boo heard a booming voice chiding some of the wayward children of the village who were up to some sort of mischief.

'Now come down from that tree this instant, children, you know you're not supposed to climb up there, you little rascals!'

'Yes, Mrs Eldridge' the children called out, who were still laughing as they climbed down from wherever the little tykes were. At least, with Mrs Eldridge they knew that they weren't going to get a cuff around the ear.

'Morning, everyone' Primrose Eldridge continued booming as she climbed the stairs of Old Blunder.

'Good Morning, Primrose' was the reply from everyone on the bus as noses were removed from deep inside books. Interestingly, Miss Lavender noted, everyone was smiling.

'She's like a breath of fresh air' Boo concluded as she joined the smiling club.

'And how are you, Boo?' the booming chider of children asked.

'Very well, thank you, Primrose. And yourself and John?' The Reverend John Eldridge had been the vicar of All Saints in the village for almost twenty years.

'Oh, the usual. You know John, Boo. If he's not ministering to his flock, he's translating some mediaeval religious text or other' she replied as she spotted two of her husband's parishioners, the Misses Whittam. 'And how are you girls?' she enquired of the two Misses whom everyone referred to as 'the girls' even though they were eighty if they were a day. 'Looking very sprightly on this gorgeous Spring day if I may say so. Oh, I could write poetry on days like this' she gushed.

'Well, thank you, Primrose...and I do know what you mean about days like this. Don't you agree, Elizabeth?' Margery asked in her sweetest voice, '... which may have been tinged with just a hint of sarcasm' Miss Lavender thought '...or a large dollop'

'Er...er...yes, I suppose one could' Elizabeth, who would never disagree with the clergyman's wife, admitted grudgingly.

'Game, set and match to Margery unless I'm misreading that Cheshire cat grin on her face' Miss Lavender decided.

'Sorry,' Primrose went on 'I've distracted you all from your reading but I couldn't help it. I just wanted to share the joys of days like these. We should have more of them, I say'

'Hear, hear!' echoed Mrs Phillips of Trout Cottage, who'd just picked up that new biography as the commotion was going on.

If looks could kill, Mrs Phillips would have had serious need of the vicar's services.

'There go those mood swings again' Miss Lavender observed as she sat at her desk watching the proceedings. 'Sometimes we don't get two in the same day and here we've had two in the space of ten minutes. One minute Margery's celebrating her victory with a smile that could sell a million tubes of toothpaste and the next, a glare that could stop a rampaging bull elephant in its tracks'

Luckily for poor old Mrs Phillips, she read the first paragraph and then returned the book to the shelf completely unaware that her life had been hanging by the borrowing of a book!

'Phew, thank goodness for that' thought the relieved Librarian, slowly releasing the breath she'd been holding. 'I don't think I could cope with any more drama today'

A very relieved Margery immediately scooped up the book before it had time to settle down properly between Marie Lloyd and Lord Nelson.

'Margery's clearly taking no chances on someone else taking a peek at it' Boo assumed as she stamped out Elizabeth's books.

'Wait for me, dear' Margery called out in a slightly panicked voice to her sister.

'Well, hurry up then! I haven't got all day. I've got important letters to write' insisted the temporarily beaten but definitely not defeated sister.

'Yes, dear' came the chastened reply.

'Bless!' Boo thought. 'That was one of the shortest victory celebrations I've ever witnessed'

Margery had her choices duly stamped out. Fortunately for Miss Lavender, there were no further incidents before she closed the doors and indulged in her eleven o'clock ritual.

The eleventh hour of the day: sheer and utter bliss! Since childhood, Boo came as close to Paradise as is possible for a member of the human race to experience ...without having to die.

Put another way, the three (not two, which, of course, were totally inadequate or four, which could be seen as completely overindulgent) ginger nut biscuits were the secret route to Boo's Heaven.

While Boo poured a steaming hot cup of tea from her flask and gently nibbled on the first biscuit, her thoughts turned again to Mrs Phillips and her membership of a curious club. It consisted of a band of people whom Miss Lavender referred to as her 'interesting readers'. Whereas most of her readers had a particular niche interest such as autobiographies or crime or science fiction, the 'interesting readers' (of whom there quite a few dotted around her fiefdom) chose their reading material for 'the content' rather than sheepishly following a writer or subject. Membership of the club was completely at Miss Lavender's discretion and none of the members were aware of their elevate status.

For instance, on her last visit, Mrs Phillips borrowed 'Existentialism is a Humanism' by the philosopher Jean-Paul Sartre alongside one of Enid Blyton's 'Secret Seven' adventures together with 'Genghis Khan: Emperor of All Men'...and so it was with the rest of the club. The diversity and eclectic nature of their choices fascinated the Librarian.

She often wondered if their reason for doing so was about exercising different parts of the brain based on the old theory of "use it or lose it".

After twenty minutes of crunching on her Heavenly manna, Boo sat herself down in the driving seat and drove off towards her next stop: the village of Burford.

Three

The visit to Burford passed without Miss Lavender having to don her referee's hat; the people of Burford clearly less quarrelsome than their neighbours in nearby Bibury.

By two o'clock, Old Blunder had been parked back at the Library in Cheltenham and Boo drove her little green Austin of England motor car back home in the gayest of moods humming the Bach-Gounod 'Ave Maria'.

'We shall crush the enemy!' Boo declared in a loud voice as she parked up outside Dumpty's. 'Kitty and Mildred won't know what's happened to them. Sir Sextus the Conqueror and the fair Lady Lavender shall be victorious!'

'What was that?' Dumpty asked as she stood upright, rubbing the stiffness out of her back from weeding the flowerbeds in the front garden. Miss Lavender had failed to notice her friend.

'You're never far away from a pair of ears' Boo realised. If only she knew how prophetic that thought would turn out to be.

'Oh, Dumpty, I didn't see you there. I was just getting excited about tonight'

'I dunno. Bloomin' bridge! It's so complicated, Miss Lavender. I likes trumps myself'

'It's not that much different to trumps, you know, Dumpty. With the exception, of course, that there are occasions when a murder could easily take place!'

The conversation was cut short by the Charge of the Light Brigade around the corner in the guise of Hamish.

'Hello, Hamish. Have you been a good boy for Dumpty?' she asked as she picked him up and surrendered to more kisses than Casanova had had in his entire life!

'Good as gold, he's been' a beaming Dumpty answered.

'Well, we'll be off then. I've got a lot to do for this evening. Bye-bye, Dumpty. See you tomorrow. Give Dumpty a kiss before we go, Hamish'

With that, Hamish ran over to Dumpty, tail wagging like a metronome at top speed.

'See you tomorrow, little man' Dumpty said succumbing to the onslaught of licks.

Four

As soon as she was through the door, Boo started. She buffed cushions, flicked the duster at the bridge table and chairs, which occasionally doubled as a dining suite, straightened an ornament here, an antimacassar there and then it was into the kitchen.

Meringues: one of Sextus' favourites. Boo whisked up a bowl of egg whites and castor sugar in no time at all and then popped them into the oven on greaseproof paper while she opened a tin of red salmon and sliced the cucumber very thinly.

'This should keep us going' she decided piling the generously-filled thick crusty bread sandwiches onto a large plate. She covered them with a slightly damp tea towel. '…and that should keep them fresh. Hmm, another thirty minutes and those meringues will be ready but I'd better hide them then before...'

She didn't even have time to finish the thought before there was a loud rat-a-tat tatting on the doorknocker. 'So much for that idea' she thought resignedly as she passed along the hallway to open the door to...surprise, surprise...her bridge partner, Mr Sextus Phipps MPS (retired).

'Oh, hello Boo' he beamed. 'Thought I'd get here early to see if you needed any help' he lied beautifully.

'Sextus Phipps,' Boo said in her sternest voice, 'the only hand you want to offer is the one which moves food from the plate to your mouth' She paused before sighing and saying: 'I suppose you'd better come in'

'Oh, Boo, how could you?' Sextus retorted in his most offended tone as he sniffed the air looking for clues as to what was on the menu that night.

This was part of the ritual between the two friends when it was Boo's turn to provide the refreshments, where Boo would pretend to be terribly annoyed at his early arrival whilst Sextus would feign complete mortification at Boo's cynical belief that the only reason he was there early was to fill his boots before the competition arrived. Which, if the truth be known, had more than a slight ring of truth to it.

'Seriously though, Boo, is there anything I can do?' her crestfallen friend asked.

'Yes, there is actually'

'Ask away' Sextus replied perking up.

'Yes! You can...not eat the meringues' the hostess said sternly.

'You're making meringues?' asked the man with the rumbling tum, his hopes rising. (but alas, as yet, not the meringues)

'Yes, I am...and they're not ready yet. So there!'

'Oh, Boo, how could you be so cruel?' came back the riposte.

'Very easily, actually. I'm not long in so I couldn't have made them any quicker'

'Then you are forgiven, my child' intoned her bridge partner, dropping his voice in that 'Bless you, my child' voice a vicar uses to one of his flock.

'Why, thank you, Bishop Phipps' she replied laughing. 'Talking of which, I need to have a word with you about an unusual request we've had at the Library'

'Pray tell...what would that be?' asked the man who recognised 'the signs'.

'Sextus, I can't believe all these references to religion. It's almost like it's an omen'

'Whatever do you mean, Mother Superior Lavender?'

'Oh, Sextus you really are the limit!' Boo chortled. 'Alright, just let me check my meringues and then we can have a cup of tea...'

'...and perhaps a little sustenance to keep Mount Etna from rumbling?' interrupted Sextus, whose brain appeared to be located adjacent to his bellybutton.

'Yes, of course, you poor lamb! How long has it been since you last saw food? Minutes...hours?' The friendly banter was never far away between these two.

'Hours, actually' the Mortally Offended One sniffed.

'Come on then, let's see what we can do to alleviate your suffering' Boo relented leading the way through to the kitchen.

'Mm, mmm!' was all Sextus could say as he entered the kitchen and wafts of gorgeous smells floated out to greet his olfactory protuberance.

'Just in time' announced Boo. 'Another minute and you'd have needed a sledgehammer to get through these'

'Funnily enough, Boo, I just happen to have one in the boot of my car' was the response from the man who would not have let a minor detail like that get in the way.

Boo removed the meringues and left them on the side while she made a fresh pot of tea and cut some of her thick crusty bread and applied lashings of butter and homemade strawberry jam for her victually-deprived friend.

'That's it, Sextus Phipps, you can like it or lump it. Now that Etna's in the process of settling down, may I please tell you my interesting little story?'

'Abso...loo...telly' replied the mouth with the jam-fringed moustache.

'I thought I might pass it by you because you are of the faith, if you know what I mean' Boo started.

'Pardon?' managed Sextus.

'You are of the Roman Church?'

'Oh, you mean Catholic?'

'Quite so' Boo confirmed. 'Well, we, and specifically myself, have been asked to catalogue the library of the Dominican monastery near Moreton-in-the-Marsh. Apparently one of my regular borrowers recommended me to the Abbot, whom I believe you know, Sextus?'

'Do you mean Dom Ambrose?'

'The same. It will take a week or so to complete. It's quite small but sorely in need of some TLC...and organising, of course'

'That could be quite interesting, Boo. Do you fancy it?'

'Actually, I'm not sure, Sextus'

'What do you mean?'

'Well as you know, I am of the Anglican faith and at the 'Low' end of it at that and I'm not sure about all the Latin and...the incense and all the paraphernalia'

'But Boo, I thought you were cataloguing the Library, not converting, darling'

'Well...yes...but...' Boo was lost for words.

'And let me tell you,' continued Sextus 'the smell of incense brings back happy childhood memories for me of when I was an altarboy. And a very happy childhood it was. And having used Latin for most of my working life as a chemist, I have no problem with that either. In fact, I rather enjoy High Mass being sung by the monks in the Abbey. You should try listening to it sometime, Boo. It's beautiful'

'Y...e...s' replied the not terribly convinced Librarian. 'And what about the monks themselves? How do you address them and do they speak? Are they allowed to speak to women? I mean...' Sextus could hear the uncertainty creeping into her voice.

'You'll be fine, Boo. Come to think of it, I wouldn't mind doing a bit of a retreat for a few days myself. Perhaps I could do it at the same time as you're doing your cataloguing and then we could meet up in the evenings. A little silent contemplation might do me the world of good. Hmm, you've got me thinking now'

'That would be excellent, Sextus. I wouldn't feel quite so alone then. So, if you're going to do it, then I'll agree to do the job' a relieved Boo said.

'Righto! It's a deal, Miss Lavender. I'll keep quiet during the day and let you get on with your job and at night we can raise the roof'

'I don't think that would be appropriate, Sextus. Do you?' asked the momentarily- flustered Librarian.

'Only joking, Boo. But I tell you what; Dom Ambrose is a pretty sharp bridge player when he gets the chance. And I'll bet there will be one of the other monks who plays. So, with a bit of luck and a fair wind, we might be able to get a game in, in the evenings'

'Gregorian chant to my ears, my dear Sextus. I can't wait to go now' replied a much re-assured Boo. 'Now let me get back to my meringues, will you?' She was so excited, she floated over to the other side of the kitchen humming Saint-Saens' 'The Swan'.

'There's no need to watch my back so intently, Sextus Phipps!' Boo called out as she carefully transferred the meringues from the greaseproof paper to a plate. 'Not only have I been watching you through my 'all-seeing' spectacles but I could feel your eyes boring into my back. It was like a very sharp knife being slowly twisted between my shoulder blades. You are a...monster!'

'Well I'm glad I'm not the only one prone to exaggeration'

'Whatever do you mean?' an astonished Boo asked now that the roles were reversed. Nevertheless, she brought one of the meringues over, knowing that Sextus probably had left a little 'space' to 'test' her handiwork.

Fangs were sunk in and complimentary comments mumbled between mouthfuls.

'Now then, Sextus, Mildred and Kitty beat the pants off us last week. So, what are we going to do about it this week?'

'It was a fluke, Boo. I miscounted the spades on the last deal and it did not help that they were vulnerable, doubled, redoubled. Lucky cats' Sextus said referring to the opponents in rather uncharacteristic, uncharitable language. Only those of us who understand the world of bridge-speak will have any understanding of his previous sentence.

'They may be, as you say, Sextus, lucky cats, but we simply cannot allow it to happen again this week'

Boo Lavender could be, and was, the most charming, kind-hearted, considerate person one could ever wish to meet but when it came to competing at bridge...that was another matter altogether. It brought out the tigress in her.

'We won't, Boo. Never fear' was Sextus' reckless reply.

'I do hope so, Mr Phipps. I'm relying on you to count properly this week' the optimistic hostess chirped.

After ten minutes of running through their bidding sequences, there was a knock at the door.

'Probably Mildred' Boo said. 'Kitty could never get away this early from the shop. She's always the last to leave. But that's what happens when you're the boss'

It was Mildred.

'Hello, Mildred' Boo said sniffing the air. 'I've heard of people bringing their work home with them but this is ridiculous'

'What'd you mean?'

'Based on the reek of smoke from your uniform, Mildred, I'd say most of the trains were on time today. Would I be correct?'

'Well, yes, they were. But...does it smell?' Mildred asked sniffing at the lapels of her three-piece suit.

'Unsurprisingly, Mildred dear, like a train station'

Little did she know that her short, dark, slick-backed hair was not entirely free of the pungent smell either!

'Well I'll be blowed! I can't smell a thing. Amazing, isn't it?' she said as she continued to sniff the air, trying to catch a whiff of what Boo was talking about. 'I dunno' she mumbled shrugging her shoulders, more to herself than to Boo.

'Good evening, Mildred' Sextus bellowed from the kitchen as he wet his fingers to pick up the last remaining crumbs of his meringue. 'Are you ready for battle?' he said throwing down the gauntlet.

'I am' Mildred replied defiantly. 'And are you ready to be pulverised again like last week?' Mildred could come back as quick as a flash. Over the years of dealing with the public, she'd learned when to bite her tongue and when not to. And this was a 'when not to' situation...take cover!

'Er...er' was the feeble response.

'Exactly, Mr Phipps. Put that in your pipe and smoke it' Mildred declared, pushing her advantage.

'Please, no more smoke' pleaded Boo. 'Apart from your Senior Service, Mildred, of course'

'I don't mind if I do' said Mildred lighting up and doing her impersonation of one of her trains at full throttle.

'For goodness sake, Mildred' Sextus said exasperatedly as he left the kitchen waving his hands around like a Dutch windmill to dissipate the clouds drifting towards him.

'Serves you right, Mr Phipps' Mildred replied smirking, belching smoke like the Flying Scotsman.

'Enough!' Boo cried out. 'Let's call a truce until Kitty arrives'

'Ag...re...ed' Mildred offered reluctantly. She hated not being allowed to press her advantage.

'Oh, alright' agreed Sextus who was secretly relieved because when Mildred got the bit between her teeth...! Enough said.

They adjourned to the dining room and sat shuffling and re-shuffling the packs of cards at the card/dining table waiting for Kitty to arrive, which she duly did, five minutes later.

'Sorry I'm late' Kitty said as she sashayed in, smelling like the perfume counter of Swan & Edgars.

'Kitty, darling,' Sextus raved as he got a whiff of her 'you smell divine. What's that you've got on?'

'Oh, I never know' Kitty lied slickly. 'I just picked up one of the bottles from the counter and gave myself a quick squirt'. Anyone who knew Kitty Wardrop knew that nothing was left to chance. Even her entrance this evening was choreographed. The rustle and swish of the exquisite blue silk Italian dress whose colour matched her eyes perfectly; the carefully applied makeup, maybe just a touch too perfect; those elegantly sculpted silk-stockinged legs and, of course, the latest hairdo straight out of Vogue magazine. No, nothing was left to chance with this lady.

'Well, whatever it is, it's gorgeous!' he enthused.

'Well, that's not what you said to me' Mildred countered, throwing a spanner and caution into the works. Mildred had decided to press her advantage and wrong foot Mr Sextus Phipps MPS (retired) in the hope of unnerving him for the game tonight. 'After all' thought Mildred '...all is fair in love and war'

'What...I...' Sextus stuttered.

'Gottim!' thought Mildred gleefully, from behind a great belch of smoke.

'But I never...'

'Mildred Bennett, I know what your game is, you fiend' Boo declared vehemently as she realised what Mildred was up to. 'Don't let her get to you, Sextus. She's trying to throw you off your game tonight. Now then, ladies and gentleman, would you care for a cup of tea before we start?' she suggested, moving swiftly on.

'Oh, Boo, you ask us the same question every time and you know the answer. Let's get started' the glamourous one protested. 'By the way,' she continued, sniffing the air '...what is that smell?'

'Do not go there, Kitty' Boo said sternly.

'I only asked' was the chastened reply.

'Can we cut for deal?' Mildred declared, keen as mustard to get started.

Boo won with the King of Hearts and Sextus duly shuffled the cards and placed them in front of Kitty for her to cut.

'Phew' thought Boo as she dealt, 'that's the second time today we've just managed to avert World War lll'

The usual thrust and parry took place over the next hour or so with neither team gaining the upper hand. The only good news for Sextus and Boo was that their opponents missed a potential small slam.

'I think we'd have found it, Boo' Sextus goaded, playing Mildred at her own game.

'Oh, do shut up, Sextus' Boo and Kitty hollered in unison.

Mildred merely fumed, literally, with great gusts of smoke spewed out from her side of the table.

'Vengeance is mine saith the Lord' Mildred muttered under her breath and sure enough, two minutes later she brought home a difficult three hearts pre-emp to win the rubber.

'I think we'll break for some sustenance' Boo announced, sensing an atmosphere.

'Jolly good idea' agreed the sparrow in the blue silk dress.

'Boo, darling, if I can't fit into my dresses and look as gorgeous as possible, then how can I expect my clients to feel that they can achieve the same?' was Kitty's stock reply to Boo's enquiry about 'Not feeling hungry again, dear?'

So, everyone helped themselves to their own level of hunger, which meant Sextus was first and last at the trough, while Kitty inserted her first Sobranie of the evening into the bejewelled cigarette holder while nibbling at the edges of one of Boo's salmon and cucumber sandwiches. Boo was always amazed at how some people could eat and smoke simultaneously.

'I wonder what it tastes like, all that smoke and food mixed up at the same time?'

But, of course, she would never be so presumptuous as to ask.

This was the time of evening where the latest gossip would be exchanged.

'So do tell, Kitty; what's the latest news from the upper echelons of Cheltenham society?' Boo, who knew most of it already, enquired, thinking it polite to ask.

'Well...' and ten minutes passed as they listened spellbound to Kitty's revelations.

'So...it's true?' Mildred gasped in shock. 'The Honourable John Greyworth actually did...?' and Mildred wobbled her head from side to side, unable to say the actual words.

'Absolutely!' replied Kitty as she inhaled some more expensive smoke.

'Can you believe it?' Mildred asked still in shock and they all burst out laughing.

'I have a bit of news myself' Boo offered. 'But nothing of the magnitude of Kitty's' she said of her impending visit to the Abbey.

'...and so what it means is I shall have to give next week's session a miss. And such a pity because...it's Mildred's turn to cook. You have all the luck' Boo said to her friend, Mildred, whose turn would now pass her by.

The truth be told; they were all secretly relieved. Mildred's cooking was...how to put it delicately...well, the words 'sand mixer' and 'concrete' come to mind when one thinks of Mildred's valiant efforts!

Play resumed when there was no tea left in the pot to wash down the last remnants of Boo's spread. That, however, did not stop Sextus looking forlornly at the last meringue on the plate as he joined the others at the bridge table.

'Really, dear,' Kitty said at the end of the first hand, 'don't you think putting me into four spades with only four points was a little rash?' All of this said with the aforementioned bejewelled cigarette holder clenched sideways in the perfectly lipsticked lips as she dealt the next game.

'Shape. That's why I did it. Shape!' was Mildred's animated response. 'I thought you would have a chance to establish my clubs'

That Kitty had not mentioned clubs at that point seemed to have eluded Mildred.

However, her card-counting abilities redeemed her on the next hand when she doubled Boo's rash contract of four hearts vulnerable, which Boo later admitted to Sextus "...was probably a little too high" for what she was holding. The result was two light and five hundred penalty points to Kitty and Mildred for which Kitty duly congratulated her partner.

Despite that, the evening ended with a win for Boo and Sextus after one particularly bold bid and play by Mr Phipps.

As they donned their coats to leave, Kitty uttered what would turn out to be one of those 'how wrong can you be?' statements when she said: 'Oh well, enjoy your stay at the Abbey, Boo. I don't suppose you'll have much to report back when you return from your little jaunt'

Wrong!

Five

Two days later having returned Old Blunder to its parking spot at the rear of the Library, Boo made a detour on her way home into the centre of Cheltenham on an errand for one of her regular readers.

For a number of years now, Miss Enid Cosworthy had been housebound but thanks to Miss Lavender, she retained her sanity with an endless flow of books, books and more books.

'The Good Lord may have decided that this body should be confined within these four walls for the last remaining years of my life but the contract says nothing about my imagination!' she would often think as her precious books took her to places far beyond the four walls of the home she had lived in for her entire life.

It was on one of her regular drop offs that Miss Lavender found herself promising to pick up a certain item which had been sent for repair to a jeweller in Cheltenham.

'Why, Miss Cosworthy, I didn't even know you wore one' Miss Lavender remarked with surprise.

'Well, Miss Lavender, it wouldn't do to let too many people know, would it?' Miss Cosworthy admitted pulling back her hair to reveal a bulky hearing aid attached to her right ear with a wire leading down to a small box hanging from her neck by a strap and concealed behind a bulky Fair Isle sweater.

'Now don't go putting yourself out, Miss Lavender. It's my spare one but I have to have it just in case the batteries go on this one'

'Then I shall make sure I pick it up on my next visit to town' the kindly Librarian had promised.

Boo Lavender always kept her promises. Just as well.

Six

Boo reached Jackson's the jeweller as the owner, Mr Jackson Snr, was closing the door for the night. With one of those looks that say: 'why do people always leave it to the last minute?' he held the door open for Miss Lavender and invited her in. Miss Cosworthy's hearing aid duly retrieved and stored safely in her handbag, Boo set off homewards.

'Goodness gracious! That was a close one!' she muttered driving along the narrow lane leading to Daffodil Cottage, her home since childhood.

Wanting to get to the Abbey before dark, Boo rushed in, picking up her suitcase and shooed Hamish into the passenger seat of her little green Austin of England motorcar before dropping him off to Dumpty's for the duration of her stay at the Abbey.

She knew where Moreton-in-Marsh was, she just wasn't entirely sure she'd be able to find the Abbey but, as her mother had always told her: 'you've got a tongue in your head': she would use it if it became necessary.

Less than an hour later, she'd managed to find the monastery and pulled up in front of the rusting gates.

As she left the car, an unexpected gust of wind almost blew her black felt dress hat, adorned with a small brooch of diamante, off. Catching the hat and her breath, she absentmindedly flattened down the pleats of her light grey skirt in her favourite pattern, the Prince of Wales check. A short black jacket and plain, if rather severe, high-collared white blouse completed her outfit; all of them had been chosen the night before as appropriate for the job ahead. And thanks to Sextus, she had added one other important accessory to her wardrobe: a mantilla. Apparently, it was 'expected' that women should cover their head in church. So, always mindful of others' beliefs, Boo was happy to comply.

In the fading light, she approached the gates, her powers of observation on high alert, noting the high Victorian brick wall in a state of some dilapidation, the much earlier ornate building squatting behind them, the bright red telephone box which looked so out of place in these surroundings. The overall effect of the place made her shiver in the way that people do when they enter a crypt. Is it the chill in the air of those places or can some of us feel a presence? Whatever it was, Boo felt it right now, looking through the rusting bars at this place.

A noise behind her made her start but before turning, she checked in her mirrored spectacles, observing a cowled figure in black and white robes striding towards her.

'Hello' announced a very sonorous voice from inside the hood, the face yet to be revealed. 'Can I be of help?'

Boo swung around to face the approaching figure. Whoever it was could certainly move fast; before Boo even had a chance to reply, his long, loping strides brought him to within three feet of her.

'I hope you can, Father. My name is Miss Lavender and I'm here at the invitation of Dom Ambrose, the Abbot. I work as a Librarian at Cheltenham District Library and I've been requested to catalogue your book repository'

'The cataloguing!' exclaimed the still hidden face. 'Of course, it's part of our preparations for our anniversary. Welcome, Miss Lavender, I am Dom Ignatius, the Prior of Brackenbury Abbey. I am Dom Ambrose's Number Two. Let me open the gates for you and you can park your car inside'

As he moved forward, the cowl fell back to reveal a face which, to Boo's mind, in no way matched the pleasant, mellifluous voice.

'A cross between the bark of an old tree and a Basset Hound' was Miss Lavender's first impression. The face, weighted down with heavy wrinkles and jowls, was not at all a pleasant sight; the eyes, a faded watery blue. The head was topped with a smattering of white hair surrounding what looked to Miss Lavender like a tonsure. There was a brightness in the eyes and...something behind them which Miss Lavender couldn't quite place.

Uncomfortable images from the past began jostling in Miss Lavender's imagination as she returned to the car. She shook her head to disperse them.

'Now Boo,' she reproved herself as she opened the door 'control that imagination of yours. Honestly! You're visiting an

English monastery...and according to Sextus, one which is renowned for its deep spirituality and tranquillity'

Dom Ignatius threw open the reluctant gates and Boo sailed through driving up the short incline and parking the car at the front of the medieval building beside two others already parked there. The keen-eyed Librarian noted that none of the cars could be seen from the road due to the surrounding dense foliage.

As Boo stepped from the car, Dom Ignatius checked his watch saying: 'Supper will be served in the Refectory shortly, Miss Lavender. You'll join us, of course? One of those things about monastic life; routine. Everything happens at the same time every day. I'll also let the Abbot know that you've arrived and then he can chat with you about what exactly needs to be done'

At that point his offer became redundant as two figures, clad in the austere habit of the Order and deep in conversation, came around a corner of the building and saw Boo with the Prior. One of them broke into a smile.

'You must be Miss Lavender. Good evening, good evening. How do you do, I'm Dom Ambrose, the Abbot and this is Brother Joseph, our Bursar. I see you've already met our Prior, Dom Ignatius' announced the tall, silver-headed man in his early sixties with a sideways nod to the Prior. Brother Joseph was obviously a man of few words as he simply inclined his head, acknowledging Boo.

Although Sextus had titillated Boo with some of the more 'colourful' details of the Abbot's life before entering orders, it was his companion who drew her attention.

A towering rake of a man with cropped pepper-and-salt hair with what Boo would describe as a 'haunted' look about him. As their eyes met, Boo felt an involuntary shudder slither down her backbone as that face broke into its crooked smile.

Boo smiled back, drawing on those skills acquired on the Library bus which enabled her to hide her true mental and physical response.

'Brother Joseph won the bronze medal at the 1932 Los Angeles Olympics. But that was before he found God and the Order. Isn't that right, Brother Joseph?

'That is true, my Lord Abbot...' the face said reluctantly, which had returned to its comfort zone of mirthlessness, '...for the hundred yard sprint': it was obvious he preferred silence.

'How very interesting. Yes, indeed...very interesting!' the librarian answered, unable to think of what else to say.

'Well then,' declared the Abbot, clapping his hands 'let's show Miss Lavender to her room, then please join us for a bit of supper and tomorrow morning we can get down to business with our library. However, I put you on notice, Miss Lavender,' said the head of the Abbey with a glint of humour in his eye '...it...is...a...complete...shambles! No-one's bothered with it for years. But I can guarantee that you will find some rare historical documents as well as some...' and here he hesitated '...interesting little curios'

'Then I shall look forward to that, Father' she replied with relish, her antennae already a-twanging. 'But what exactly did he mean?' she thought curiously.

Without further ado, the Abbot picked up Boo's suitcase and said 'Walk this way, m'dear' and led the way to the great weather-beaten oak doors which in turn led into a vast, poorly-lit hall festooned with dark, foreboding pictures of saints being martyred; beatific saints with hands clasped in prayer under golden halos; small wooden statues, large marble statues, all of them, Miss Lavender presumed, of more saints together with a very distinct, and for Miss Lavender unsettlingly powerful smell: incense. Although to be fair, it was mingled with another smell; floor polish, which she didn't mind at all.

'Oh dear,' she thought feeling slightly panicked 'I know I am being quite irrational but that smell just gives me the heebie-jeebies'

'I'll leave you with Dom Ignatius who'll show you to your room, Miss Lavender. Do bring Miss Lavender along to join us for an aperitif before supper when she's finished unpacking' instructed the Abbot who went off with Brother Joseph along one of the many winding corridors, clearly returning to their earlier deep conversation.

As Miss Lavender took in the surroundings, the Prior kept up a running commentary as he led the way up the main stairway taking a left turn along a short corridor to one of the guest rooms.

'With it being a rather special anniversary about to happen, we're trying to get everything shipshape for the occasion. There will be a special celebration soon attended by the great and good of the land including the descendants of our benefactor, Sir Fergus MacDorn-Smythe. So, it's all hands on deck, so to speak'. He continued: 'As you wander around the place, you'll probably notice that while the main part of the building is original, there have been a lot of later add-ons like our cloistered gardens: most of our visitors find them very peaceful. They do have a very calming effect on the soul'

'I shall look forward to seeing them' Miss Lavender said still at a slight loss as to how to converse with this man of the cloth, clothed in the austere habit of his Order.

They arrived at her sparsely-furnished room with its single bed, bedside table and lamp with a crucifix hanging on the wall above the bed. These, together with a small writing table and chair completed the room's fixtures. A small pair of outward opening windows overlooked the inner courtyard and the cloistered gardens.

'Oh my goodness!' Boo burst out as she took in the landscape beyond the window in the dwindling light of the day.

The Prior mistook her outburst and apologised. 'Yes, I'm sorry, Miss Lavender, The Ritz it's not'

'No, no, Father. My surprise did not concern the room. It's the view. Beautiful! How magnificent' enthused the lady, rarely taken by surprise. 'You know, Dom Ignatius,' continued Boo as she checked her wristwatch 'I think I'll leave my unpacking till later, if that's alright? Shall we join the others?'

'Of course, follow me' he replied in his gentle melodious tenor voice.

Seven

As they meandered along a collection of non-descript corridors, Dom Ignatius chattered away to Miss Lavender while she took note of statues and paintings positioned in alcoves and crannies which would help her get her bearings for the coming days.

'Sir John and Lady MacDorn-Smythe and their children arrived earlier this afternoon. You'll meet them before supper.'

They approached a large pair of old oak doors where a general hubbub of conversation could be heard coming from behind it.

Dom Ignatius pushed the door and its unoiled hinges protested loudly. Heads turned and conversations halted as they entered. Miss Lavender found herself in a rather large sitting room which reminded her of a gentlemen's club in Cheltenham where she'd once been invited to dine. Like the club, it was filled with an assortment of leather club and winged chairs and a number of overstuffed, dark coloured sofas. None of them were being used at the time as the dozen or so people in attendance were all standing, drinks in hand. To the right of the group, a young monk stood beside what appeared to be a well-stocked cocktail cabinet pouring drinks.

'Ah, Miss Lavender,' the Abbot, who was conversing with some smartly dressed people in non-clerical garb, called out 'do come and join us. Let me introduce you to our other guests'

The Abbot gently took Miss Lavender by the elbow and led her towards a very distinguished-looking elderly gentleman dressed in what Boo guessed from the cut of it to be a Savile Row suit. It was of the deepest blue and made from the finest worsted mohair. The white shirt he wore, in contrast, had a softness about it which suggested French or Italian and the grey and red tartan tie, knotted in the Windsor fashion, indicated perhaps a Scottish connection. Connected to the ends of the perfectly creased trousers ('Charlie Chivers has got competition' she thought of her friend, Chief Superintendent Charles Chivers of Her Majesty's Constabulary) were immaculate black brogues which had been buffed to perfection. And to complete the outfit, a gold Albert spanning the waistcoat of his suit which was probably, Boo guessed, attached to an exceedingly fine timepiece. There was an air of leadership and quiet courage about the man, 'not one to be boastful or full of self-importance' thought Boo unlike some aristos Boo could mention, but at the same time, someone who would brook no nonsense...from anyone.

'Miss Lavender, I would like to introduce Sir John MacDorn-Smythe, head of the clan MacDorn and his wife, Lady Dorothy' the Abbot announced formally.

'Pleased to meet you, Sir John and very nice to make your acquaintance, Lady Dorothy' Boo replied demurely.

'And very nice to meet you too, Miss Lavender. Please...call me Johnnie, everyone does' was the easygoing reply.

'Knew it!' thought Boo 'Not a snooty bone in his body. Probably ex-army...not at all like Colonel Forbes' but she replied: 'I most certainly shall...Johnnie!' and they all laughed and one could feel the tension leave the room.

'And this is the family' the Abbot said with a wave of the hand in the direction of the young man and lady. 'Young Gertie, or as she is known to one and all: The Honourable Gertrude Theodora Sybil Mary Elizabeth MacDorn-Smythe. Whoo!' the Abbot said, pretending to wipe the sweat from his brow to hoots of laughter from the rest of the group.

'Dom Ambrose, you're such a tease' Gertie laughed gaily.

'How do you remember all of those names, Father?' Boo asked in complete amazement.

'Miss Lavender, I am here to tell you that I am probably the only person in this room who knows them...but only because I baptised her' the Abbot revealed to more laughter.

'Hmm, they all seem to be quite comfortable and relaxed with each other' mused Boo. However, sometimes, first impressions are not exactly as they appear.

'And not forgetting young Angus' the Abbot continued about the thirty-something young man standing to the side, dressed similarly to his pater but in a slightly more modern, nattier sort of a way, whose obvious good looks he'd inherited from his father's side of the family.

'How do you do, Miss Lavender'. The forthright young man smiled, extending his hand for her to shake.

'And jolly firm it is too' was what Boo thought.

'I won't bother to tell you all of his names otherwise your supper will be cold by the time you get to it'

'Miss Rosemary's here to catalogue our Library' the Prior piped up.

'Er...Lavender, Father' corrected Boo. 'My name is Lavender'

'I'm so sorry, Miss Lavender. Wrong plant' offered the Prior by way of explanation.

'Typical Dom Ignatius, I'm afraid, Miss Lavender. Gardens, flowers and plants are very special to him but had it been the name of a particular fish, he would have gotten it right first time. Originally, you see, we were an order of preachers and we still hold on to that but over the years here at Brackenbury, we have spread our wings and so we have sheep, cattle and pigs as well as a well-stocked garden and herbarium'

Boo could only stammer: '...pardon?' She wasn't quite sure where this conversation was going...let alone where it had been.

'Now it's my turn to say sorry' the Abbot offered. 'Father Ignatius used to be a naval man. Sailed the Seven Seas for many a year'

'Over thirty to be precise' put in the Prior.

Miss Lavender did not question the statement that 'over thirty' was not at all very precise but at least things made a little more sense as she recalled his reference to 'shipshape' and 'all hands on deck' in their earlier conversation. 'Perhaps weather-beaten would have been a more charitable description.' Boo thought of her earlier portrayal of the Old Salt/Prior.

'Sherry, Miss Lavender?' the Abbot enquired.

'Thank you, Father, that would be very nice'

'Dry or sweet?'

'Dry, please, Father'

'Brother Fabian, would you mind pouring a dry sherry for Miss Lavender?'

'Certainly' the young novice replied and handed Miss Lavender her drink.

'You'll get a chance to see our magnificent gardens tomorrow, Miss Lavender, It's Brother Fabian here we have to thank for them. Is that not so, Brother Fabian?'

'I do my best, Father Abbot' he responded humbly bowing his head.

'I caught a glimpse of them from my room just before darkness fell, Father. They do look rather splendid' she said looking around, noting that some of the others were well into their second snifter.

'Excellent malt, Ambrose' Johnnie called out as he swapped his empty glass for another presented by Brother Fabian on a silver salver. As he raised his glass to Boo, she noticed a frown flit briefly across his soft features.

'Good health, Miss Lavender' he toasted her, raising his glass and smiling.

'...and to you' Boo responded with gusto raising her own glass.

The door to the sitting room opened and in walked a gentleman dressed in a rather rumpled, dark grey three-piece suit, the waistcoat of which was covered in cigarette ash burns.

'Typical absent-minded academic who ends up with, what my mother called, "a Leaning Tower of Pisa" of cigarette ash. Feh!' she concluded, rather disapprovingly.

She was very quickly disavowed of that notion.

'Ah, Professor Beech, a warm welcome to you' the Abbot called out. 'Please come and join us. What will you have? We've got dry or sweet sherry and a very nice malt according to Sir John'

'Whisky would be fine, Father'

Judging by the wheezy, gravelly-voice, he sounded like a sixty-a-day man; probably Capstan.

'Let me introduce Miss Lavender who's here to sort out our Library which is in a bit of a mess'

'I've noticed' the Professor admitted brusquely.

'Oh, and did you find anything interesting, Professor?' Boo enquired in her best Librarian's voice.

'Er...er...not really' was the rather swift response. 'I only popped my head around the door, saw the disarray and left'

'Not a very convincing liar' was Boo's conclusion.

'Oh really?' she replied in a tone which carried more than a soupcon of disbelief in it.

The Abbot quickly stepped in.

'Yes, Professor Beech is retired now. He taught for many years at Balliol. Ancient History was his field'

'Is, Father, is. I've not snuffed it yet' the elderly academic retorted grumpily.

'Hmm,' Boo reflected 'not quite the old fuddy-duddy type I thought. No sense of humour...and miserable to boot'

'Yes, well' he continued '...I've come here for a spot of peace and quiet and to check a few things out' he let out.

'And what sort of things might they be, may I ask?' Boo enquired nonchalantly.

Boo didn't miss the look of panic which passed across the crinkled eyes.

'Er...nothing...nothing...sorry, I don't know what I was thinking about when I said that' he announced huffily, downing the generous measure which Brother Fabian had only just served him and storming off to get another.

'Sorry about that, Miss Lavender. He just arrived yesterday; last minute booking. I'm sure his bark is worse than his bite' the Abbot said charitably. 'But enough of this idle chatter, Miss Lavender, I am very much looking forward to a rubber or two after supper, if you're up to it? To be honest, if there's one thing I miss from my life in the secular world it's the hours I spent in smoky rooms playing with some of the grouchiest people on the planet. But boy, did I enjoy it! There were times when I left the club with the most blinding headache having had the most wonderful evening. But, as you know, only a member of the bridge-playing fraternity would understand that one'

'Indeed, Father, I can see you're looking forward to your next splitting headache already' Boo said jokingly. 'Who are you pairing up with tonight?' Boo asked, mildly curious.

'One of our Brothers is willing to make up a foursome. He came to us five years ago. Used to be a big City lawyer before joining our community; represented some big oil exploration company that hit it big'

'Did he really?' asked the lady whose stomach felt a little queasy at the mention of City lawyers and oil exploration in the same breath. It was not that long ago that Miss Lavender had had to deal with another gentleman of the same profession in 'The

Case of the First Case' as Sextus had dubbed it. It had nearly cost her, Sextus and their friend, Chief Superintendent Charlie Chivers, their lives.

But then something at the back of Boo's mind crept into the forefront of that formidable brain of hers.

'His name, Father?'

'His name was Anthony'

'And he worked in the City' Boo said, more as a statement rather than a question.

'Yes, Miss Lavender, that is correct' confirmed the Abbot now furrowing his brow at the strange turn this conversation seemed to be taking.

'Hmm, I wonder' Boo paused in thought. 'Was his surname Malone, would you know, Father?'

'Why, yes, I believe it was. Why do you ask?'

'Tony Malone' Boo stated resolutely. 'I'll bet it's him'

'Who?' the puzzled priest asked.

'You mean you don't know?'

'Don't know...what?' the Abbot asked getting more and more frustrated.

'Well, if it's the Tony Malone I think it is, he represented Britain in the European Championships in...oooh, let me see...was it '37 or '38?' she said, racking her brains.

By now the Abbot had completely lost the thread of the conversation. '...represented Britain in what Championships, Miss Lavender?' he requested, mystified.

'Why, bridge, of course. You mean you really didn't know?'

'To tell you the truth, Miss Lavender, no, I did not know. What a surprise!'

'If you don't mind me asking, Father, what does he look like?' Boo wanted to know, unable to conceal her excitement at the thought of playing against a former member of the British team.

'Well...'

'Does he have a shock of rather long lustrous fair hair?' Boo interjected as she recalled the suave, sophisticated 'golden boy' of the bridge circuit who used to set the ladies' hearts a-fluttering.

'Well, he may have had a long time ago but...' the Abbot laughed '...but how can I put it? Let's say his tonsure has grown

44

larger over the years. I suppose that would be the charitable way to say it'

'I beg your pardon, Father?'

'He's bald, Miss Lavender. Bald as the proverbial' the Abbot sighed when he saw the look of disappointment on the Librarian's face.

'Oh well, never mind. If I remember rightly, he was a demon, if you'll pardon the expression, Father, at being able to force the opposition into impossible contracts and then making them pay dearly for it'

'I do hope so, Miss Lavender. I'm looking forward to our little evening skirmishes even more now. They should prove to be most interesting'

'Is that a challenge I hear, Father?' Boo asked tingling with anticipation.

'Absolutely' declared the feisty Abbot.

'Then, on behalf of Mr Phipps and myself, I accept!'

As Boo enjoy the banter with the Abbot she'd continued to follow the Professor's movements in her mirrored spectacles. He'd pulled out his cigarette case in a fit of pique, his hand clearly shaking as he attempted to remove a cigarette from the band of elastic used to stop them falling out when the case was opened.

'What was that all about?' she deliberated. 'The one thing one can be sure about is that he's here for something. But what?'

As the old academic puffed away frantically, he was joined by a man in a dog collar wearing a brown tweed suit with an air of what reminded Miss Lavender of one of her least likeable characters of Mr Dickens, Uriah Heep: all hand-wringing and unctuousness.

The two of them seemed to be glad of each other's company but nevertheless both continually looked around as if waiting…for something. 'Other arrivals, perhaps?' she wondered. 'And surely that is not the usual garb for a member of the Roman clergy. Don't they always wear black?'

Finally, curiosity got the better of her.

'I couldn't help noticing the gentleman talking to Professor Beech. Is he a member of this community, Father?'

'No, no, Miss Lavender, that is the Reverend Richmond. I understand he's a country parson from...' he hesitated '...Hertfordshire, I believe. Another last-minute booking. Apparently, he'd heard good reports about us and decided to join us for a few days of quiet reflection' he added.

Before Miss Lavender could probe any further, Sextus sidled up.

'Good evening, Boo'

'Oh, hello, Sextus. Been here long?'

'I arrived about an hour ago. Boo, do you know who we're playing against tonight?' he hissed under his breath. 'Tony Malone! The Tony Malone!'

'Yes, Dom Ambrose has just told me. Exciting, isn't it, Sextus?' Boo's reply was very devil-may-care. Casting an eye around the room she continued: 'Which one is he?'

Sextus casually looked around the room:

'He's right behind you talking to Lady Dorothy. He is known as Brother Augustus now. Must have changed it when he took his vows'

Boo had a quick squint in the mirrors on the inside of her glasses.

'No...o...!' she exclaimed a little too loudly. Heads turned. Boo blushed.

In a disbelieving whisper, she said:

'Many a heart was broken, Sextus, when he gave up playing on the circuit, I can tell you. But I didn't recognise him. He's changed so much' Boo said as she scrutinised the rotund figure with a few strands of wispy grey hair straddling the top of his pate.

'We've all changed over the years, Boo' Sextus sniffed.

'I know, but...' there was no chance to finish as Brother Augustus waddled over to   join them.

'Miss Lavender, I believe we have a game on our hands tonight. What joy!' he proclaimed heartily.

'Indeed we do but I put you on warning, Brother...I shan't allow you to push us into impossible contracts. I remember that used to be your forte'

'We shall see, Miss Lavender, we shall see!' the plump friar teased rubbing his hands.

With battle lines drawn, Boo and Sextus followed the others into supper.

In the meantime, Sir John and the Abbot strolled along together, arm in arm with heads almost touching, as people do, who have known each other for a very long time. The elderly knight of the realm leant in even closer and whispered:

'I must have a word with you after dinner, Ambrose. There's something of a delicate nature which I need to discuss with you'

The Abbot looked askance at Sir John but the old man shook his head; it would have to wait.

A long night was just about to begin.

Eight

A jolly mood hung over the diners as they sat down and continued their conversations where they'd left off after the Abbot said Grace.

Before he sat down, the Abbot rang his bell to get everyone's attention.

'Just before we start, I would like to welcome all of our guests and retreatees...'

A groan went up from the Community at the Father Abbot's much repeated jokey reference to those on retreat.

'Thank you, thank you' the Abbot said by way of acknowledging and dismissing their censorious observation.

'As I was saying,' he continued 'to welcome our special guests tonight, I thought it would be appropriate to open up our well-stocked cellar'

This time, a cheer went up and the Abbot sat down.

'That seemed to go down well' he announced to those within earshot. Turning to his right he said to Sir John: 'Johnnie, we have a bottle of Margaux '26 which we've been holding onto for a special occasion and I think this is it. I know you're a bit of a connoisseur. Will you do us the honour of sampling it?'

'With pleasure!' Johnnie agreed, beaming. 'You know me, Ambrose, never one to turn down a good vintage. '26, you say? Wonderful!'

The Prior, Dom Ignatius, carried the bottle over, holding it carefully in both hands as if it were a new-born baby, and presented it to the knight: Johnnie inspected it and nodded his approval.

The Prior then opened the bottle and held the cork for Johnnie to sniff, which he did and again nodded his appreciation.

The monk carefully poured a small amount of the hugely expensive liquid into Sir John's glass for him to sample. The elderly knight lifted the glass up to eye level, checked its colour before swirling the precious contents around and finally sniffing it. Satisfied, he sipped. Smiling with delight and appreciation at the wonderful nuanced notes of blackcurrant and herbs, he swallowed.

'Yes, indeed, Ambrose, a superb vintage! Lives up to the MacDom-Smythe's family motto: "Virtus Exspectatur"' he declared grandly. '"Excellence Expected" for those of us not familiar with Latin.' he translated before raising his glass again and saying:

'Absolutely su...' Suddenly the smile fell from Sir John's face as his eyes widened and his whole body went limp.

'Oh my goodness! He's having a heart attack. Quick, someone, call a doctor' the Abbot shouted in panic.

Brother Robert, the Head Gardener called out: 'I'll do it' and ran off towards the Abbot's office.

Initial inertia was quickly followed by panic as everyone in the room rose from their chairs; some of them pushed back with such force that the sound of them clattering to the floor together with the ear-splitting noise of raised voices added to the chaos. Everyone rushed to the High Table as Sir John's body began to slide from his chair.

Dom Ignatius placed the wine bottle on the side table before moving swiftly to join the others.

'Give him space!' someone cried out. 'Move back!' another voice called out.

The whole place was in uproar; meals were abandoned, all thoughts of pleasure, forgotten.

In the melee, one of the monks rushed over and cleared the surface of the table with a sweep of his arm: plates, cutlery and glasses crashing and smashing everywhere.

Father Ambrose called out:

'Someone help me to lay him on the table' as he gently held onto the elderly knight under his arms. Brother Joseph hurried forward.

'Gently, Brother' the Abbot exhorted. They lifted the frail body of Sir John and tenderly placed him on the cleared surface of the table.

By then, the aged knight had turned the colour of Dom Ambrose's dog collar. Froth slowly trickled from his mouth. He made no sound as the spume formed a lather around his lips. Suddenly, his whole body shuddered violently.

The Abbot and Miss Lavender, who were the closest to him, bent over to see if there was anything they could do but silently looking up at each other, their eyes said it all: Sir John's unblinking eyes saw no more...he was gone.

While the Abbot moved to comfort Her Ladyship and Sir John's children, Miss Lavender, unnoticed by anyone, leaned over closer to the body; there was a distinctive smell. She had come across that smell before.

She moved away to the end of the table and gestured to Sextus.

'Sextus, will you follow Brother Robert and ask him to make one more call, please?'

'Certainly, Boo. To whom?

'The police. I think we're going to need them'

There was no question: Sir John MacDorn-Smythe, Head of the Clan MacDorn, had been poisoned. But was it by accident or on purpose, speculated Miss Lavender?

Nine

It took twenty-five minutes for the ambulance to arrive: the police made it in fifteen.

Chief Superintendent Charles Chivers, late of Scotland Yard came charging through the open door to the main hall with a sergeant and two constables in his wake. The Prior, Father Ignatius, under strict instructions from the Abbot was waiting for them and led them straight to the Refectory. The two minutes that it took to reach the dining room was conducted in complete silence such was the black thunderous look the Prior perceived on the face of the Chief Superintendent.

The dead knight's body lay still on the High Table where his last breath had been painfully drawn on this earth.

'I am Chief Superintendent Chivers. Who's in charge here? And will someone please tell me what has gone on?' he demanded sharply.

The Abbot stepped forward and answered:

'I am Dom Ambrose, the Abbot of Brackenbury Abbey and this...' he choked as he pointed towards the inert body of his lifelong friend. For a few moments no other sound could be heard except the piteous wracking sobs of the Abbot. Clearing his throat, he struggled to pull himself together and continued '...this is Sir John MacDorn-Smythe, our very dear friend and benefactor. I think he's had a heart attack. Poor man. Requiescat in pace'

The Chief Superintendent scanned the room catching sight of Miss Lavender and Mr Phipps. He was well acquainted with them both: all three had worked together on a number of cases in the County. With only the briefest incline of the head, acknowledging their presence, he continued scanning the faces around the room.

'I would be grateful if you would all remain in this room for the time being to give myself and my men a chance to assess the situation and then we'll need to take statements from you all'

His request was greeted with silence apart from one gruff voice which spoke up; Professor Beech. As the police entered the

Refectory he'd lit up and was puffing away nervously on his cigarette.

'Chief Superintendent, my name is Beech and I strongly object to being held here. I...we've...' he said waving his hand with the cigarette in it '...done nothing wrong. So I would be grateful if you would allow me to return to my room. I assure you I do not intend to flee and will make myself available to make my statement to your men when it is required of me'

Chief Superintendent Chivers had come across his "sort" many times: "I'm a personal friend of the Chief Constable" or "...if you insist on keeping me here I shall instruct my solicitors" Blah, blah, blah.

All water off this very old duck's back.

'Permission denied. Now are there any other questions?'

Apart from the Professor's huffing and puffing, the rest remained silent.

'Good' the Chief Superintendent said forcefully. 'Then let's get on with it'

Before speaking, Miss Lavender noted that the Chief Superintendent's normally impeccable appearance was somewhat dishevelled. 'Probably just about to finish his shift and make his way home when the call came in' she assumed.

'Chief Superintendent,' Miss Lavender addressed her friend and stepped forward to join the Abbot 'Father Ambrose and I were seated beside Sir John when he imbibed some wine and became ill'

As she said it, her eyes directed the Chief Superintendent to the wine bottle sitting on the side table behind the High Table.

Charlie caught her drift and called out:

'Constable Smith, take charge of that bottle and don't let it out of your sight'

'Yes sir' the constable answered, saluting.

One of the diners quickly covered his mouth, pretending to cough as an involuntary smile appeared on his face.

'Perfect...' was the gleeful thought running through his mind. '...couldn't be better'

However, the one mistake most murderers have in common is that they believe they've committed the perfect murder.

For the time being, this murderer may have been right in thinking that...but not for much longer because it was about to be put to the test by someone.

That someone was Miss Hilary B Lavender.

Ten

It was nearly midnight by the time the statements of the residents and guests of Brackenbury Abbey were taken and despite Professor Beech's protestations, he took his turn like everyone else. All of the statements said virtually the same: Sir John MacDorn-Smythe sampled the wine and appeared to have a seizure. All, that is, except one: Miss Lavender's, which just happened to be taken by the Chief Superintendent himself.

In hushed tones, the Librarian told Charlie of her suspicions.

'It's possible he may have been murdered, Charlie' was her opening statement as she looked directly into Charlie's eyes looking for support/rejection of her theory...but she got neither.

If Charlie Chivers was taken aback by her statement, it didn't show. He was used to Miss Lavender's manner of coming straight to the point. And more importantly, she had always been spot on. No flights of fancy from this lady Librarian; only facts and reasoned argument.

'...and the grounds to back up that belief, Miss Lavender?' enquired Charlie, hanging on her every word.

'Well, for one, did you see Sir John's lips, Charlie? The white spume around his mouth?' She hesitated before continuing, '...and there was a smell, Charlie; one that I recognised, but, for the life of me, couldn't put a name to; still can't. But he was poisoned, Charlie. No doubt in my mind. The question is: was it an accident or is there someone in this Abbey who would commit such an act and if so, who on earth would do such a thing...in a place like this? He seemed such a gentle, amiable sort of man. Now, don't get me wrong. I know from the conversation I had with him before we went into supper that he wasn't one to suffer fools gladly, I could see it in his eyes. But why would someone kill him...and choose this particular location to do it?'

'I have no idea, Miss Lavender but we will find out. I'll get that bottle over to our lab straightaway and I appreciate the information and for sharing your thoughts about it'

'I'd better finish now, Charlie. If we do have a murderer in our midst it would be prudent, don't you think, to keep our past association to ourselves. Would you agree?'

'Absolutely, Miss'

He stood up then and announced in a voice loud enough to be heard by those nearby:

'Thank you very much for your help, Miss. If we need any further information, we'll be in touch': exactly as he'd said to three others before her.

Needless to say, all hope of a game of bridge that night or, as events turned out, any other night in the near future were well and truly forgotten.

Eleven

Throughout the night, lights could be seen going on and off all over the building as different things played on different people's minds...in very different ways.

For the majority, feelings of sadness at the death of their benefactor and sympathy for his family were what kept most of them awake: many spent the night on their knees praying for his immortal soul.

However, there were other rooms where the occupants' minds were turning over completely different thoughts.

In particular, a faint light could be seen coming from under Miss Lavender's room door, flickering on and off throughout the night; just like her formidable brain. It refused to let her eyelids stay closed for very long as it wrestled with facts, turning them this way and then that, attempting to impose some kind of order on the situation. But the more she tried to slot the facts, as she saw them, into logical boxes, the more they refused to fit.

'Come on!' she thought frustratedly when her eyes flew open for the umpteenth time and she switched on her bedside lamp '...there has to be a reason why someone would choose to perpetrate this foul deed at this time and in this place...if indeed it is murder' she thought, allowing for the unlikely possibility that it could still have been an unfortunate accident.

But no matter how she tried, the facts declined to be fitted into neat tidy compartments.

Meanwhile, in another room different "things" were being considered.

Just as Miss Lavender's brain kept turning over the facts and trying to make sense of them, this murderer was turning over the same facts but complimenting himself on a job well done.

'...that was a close one. All that planning nearly ended up down the Swanee. But in the end, it couldn't have worked out better. That little twist at the end was a stroke of genius, the coup de grace. Should keep the coppers busy for a while as I concentrate on the real reason why I'm stuck in this damn place. But the day after tomorrow...freedom. Almost there. Can't wait!' the killer thought gleefully.

However, plans have a way of not always going exactly the way they're supposed to...as this murderer was about to find out...the day after tomorrow.

Twelve

The police returned to the Abbey the following morning to conclude their enquiries, leaving just before lunch.

In the meantime, the Community and guests continued to move around in their silent world; only the sound of sandals flopping on well-trodden flagstone floors could be heard as each member of the community came to terms with the previous night's sad affair in their own way.

At breakfast, it was arranged that Miss Lavender would meet the Abbot in his office mid-morning to discuss what would be required, although Miss Lavender could see that his heart wasn't in it. He was taking the death of his friend badly.

'Come in' the Abbot called out when she knocked. 'Ah, Miss Lavender,' he began 'I don't know if your superiors informed you or not but what you are about to do for us is very important: it's for our anniversary. Strictly speaking, "Old Coppernose" or as the rest of the civilised world knew him, Henry VIII, interrupted its continuity with that marvellous idea he had for the Dissolution of the Monasteries, but the fact remains that the original monastery was built on this site in 1256...and there is still a monastery here today. So, we have one or two 'things' lined up to celebrate it. One of which is getting the Library organised. Perhaps now you can see how important it is to us what you're doing'

Boo nodded her acknowledgement of its significance. Equally, she hadn't she missed the emphasis the Abbot had placed on the word 'things'.

'Time to go fishing, methinks. I wonder if I can wheedle out of him what these other 'things' are?' So, the 'fisher' of facts went after the 'fisher' of men.

'Oh yes, Father, I do see. And, of course, it goes without saying that I will make a special effort to get everything in order in time for your celebrations. But how very interesting. You...you mentioned that you have some other things planned?' she enquired in her most hesitant, innocent, fishing voice.

'Alas, dear lady, I am not at liberty to divulge what they are at the moment. But suffice to say that what it is will be quite fascinating, even to those who are not of our faith'

'Now you have got my curiosity going, Father. When will you be able to tell us?'

The 'us', of course, referred to the 'fisher' whose line had come back with not even a minnow attached.

'Oh soon, dear lady, soon' was the cryptic reply, which, of course, was of no use to Miss Hilary B Lavender.

In the time it took for this brief conversation to take place, the Abbot and Boo had arrived at the tall double doors to the Library. Above the doors was a plaque written with the word 'Bibliotheca' in medieval script.

When the Abbot pushed the door and held it open for her, Boo gasped. For it was the second time in twenty-four hours she'd been caught unawares.

The whole of the room was bathed in dazzling shards of multi-hued colours from the breathtaking stained-glass windows. For Boo, it felt as though she was standing at the end of a rainbow. Only now as she stood there, did she understand how the monks who worked in the 'Scriptoria' of such monasteries in a bygone age, produced such exquisite works as 'The Closworth Missal' which she'd first seen in the Bodleian Library in Oxford when she was taken on a tour as a newly qualified Librarian.

The thought occurred to Boo again that '...with light like this, a lot of our most famous painters would have taken up holy orders instead of wine, woman and song' But out loud she said:

'How utterly beautiful, Father. I can't wait to get started'

'Then why not now?' asked the bemused cleric.

'Absolutely!' declared the curious Librarian whose appetite had been more than whetted by the visual feast in front of her.

However, Boo had been so taken by the sun-swathed room that she had failed to notice the higgledy-piggledy state of the bookshelves.

'I can see I've got my work cut out for me, Father' Boo confessed as it dawned on her just how much of a task lay ahead. 'Did no-one return their books to the shelves they came from?'

asked the lady whose daily life was the embodiment of orderliness.

'It would appear not, Miss Lavender' the Abbot chuckled. 'I must say it's been years since I've been in here myself but there does seem to be a level of disorganisation'

'What an interesting way to describe chaos: "A level of disorganisation" Boo repeated. 'I think you may have missed your calling, Father. Perhaps you should have been a politician.'

'And who says I'm not?' the priest came back, quick as a flash, matching Boo's laughter. 'As the leader of this community, I have to wear about half a dozen hats which I am continually juggling in the air...if you'll pardon me throwing my metaphors into the mix as well'. He then started ticking them off on his fingers.

'Firstly, I have to be an accountant, looking after the income and outgoings of the community. We have a Bursar but, at the end of the day, all responsibility for what happens within these walls rests on my shoulders. Secondly, although I am the leader of the community, I still have to be an active, contributing member. Oooh, Miss Lavender, I'm beginning to sound like an old moaner, don't you think?'

But Boo, employing one of her favourite tactics of silent nodding, just continued to smile. ("It actually works, my dear Sextus" she would say to her bridge partner. "The silence makes people uncomfortable and so they feel compelled to keep talking")

The Abbot in accordance with Boo's dictum duly obliged. 'But, by far, the hardest hat of all to wear is my referee's hat'

'Do you mean for sport?' the confused Librarian asked.

'If only, Miss Lavender, if only. No, I'm afraid it's the one I dread having to wear the most. But don it I must, to keep all of the...' and here there was a very obvious hesitation, '...blessed egos of our community apart and it's only doffed when all parties have been mollified. You'd think in a place like this,' he said waving his hand to encompass the building and all who lived within, 'most of those egos would have been left outside the front door when they entered. Not a bit of it, I can tell you. But let's not dwell on that'

'Why not?' the Librarian thought, her natural curiosity heightened. 'That could turn out to be the most interesting part of the job'. However, she let it pass, much to her regret, in the not too distant future.

'I'll leave you to then. Good luck, Miss Lavender' and he left.

Boo was left standing in the middle of the room, wondering where she should start. For a full minute, she stood pirouetting on the spot, turning this way then that, deciding how to divide up the room before coming to her conclusions.

'Right, let's get started'. For the next two hours, she shuffled mounds of books, large and small, into neat manageable piles around the room. There was no point in trying to arrange them into categories, not yet anyway, with titles as varied as 'Celtic Runes of the Fifth Century' and 'The Life of Saint Ledewigis' by Thomas a Kempis. She set aside two of the half dozen desks dotted around the Library, to lay down first editions (of which there was more than a few) and those books which were clearly in a fragile state. All the while she was lifting and sifting, she would pass her gaze over the titles on the spines. At one point, she became quite excited at discovering an early edition of 'Discourse of Method' by Rene Descartes which Boo distinctly remembered from her student years had been put on the Prohibited Books list by one of the Popes.

'I just can't believe the treasures hidden here under this pile of old toot' she thought as the excitement ebbed and flowed in whichever part of the brain is responsible for curiosity. However, this excitement was to happen again and again over the next few days...but not always about a collection of old books...or bridge.

Elevenses and lunch came and went with most maintaining the "Grand Silence", a silence which normally only lasted from 9pm until breakfast the following morning.

However, by the time the evening meal arrived, the atmosphere had eased a little and the odd whispered snatches of conversation could be heard.

At one of the tables, however, there was something else: a sense of anticipation.

Plans were finally coming to fruition in less than twenty-four hours...but not quite as anticipated.

After the previous sleepless night, lights were extinguished very early: which was just as well...they were going to need it. It was about to happen again.

Thirteen

The following morning, everything seemed to be getting back to normal until Boo heard an anguished, strangled cry just as she was stooping to pick up a fresh pile of books from the floor surrounding the table she was working on; she just knew it meant trouble. She rushed and threw open the Library door, almost colliding with The Honourable Angus MacDorn-Smythe as he careered along the corridor towards the main staircase leading upstairs, where the noise appeared to come from.

'Did you hear that scream, Miss Lavender? Whatever could it be?' the young man asked in a state of some excitement. For someone who was in mourning for his recently deceased father, he seemed...normal, happy even. Miss Lavender assumed he was glad of any kind of distraction to take his mind off his loss.

'I don't know, Angus, but whatever it is, it didn't sound good' the worried Librarian answered who knew the difference between a cry of sheer terror and someone involved in a minor mishap: this one definitely fell into the former category.

They both rushed along, meeting a dishevelled, out of breath, Father Ignatius on the way.

'What's going on?' he asked breathlessly. 'I was asked by the police to check if there were any other bottles of the Margaux '26 in the cellar when I heard this awful cry. D'you know where it came from?'

'It sounded like it was upstairs' Angus suggested. 'I was in the gardens when I heard it and thought it came from one of the upper rooms'

All three mounted the stairs, young Angus taking them two at a time and Miss Lavender assisted by Father Ignatius following as quickly as they could. In the meantime, Angus careered ahead of them to join Father Ambrose and Brother Fabian who were opening and shutting doors, calling out to whoever had cried out.

'Hello? Is anybody there? Are you alright?' Father Ambrose was calling out. For his age, Miss Lavender noted, he could move pretty fast.

Nothing.

They were joined by Gertie and Brother Joseph, the Bursar.

'Did anyone recognise whose voice it was?' Miss Lavender posed the question to the assembled group.

'No, I can't say that I did' the Abbot answered straight away.

'Neither did I' Brother Joseph called out, continuing the search, yanking on another door.

It was Gertie who solved the mystery. Opening the door to the guest room, she screamed and fell to the floor in a faint.

The rest of the group rushed along the corridor towards the open door.

'Why would anyone be in there?' the Abbot shouted out as he neared the door. 'This room has been reserved for...' He never completed the sentence.

The body lay on its side by the window where it had fallen, a pool of blood oozing onto the faded Persian rug from the massive wound to the man's head.

'Is he dead?' Brother Fabian asked stunned.

'I...I...don't know' stuttered the Abbot as he leant over the body, feeling for a pulse at the corpse's neck. At his touch, the body moved and Dom Ambrose found himself staring into the bulging, staring eyes of the dead stranger. He recoiled.

He shook his head despondently but out of respect knelt down again and closed the eyelids of the lifeless stranger.

'Whoever this person is...was, he must have hit his head on something and called out as he fell' he postulated.

Making her apologies, Miss Lavender gingerly stepped over Gertie as Angus ministered to her in the doorway. Quickly surveying the scene, she leant over the Abbot, observing the wound and the huge amount of blood already soaked into the carpet, she knew that this was no accidental fall; for sure, this was murder.

'Father,' she stated, putting her hand gently on the shoulder of the Abbot 'if I were you, I'd step back and leave the body where it is until the police get here. I'm afraid this gentleman, whoever he was, has been...murdered'

'Wh...at?' the Abbot cried. 'Murdered? But...but how do you know?'

'Father, look around you. Do you see anything which might have inflicted this injury, something which might have fallen on him or something he might have knocked his head on as he fell? Can you see anything in this room with blood on it apart from the carpet? A sharp edge, perhaps?' She waited as the dazed superior of the monastery looked around. She continued, 'No, Father, there's nothing like that that we can see. The only blood is on the floor which means he was hit by something and that something, so it would appear, has been removed'

'But...' said the Abbot struggling to make sense of the questions that were hurtling around in his befuddled brain '... but who is he? Why was he in this room? And...who would have murdered him...and why?'

He pondered these questions until the realisation of what Miss Lavender had said, hit him. He turned to face her, disbelief clearly in his voice:

'Are you saying, Miss Lavender that it was someone within the walls of this monastery who has committed this...this despicable act?'

'It would appear so, Father. But this man is a priest...don't you recognise him?' Boo asked perplexedly.

The Abbot studied the battered face again, noting the clerical garb, searching his long, excellent memory for some, any, kind of recognition. But his brain was frozen with shock: it was incapable of coming up with an answer.

Finally, he shook his head again and said 'No, Miss Lavender, I've never seen this man before in my life but I can tell from his clothes that he was not just a priest, he was a Monsignor, a higher rank in the Catholic Church. Do you recognise him, Father Ignatius?'

'No, Father. I'm sorry, I don't' the Prior offered nervously.

'Obviously everyone is highly strung after what happened to Sir John' Boo concluded.

'What about you Brother Joseph?'

A shake of the head was the Bursar's silent reply.

'Perhaps if we look in his pockets we might find a wallet or something which might tell us who he was' Brother Fabian, the novice, also clearly agitated, suggested.

'I really don't think that's a good idea, Brother. The police would not want the body moved in any way' Miss Lavender asserted.

The young monk nodded nervously in agreement.

They all stood, rooted to the spot in silence, gazing at the body, each with their own thoughts until Gertie, recovered from her fainting fit, interrupted and demanded: 'Well, is someone going to call the police?'

This brought them out of their numbed shock and the Abbot said: 'Of course. Brother Joseph, would you mind?'

The Bursar nodded and hurried back along the corridor and down the stairs towards the Abbot's office on the ground floor where the only phone in the monastery was kept.

He picked up the candlestick-shaped telephone, dialled 0, and waited for the operator to answer. While he waited, his eyes roamed over the sparse furnishings in the room.

It was then he saw the telephone wire lying on the floor: it had been ripped out of the wall.

The telephone was dead.

'Jesus!' he blasphemed. 'What is going on here? This isn't how things are supposed to be turning out' he uttered under his breath.

A deep, calm-inducing breath later, he remembered the telephone box outside the gates of the monastery. Whoever had destroyed the telephone might have forgotten about its existence. Or had they? Would he find that vandalised as well? He sped off along the corridor towards the main door throwing it open and dashing down the drive towards the rusting gates.

He was right: whoever it was had forgotten about the phone box.

He lifted the receiver and dialled 0. This time the operator came on the line straight away.

'Put me through to the police. There's been a murder!' he shouted in a voice laden with fear.

Fourteen

Back at the murder scene, Miss Lavender kept watch over the body while the others drifted out into the corridor and stood waiting for the police to arrive. The Abbot had fetched his Holy Oils to anoint the body but Miss Lavender had gently explained to the Head of the Abbey that '...it would be best if he waited for the police'. Without disturbing the crime scene, Boo carefully examined the area around the body, looking for anything which might give them a clue as to the identity of the dead man or what the murder weapon could have been.

While she expanded the area of her search, Boo couldn't help but notice, in the small mirrors she'd had specially inserted on the inside of her spectacles, Brother Fabian behind her, loitering by the doorway, hopping from foot to foot. His eyes too were restless, continually on the move.

'Probably never come across anything like this in his sheltered life' she assumed. But his presence was nevertheless distracting.

Brother Fabian, would you mind fetching Mr Phipps and bring him here as quickly as possible, please?'

The novice scurried off in the direction of the Chapel where the retreatants tended to meditate in the morning.

Boo continued mooching around the room but there was very little to glean apart from the presence of a damp coat, hat and scarf thrown over a chair together with a small valise. However, there was a very telling space in the dust on the mantelpiece. She resisted checking the pockets of the coat or opening the case.

'Better leave that until the police get here'

Suddenly, outside the window a black and white blur caught her eye, startling her: it was the Bursar rushing towards the gate.

'What on earth is going on? Isn't he supposed to be calling the police?' she thought anxiously. Then a dreadful thought occurred to her: 'Is he the murderer and he's making his escape? Surely not'

Two anxious minutes wait later, Brother Joseph returned through the creaky gates, putting her mind at rest that whatever he was doing, it was not an attempted getaway ...at least, not yet.

'Hmm, but he looks....' Miss Lavender studied the aged face and the expression etched into it but couldn't decide what it represented. Was it fear? Anger? Anxiety? What was it?

The Bursar, sensing he was being watched, looked up at the window of the guest room only to catch sight of a twitchy-looking Miss Lavender returning his gaze. He called out something but she couldn't hear him.

Five minutes later, the corridor outside the guest room had filled with black and white robed figures, members of the community, standing in small groups muttering and mumbling. Dom Ambrose quickly took charge and ordered them back to their duties.

'...and pray for the soul of this poor man who has been murdered in our midst' he commanded.

As an outsider, Miss Lavender could only wonder at the calm way in which this second death was received within this insular world she had been invited into.

'What is going on here? Why is this happening?' she fretted for the thousandth time, but on this occasion the thought was interrupted by the arrival of Sextus and a few minutes later, Professor Beech.

'Boo, are you alright?' the out of breath retreatant asked worriedly. 'Brother Fabian said there'd been another death! Who's dead? I mean...'

Words were pouring out of Sextus' mouth at a rare old rate of knots until Boo held up her hand for him to halt.

'Sextus, slow down!' she insisted. 'Yes this is definitely a murder but as of yet, we do not know the identity of the dead priest'

'A priest?' Sextus, horrified, blurted out. 'What is happening here, Boo?'

'I wish I could tell you, Sextus, but I am as mystified as you; not for much longer though. The police have been called and when Charlie Chivers gets here, he will not be a happy man. One suspicious death and a definite murder on his patch within two days? God help whoever did this' predicted Miss Lavender.

As Boo spoke these words she observed the figure of the Professor slowly and quietly receding into the background before skulking, yes, definitely skulking, she decided, along the corridor towards his room.

'Why do I get the feeling that he's gone into hiding?' she speculated. 'For a so-called respectable man of letters, he has a very strange way about him'

And so, until the police arrived, Boo fell into a silent analysis of the Ancient History Professor: something wasn't right. And when it wasn't right...it was wrong.

Fifteen

Considerably less than the fifteen minutes it had taken on their first visit, but as predicted by Miss Lavender, the bells, or 'Winkworth Gongs' as they were sometimes called, on the police cars could be heard as they hurtled along the narrow country lanes towards the Abbey. Three black Wolseleys screeched to a halt outside the gates of the abbey.

'Hmm, three of them' mused Boo as she saw the cars pull up outside the gates. '...they definitely mean business this time'

A sergeant jumped out of the driver's side and pushed open the gates which seemed to squeal louder than ever; the three cars drove in and came to a halt just below the window where Miss Lavender was keeping watch.

As the three cars disgorged their passengers, she counted a total of ten policemen approaching the main door with Chief Superintendent Chivers at their head.

The keen eye of the Librarian noted that his immaculate double-breasted navy blue suit looked as if it'd just been returned from the dry cleaners.

'That's more like the Charlie I know'

His trademark black Homburg was at, what Miss Lavender had always considered, a rakish angle whilst the white handkerchief in his breast pocket had a tendency to flop out. The pearl tiepin he always wore sat so perfectly in the middle of his burgundy and white polka dot tie that Miss Lavender often wondered if he used a tape measure to position it.

Again, it was Father Ignatius, the Prior who was standing waiting for their arrival. Unbeknown to any of them, he was standing at the same spot where the murderer had stood less than two hours earlier, waiting for the victim. He pulled open the door.

'The body's on the upper floor, Chief Superintendent. I'll take you there'

"Right you lot," began the Chief Superintendent "spread out. I want everyone, and I do mean everyone, gathered together in the Refectory and we'll interview them one by one. Two of you come with me now. Lead on, Father' commanded the policeman. He was in a no-nonsense mood. Enough was enough.

The Chief Superintendent marched along behind the Prior to the guest room where the Abbot, Brother Fabian, Brother Joseph, Angus, Gertie, Sextus and Miss Lavender were waiting.

He turned to the two police constables saying: 'No-one gets in here without my permission. Got it?' The two constables nodded. He walked through the open door and offered a brusque 'Good morning'

'Now then, what do we have here?' he continued, scrutinizing the body by the window. 'Would anyone like to tell me what happened?'

Dom Ambrose took the lead. 'Brother Fabian and myself were replacing a broken window in one of the rooms at the far end of this floor when we heard a shout...except we now know that it was a cry for help and we immediately started searching for where it had come from. As we were going from room to room, we were joined by Miss Lavender with young Mr Angus and Father Ignatius who came from downstairs. Then, Brother Joseph and Gertie arrived and joined in the search. Sadly, it was Gertie who found the body. She fainted at the sight of all the blood' he concluded.

'I can corroborate that Chief Superintendent' added Miss Lavender. 'I was in the Library when I heard it. I almost collided with Angus as I rushed out to find where the shout had come from. Angus was in the garden and Father Ignatius was in the cellar when they heard it. We all rushed upstairs and that's when Gertie stumbled on the body. Such a shock for the poor girl' and she tut-tutted, shaking her head.

'Okay, that'll do for now but you will all need to give statements later. So, who have we here?' Charlie said as he leant over the body. 'When did it happen?' he asked over his shoulder.

Checking his wristwatch, Dom Ambrose answered:

'...less than forty minutes ago at about 10.30. Would you agree, Miss Lavender?'

Boo thought about it for a few seconds before observing:

'I can tie it down even tighter than that. I looked at the clock as I left the Library and saw that the time was 10.36. Also, Chief

Superintendent,' she continued 'I have since observed that there is only one rather large candlestick standing on the left-hand side of the mantelpiece...' Boo pointed towards it '...while on the other side there is only the outline in the dust of what looks like an identical candlestick base. I believe the missing one may well have inflicted this poor man's fatal injury'

'So, where is it?' the Chief Superintendent demanded looking around the room.

He was greeted with silence.

'Well, thank you anyway for that information, Miss Lavender, that really does narrow down both the time and the potential cause of death. I'll need to know where everyone was at that precise time...and clearly we need to find that missing candlestick' the Chief Superintendent concluded writing down those important facts in his notebook before replacing it in his pocket. He bent over and carefully flipped open the murder victim's jacket with his pencil, extracting a wallet and some papers from his inside pocket.

'Now then, my man,' began the Inspector 'at least we should be able to give you a name'

He sifted through the assortment of items.

'Good Lord!' he exclaimed suddenly. 'This is a Diplomatic passport. Oh...my...God!' ...excuse my language, Father.' Like Miss Lavender, he was not of their faith but that didn't stop him from being respectful of other people's belief.

'Whether we're all equal in the Good Lord's eyes is debatable but in the eyes of the Law everyone is equal' was a motto of his which he would regularly remind the men under his command, of.

The Abbot dismissed the minor slip of the tongue with an impatient hand gesture, waiting to hear the name of the dead man.

But in his heart of hearts, he already knew; it had to be.

Now, with his stomach heaving like a sailing dinghy in the middle of a Gale Force 8 storm, it was the turn of the Abbot to blaspheme, albeit in his own head.

'Sweet Jesus Christ, please don't let it be him'

But it was.

'It says here that he was a Vatican Diplomat and his name was...Avrili. Monsignor Luca Avrili. Does the name mean anything to anybody?' the Inspector requested, looking around the assembled faces of the group.

'Inspector...' the Abbot started to say before his knees began to buckle under him.

'Steady, Father, steady. Are you alright?' the Chief Superintendent asked, taking hold of the Abbot's elbow to support him.

'To be honest, Chief Superintendent, I didn't think things could get worse after the death of Sir John...but it just has'

He took a deep breath to steady himself and then announced to those present:

'This man,' the Abbot began, indicating the corpse 'Monsignor Avrili, travelled here under the assumed name of Senor Tartaglia, and until one hour ago, he was a special adviser to His Holiness, the Pope'. He sighed and continued. 'To celebrate our 700th Anniversary and after much negotiation, the Vatican had agreed to lend the Abbey two very precious items which had not been seen on these shores since the time of the Reformation'. He hesitated.

'Please continue, Father' the policeman urged.

'For you to understand...' the Abbot picked up the story again, '...you will need to know a little of the Abbey's history. Back in 1156, the Queen, Eleanor of Aquitaine, not only granted us our magnificent Charter but made a gift of her own personal Rosary beads, a gift which had been given to her by the Pope at that time, Alexander IV, on the occasion of her marriage to King Henry III. I can tell you that I had the privilege to view both the Charter and the Rosary many years ago when I visited Rome. Apart from their historical significance, they are the most magnificent examples of medieval craftsmanship that I've seen; the Rosary itself being made from the finest gold, diamonds, rubies and pearls. They are both...priceless'. He halted again.

'There's more, isn't there, Father?' probed Miss Lavender as the others waited in silence.

'Yes, there is' admitted the Abbot. It only took a split second for him to decide to tell them everything. After all, it couldn't get any worse. Could it?

He resumed his tale: 'At the time of the Reformation, Henry the Eighth, you probably remember from your school lessons, was badly in need of money and at that time the great monasteries of England were awash with lands and riches. I won't bore you with the whole story of the Reformation but our monastery was gifted to one of the King's favourites, Sir Roland Black. However, unlike most of the monastic buildings of that period, this one wasn't pulled down. No. The story goes that Sir Roland fell in love with it and thought it too beautiful to demolish. So, most of what you see today is pretty much how it would have appeared when it was originally built in the twelfth century. But I'm rambling. The Charter and the Rosary were smuggled out of England and taken to Rome where they have been on display ever since...until now. Monsignor Avrili was bringing them back here, to the Abbey, to go on display for our Anniversary before being returned to Rome'

The Abbot's eyes drifted over to the inert body of the prelate, he sighed and added:

'Such a terrible shame: this was his first visit to our Abbey'

He seemed to have run out of steam but then as an afterthought said:

'And so, my dear Chief Superintendent, it appears that not only do you have two apparently unexplained deaths to solve but, in order to avert a major diplomatic incident, locating and returning the missing treasures to The Vatican...because... they 'aint 'ere' he finished, in rather coarse, uncharacteristic language, waving his hands around to encompass the room.

'And I, for one, have every confidence in you' Miss Lavender declared robustly.

'Hear, hear!' chipped in Sextus Phipps.

'I may need a little help' the Chief Superintendent hinted, looking sideways at Miss Lavender.

Misunderstanding Charlie's plea the Abbot answered:

'Of course we will all pray for you, my son'

'No, Father, I was thinking closer to home' replied the wily policeman catching Boo's eye again.

Her response was suitably vague so as not to arouse any suspicion or interest from the others but Charlie and Sextus understood.

'I'm sure we will all do what we can for you, Chief Superintendent'

The bells began to ring out: ten forty-five, time for elevenses. Time waits for no man...not even for a murdered one whose time had come.

'Would you care to join us for a cup of tea?' the Abbot enquired of the Chief Superintendent.

'Very nice, thank you, Father'

Much to Miss Lavender's relief, they made their way to the Refectory.

'The troops should have gathered everyone there by now for the interviews. So, I can kill two birds with one stone' the policeman thought.

It was only afterwards he realised the impropriety of his unfortunate analogy.

Fortunately, he hadn't shared it with anyone.

As he left the room, the Chief Superintendent reminded the two PCs of his last order:

'Remember, no-one in...or out' he growled.

Perhaps the Chief Superintendent thought Monsignor Avrili might think of joining them for elevenses?

Sixteen

As they made their way along the corridor towards the staircase, the entire group could clearly hear the hubbub emanating from the Refectory below even though they were some considerable way away from it.

'The gossip mill will be running full steam ahead, I expect' Miss Lavender worried. 'Can Charlie Chivers, Sextus and myself stop this before it goes any further?'

Twenty different questions without a single answer were spinning around in her brain like they were stuck in a revolving door as they all marched along the corridor toward the Refectory. 'Two deaths within three days: will there be more? Who will be next?'

Miss Lavender, marshalling her thoughts, halted these time-consuming, pointless conjectures in their tracks.

'No good going off at tangents, Boo. Stick to the facts and something will crack' she reproached herself. 'So what do we have? One: the poisoning of a very decent man and two, the very brutal murder of a Vatican prelate. Whoever the murderer is, they're not pussyfooting around. The targets were both VIPs but that didn't stop them from taking drastic action. A huge amount of planning must have gone into this: the sheer boldness and meticulous timing of each of the murders attest to that. So far the murderer hasn't put a foot wrong. But fortunately, there are some interesting aspects which I will consider...after elevenses' she vowed.

In one respect, Miss Lavender was correct but in another she was completely wrong. It would only be much later that she realised the error in her logic.

The Abbot, at the head of the group, his robes flying out behind him, strode along at a fair pace, stony-faced and in silence. Reaching the two massive doors to the Refectory, he hesitated for a moment before flinging them open very dramatically. It had the desired effect: he got their attention as all within fell silent.

He stood in the doorway for that brief moment, a powerful, commanding figure, a man not afraid to take charge. He was aware that the situation was getting out of hand and, if allowed to continue, would result in chaos. He needed to maintain discipline and wasn't afraid to stamp his authority on the situation.

'Please, everybody, sit down' he commanded. He waited while chairs were dragged from under the tables before he began.

'The situation we now find ourselves in is very sad and something that we, at Brackenbury Abbey, are at a loss to understand. However, we still have a duty to God and our fellow man; our work will always be dedicated to the greater glory of God and it is our duty to pray for our fellow travellers on this earth, no matter what they may have done...in moments of weakness. To that end, the police will be interviewing everyone. Please, do not waste their time. Answer their questions, say what you have to say but then, return to your work' he concluded forcefully.

It did the trick. Conversation for the rest of the break was conducted sotto voce.

After a quick cuppa with his men, the Chief Superintendent gathered them together and gave them their orders.

'Alright, listen up, gentlemen. I want four of you to check this entire building. Every room is to be checked, every door of every cupboard opened. No stone left unturned. When you've done that, I want the grounds searched for anything that might appear suspicious. If you do find anything, you come straight to me. Got it?' Their silence was acknowledgement that they'd 'got it'. 'The rest of you will be taking statements. Use the Refectory tables. I want this...' and here he lowered his voice as he looked around to make sure only his men heard him, '...swine caught and quickly. Now, any questions?' Again, the silence. 'Right, well get on with it then. Chop, chop!'

While Charlie was addressing the troops, Miss Lavender had quickly demolished her three ginger nuts, not quite at the leisurely pace she would have liked because "the catching of this fiend must take priority" she thought. She now appeared to be engaged in conversation with Sextus, her back to the company of policemen gathered around their Chief. But she was only half listening to Sextus' witterings as she watched the proceedings in the mirrors attached to the inside of her spectacles. When Charlie began to move away, Boo interrupted Sextus and asked him to pass a message to the Chief Superintendent.

He caught up with Charlie as he walked out the Refectory.

'Boo said, if it's convenient, could we meet in the Bibliotheca in five minutes, Chief Superintendent?'

'Five minutes, it is then'

When Boo and Sextus were leaving for their rendezvous with Charlie, one of the young constables was escorting a somewhat unwilling Professor Beech firmly by the elbow into the Refectory.

'Alright, young man, please remove your hands from me! Really...this is too much!'

To Boo, his high-handed attitude came across as more frightened rather than angry.

Seventeen

The murderer's scheme had taken a long time to come to fruition, he wasn't going to jeopardise it by doing anything to arouse suspicion now.

He sat quietly, waiting his turn to be called in the row of chairs which had been arranged along the wall of the Refectory for the interviewees. He answered all of the questions put to him by the young constable in a calm, sensible and thoughtful manner. They sat opposite one another at the end of the senior clerics' table, the constable writing the replies in his notebook, just like all the others.

He had the perfect alibi and he played it out to perfection with just the right amount of shock and grief in his tone.

Within minutes, he heard the magic words: 'Well, I think that's all, Sir. Thank you for your patience and again, please accept our condolences'

That was it; he was off the hook. No suspicion. But then again how could there be when he was who he was?

Leaving the Refectory, he began to make his way back to the secret passage he'd emerged from in time to avoid rousing any suspicions. Walking in a slow pensive way, he would turn around unexpectedly halfway along a corridor, looking to see if anyone was following him but he was in the clear. No-one had an inkling...and he intended to keep it that way.

One last look and he dodged into one of the many rooms which had fallen into disuse over the years. The windowless room, known as the Lumber Room, was used as a storeroom for broken furniture and other domestic items which could not be repaired but, equally, could not be thrown away either. There were old standard lamps with their multi-coloured shades akimbo, assorted kitchen paraphernalia and various electrical items together with a variety of broken chairs and tables strewn haphazardly around the room. The murderer cautiously sidestepped the junk and moved towards an old kitchen range on the far wall which had a fine coating of dust showing how little it or the room had been used over the years.

The murderer's hand moved down the left side of the range, counting down the raised decorative flower motifs until he got to the fifth one. He tugged it and the range fell away from the wall about eighteen inches, just enough for a man to squeeze through into the darkened space behind. He immediately pulled the range back to its original position: with the police searching everywhere he couldn't take any chances.

He bent down to pick up the package he had plotted and murdered for, just as the door to the room opened; he stopped mid-stoop, returned to the upright position and held his breath.

Pressing his ear to the back of the range, he listened. There were two people moving around among the clutter.

'Not much to see in here' the first one voiced.

'Yeah, but remember what the Guv'nor said "Leave no stone unturned". If he finds something later on in one of these rooms that we're supposed to have searched he'd have our guts for garters!'

'He is a stickler for detail, you know, but one of the best I've worked for' replied the one the murderer assumed was Plod No.1.

Next, the murderer heard a scraping sound like something being lifted off a table and dumped on the floor.

'Look at this dust' said No.2 blowing the dust off the top of the table.

The murderer heard a loud sneeze.

'Now look what you've done' No.1 called out before erupting into a succession of louder and louder 'Achoos!'

'Oh, come on, let's go. No-one been in here for years and we've still got to search the grounds. That's going to take bloomin' ages'

'Okay,' agreed No.1 'but no more blowing dust!'

The door closed and all was silent again.

'That was a little close for comfort' the murderer thought apprehensively, wiping the tiny cold droplets of sweat which had formed on his brow with his handkerchief. 'I daren't take any of this back to my room. Not while the police are combing every square inch of the place. It'll have to stay here' he concluded. 'Good job I'm the only one who knows about the secret passages'

Like Miss Lavender's logic, he was right...for the present.

He opened the parcel.

'At last!' he whispered in triumph to himself and any spectres of the past who still lingered there.

Carefully removing the Rosary, he caressed the precious jewels, allowing them slip through his fingers, as if in prayer, just as Queen Eleanor would have done nearly eight centuries before.

'I'd love to keep you, my beauties, but sadly, you have to go' he thought regretfully. It was all part of the plan.

However, what the murderer was unaware of was that the police weren't the only ones looking for him: the other murderer was keen to meet him too.

Eighteen

Charlie was a couple of minutes late for the meeting with Boo and Sextus, which was unusual for him, in fact, almost unheard of. He'd been quietly padding around the Refectory, listening to responses, watching faces; were they uncomfortable, nervous, fidgety? He also scrutinised all of the monks and retreatants sitting along the wall of the Refectory, waiting for their turn. All the time, he was waiting, waiting for something to jump out at him, that something which might give the murderer away...but there was nothing.

'Sorry I'm late. If there is a murderer here, then he or she is as cool a customer as I've ever come across. And in all my years in the force I don't think I've come across anyone so bold' he remarked.

'You really don't expect these kinds of going-ons in a place like this' commented Sextus.

'No indeed' concurred Boo. 'But it's happened. So what can we do about it?'

'Any thoughts, Miss Lavender?' asked the policeman.

'A couple, Chief Superintendent. Firstly, I noticed that the monsignor's coat and hat were barely wet even though we had a fair amount of rain this morning. Therefore, it is not unreasonable to conclude that he did not walk from the station but took a taxi. If we can find the taxi driver, he should be able to give us the precise time the victim was dropped off. We already know when the murder took place. But how long had the victim been here and where had he been during that time? Anyone who cannot account for their time during that period could potentially be our murderer. The timing of that window of opportunity will be crucial in finding the perpetrator. Another thing we could look at is: how did the murderer know he was coming? How many people were privy to that information? How did the murderer know when Monsignor Avrili was due to arrive? And where did the murderer wait for the victim? He or she would not have left that to luck. No, our murderer has planned this down to the smallest detail. Did any of the monks or visitors see anyone acting suspiciously or out of character or maybe somewhere where they ought not to have been?'

Miss Lavender paused. 'Hmm, talking of that, there's something I want to check. Would you wait here for a moment, please, gentlemen?'

She left the Bibliotheca returning a few minutes later, holding the handle of an umbrella with her handkerchief.

'This was lying in the coatstand by the door; from its design, it's obviously foreign and it's wet, so it's been used recently. Could this be the victim's? If it is, there may be fingerprints other than the victim's on it. Could they be the murderer's?

Charlie took hold of it saying: 'I'll get it checked for dabs right away'

'You know, Chief Superintendent,' Miss Lavender said picking up where she left off 'I understand the murder of the Monsignor; he had what the murderer wanted. But, if it turns out that Sir John was murdered: why? It doesn't make sense'

'It's a rum one right enough, Boo' agreed Sextus.

'You're right, Miss Lavender.' concluded Charlie 'At the moment, nothing is making sense but we will piece it together bit by bit and we'll catch the blighter. Oh yes, they're not going to get away with that kind of behaviour on my patch. But in the meantime, we'll keep this to ourselves. Mum's the word' said Charlie tapping the side of his nose.

'Oh, hold on, Charlie, I've just thought of something else!' exclaimed Miss Lavender excitedly. 'Dom Ambrose began to say something about "what was he doing there? It had been reserved..." and then he stopped. I'll bet he meant that it was reserved... for the victim. But if that is the case, how did he get there? How would he have known that it was reserved for him? I believe the Abbot said that this was his first visit to the Abbey? So, was he taken there? Was it the murderer who led him there...and then killed the poor man? Hmm' Miss Lavender halted again deep in thought. Suddenly, the thoughts turned themselves into words which began to tumble out of her mouth. 'I mean, there was no sign of a struggle and he had removed his hat, coat and scarf and placed them neatly on the chair. So, I don't think he was suspicious or concerned in any way. In fact, I think the opposite was true...I think he was...' Boo struggled for the word but finally found it '...relaxed'

'Interesting, Miss Lavender, very interesting' commented the Chief Superintendent making a mental note of what she'd said. 'I'll get this checked for fingerprints' he replied enthusiastically, holding the umbrella carefully with Miss Lavender's handkerchief '...and I'll have one of my men check out the taxi driver theory. If we can find out the precise time the victim was dropped off, it'll narrow down the list of suspects. In the meantime, I'll make sure my men are on the lookout for that candlestick like the one that appears to be missing from the crime scene. Well, not so short of clues after all, are we?' the Chief Superintendent concluded grimly. 'Maybe we could meet later to talk about what developments there've been...if any'

'Good idea' agreed Boo and Sextus.

Nineteen

When the door closed behind Charlie, Boo asked Sextus what his thoughts were on the matter.

'Shocked really, Boo. This retreat is over for me now but I'll stay to try to help you and the police catch this villain. As it happens, I am acquainted with the police doctor, Peter Davenport, who examined Sir John's body two nights ago and he's agreed to give me a small sample from the wine bottle'. Boo's jaw dropped open: that was police evidence. Sextus, noting the shock on Boo face, continued '...only with Chief Superintendent Chivers' permission, of course' Boo's mouth duly closed. 'I'm going home later today to test it in my lab at home. At least my knowledge of poisons might be useful to the investigation'

Since the earliest days of his studies as a chemist, Sextus had had a fascination for poisons that had remained with him throughout his career; it had proved to be quite useful on more than one occasion to Boo as she assisted the police in previous investigations.

'Then while you're away, I shall have one eye on cataloguing the Library and the other on the inhabitants of this establishment. A dreadful business, Sextus' Boo admitted. 'Let's hope that the murder of Monsignor Avrili will be the end of it'

Logic seemed to dictate that Miss Lavender should be right; the killings would now stop.

But Miss Lavender also knew that the world was not always a logical place.

Twenty

Two hours later, the sergeant reported back to the Chief Superintendent that his men had found nothing untoward in the grounds; they were still checking the interior of the building. Although the rain during the night had softened the earth, there were no footprints of any significance to be found, let alone signs of an intruder.

'No two ways about it, Bert...' the Chief Superintendent, puffing on his pipe, insisted to his sergeant and confidante of twenty years in the nicking business as they walked around the abbey's gardens '...I can't see any other interpretation of the facts; it has to be an inside job. There's just no sign of any attempt to break in'

'I'm with you there, boss' agreed the sergeant, Bert Butters, who'd won the "Flattest Feet in the Gloucestershire Constabulary" in 1948 and still held the record; his rotund eighteen stone frame didn't help, of course...until it came to restraining those of a felonious nature.

'PC Gibbs found the taxi driver who brought the clerical gentleman from the station this morning. He informed him that he dropped off the 'foreign gentleman' about 10.15am and he did have a parcel with him. So now we know that the murderer had only twenty minutes to carry out his work. Twenty minutes. That's cutting it a bit fine, don't you think, Bert?'

'Whoever it is must have ice running through their veins. Phew, they're a cool customer right enough' replied Bert. 'The timing and the nerve you'd have to have to...leaves me dumbfounded' he conceded, lifting his helmet and scratching his head.

'Aye' his Chief concurred '...you're not wrong, Bert. And there's still no sign of the murder weapon. Where could that be? I mean, within minutes of hearing the victim cry out, people were on the spot. Come to think of it, where did the blinking murderer get to? I'm telling you, Bert, I'm beginning to think this place is haunted'

'I'm with you there, boss' repeated the sergeant.

'Well, I've checked through the statements they've all given and the only ones I can see who didn't have an alibi for that twenty minutes period were: Father Ignatius who was in the Abbey's cellar checking for any other bottles of that wine which Sir John drank; The Honourable Gertie who was in her room having a lie down; The Honourable Angus who was in the gardens; Professor Beech who had been in the chapel meditating but, apparently, had a call of nature and four of the monks; Father Edward, the Master of Discipline, who said he was fast asleep in his room; Brother Martin, the organist who was in the organ loft trying to repair a wonky wooden trombone pipe; Brother Peter the Infirmarian, who was weeding the Abbey's herb garden at the time; Brother Jerome, the cook says he was preparing the lunch menu in the kitchen and finally, Brother Joseph, the Bursar, who was going over the accounts in the Abbot's office. So, eight people who were in places where no-one else can verify their alibi. And that, my son, is the list of potential suspects we have for the moment. Oh, and Miss Lavender but I don't think we'll count her' joked the Chief Superintendent.

The sergeant scratched his head again, a thing he regularly did when there was something bothering him. 'D'you think we can cut that list down even further, Sir? I mean surely the two Honourables, Gertie and Angus, could be discounted? Would they be involved in their own father's death? According to everyone we interviewed two nights ago, they doted on the old man and were very upset when he croaked it. Although thinking about it, Sir...who inherits the estate? You never know, they might come into a tidy sum on the father's death. For all we know, they could be in financial straits. And let's be honest, they wouldn't be the first son or even daughter who bumped off a relative to get their hands on their inheritance'

'I know what you mean: they seem such decent people, but you're right Bert, we'll need to check out Sir John's will. That might give us a clue. However, if your original hypothesis is correct, then we're looking at five monks and that Professor Beech fellow. He's a rum one, right enough, but is he a murderer? Oh, it's at times like this that I wish we could bring back the rack. We'd have a confession in no time!'

Twenty One

Later that day, having already cleared it with Chief Superintendent Chivers, Sextus drove home to begin testing the small sample of wine which the police doctor, Peter Davenport, had supplied to him.

The drive to Bishop's Cleeve, the small hamlet where Sextus had lived and led his bachelor existence for the past 35 years was uneventful...unless you count shoo-ing a stray sheep off the road and back into the field it had escaped from.

The whitewashed, ivy-covered cottage was as he'd left it with the front door key still under the mat. But before he got down to work, he made a call to Police Headquarters and was put through to Charlie, who'd arrived back at HQ about the same time as Sextus had arrived home.

'Chief Superintendent, I'm just about to start working on that phial of the wine. Any word from your own people?'

'Yes, as a matter of fact I have. I've just seen the report in my in-tray. Hold on a minute.' and he began to read. 'Hmm, looks like they've tested the cork and they say that it definitely wasn't tampered with. No needle marks...blah, blah, blah...the cork hadn't been extracted and then replaced. They seem quite sure about it: it was intact when it was opened. The lab boys assume that it must have been some kind of freak accident' he finished.

'You and I both know that's not correct, Chief Superintendent, especially now we've had another murder. Or could that be just another accident perhaps?'

'Well, no. I see what you mean, Mr Phipps. Mmm...I wish you luck with the tests; our people haven't started on the contents yet. They've been pulled onto another case which needed their urgent attention. So what's this one supposed to be? A naughty schoolboy prank? I dunno, I can remember when we'd get a case like this once in a blue moon. Now, it's almost one a week. What's the world coming to Mr Phipps, eh?' he asked dolefully.

'I wish I knew, Chief Superintendent, I really do. But I'll get started now and call you when I have something' Sextus offered, empathising with the Chief Superintendent's position but unable to offer a suitable answer or solution.

'Much obliged, Sir. Thank you again for your help'

This was the part of his life where Sextus had always chosen to work alone. Working with others had its advantages; but it had its drawbacks too. He was the lone scientist but wasn't above picking the brains of friends in the field.

The test tubes beckoned and Sextus answered; he donned his lab coat and lit the Bunsen burner.

It didn't take anything like the time he had expected. Forty-five minutes later, to be precise, he had his answer.

'Unbelievable. Simply unbelievable'

Picking up the phone again he dialled a London number.

'Mayfair 215' announced the deep, sonorous voice of the occupant.

'Peter. Hello, it's Sextus. How are you old man?'

Peter Crossland OBE had trained with Sextus before they embarked on their separate careers. Unlike Sextus, Peter decided to go into Industry and ended up as the Managing Director of one of the biggest drug manufacturers in Europe.

'Well, knock me down with an ostrich feather! How are you, Sextus, you old devil! Still assisting that sleuthing friend of yours; what's her name, Miss Wisteria, isn't it?' he barked.

'No' explained Sextus patiently for the umpteenth time to his friend 'Lavender's the name.'

'I knew it was something Marjory grew in our garden. Of course, I remember now. So, to what do I owe the pleasure, old friend?' he continued, getting down to business.

'Just wanted to check a couple of things with you that I'm working on, Peter. It's to do with that terrible business at Brackenbury Abbey; I suppose you've read about it in the papers?'

'What? Is that the one where old Johnnie MacDorn-Smythe died after a tipple of vintage claret? He knew his wines, did Johnnie. A real connoisseur. Terrible way to go. I knew him personally. Nice chap. He was a member of my club and a more decent fellow you couldn't meet. So what's it about, Sextus, hmm?'

'I just wanted to pass something past you, Peter. I've checked and rechecked my findings and I can't see that I can draw any other conclusion'

For the next ten minutes, the two men talked about things that would sound like complete balderdash to the public at large; all about molecules changing their shape and things like that.

'You're conclusion is spot on, old chap. No two ways about it: the only possible answer. Poor Johnnie. Never hurt a fly. So it was murder. Find the swine that did this and give him a thump for me will you, Sextus?'

'I'd love to Peter but I don't suppose the police will allow it. But thank you again for your help. Best regards to your Marjory and the children'

'Sextus,' Peter chortled, 'the children, as you call them, are middle-aged parents with grown up children of their own!'

'Where does the time go?' Sextus, the disbelief clear in his voice, asked. 'Well, goodbye, Peter'

'Bye-bye, old man. Look after yourself'

Twenty Two

Late evening, with a general lack of appetite among the Abbey's residents and the dishes from the sparsely-attended supper cleared out of the way, two cruel, heartless murderers sat on the edge of their respective beds, no more than forty feet apart plotting their next move.

One murderer, the possessor of the contents of the mysterious packet, was about to unleash a trompe l'oeil whose purpose was simple: to distract the Upholders of the Law as he began the final chapter of his grand scheme. But he had a problem: to complete the distraction, he needed another victim.

'Who? Who? Who?' deliberated the man who, long ago, had sold his soul in the search for this prize, now in his possession. His mood, despite everything that had gone on, was almost light-hearted: he was nearing the end of his quest.

'No-one would believe it if I told them. Hundreds of years and not a single one of them, in all of that time, realised what they had'

Forty feet away, his fellow lost soul was not in such a buoyant mood. 'This is not how it was supposed to bloody turn out. We should have been out of here by now. What went wrong? And who the bloody hell's stolen the goods? Damn!' He fell into a deeply melancholic mood, interrupted only by spasmodic feelings of anger towards his opponent, whoever that was.

In the meantime, as this murderer considered his next move, the other murderer had elected his next victim.

'Perfect! Fortunately, the timetable is so rigid. Or maybe...', his thoughts were colliding so fast they almost caused sparks in his twisted brain '...yes, that's it. I think that will work well. In fact, very well indeed'

The second murderer still hadn't worked out his plan of action.

Around the same time, Sextus, who'd arrived back at the Abbey forty minutes earlier, was discussing his findings, in depth, with Boo.

'No question, Sextus?'

Her friend shook his head. 'Absolutely not, Boo, I consulted an old friend from my college days who knows what he's talking about and he concurs'

'So it was cyanide. Have you told Charlie yet?'

'Yes, I called him; he didn't seem unduly surprised. Apparently, he'd been involved with a murder case at Scotland Yard some years before he joined the Gloucestershire Constabulary where a woman had murdered her abusive husband using it: she was still hanged, apparently'

Miss Lavender harrumphed. Although she was a firm supporter of the great British justice system, there were times when she had her doubts...and that particular situation was one of them. However, she let it pass; she did not want to digress from the serious issue at hand. But another time...

'So how did it get in the bottle? Can that happen with vintage wines or was it a freak of nature or was it deliberate, Sextus?'

'I discussed that too with my friend, Peter, and we both agree that no amount of fermentation, no matter how long, could produce that sort of substance. Neither, Boo was it a "freak of nature" as some people have referred to it as: it was murder. But how it got into the wine is a mystery...the only thing we know for sure is the outcome'

'Yes, Sextus, it is so incredibly sad. He was a lovely man'

The call to compline, the last prayers of the evening, rang out, interrupting their conversation and the troubled thoughts of a murderer trying to work out his next move.

'Blast!' he cursed and began making his way along the corridors towards the Chapel, mingling with the monks and lay people as they all made their way there in silence.

The laity, including Sextus and Miss Lavender, who had remembered to don her mantilla, sat apart from the religious as they waited for the Abbot to begin the prayers. Miss Lavender was again keenly aware of the smell of the incense imbued in the very fabric of the building over hundreds of years of thurible-swinging.

In those few moments before the Abbot intoned the opening of the first prayer, most of the congregation's eyes drifted towards Lady MacDorn-Smythe. Sitting upright in the front row of the lay pews, with her children sitting either side of her, her grief, clearly etched in the sunken, dark sockets of her red-rimmed eyes, bore testament to the loving relationship she had had taken away from her. Her children patted her hand occasionally in comfort even though it looked like they'd both done their own fair share of tear-shedding. What more could they do for their mother? How do you console someone whose life had been destroyed for no apparent reason?

Of the two of them, Angus seemed to be bearing up better than his sensitive sister but then, he was from a long line of British male aristos who, for centuries, had had a "stiff upper lip" thrashed into them at public school.

As the short service progressed, Miss Lavender kept watch on those with the roaming eyes, both fore and aft, intently. It did make her slightly giddy: one minute scanning those behind with her specially adapted mirrored spectacles and the next, checking out those at the front. But she could see no sign of 'Guilty' displayed in those eyes or faces...at least, not yet.

The whole congregation appeared to Miss Lavender, to be on a knife's edge: the fear manifesting itself as eyes locked briefly with others present in the congregation. 'Are you the murderer...' the eyes seemed to ask '...or can I trust you?'

'Dear oh dear,' thought Miss Lavender 'this situation can't go on. The Lord only knows what it will lead to. Nervous breakdowns? More violence? I mean anything could happen'

Boo was jolted out of her intense scrutiny of the congregation when the Abbot stood up and announced: 'Now let us pray for the souls of the faithful departed'

The monks began to recite the 'De Profundis' in Latin which Boo, unexpectedly, found very moving.

The service ended and the majority of the congregation, including Miss Lavender and Sextus, quietly made their way back to their rooms for an early night. But a few monks and one or two of the laity stayed behind.

Some of the monks opened their breviaries, no doubt offering further prayers for those recently deceased while others produced their Rosary beads.

As one of the monks opened his prayer book, a small scrap of paper fluttered slowly to the floor. He retrieved it and saw that something had been scribbled on it. He read the message.

It read: "Father, I think I know who is responsible for these terrible deaths but I cannot prove it. I need your help. Please meet me in the Lumber Room in fifteen minutes. I need your advice"

It was signed from a member of the Community.

He closed his prayer book and stood up slowly before genuflecting and leaving the Chapel.

His actions did not escape the attention of the murderer.

Twenty Three

'Just enough time to get things set up' deduced the murderer almost cheerfully as he left the pew, checking his expression was suitably sombre before genuflecting and bowing his head reverentially as he made a slow, pious sign of the Cross.

The enormous contrast between the untroubled cheerfulness going on in this murderer's head and his external appearance of solemn mourning would, for most people, have been unsustainable but not this murderer.

The Lumber Room, where the young policeman had had the sneezing fit earlier in the day, was conveniently situated far enough away from any prying eyes or ears for the work which had to be done, thought the murderer.

During the hours of darkness, it was customary for all lights in the monastery to be extinguished and candles used. The practice had grown during the war years when the curfews and blackouts were in operation: it had been noted at the time that the electricity bills had been considerably smaller and so the system was kept in place. The only natural light was garnered from stray moonbeams slipping through narrow windowpanes into corridors and rooms giving some small amount of illumination. That night, the cloud cover was thick and heavy with very little light seeping into the building.

The murderer crept along the corridors towards the Lumber Room, listening all the time for any sounds which might indicate that he was not alone. There was not a sound. Reaching the door of the Lumber Room, he gingerly felt his way past the jumble of furniture to the range where he counted down the raised flower motifs to the fifth one, pulling and releasing the catch.

He retrieved the two items he needed. First, the still-bloodied candlestick used to such devastating effect on the Italian prelate. The second, the habit, stolen from the Laundry Room and used to protect the murderer's own clothing from any blood splatter. So far, no-one had reported the robe missing.

Donning the habit and pulling the cowl over his head and with the candlestick clasped firmly in his left hand, he crept from behind the range, closed it and ducked down behind one of the broken pieces of furniture...then settled down for the wait.

While he crouched there, he commended himself on his tenacity: 'You have the patience of a saint'. He almost burst out laughing at the irony of the thought until the soft slow shuffle of sandals together with the rustling of a habit dragging behind on the stone floor could be heard outside the door. The murderer tensed.

Just as quickly as the noise was heard, it stopped; that was when the murderer observed the faint glow of a candle under the door.

'He's come'

The handle rattled slightly as the doorknob was turned and the door creaked opened slowly. The murderer made out the figure of the slightly stooped, elderly figure still in his robes, by the light of the flickering candle he was carrying.

'Brother, are you there?' the monk called hesitantly.

'I'm here, Father' the murderer answered softly.

The monk sighed and pushed the door closed behind him. He turned back slowly as the weak light thrown out by the candle caused the room to come alive with a thousand shadows: the murderer stood up.

'Here, Father' he repeated.

The weak watery eyes of the priest saw the robed shape and said:

'How is it you think I can help, Brother? What is it you know of these terrible crimes?'

'I have the proof, Father' the murderer replied 'It's over here on the table. Come, have a look'

The old priest shuffled over towards the table, wax dripping from the small brass candlestick onto the floor as he moved. He placed one hand on the table, screwing up his eyes as he bent over looking for what it was the murderer said was there.

'I can't see anything, Brother' he observed perplexedly, looking upwards into the face standing on the other side of the table. The guttering candle momentarily lit up the face framed by the cowl. Puzzlement then alarm registered on the deeply lined face. 'You're not...!'

'No, Father, I'm not' was the reply before the murderous weapon crashed down on the priest's tonsured head.

The candlestick had performed its vile work yet again...only soundlessly this time. Father Edward, the Novice Master, fell to the ground with barely a sound. No need for panic this time.

The murderer hummed part of the 'De Profundis' to himself as he dragged the crumpled, lifeless body of the old priest behind the range.

Wedging the body into the sitting position, the murderer disrobed and covered the body over with the bloodied habit.

'And now for the fait accompli...such a shame' he thought wistfully as he removed the precious Rosary from its package and stuffed it into his pocket.

He then made his way cautiously along the darkened, silent corridors. No sound; everyone in the Abbey was asleep or as close to it as their troubled minds would let them.

Reaching the sidedoor to the Chapel, he tentatively lifted the latch, hoping it wouldn't make a sound. It opened silently.

The only illumination in the deserted church came from the red glass candleholder raised high above the altar, the flames flickering lazily around the sanctuary bouncing dully off the stained-glass windows.

He approached the altar, out of habit, genuflecting. Walking up the three steps to the altar he stopped, standing in front of the tabernacle.

For the briefest of moments his conscience surfaced, then quickly slid back to its dark place.

He placed the Rosary beads on the altar alongside a single folded sheet of notepaper.

'That should keep them busy, now to get on with solving the mystery'

Twenty Four

It was a few minutes to four o'clock, Matins, the first prayers of the day, were about to begin when the Rosary and letter were discovered. For a place where peace and tranquillity permeated its very fabric alongside the all-pervading smell of incense, mayhem was fast replacing it.

Brother Augustus, the sacristan found them.

He was about to open and read the note when the Abbot strode into the Chapel. Brother Augustus tried, unsuccessfully, to surreptitiously attract the Abbot's attention. But with every pair of monks' eyes looking and waiting for the Abbot to arrive that just wasn't going to happen.

The Abbot's brow furrowed, confused and worried by the animation he could see on the normally placid sacristan's face. What now? And is it good or bad news? Then he saw the Rosary hanging from Brother Augustus's hand he murmured 'Praise be to God and his Blessed Mother', thinking that the thief had had a change of heart and returned the precious artefacts. Only when he approached the sanctuary did he see the note in the sacristan's other hand.

He read the brief note.

'It can't be true. This just cannot be true' he thought desperately.

But it was written there in black and white. Could there be any room for doubt?

'Why, oh why, did I ever start this?' he berated himself, his eyes darting from the note to his congregation and back again. 'It was pure vanity. Nothing less. And now look how it's turned out'

The rest of the monks sat waiting in anticipation, Matins forgotten.

'I'll have to tell them' the Abbot decided '...but then what?'

A deeply troubled sigh later, he cleared his throat and announced:

'Father Edward has confessed to stealing our historic artefacts'. The Abbot lifted the note and read: 'I could not...stop myself' he began falteringly. 'I feel that I have brought shame on our House and my Brothers in the community. I have left the monastery never to return' The Abbot let his arm drop, the note hanging limply in his hand at his side.

With enormous strength of will he concluded:

'He asks for our forgiveness and our prayers'

For a few moments, there was silence and then a chorus of 'No's!' and 'Impossible!'

Finally, when the shock had sunk in and only silence remained, the Abbot announced: 'Let us say our Holy Office and prayer for our fellow Brother in Christ's eternal soul'

To say the Abbot's mind was only half on Matins would've been a gross exaggeration. The truth was for most of the morning prayers, his thoughts were on how to tell the rest of the Abbey when they woke up about Father Edward's terrible admission. But it didn't end there. Where was the Charter? Why didn't he return that? Was he responsible for the death of those two people? Father Edward? The Abbot pondered on it. How long had he known the Novice Master? Twenty, maybe twenty-five years? Everyone knew him to be a bit of an old grump at times but...this? Murder and theft?

No matter how he looked at it, he just could not have seen this coming.

'I need to inform the Chief Superintendent and Sextus... and his friend, Miss Lavender' he decided. 'I suppose the police will have to catch him. Oh, the shame! What will our bishop say? What will the newspapers make of it?'

Matins over, the monks went about their daily routine while the Abbot retired to his study to prepare for what he had no doubt would be a very daunting day.

Twenty Five

At a quarter to eight, the slow melancholic toll of a bell began to ring out, calling those toiling in the fields along with the members of the community at work in the repair of the massive building's fabric, to come and break their fast.

All gratefully laid down the tools of their trade and began making their way towards the Refectory and the brief respite from their labours it afforded them: the lay visitors would be joining them there.

Ten minutes earlier, Sextus had knocked on Boo's door to see if she was ready, which she was. Today, she had chosen a very smart black and off-white Prince of Wales check skirt, short black Jacques Fath jacket, both purchased from Kitty Wardrop's couture shop in Cheltenham. It was finished off with a plain white starched cotton blouse adorned at the neck with an amethyst brooch, making her look every inch the smart Librarian. The understated, sensible flat black shoes with a delicate gold clasp were new and pinching the little toe of her right foot.

Both she and Sextus admitted that they hadn't slept particularly well. Like most of those lodging under the Abbey's roof that night, they'd slept with one eye open and an ear half-cocked.

Making their way down the wide staircase, Sextus wondered out loud what the day might bring. Boo didn't speak it out loud but she secretly hoped that today would be the day that the murderer might make a slip; little knowing what was about to be revealed before they'd even broken bread.

'Good Morning, Sextus, Miss Lavender' the Abbot greeted the friends as they entered the Refectory. Boo didn't miss the angst in the eyes nor the voice, which matched it.

'There's more trouble afoot, Sextus' warned Boo. On reaching their table, they dragged their chairs out from under the table scraping them along the stone floor noisily and sat down.

'Surely there can't be anything more, Boo' Sextus said more in hope than expectation.

As predicted by Boo minutes earlier, the Abbot rang the small bell which he used to bring silence to the proceedings.

'Can I just have a moment of your time, please, everyone?' he called out over the hubbub of early morning chatter.

Instant silence. All heads turned towards him, expectant.

The Head of the Abbey stood up.

'Most of you already know what I'm about to say so I ask you to bear with me' The Abbot took a deep breath before pulling out a sheet of paper from the folds of his habit.

'When we met this morning to say our Holy Office, this note was found on the High Altar together with this' He pulled something from the pocket of his habit and held it aloft. The light streaming through the windows of the Refectory quickly caught the sparkling diamonds and rubies of the Rosary as it twirled slowly in the Abbot's hand: refracted red and white lights slowly spilt over the faces and bodies of all those present like a glitter ball in a dance hall.

The Abbot read the note out loud, this time with only an occasional glance at it, while he surveyed the faces around the tables.

He wasn't the only one looking. Boo was on high alert, analysing the reactions of those present. On the faces of the community, she could see nothing but surprise and shock: '...but that's probably because they'd already been told' she thought. With the lay people present, she expected them to be surprised but what else might be seen there?

Lady MacDorn-Smythe was clearly shaken. 'Is this the man who murdered my husband? A man of the cloth: a respected, long-serving member of his community?' These were the sort of thoughts Boo assumed were going around in Her Ladyship's head, judging by the expression on her face.

From the looks on their faces, it seemed the two Honourables were thinking along the same lines. Or were they, thought Boo?

Angus seemed to be struggling to keep his stiff upper lip under control. Boo wasn't sure what was going on there at all. Gertie wasn't even trying; she was quietly blubbering into her handkerchief until the Rosary was displayed; then suddenly the waterworks dried up and she sat upright and concentrated on what the Abbot was saying...or at least that was Boo's initial reading of the situation.

'Hmm. Were they real in the first place?' was her thought about those tears.

Her heart went out to the family but she had trained her brain to focus on the facts only.

She noted that the Reverend Richmond, the cleric she'd observed in conversation with Professor Beech a couple of days earlier, seemed stunned. But was there anything else there? No...wait, yes. There definitely was something else, Boo decided. But what? Then it hit her. He was staring so intently at the Abbot it was as if he was hypnotised. He couldn't take his eyes off the Abbot. 'But why?' Boo wondered.

For a brief moment, Boo's eyes drifted over towards Professor Beech. The scholar seemed equally transfixed. Mesmerised.

'Why would these two gentlemen be listening to the Abbot quite so intently? Or had they foreknowledge about what the Abbot has just revealed?' she asked herself.

She turned her attention back to the Reverend Richmond just as the Abbot's hand holding the Rosary dropped. At exactly the same time as the Abbot's hand fell, the Reverend's head followed it. She quickly looked back at the Professor: his head had fallen too.

Then she twigged. 'It's the Rosary. They...are...completely enthralled by it!' They probably can't even hear what the Abbot's saying' she realised. 'But is that significant, I wonder? Does it point the finger at either of them? Or is everyone's reaction the same as theirs?'

Boo continued to scan the faces of the others and saw that their reactions were pretty much the same. No, not quite. There was one, she saw, whose attention seemed elsewhere? Almost as if he was daydreaming. 'Now why would that be? Why would his reaction be different to everyone else's' she thought. 'Is it significant that he doesn't seem surprised or overawed by this object in front of...?'

Before she could complete the thought, young Brother Fabian stood up.

'I just cannot believe this, Father Abbot' he said, verbalising what the rest of the community was thinking. 'We all knew

Father Edward. He would never do such a thing. This is wrong. There is something wrong here'

There were murmurs of agreement from other members of the community.

'Silence!' the Abbot commanded. 'Please Brother Fabian, sit down. I will not have such outbursts' he hesitated, unused to such indiscipline. 'Has anyone seen Father Edward this morning? When was the last time anyone saw him?'

There were a few moments of tense silence before Brother Jerome, the cook, spoke up, his West of Scotland accent noticeable for the first time to Boo: 'Well I heard him in the corridor last night around ten o'clock. I recognised his shuffle...' here some of the other monks laughed; in such a close community, everyone's habits were well known to the others.

'Silence!' the Abbot insisted even more forcefully this time.

'...and saw a dim light pass along under my door. I assumed he was going to the lavatory; he often did at that time of night'

Nothing else was offered.

'Well, I shall pass these items and that information onto the police and let them deal with it' The Abbot paused, bringing matters to a close by saying: 'Let us say Grace'. He continued, 'Bless this food, O Lord. Bless those who have prepared it and provide food for those who have none' and everyone joined in with an 'Amen' at the end.

Of course, the talk was all of Father Edward and the Community's utter amazement at his disappearance and the re-appearance of the precious artefact.

Boo was sitting next to Sextus, who was chomping his way through some heavily buttered toast while the conversational cacophony increased in intensity as the meal progressed.

'What do you make of it all, Sextus?' she asked as she herself nibbled her thinly buttered toast with a smidgen of orange-cut marmalade.

'From what I saw of him, he didn't strike me as a murderer or indeed a thief, if I'm being honest, Boo. Strange. Definitely strange'

'Nothing else?'

'Er...er...no. I don't think so. Why, what are you thinking?'

'Let's wait till Charlie gets here and we can discuss it then. You never know' she finished mysteriously. Sextus turned to see what she meant, toast half way to his mouth, when he saw Boo tugging on her ear as if to suggest there might be someone ear wigging.

'Quite, quite' responded the man returning to his toast with gusto, only this one had a generous helping of butter with rather a large dollop of marmalade precariously balanced on top.

'In fact,' thought Boo mischievously regarding the quantity of preserve piled on the bread, '...if he had a shovel...'

Twenty Six

Breakfast over, Boo returned to the Bibliotheca to continue cataloguing. The range of first editions and esoteric titles absorbed her in a way that often found her forgetting to take breath.

With every pile of books she lifted onto her table to examine there was something which brought a small gasp to her lips. Within the hour, Sextus and Charlie Chivers arrived and Boo was forced to abandon her treasure hunt.

'Goodness gracious, gentlemen, you gave me a start! I take it you've been brought up to speed with the latest developments, Charlie?'

'Yes, thank you Miss Lavender. Mr Phipps here said that you had some thoughts which you'd like to share?'

'Well, yes I do, but before we get to that is there anything which strikes you as odd about what's happened?'

'I'm...I'm...not sure' he admitted uncertainly. 'I've only just heard and haven't had time to think it through'

'Well, if you'll allow me...' she waited until she got the nod '...what really strikes me as odd is the way it has been done'

What do you mean, Boo?' Sextus asked.

'Here we have a priest who has lived within these walls for the best part of thirty years but who, with the imminent arrival of these treasures, has the urge to murder two strangers and steal these priceless artefacts. And if you think that's strange, what about the significance of the item which he supposedly returned?'

'My turn, Miss Lavender,' Charlie Chivers said 'what is its significance?'

'It's now my belief that it was the Charter that the murderer was always after'

'May I ask how you came to that conclusion?' Charlie asked on behalf of both of them.

'Let me put it this way: if you'd gone to all of the trouble of murdering two innocent people to get your hands on these priceless objects but later had an attack of guilt or remorse or whatever this highly-suspect letter offers by way of explanation, would you return one but not the other?' Boo paused before continuing: 'So, I believe that it was the Charter that our murderer was after all the time. The return of the Rosary is simply meant to...distract us. But from what I couldn't tell you' she admitted candidly.

'I see what you mean' the Chief Superintendent gathered when he saw the sense in what Miss Lavender proposed.

'Yes, when you put it that way, Boo, so do I' Sextus concurred.

Now that she had the bit between her teeth, Miss Lavender wasn't about to let go.

'The question is,' she pressed on 'what is it about the Charter that they wanted? What is there about it that is significant? Maybe the Father Abbot might know. I think he should be our first port of call: ask what the history is behind it. Maybe there are legends or myths attached to it that made it so irresistible to whoever has possession of it now'

'Well, there's no time like the present. Just stay here and I'll see if the Abbot's free' offered the Chief Superintendent removing the bit from Boo's teeth and getting it between his own.

This was Sextus' first time in the Bibliotheca and so Boo, unable to resist the opportunity to dazzle her friend, spent the next ten minutes producing eye-popping books like rabbits out of a magician's hat. Sextus was dumbstruck.

'Wonderful!' 'Marvellous! 'Incredible!' were the only one word statements he could muster each time a volume of stunning magnificence appeared.

Finally, Sextus found his tongue.

'Boo, some of these should be in the British Museum'

'You're telling me, Sextus' came back the swift reply.

'It's almost like discovering Tutankhamen's tomb all over again'

'I say, Sextus, steady man! Steady!'

But it struck a chord with Miss Lavender. 'Is that what he meant about "check things out"?' she thought but as had so often happened recently, her train of thought was interrupted by the door of the Bibliotheca squeaking open.

The Chief Superintendent returned without the Abbot.

'Can't find him' he reported. 'I've sent a couple of men around the grounds to find him and ask him to come here for a meeting'

Boo replaced the latest book she'd been showing to Sextus back on her desk before turning and putting into words some thoughts which had been bothering her.

'Surely the precious stones in the setting of the Rosary must be worth a king's ransom, don't you think, gentlemen? So why give it up? Especially when there's no need? I mean, it's not as if we have any clues, as yet, to the identity of the murderer...or do we, Charlie?' she asked of the Chief Superintendent.

'Er...er...no, Miss. We've drawn a blank so far. Not only have we been unable to work out how they managed to introduce the poison into the wine; the only fingerprints on the umbrella belonged to Monsignor Avrili. Damnation! Whoever this character is, they've gone to a lot of trouble to cover their tracks'

'Yes, that is a pity, Charlie' commented Miss Lavender matter-of-factly. 'So, our only hope is that the murderer makes a slip. However, as they have what he or she wants, I'm unable to see how we'll be able to flush them out. To my mind, we have two good scenarios and one bad one. The good scenarios are: one, the murderer makes a mistake or, two, we have a breakthrough. However, if the murderer decides to lay low and wait then we have the bad scenario and that, put simply, means we're stumped! But in the meantime, maybe it'll be for the best if we keep my theory that the Rosary is a red herring to ourselves'

'But why?' Sextus wanted to know. 'Isn't it better for us to let the murderer know that we're on to them and that their ruse hasn't worked? I mean, that might flush them out'

'No, Sextus' Boo replied patiently, 'if the murderer thinks that he or she has gotten away with this, they might get cocky and make a slip. Trust me, Sextus, at this point; we really do need for them to do that'

'Agreed' remarked the Chief Superintendent honestly.

'Our immediate concern, I feel, is finding Father Edward. I have a bad feeling about this' continued Boo.

'We've put out an all-points bulletin on him, Miss Lavender but like you I can't understand how or why someone would suddenly, after thirty years, become a murderer overnight. It just doesn't add up'

'As our old head Librarian used to say, Charlie: "if it doesn't add up, you've got your sums wrong: so start again"' concluded Boo.

That thought provoker was interrupted by the arrival of Dom Ambrose.

'Ah, Father, thank you for coming' the Chief Superintendent said.

'Sorry you couldn't find me, I was up on the roof. After the rain the other day, we found several new leaks had sprung up, although in this case they didn't "spring up" they poured down into the chapel. The truth is we need a new roof...but then again we need a new...' Suddenly the Abbot stopped and chuckled before continuing: 'Apologies, everyone, I'm rambling. Once I get started with the list of new things we need, I usually can't stop. Now how can I help you, Chief Superintendent?'

'We were wondering if you could tell us a bit about this Charter, Father?' the Chief Superintendent enquired.

'What's there to tell?' the Abbot said frankly. 'It was given to us in 1156 by the Queen at the time, Eleanor. It was kept here in the monastery until King Henry the Eighth's Dissolution of the Monasteries Act in 1536 when it was smuggled out of the country to Rome and there it stayed until last week'

When he'd finished, Sextus and Charlie looked at one another and shrugged their shoulders as if to say 'nothing to be gained there'.

Fortunately, a tingling sensation in Boo's tummy region meant she wasn't ready to let go of her theory quite yet.

'I wonder, Father,' began the lady as she went fishing, 'there must be lots of rumours and myths surrounding the Charter. I mean, how romantic was it that it was smuggled right out under the noses of the King's men'

The Abbot hesitated, opened his mouth to speak and then closed it again.

'Yes, Father?' the fisherwoman pressed.

'Well,' he started, 'there have been many rumours and tales which have been passed down by word of mouth, nothing written down of course, over the last few hundred years about it...but they were only stories, nothing else'

'I see' Charlie uttered, thinking that that was an end to it: the brick wall had finally been hit. Not so, for Hilary B Lavender.

'Oh, Father do humour with a rumour...or regale with a tale!' she cajoled.

They all laughed at her unintended rhyme.

Yes, please tell us some of them' Sextus agreed.

'Well, if you really want to hear them...' the priest offered reluctantly.

'We do. Truly, we do' the Chief Superintendent chimed in.

'Right then. Well I won't bore you with the more...shall we say...fanciful ones. It would appear that each time they were passed on by word of mouth, the bigger and more fantastic they became'

'The more fanciful the better, Father' Boo said with gusto.

Charlie and Sextus exchanged puzzled glances again.

Dom Ambrose was slightly bewildered at Miss Lavender's enthusiasm but took her at her word.

'Very well,' the Abbot began 'the most enduring anecdote concerns one of my predecessors; Abbot Eustace who according to the Abbey's chronicles ruled the monastery 1425-1440. According to legend, there was a plague sweeping the land at the time. While tending the dying, Abbot Eustace was laid low with the affliction himself and was within knocking distance of death's door' he paused, looking at all three to see if they wanted him to carry on.

'Yes, yes?' responded an excited Miss Lavender.

'According to the story,' the Abbot continued 'he asked to see the Rosary and Charter one more time before he died and...'

Before he could finish Sextus piped up '...and he was miraculously cured'

'Well yes...yes, exactly' the Abbot agreed, slightly miffed that Sextus had stolen his thunder.

'How very interesting, Father' observed Charlie making a great show of pulling his pocket watch from his waistcoat pocket and checking the time. ''I'd love to stand here listening to these fascinating stories all day long but I really must get on'

'Me too' announced the spoiler of punch lines. 'I promised myself I'd say the "Glorious Mysteries" for great Aunt Bethany when I came on retreat'

Boo gave Sextus a look which left him in no doubt that she expected his nose to grow considerably longer, before turning back to the Abbot.

'So interesting, Father! I can't wait to hear the rest' declared Boo with enthusiasm.

'Well, we'll be off then' Sextus announced beating a retreat with Charlie from the Bibliotheca.

'Cowards' Boo decided, looking daggers at their disappearing backs.

The Abbot began slowly pacing up and down in front of the desk which Boo had been working on as he endeavoured to retrieve the long-forgotten oral myths concerning the Abbey's treasures from a rarely used compartment of his memory.

It took a little more than fifteen minutes for Miss Lavender to find her 'Eureka' moment.

'It just goes to show that everything comes to those who wait. Now I know why the murderer wants the Charter. Wait till I see those two later. Boys...' she tutted mentally '...they've got no patience'

Now that she'd found what she was looking for Boo wanted to stop the Abbot. However, he'd quite gotten into his stride but as luck would have it, the bell for the mid-morning break began to toll.

'...shall we continue after our break?' the Abbot enquired hopefully.

'That won't be necessary, Father. I think I've heard enough to be going on with' replied Boo charitably.

'Oh...very well then. Maybe later?' asked the crestfallen priest.

'Yes, maybe, Father. Maybe' and she left it at that.

Five minutes later, Boo could be found in the Refectory crunching on the first of her three ginger nuts.

Twenty Seven

That afternoon, Miss Lavender was busy ferreting through a particularly dusty pile of books when she came across one whose cover caught her attention. Most of its pages were stuck together with mould but for a few interesting minutes she flicked through the unstuck folios not realising their significance. It would only be later that evening after a chance remark during supper she would realise what she had been holding in her hand earlier.

'Fascinating' she uttered as she flicked through the pages.

About a quarter to four, Sextus re-appeared.

'Just in time for afternoon tea, I see' Boo noted sarcastically...but truthfully.

'Hello, Boo' was the very sheepish greeting offered from the head poking around the door of the Bibliotheca.

'Hah!' was the waspish reply.

'Am I forgiven?' bleated the sheep.

'If...I must' she replied sternly.

'But Boo,' pleaded Sextus in mitigation 'it was so boring.'

'Not from where I'm standing' replied Boo smugly, not giving anything away: Sextus was going to have to do a lot more begging. 'I don't want to have to repeat this twice, Sextus, so would you go and find Charlie and bring him here?'

'A hint?' begged Sextus.

'Go!' commanded the Librarian with an outstretched arm at the end of which was an imperiously extended finger.

A few minutes later, the other member of the herd appeared at the door with Sextus by his side.

'You wanted to see me, Miss Lavender?'

'Do come in and close the door, Charlie, you're making the doorway look untidy'

The two of them stood in front of Boo's desk like two naughty schoolboys, hands clasped in front of them, having been summoned to the headmistress's study.

'I was going to lecture you both about patience being a virtue etc. However, we don't have the time. I've found out why the murderer wants the Charter' she declared bluntly.

A pair of jaws dropped in shock but they both waited in respectful silence.

When she felt they'd suffered enough, Miss Lavender put them out of their misery.

She uttered one word: 'Treasure'

'Pardon?' asked the first to recover, Charlie.

'Treasure' she repeated. 'Apparently, so legend has it, when the Monasteries were being ransacked, the quick-thinking incumbent at the time, Abbot Francis, hid the Abbey's enormous cache of treasure...but to this day it has never been found. According to Dom Ambrose, the Charter is reputed to hold the answer to the mystery of its whereabouts. However, he also informed me that many scholars have pored over it for the last several centuries without any success. And so, it remains part of folklore: either gone forever or never existed in the first place. And, may I say, I found that out by being patient, gentlemen. Once the Abbot got into his stride, I couldn't stop him' she added as an aside.

'That's what we were afraid of' mumbled Sextus giving Charlie a surreptitious sideways glance.

The room went quiet for a minute or so before Charlie broke the silence: 'Well that puts things into perspective. Now we have a probable motive'

'It would seem so. I suppose the Charter would have been kept under lock and key in Rome or in some display case where it could be seen but not touched without arousing suspicion' Miss Lavender postulated.

'Then let's catch the blighter' retorted Sextus vehemently. 'What a vile creature they must be to murder two innocent people to get their hands on it'

'Maybe three' speculated Miss Lavender.

'What?' the Chief Superintendent said distractedly.

'Well,' Miss Lavender opined 'Let's put it this way; they haven't found Father Edward yet. Could he be the latest victim?'

'What makes you say that, Boo?' Sextus queried.

'Look, we all agree that his disappearance and apparent confession is highly suspect. Supposing the murderer has claimed yet another victim, eh?'

'But what could the motive be, Boo?' Sextus asked trying to follow her reasoning.

'Good question, Sextus. But can I turn that question back on you? Why were the other two killed?'

'Well, we don't know' replied Sextus straightforwardly.

'Exactly!' insisted Boo. 'So what's different with Father Edward? Apart, that is, from a very dodgy confession. Wait. Let me think about what I've just said'

The other two stood in silence.

Boo's brain shuffled events into different orders. 'No, that doesn't work' she muttered as she absentmindedly picked up a pencil and began tap, tap, tapping on the desk.

The other two just looked at one another.

'Hmm. Neither does that. Drat'

For the second time that day, the eureka moment pushed its way to the front of the queue of thoughts in her methodical brain.

'Yes, that fits' she concluded finally. 'Tell me what you think, gentlemen and you can be as brutal as you like in your criticism. I am not afraid of an honest critique; it's the only way to separate the wheat from the chaff. So, here goes. The events, if I've got them correct are as follows: Father Edward disappears: the dodgy confession then appears with the Rosary and...this is where I think our murderer's plan falls down...because he or she wants us to believe that Father Edward has run off out of guilt or remorse. Except why take the Charter, why not leave that too? If this murderer has their way, Father Edward will be blamed for the murders, while the murderer keeps the Charter and is completely in the clear. What d'you think?'

'So you think the murderer has killed Father Edward in order to cover their tracks?' Sextus hypothesised.

'Absolutely, Sextus. It fits. It doesn't make sense to me that a man of the cloth would do those things which are so terribly out of character with how he's behaved over the past thirty years. I keep asking myself: 'Why? Why would he decide to give up the spiritual life he's led for all this time and commit murder for the sake of money? Something he's eschewed for his entire adult life. But the problem we have is: who has committed these abominable crimes and how do we flush them out?' she finished frustratedly.

Boo turned to Charlie who'd stood silently chewing his lip all the time she was talking: he was putting the theory through its paces from a police perspective. Finally, he spoke:

'I have to say, Miss Lavender, it holds water. But where does it leave us?' Charlie counted off on his fingers: 'we know the probable motive, the treasure. We know two people have been killed and now possibly three...but that's it: all theory and no facts'

Boo and Sextus' initial excitement at discovering the murderer's motives suddenly lost its shine.

'Ah, but wait!' Sextus said taking up where his friends had left off. 'There's one thing you've both forgotten'

'Go on' encouraged Boo.

'If the murderer has killed Father Edward where's the body? It can't be far. No-one has left the Abbey, have they?'

It was Chief Superintendent Chivers turn to get excited.

'No they haven't...unless there's a secret way out of here that we don't know about. My men have been patrolling the grounds for the last couple of days'

Boo interjected: 'So, what you're saying is: either Father Edward is still here...alive...or the body is'

'Precisely' concluded Sextus.

'Right then,' Charlie said forthrightly 'I'd better organise a search party and take this place apart. I'll get onto it straightaway'

'Hold on, Charlie' Boo jumped in '...we don't want the horse to bolt'

'What do you mean?' Sextus asked.

'Well...' thinking out loud, Boo said '...if we mount a full scale search of the Abbey and the grounds, the murderer will realise that we've rumbled him or her and they may go to ground and then we might never get the chance to catch them. No, we have to be more subtle in our approach. Wouldn't you agree, Charlie?'

'I see what you mean, Miss Lavender. Hmm, what can we do? What can we do?'

Silence fell again as three thinking caps were donned and the brains beneath them got into gear.

'What if...' began Sextus before fading away with a shake of the head.

'I think there's only one way to do this' concluded Boo. 'We have to do it ourselves: just we three, no-one else and no uniforms setting off alarm bells'

'It took all of five seconds of thinking time before the others replied: 'Agreed'.

After all, it wasn't the first time they'd solved crimes between the three of them.

Twenty Eight

By the time they'd reached the Refectory, the how, when and where, had been worked out.

Chief Superintendent Chivers would continue to act as though Father Edward's confession was genuine, while Boo and Sextus would work in tandem and methodically check every room on both floors of the Abbey for any signs of disturbance before moving onto the outbuildings and grounds.

And it was decided that Charlie would keep the police presence to a minimum thereby allowing the murderer to think that they were out looking for the thief, murderer and general villain that Father Edward was supposed to be.

At the opening of the Refectory door, the general murmur in the dining room dropped as everyone turned to see who had entered; it had been agreed that Charlie would delay his entrance for a few minutes so as not to arouse any suspicion in the mind of the murderer of any collaboration going on.

Dom Ambrose slowly strode across to them: the strain clearly etched on his handsome features.

'Oh hello, Miss Lavender, Sextus' he said, nodding to his friend before turning back to Miss Lavender. 'How is the cataloguing going, my dear?'

'We're getting there, Father. You know, you really have the most wonderful library: such a marvellous collection'

'Indeed, I can vouch for that, Ambrose' interjected Sextus. 'Boo's been showing me some of the little gems you have there. I'm sure you could raise a tidy sum of money from them. You might even be able to raise enough to have the roof of the chapel repaired'

'Maybe once this is all over...' the Abbot sighed. 'But in the meantime, I've had a call from the bishop; my ear's still recovering. Apparently, we're "...bringing the Church into disrepute" he offered in a squeaky hoity-toity voice which, Boo presumed, was meant to sound like the bishop. It must have been close because Sextus guffawed.

116

The Abbot continued: 'Oh, when he gets a bee in his bonnet about something, that man can go on for hours. Wait till he finds out that Father Edward's gone missing. He'll probably have apoplexy!'

Boo and Sextus glanced at each other. In that split second, Boo read it in Sextus' eyes: he was about to divulge their theory to the Abbot. Whether out of guilt or feeling sorry for the poor man, Boo couldn't tell but she quickly tugged Sextus' sleeve to distract him.

'Come on, Sextus, otherwise all the food will be gone'

'Wh...a...t? Er, yes' stammered Sextus slightly bemused as he moved over to the table laid out with sandwiches, tea and cake.

The moment was gone. Boo had distracted him long enough to stop him revealing what they had discovered.

'Why the sudden rush?' Sextus wanted to know.

'What were you thinking of, Sextus?' Boo murmured under her breath.

'What do you mean, Boo?'

'You know what I mean, Sextus Phipps! You were on the brink of telling him, weren't you?'

'Oh, Boo, the poor man looks so stressed, I just wanted to comfort him' Sextus admitted as he filled his plate with assorted goodies: nothing put Sextus off his food.

'I understand your compassion but you must not do that. It could jeopardise our plans. And besides, what were you going to tell him: "Oh, good news, Father, we think there's another dead body hidden somewhere in the Abbey?" 'Or, maybe, "we think the double murderer, i.e. Father Edward might be hiding out somewhere within the confines of the Abbey?" 'Either way, I don't think it would have given him very much comfort, Sextus'

'Sorry, Boo...a momentary lapse'

Boo was tempted to say that it was momentary lapses which had caused some of the world's greatest disasters, but she resisted.

'Right,' she said with just a pinch of sarcasm in her voice 'when there's nothing left on the table we can make a start of it'

It sailed straight over Sextus' head.

There would be no shifting of Sextus from the vicinity of a table while there was still something to eat on top of it.

'Have you ever left anything on a plate, Sextus?'

'Oh Boo, how can you be so cr...u...el!' said Sextus stretching the last word out. 'But now you mention it...' he paused to think '...yes, I did once. It was...' he began.

'I was only joking, Sextus'

'Oh'

'While you're munching away I can tell you that I have decided to knock the cataloguing on the head for a couple of days. I don't think anyone will notice with everything that's going on and it'll give us the time we need to search the place'

'Jolly good, Boo. Whatever you think' her friend replied absentmindedly while he concentrated on satisfying the large bump which preceded him into any room.

Ten minutes later with only crumbs on the plates, Sextus reluctantly took his leave of the Refectory accompanied by Boo to begin the search.

Within two hours, most of the top floor of the Abbey had been searched and they were no further forward top finding answers or bodies in the hunt for Father Edward.

Supper would change all of that.

Twenty Nine

For supper that evening, Boo changed into a full-length dark grey Prince of Wales check skirt but wore the same simple white blouse with the amethyst brooch which she'd chosen to wear earlier in the day. A short black jacket with matching black felt hat held with a beautiful natural pearl hatpin completed her outfit.

Miss Lavender took her seat to the Abbot's left while Lady MacDorn-Smythe sat on his right, dressed head to toe in black. It really wasn't necessary for her to wear widow's weeds, everyone could see her loss; the devastation was written all over her face.

The Abbot was trying, gently, to draw her into conversation but her replies, as she shuffled bits of food around her plate, were desultory. Clearly she did not want to enter into a dialogue.

However, the Abbot persisted, seemingly oblivious to Her Ladyship's desire for solitude. So, Boo decided to intervene and distract the Abbot with a subject she thought would engage him: the possible sale of rare books from the Library to go towards the cost of repair of the chapel roof.

'Father,' she butted in quickly when there was a lull in the one-way conversation, 'I know that Sextus mentioned about a number of valuable tomes the Abbey has within the Library and I understand that you would prefer to deal with it when everything calms down. However, I just wanted to say that I have an acquaintance who works for a highly-respected auction house in Cirencester whom, I'm sure, would be happy to value the collection with a view to raising money for the church roof restoration fund'

'Thank you, Miss Lavender,' he responded, his shoulders slumping 'maybe you're right. Perhaps I should think about it now rather than later' he leant over and whispered sotto voce 'I could do with something to take my mind off our current situation even though I am reluctant to sell off any of the Abbey's heritage'

'I have to confess, Father, that over the last few days I have been distracted myself when I've found one of those little treasures. Just this morning there was a mouldy old volume that must have been at least two or maybe three hundred years old about a monastery called "Chalfontbury Friary". It was fascinating, what I could read of it, most of the pages were stuck together...with the assistance of some very nasty mould' she finished archedly. For Miss Lavender, one of the biggest sins on the planet was the neglect of any book, no matter its content.

'My dear Miss Lavender, you've just cheered an old man up' the Abbot conceded smiling for the first time in days. 'That was the original name of this Abbey. It was Sir John's...great grandfather, I think, changed the name from Chalfontbury Friary to Brackenbury Abbey. For the life of me I can't remember why but goodness me, that name hasn't surfaced in years'

It wasn't very often that Miss Hilary B Lavender was so stunned that she couldn't follow up a revelation like that but over the course of the last few days, it had actually occurred on several occasions. Questions stuck in her throat.

The Abbot continued to ramble on but it was as if Boo couldn't hear. She could see his lips moving but the voice sounded like it was coming from the end of a very long tunnel. This was Chalfontbury Friary? Then that meant...

Boo had to pinch her hand hard to bring herself back.

'I'm sorry, Father, but did you say that the Abbey used to be called Chalfontbury Friary?'

The Abbot gave her a funny look.

'Er...that is indeed what I said, Miss Lavender. Why?'

Recovering her composure, Boo gave a little cough and said:

'Oh, nothing in particular, Father. It's just that...a lot of things have just fallen into place'

'What do you mean?'

Realising she'd made a "boo-boo", her own way of saying to herself that she'd made a mistake, Boo quickly recovered by asking a question which would appear relevant to the person a propos of what they were talking about, but was in fact a distraction.

'I'm sorry, Father, but did you say it was Sir John's great grandfather who changed the name?'

'Now you've got me doubting my own memory, Miss Lavender'

He turned to Lady MacDorn-Smythe and asked:

'It was Johnnie's great grandfather who changed the name of the Abbey was it, Dorothy?'

Still not in any mood for chit-chat, Her Ladyship answered:

'Yes, I believe it was Sir Mungo, Johnnie's great...' a slight hesitation 'yes, his great grandfather, if I'm not mistaken, Ambrose'

'Thank you, Dorothy' he turned to Miss Lavender 'There you have it, Miss Lavender'

The food on Boo's plate remained untouched after that; she could not wait for the meal to finish. When Dom Ambrose rang the bell to signal the end of supper, Boo was out of her chair faster than a farmer out of the bull's paddock in the mating season.

'Bridge tonight, Miss Lavender?' the Abbot called after her.

'Oh, I'm sorry, Father, I have some personal matters to deal with' she lied.

'Oh well, never mind...' he replied despondently '...maybe tomorrow night. Yes?'

'I'm sure I'll have cleared everything up by then, Father' was the evasive reply he received.

'Excellent' responded the Abbot not very convincingly before accompanying Lady MacDorn-Smythe to the sitting room for what he felt sure would turn out to be...a very long, challenging night.

Boo pressed on, trying to catch up with Sextus whose back she had just seen exiting the Refectory door.

'Sextus...Sextus!' she called out hoarsely as he walked along, deep in conversation with the Prior, Father Ignatius.

'Will you excuse me, Father?' Sextus said, holding back while the monk walked on and Boo caught him up. 'Whatever's the matter Boo? You look as though you've just seen the ghost of Monsignor Avrili'

'Sextus,' Boo answered breathlessly, '...you really must find Charlie and get him to meet us both in the Bibliotheca...no wait. Better not meet there; someone might see us' she paused, in her mind she ran through possible meeting places where they might not be seen. 'Tell him to meet us outside by the telephone box in half an hour' she decided, checking her watch. 'And tell him I think I've stumbled onto something which could help us solve the case. Now hurry!'

Sextus knew better than to question Boo when she used that tone of voice.

Thirty

The murderer retired to his room on the pretext of being tired but the truth was this would be the first chance he'd have to scrutinise the Charter in detail.

With the police presence seeming to pervade the entire Abbey; you couldn't go anywhere without bumping into someone with silver buttons on their shoulders, or at least that's what it felt like to his paranoid mind. 'Every corner I turn, there seems to be one of them there'

Years ago, on his first visit to Rome, the murderer had been completely spellbound at his first sighting of the Charter and the stories he'd heard of untold wealth surrounding it. He became convinced that only he would be able to crack the secret of its code.

However, because of its historical significance, the Charter was kept permanently under lock and key and the only option open to those wishing to view it was to stare at it through plate glass. It was then that the murderer concluded he'd have to get a closer look: a plan began to form in his warped mind. That plan had finally come to fruition; in fact, almost to a perfect conclusion except for one unexpected occurrence. He'd have to deal with the fallout from that later but for now...he opened the case and carefully unravelled the Charter, laying it flat on the table in his room which doubled as a writing desk.

His eyes pored greedily over the document he'd dreamt of for years. It was incredibly fragile but then it was '... nearly eight hundred years old', he reminded himself.

Withdrawing a powerful magnifying glass from his pocket, he began scrutinising the document, looking for any imperfections which might need further investigation: nothing. For a further hour, he focussed intently on each individual letter viewing them through the magnifier, checking if any of them had been indented or overwritten in some way so as to spell out a clue or a location.

After the hour of intense study, he was none the wiser.

'Damn!' he swore but then it occurred to him '...if it was going to be easy, someone would have found the answer a long time ago. No, I have to look at it from a different angle. Mmm'. He was closer to the answer than he realised when that thought presented itself.

He began looking around the edges of the document paying particular attention to the margins and extreme edges, looking for any marks or indentations or writing around one of the edges which might hold a clue but no matter how closely he looked at it, nothing came up which might warrant further investigation. Nothing, nothing, nothing.

What to do?

'I know it's here somewhere, but where?' the murderer contemplated. 'Surely I haven't done all of this for nothing? No, it is here' he asserted firmly. 'I know it is. So, I have to work out how and where those stupid monks in the Middle Ages hid the clues'

His studies were interrupted by the bell calling everyone to Compline, the last prayers of the day.

'For God's sake!' he cursed exasperatedly and hid the precious document away until his return.

Thirty One

In the meantime, Boo was hurrying along to the Bibliotheca. She rummaged through piles of books scattered around the Library, all sorts of thoughts swirling around in her brain as she did so.

'Where did I put that blessed book?' she tried to recall, panicking as each pile she checked refused to give it up. 'It's here somewhere, I distinctly remember...' she stopped, resting her hands on the desk she took a slow inward breath before releasing it unhurriedly to calm herself down...and make herself think logically. 'It's the only way to do it' she reminded herself. It took thirty seconds to marshal her thoughts...nothing at first, then in her mind's eye she saw it. 'Ah ha, there you are!' she cried, walking over to a bundle of books she'd put aside as being too damaged to be worth keeping. 'I'm glad I didn't have the opportunity to suggest to the Abbot to get rid of them' she realised, breathing a sigh of relief.

Carefully thumbing through the matted pages, she realised that most of the information contained within was gone forever: its gradual destruction over many decades guaranteed by the mould from the damp air and lack of heating that is common in those sorts of old buildings.

But, there was still some information to be gleaned from it.

'Can you imagine,' she reflected 'this Abbey was originally known as Chalfontbury Friary. No wonder we couldn't find any sign of...'

Before she'd completed the thought, Sextus and Charlie burst through the door.

'I said to meet by the telephone box' Boo called out, annoyed that they'd ignored her instructions.

'Sorry, Miss Lavender, my fault, I couldn't wait' admitted Charlie candidly. 'Is it true then, Miss Lavender?' Charlie asked excitedly 'Is it really true? Mr Phipps tells me you might have had a breakthrough. Please tell me it's true' he pleaded.

'I have, Charlie' she stated simply. 'Come and let me show you'

Charlie and Sextus strode eagerly to the desk where the tome lay.

Donning his spectacles Sextus announced: 'The History of Chalfontbury Friary' from the highly damaged front cover.

'Oh...I see' was Charlie's rather disappointed reply. Clearly he didn't see.

'I won't keep you in suspense...the original name of Brackenbury Abbey was...Chalfontbury Friary' and waited for their response to this revelation.

'So?' Sextus still couldn't see the relevance.

'Have a look inside this little beauty' she insisted. 'This place is riddled with secret passages. No wonder we couldn't find the murderer. He obviously knows about them and was almost definitely hiding in one when we found the body of Monsignor Avrili!'

'Well I'll be...' began Charlie, cautiously leafing through the damaged pages, mindful of its fragility.

''Now you can't see everything...' Boo conceded earnestly '...but you can see enough; enough for us to start over again, only this time...we know what we're looking for'

Charlie was turning the book this way and that before he thundered:

'Look, there is a secret passage in that room where the body was found!' He squinted to read what it said: 'The passageway is located behind the fireplace. Twist the carving of the angel on the left side of the fireplace to gain access. I'll get my lads onto it straightaway and they can check for any evidence or fingerprints. By God! We've got whoever did this now!' he averred punching his fist into the palm of his other hand.

Now, if there was one teensy-weensy thing which caused Miss Hilary B Lavender to despair about Chief Superintendent Charlie Chivers of the Gloucestershire Constabulary, it was his propensity to act as if he was leading the Charge of the Light Brigade when he found or was presented with...a clue.

She knew she'd have to slow him down.

'Excellent idea, Charlie. But...' she paused for dramatic effect '...but what happens if there are no clues or fingerprints? What happens if the murderer is smarter than you or I, Charlie, and hasn't left any clues, what then? You'd have let the murderer know that we know and he or she will surely disappear quicker than a ferret down a rabbit hole'

'Hmm...I see what you mean, Miss Lavender' agreed Charlie after he'd thought it through.

'So do I' Sextus, of a similar disposition, concurred. 'What are you suggesting, Boo?'

'Far be it from me...' Boo started to say.

'No, please, Miss Lavender, what are you thinking?' asked Charlie who had been grateful for her support in the past.

'Well, if you insist...'

'We do. We do!' protested Sextus.

'Very well then...what I propose is that we...and I do mean we, Charlie, no uniforms that'll scare our murderer away, begin to check each of the rooms which have secret passages attached to them. And I propose that we start off with the room where we found the body of Monsignor Avrili. There is a chance that the murderer may have left incriminating evidence when he or she fled the scene but we'll have to be careful not to arouse any suspicion. Any suggestions as to how we should go about it?'

As soon as the words were out of her mouth, she regretted it. Both Sextus and Charlie were like schoolboys when the teacher asks a question which they know the answer to and their hands shoot up, shouting 'Please, Miss! Please, Miss!' ...or at least that's what it felt like to Boo.

'One at a time, please' insisted Boo as they both vied to be first. 'Alright, Charlie, what do you suggest?'

'I think we should get ourselves up to that room right now and check it out'

'I was going to say that' Sextus said sulkily. Boys: they're so competitive.

'I agree, Charlie but I propose we do it in a slightly more subtle way' offered Boo.

'What do you mean, Boo?' It was Sextus' turn this time to ask.

'Well, if we do it the way you gentlemen propose, we run the risk of being spotted by the murderer as we enter the room. So I suggest we play this murderer at his own game; I noticed earlier that the secret passage in that room leads downstairs and comes out in what looks like a disused room. When everyone has gone to bed, I think we should enter via the downstairs room and make our way up to the guest room and then we reduce the chance of anyone seeing us. Yes?'

'Good idea, Miss Lavender' the Chief Superintendent conceded.

'Then we'll need at least one strong torch, Charlie. Do you happen to have one?'

'I've got a couple in the car. I'll slip out and get them'

'Excellent. At last things seem to be going our way. We know now how the murderer managed to evade us: the chink in his armour has been exposed'

The call to Compline which interrupted the murderer's examination of the Charter reached Boo's ears.

'I forgot about night prayers. They do pray a lot, don't they, Sextus?'

'That's their job' the man of faith replied simply.

'Oh, very well then' Boo decided consulting her watch. 'Shall we say, meet here twenty minutes after night prayers have finished? That should give everyone plenty of time to get themselves off to bed and then we can make our way to that abandoned room?'

'Agreed' the two men said.

Charlie went off to fetch the torches while Boo and Sextus made their ways, separately, to the Chapel.

Just in the nick of time, Boo remembered to grab her mantilla.

Thirty Two

The murderers hardly gave each other a second glance as they walked down the main staircase mingling with the other guests and monks making for the Chapel.

Mantilla in hand, Miss Lavender herself headed along the corridor from the Bibliotheca towards the Chapel and was, as always, scanning the mirrors inside her spectacles constantly for any suspicious behaviour at the rear: this time, she did notice something.

Two people, making their way, seemingly independently, to the Chapel were about twenty feet behind her when she saw one of them catch the other up and pass what looked like a note before hurrying on by. Whatever it was it was quickly pocketed by the other one.

'Now why would those two be passing notes to one another in such a furtive manner? Why would they feel the need? Hmm'

Compline was a half-hearted affair that evening; there was nothing to stir the soul. For Boo, it sounded like the drone of bees when you're half dozing in the garden in the summer; it was just a noise floating by. Or at least, that's what it felt like for Boo...and she was sure she wasn't alone

'Everyone looks totally exhausted...probably with what's been happening over the last few of days' she thought. But while her mind might be wandering, her eyes were as alert as ever, in particular, watching the note passers.

Several times during the service Boo noticed the pair glance over at each other nervously.

'What is going on? Or to put it another way,' she allowed 'there is definitely something going on, but what? I need to look into this'

The service finished and most of the congregation left immediately, the strain etched deeply on each of the faces.

Boo waited for the stragglers to leave before making her way back.

She was deep in thought as she strode along the corridor leading to the Bibliotheca, turning over in her mind what the note passers were up to and what it could mean, when Sextus suddenly loomed out of the shadows making her recoil.

'Oh, Sextus, I was a million miles away. You frightened the life out of me!'

'Sorry, old girl, just trying to avoid being seen'

'Well it certainly worked, I didn't see you; my mind was on other things' She told Sextus about the note passers.

'How very strange, Boo. Well that's another thing to add to the pot' he concluded mystified by the actions of the two involved.

Thirty Three

When they reached the Library, Boo, wanting to avoid lighting the whole place up, asked Sextus to turn on the small lamp on the desk. Opening the "Chalfontbury Friary" book, she flattened it carefully on the desktop, looking for the location of the abandoned room.

'Why it's just along the corridor from here'

The squeaking of the door hinge alerted Boo and Sextus to the arrival of Charlie.

'Come in Charlie, we've just worked out where the room is' she muttered softly. After a quick shufti out the Library window, she concluded: 'By the looks of things, most people are tucked up in bed; I can't see any lights showing. Well then...are we all ready?'

'Definitely, let's go' asserted Charlie, handing one of the torches he'd brought to Sextus.

The three of them slowly edged their way along the wall of the corridor towards the room: Sextus at the front and Boo bringing up the rear. Careful to avoid the religious objects and statues sitting on pedestals in small alcoves along their route, they had almost reached the room when disaster struck. Sextus' elbow accidentally knocked a huge medieval painting of St Sebastian which, they later discovered, had not been attached properly to the wall; it would have toppled over on him but for Charlie's swift action which managed to steady it. It shook them all.

'Are you alright, Sextus?' whispered Miss Lavender breathlessly, her heart pounding.

'Er...yes, Boo, I'll be okay and thank you, Charlie' the retired chemist responded, badly shaken.

'Okay, if I'm correct, this should be it' Boo concluded.

The handle rattled noisily when Sextus touched it.

'Shht' hissed Boo.

Sextus held his hands up in silent disgust as if to say: 'I only touched it'

'Looks like an old lumber room' suggested the Chief Superintendent as they peered into the gloomy interior.

Sextus flashed his torch around the room, casting weird and wonderful shadows, while Charlie pointed his own beam of light in the opposite direction, at the floor.

Sweeping it methodically over the floor space, something caught his eye.

''Allo, what's this?' he said, his copper's instincts rising. 'Hold this for me, would you, Miss Lavender?' and Charlie handed Boo his torch.

He bent down and touched the dark substance splattered on the bare flagstone floor. 'It's candle wax by the looks of it. It's hardened but you can see it's fresh. Someone's been in here recently'

Boo swept the torch around the area where the wax was.

'Look!' she cried out hoarsely 'On the table. There's some sort of mark, it's...it's more wax I think and...oh, I don't know, what do you make of it, Charlie?'

Charlie pulled his magnifying glass from his jacket pocket.

'Blood' he declared emphatically. 'And definitely fingerprints. But whose? That's what we need to find out'

The three of them bent over, scrutinising the surface of the table.

'I'll have to get on to Headquarters straight away' Charlie announced straightening up. 'Please...don't touch or move anything'

It was an order not a request.

'Of course not, Charlie, but before you go, should we just take a quick look at the passageway behind the range? There may be something there that could help us' insisted Miss Lavender.

His instincts told him to deny Miss Lavender's request but, how could he? Without her patience and skill, he would never have found out about the secret passages and he'd still be scrabbling around for clues and '...I suppose you never know' he finally decided.

After a brief hesitation, he agreed to her request. 'Okay but again I have to ask you not to touch anything'

'Of course' the sleuthing Librarian and her cohort replied.

Moving their torches to and fro as they made their way cautiously through the jumbled mishmash of furniture and

132

discarded household goods to the range, they reached it without any further gruesome discoveries.

'According to the book, there are some flower motifs on the left-hand side of the range. We have to count down from the top to the fifth one, I believe, and then pull it'

Both Sextus and Boo held their torchlight on that side of the range as Charlie counted down '...three, four...five' and pulled. Nothing moved. He tried again but this time, gave it an almighty tug.

The three of them leapt back as the heavy range fell forward knocking Charlie off his feet; he, in turn, knocked Boo's torch out of her hand which fell to the floor with a bang and went out.

'Damn!' uttered Charlie regaining his balance and brushing off the dust from his clothes. 'Oh, excuse me, Miss Lavender; didn't realise it to be so loose. I expected it to be quite stiff'

'That's quite alright, Charlie but, if nothing else, it could mean that it's been used recently. But is that a good thing or a bad thing?' she concluded doubtfully.

The bad thing was waiting for them when they regained their composure and Sextus flashed his light behind the range.

'Oh my God! What's that?' he cried out when he saw the bloodied habit covering a shapeless mass against the wall.

'May I, Sir?' the Chief Superintendent pressed taking control and the torch out of Sextus' hand as he peered closer at something he'd seen many times before: he knew what it was. He withdrew his pencil from his pocket and pulled the habit back to reveal a battered, blood-splattered face.

'It's the missing reverend gentleman' he stated matter-of-factly. 'Father Edward, isn't it? He's been done for, I'm afraid. Don't go any closer, please, Miss Lavender, it's not a pretty sight: looks like he's been on the receiving end of the same blunt instrument as the other reverend gentleman'

As he finished speaking, he moved the torchlight slowly around the immediate area of the body looking for any other clues when the beam from the torch bounced off a shiny object: the missing candlestick.

The Chief Superintendent moved closer to look at it. There was no doubt what the dark crimson stains on it were: blood.

'I think we've found the murder weapon'

'Requiescat in pace' Sextus murmured making the sign of the cross.

'The truth is we knew that Father Edward wasn't a murderer or a thief. But what was the murderer's thinking behind this? Why murder a perfectly innocent bystander? Why? And why hide the body here? And then...give the Rosary back?' Miss Lavender posed these questions out loud as her formidable brain got into gear.

'I've no idea, Miss Lavender but now we've got the murder weapon we should be able to get the murderer's dabs off it and then we'll have 'im!' Charlie promised. 'I may not be of this gentleman's faith but he didn't deserve this. He was a decent man. Whoever did this, will hang' he added finally.

'Indeed, Charlie, but can we sit on this for half an hour and talk it through before your forensic people are all over it? The poor man's dead and half an hour is not going to make any difference to him now...but it might to us' Boo argued. She was of the opinion that jumping in with both feet straightaway might not be the best solution.

'Why, Miss Lavender? Surely now we've got the murder weapon and the murderer's prints, why should we delay?' contended the Chief Superintendent.

'If I'm honest, Charlie, I'm not sure. There's a niggle at the back of my brain that there's still something missing'

'Half an hour, you say? Hmm'

Boo and Sextus stood and waited as the Chief Superintendent considered his options.

'Very well, then...' he said at last '...let's sit on this until the morning and see what you can come up with, Miss Lavender'

'Thank you, Charlie. I appreciate that'

They closed the range and carefully retraced their steps so as not to disturb any evidence.

The cleric lay there until the following morning.

Thirty Four

Safely back at the Bibliotheca, they gathered three chairs together and placed them around the desk before collapsing onto them.

'Oh dear!' Miss Lavender let out as she sunk into her chair.

'What I wouldn't give for a stiff drink' Charlie observed solemnly.

'Well, it just so happens...' began Sextus removing a flask from his inside pocket.

Boo looked at him in surprise.

'For medicinal purposes only, Boo' Sextus said defensively.

'Well, I'm jolly glad that you have it, Sextus, because I, for one, could do with a bit of fortification. It's given me quite a turn' Boo admitted removing the hatpin from her hat and placing them both on the desk.

'After you, Miss Lavender' Charlie said passing the flask to the lady first.

Boo took a decent swig of the amber nectar before swallowing it in one and passing it to Charlie, who didn't bother to wipe the neck of the flask and downed a good amount of the liquid before passing it to Sextus. Sextus held it, shook it and said before joining them:

'I say, you two, this is my best brandy. You didn't leave much for poor old Sextus, did you?'

Miss Lavender, feeling light-headed opened her mouth to deliver a withering response when she hiccupped.

'Oh...I do beg your pardon, gentlemen' she apologised.

Their laughter briefly relieved the tension floating over them like a black cloud on a summer's day.

'Down to business' Miss Lavender suggested. ''I don't know why I asked you to delay telling your superiors, Charlie, but please bear with me. My first and most obvious question is: why did the murderer kill Father Edward? What would be the point? Could Father Edward have found out the identity of the murderer? Perhaps the murderer had a pang of remorse and confessed to him? However, I have to be honest and say I have my doubts about that particular theory. As I understand it, even if Father Edward had found out who it was in the confessional, he would have been bound by the seal of confession not to reveal it. Am I right, Sextus?'

'Unquestionably, Boo. Anything a priest hears in the confessional stays there no matter how much the priest might want to or feel he ought to speak about it, he can't'

'Stupid rules' opined the Chief Superintendent.

Sextus glared at him. 'Do not question my faith!' he retorted.

Boo quickly intervened to stop this descending into a debate on religious mores.

'I don't think the Chief Superintendent meant to call your religious beliefs into question, Sextus'

The two men looked at each other. Sextus was not entirely sure Boo was correct but then Charlie apologised and Sextus let it go.

'Sorry, Mr Phipps, I didn't mean to imply anything by it'

'Then we'll forget about it' declared Sextus magnanimously.

'Let's move on' Boo proposed quickly.

'So why did he kill Father Edward?' the Chief Superintendent threw out.

'To be honest,' Boo confessed 'I've been racking my brains and I don't think we'll know the answer to that one until we catch the murderer and ask him or her. No, I think the reason I asked for the delay is I think there's a better way to do this.' She paused. 'First of all, I don't think it would be difficult to find out whose habit we found covering Father Edward. Whoever was wearing it, obviously discarded it because of the bloodstains. So, does that mean they had to find another one? Or is someone missing a habit? So, Charlie, what if...' she halted trying to gather her thoughts '...what if we set a trap for the murderer? What if we say...we've found a bloodied habit but omit to mention where it was found or that we found Father Edward's body? Wouldn't that confuse the murderer? Wouldn't they wonder how we could have found the habit but not the body?' she suggested.

'Hmm, that might panic him or her into some sort of action' Charlie concurred.

'I would want to go and check on the body' Sextus stated.

'My point exactly' Boo agreed jumping on what Sextus had said. 'But we're dealing with a clever, devious person, not someone who's just going to pop along to check behind the range. If...if I were them, I would assume that the lumber room would be watched...but the murderer doesn't know that we know about the secret passage leading down from the room where Monsignor Avrili's body was found. That's it. I think the murderer might try to check on the body that way...but we'll be waiting for them. Yes, I think that might work. The alternative is to wait for the forensic report and that could take days, maybe even longer and Lord knows what the murderer might get up to in the meantime' she concluded.

'You know, Miss Lavender, you could just be right' said Charlie in admiration.

'It might just work' admitted Sextus.

'I knew there had to be another way. But now,' she stifled a yawn 'I think we all need to get some rest. I get the feeling it's going to be a long day tomorrow'

Thirty Five

Never mind a long day; it was turning into a long, long night for the murderer.

Frustrated by his lack of progress, he was on the brink of doing the one thing he'd hoped to avoid: potentially damaging the Charter.

'...but needs must' he decided impassively after a "should I/shouldn't I?" debate with himself.

Nothing else had worked. He'd tried studying the parchment under a powerful magnifying glass for raised or overpainted letters; nothing. He'd tried running his fingers over it, feeling for lumps or bumps or imperfections which might reveal something; nothing. In fact, he'd tried all of the methods he'd made it his business to find out about that would reveal hidden messages; nothing. Now he was left with one last hope: he was going to hold the Charter over a candle flame to see if the monks had written the secret hiding place of the treasure in invisible ink.

Way back at the time of the Reformation, both sides were highly-skilled at passing secret messages, using combinations of readily available everyday commodities like lemon juice and grape juice.

'If this doesn't work...' the thought gave rise to palpitations. 'But it must...it will'. However, despite his attempts to avert the sinking feeling which the rising panic was inducing, he couldn't rid himself of its consequences: a positively queasy stomach.

Finally, his hands trembling slightly, he held his breath as he held the Charter above the naked flame, making sure it didn't get too close to the flame's intense heat: charred remnants of the Charter were of little use to anyone.

'Come on my little beauty, tell your Uncle...!' he stopped mid-whisper. Was that a noise outside his room door? He straightened up from his work...waiting, listening. Despite the lack of heat in the room, a fat bead of sweat slowly dripped off his forehead landing on the Charter; it was quickly absorbed and disappeared with the heat from the flame.

'I'm about at the end of my tether!' he croaked inwardly.

But this time, the absolute concentration he demanded of his senses, like the morning he waited in the vestibule for Senor Tartaglia, caused him to miss his arch-nemeses. With those senses concentrated in the entirely wrong direction, on the Charter, they had missed Boo and Sextus who passed by quietly in the darkness of the corridor, padding towards their own rooms.

Equally, Boo and Sextus, in turn, had been so intent on not being seen or heard that they'd failed to see the faint glow of the murderer's candle emanating from beneath the crack of his door.

With his nerves stretched as taut as a violin string, the murderer returned to his work, but this time, with half an ear cocked for telltale noises.

Nothing. The flame had revealed nothing. The Charter bore the scorch marks of the flame in places but nothing appeared on the Charter which hadn't been there before.

'Damn them!' he cursed angrily. 'All this time I've wasted. Believing those stupid monks had hidden the location of the treasure on the Charter. What am I going to do now?'

By then, it was gone midnight. Apart from an occasional loud snore, there wasn't a sound to be heard in the whole place: 'It's like...a graveyard' he thought not realising the irony of the thought: at least not until his conscious mind brought up the picture of the dead monk, Father Edward, lying behind the range.

'And what a pointless exercise that was'

His head felt full to bursting: all kinds of thoughts were whirling around in there. He needed to clear his head. He couldn't do it in the confines of his room, he had to get out.

Go for a long walk? That might raise a few eyebrows at that time of night. So, he decided to stroll around the covered cloisters surrounding the inner courtyard gardens.

Thirty Six

The cool night air together with the lack of moonlight, due to a heavily clouded sky, went some way to easing his tired brain. Strolling slowly around the familiar setting of the cloisters in the pitch black, he pondered his situation.

It had always been his intention to... 'Well,' he thought morosely, 'there's no point in crying over spilt milk. Turns out it was probably an old wives' tale anyway. But the problem I have now is; I've got to make sure that any evidence which could lead the police to me disappears...and fast. It won't be long before they find the body; for the moment they haven't a clue. Thank God I'm the only one who knows about the secret passages' he mistakenly believed.

Ambling around the quadrangle in the darkness seemed to calm his troubled mind and help him accept what life had dealt him. 'I'll have to find some other way to deal with my problems. Pity. But wait a minute...what if I could...'

The murderer turned this new thought around, checking for flaws.

After a few turns around the quad, he entered the gardens through the small stone colonnaded entrance which had been there since the Middle Ages and sat on the bench underneath the ancient oak tree where he had first hatched his plan to bring the Charter to the Abbey a couple of years before.

'Regrets? None. Except that if the treasure ever did exist, it's not going to be found now. There would have been no chance of doing what I did tonight with the Charter while it remained in Rome. They'd have thought I was mad. So, I knew I had to find a way to get it away from there. Shame it was a waste of time and even bigger shame that poor old...'

The thought froze in the murderer's brain. A rusty door hinge creaked a warning to him that he would not be alone for much longer.

He hurriedly hid behind the bench: on a moonless night like tonight there was little chance of being spotted.

The light from a torch entered the quadrangle from a doorway leading from the kitchens. As it penetrated the darkness, the murderer whose eyes had grown accustomed to the lack of light, strained to see who was behind the torch but whoever it was, was keeping the light low to the ground making it almost impossible to see anything beyond the carrier's outline. The murderer screwed up his eyes and concentrated. Slowly, the figure took shape: it was the outline of someone...in a monk's habit.

'What the dickens is going on? Who is that?'

The torch bearer turned and whispered something hoarsely into the open doorway but the murderer couldn't hear what was said. Judging by the continued squeak of the hinges, the door was being pushed wider and suddenly a second figure appeared carrying what the murderer assumed was a smaller torch because it gave off a lesser light.

The murderer repeated the thought. 'And who is that? Has someone seen me and come to check what's going on?'

He strained to hear what the two people were saying but a light breeze had blown up and he could only hear snatches of their whispered conversation before they were carried away by the wind.

'...shouldn't be seen 'ere together at this time of night. People will get suspicious' the habit rasped angrily.

'...can't hang around...! The cops........sooner or later' was the smaller torch's contribution to the conversation.

'An' who's to blame...?' the habit spat. '...you'd listened...out of 'ere by now'

The murderer was stunned. Although he couldn't hear every word, he was getting the gist of it; these two were up to no good. What exactly they were up to, he wasn't sure. But who were they? The murderer could only hear snatches.

The next words he heard took on a sinister implication.

'...it'll all be over by tonight...everythin' will be sorted'

'But what are you going...' was all he heard before the wind carried the rest away.

'Wait and see. You're not the one who's been stuck...'

'Jesus!' swore the small torch holder. 'The cops'll be...'

'...chance we take!' the habit spat. 'Meet me at 5 o'clock tonight by...finish it once and...'

'The one in the habit is obviously the leader' the murderer worked out frantically. 'I should know who that is and yet...? Is it a monk or someone wearing a habit as a disguise?'

The murderer realised that he ought to be able to put faces to those voices but darkness changes things, plays tricks with the senses and besides: whoever was wearing the habit had a cockney accent and from what the murderer could recall, none of the monks or visitors were from that part of the Capital. He continued to strain his eyes, looking for a clue to the identity of the habit-wearer but at the end of the day, the design of the habit was loose-fitting and adjusted by a cord to tighten according to body shape. So, there was no clue there.

The murderer racked his brains but it was no good; he simply couldn't recognise who the two associates were.

'I might not be able to work out who they are but from what the habit said it's obvious that he's planning something big for tonight. But what?'

The two obvious ne'er-do-wells, meeting over, retraced their steps back through the kitchen area. The murderer watched as the torchlight slowly moved through the kitchen and disappeared.

Without knowing it, the murderer had just encountered the other murderer and his partner in crime.

Their next encounter would be fatal.

By the time he rose from his hiding place under the oak tree, the murderer had made up his mind.

He was going to steal back the Rosary.

Thirty Seven

A lot of sleep was lost in not a few bedrooms of the Abbey that night.

In one guest room, Miss Lavender found that she could not turn her brain off as it tried to make sense of the various scenarios which had presented themselves. Facts were getting mixed up with fiction with the resultant outcome: "factions".

'Is the story of the treasure true? Or is it an old monk's tale? Is the hunt for the treasure the reason for all the murders? Are some or all of the murders connected? Were any of the murder victims involved in the search for the treasure but then fell out with their associate and paid the price?'

At that point, Miss Lavender had what she had come to refer to over the years as one of her "magic moments". That rare thing, a "magic moment", occurred when a major part of an investigation falls into place resulting from her focussed method of logical deduction. Her very first one had involved a cup of Earl Grey tea, milk and a young police constable, Charlie Chivers. The result was the exposure of a very unsavoury character during the war.

With this one, she realised that she, Sextus and Charlie had made a serious error, to wit: an assumption. That assumption being that there was only one person committing these murders. But what if the murders weren't connected? What if they'd been committed by different people? Three murders...three different people? 'Why not?' she asked of herself. At that point, Miss Lavender took hold of her paranoia: 'At this rate, I'll be suspecting Sextus...and then Charlie. So,' she continued 'is there more than one killer? Could there be two of them or even a gang? And are they all after the Charter which, when it comes to it, we're assuming?'

The thought of two murderers or even gangs of murderers acting independently sent her brain into a spin.

'I need to think this through completely' she decided. 'If...one of the murderers has the Charter...what does that mean? Is that why the other murders have taken place? Is the other murderer/murderers looking for the Charter and killing people to find it?'

Another very important theory, which had waited patiently in line, popped up.

'Three murders and two, not three, different methods of killing. Is that significant? They say that poison is a woman's method, although I don't necessarily agree with that. But whoever committed these murders is, for some reason, using two very different styles: two very violent and one, the coward's way. Why change? Or were they done by different people? Does it tell us anything about them? Does that help us in any way in our search for them?'

And so, it went on. There would be no sleep for Miss Hilary B Lavender that night.

Unlike Sextus Phipps MPS (retired) who slept like a baby whose teething days were finally over...but not so for some other residents of the Abbey that night.

The residents of two of the other rooms were also, like Miss Lavender, struggling to shut down their own whirling brains.

The murderer with the Charter was feeling distinctly uneasy as thoughts of the two accomplices he'd observed earlier in the quad kept spinning around in his mind, refusing to let him sleep.

'What're they up to? As the one who was ultimately responsible for the Charter being brought here from Rome, I know that they have no connection to it. How could they? But if it's not the Charter, then what are they up to? And if it is the Charter they're after: why? How did they find out about its so-called secrets? Except, it doesn't have any secrets...but I'm the only one who knows that...aren't I?'

That's when the murderer had his own eureka moment...but wished he hadn't.

'So does that mean it was they who murdered...?'

He rushed to the wash hand basin and vomited.

'Of course! Who else could have done it? But why would they do it? The old boy didn't know anything...but then neither did the other two but I still got rid of them. So, maybe they had their reasons...maybe he found out about their plans and they had to kill him. All these maybes are making me very twitchy'

144

No sleep for the Charter-possessing murderer that night.

Not a million miles away, one of the two accomplices lay on top of his bed smoking a cigarette, contemplating the situation. 'Not the first time a job's gone wrong' he thought coldly. 'So, might as well be hung for a load of sheep...'

This murderer's plans had taken a long time and should have come to fruition by now, instead, they'd come to naught...so far. All he had to show for his efforts was one dead body.

'Served him right...interfering old sod! But at least the cops don't have a clue' he determined with satisfaction. 'Anyway, enough of that, it's got to be done tonight. Can't wait any longer. The longer we stay here, the more chance we have that the coppers might cotton onto us. After what I've got planned for tonight we'll have to go to ground for a long time until the heat dies down, that's for sure'

He lay there smiling to himself in the darkness; this career criminal, like his Charter-possessing fellow murderer, couldn't give a hoot about the consequences of his actions. His only concern was the fabulous wealth that the Charter could bring...and not forgetting, of course, the Rosary. He and his accomplice knew the right villains to help dispose of the Rosary when it was broken up without too many questions being asked. Even on its own, the Rosary was worth a medieval king's ransom.

Alas for him, he wasn't the only one to reach that conclusion.

The Rosary was about to disappear for a second time.

Thirty Eight

The Charter-possessing murderer had earlier concluded that if he could retrieve the Rosary, it might redeem his situation...and there was no better time than the present, he decided and besides, he couldn't sleep.

So, as the rest of the inhabitants struggled to get some shut-eye, he dressed and cautiously made for the one place he knew the precious prayer beads were being kept for safekeeping – the Abbot's study.

'It wouldn't even occur to any of them that perhaps someone would try to steal the Rosary again. How stupid are they and how clever am I?' the murderer concluded impressed by his own brilliance.

Silently closing his room door, he crept stealthily along the corridor, stopping along the way, listening intently for sounds which might indicate that anyone else was abroad at that time of night.

The sudden sound of a creaking floorboard alerted him that someone was approaching; he froze in panic. Fortunately, it was only one of the elderly brothers behind the faint glow of a candle stub in his hand, seeking the lavatory. He shuffled along the familiar route, eyes half-closed, mumbling to himself, to perform his nightly ablutions. For what seemed like an eternity, the murderer held his breath as the old man passed by within inches of the hiding place he'd ducked into: one of the many alcoves complete with a plaster statue of some saint or other. He waited there until the old man had returned to his room before continuing his journey along the winding corridors. Moving swiftly, he reached the door to the study without any further mishaps.

The door was unlocked.

'How easy is this? I bet it'll be in one of the desk drawers'

In three long, silent strides, the murderer reached the leather-topped antique desk. But before turning on the torch he'd brought with him, he quickly pulled down the blind on the only window in the room. Only then did he feel safe enough to turn the torch on.

Softly tugging at each drawer, he found what he was looking for; the only locked drawer in the des

Thirty Nine

Meanwhile, in her room, Miss Lavender had finally managed to doze off, that is, until something, she wasn't quite sure what, woke her up.

Groggily thinking that she'd dreamt it, her eyes began to flutter closed again when it happened again.

'What is that?'

Rising from her bed, the old bed springs creaking as she pushed herself up, she moved over to the window.

Looking out, at first, she couldn't see anything and with a mumbled "...must have been my imagination" was about to return to her bed when the absolute darkness was broken by a moving light in one of the ground floor rooms.

Unaware that the blind he'd pulled down had slowly rolled up and was allowing light to escape through the window, the murderer's attention was completely absorbed in finding something to force the drawer open. In one of the unlocked drawers he found a letter opener.

'Perfect'

In her room, Miss Lavender quickly deduced from the pattern of the light movement that it was a torchlight. Now instantly alert, she watched for another few moments before leaping to action.

'I smell a rat'. She donned her dressing gown.

Retrieving the torch which Charlie had given her, she opened her door trying not to let it creak and walked rapidly to Sextus' door and knocked.

No response, only the steady sound of a gentle snore.

Another urgent rat-a-tat on the door brought a sleepy reply.

'Who's there?'

'Sextus, quick, it's me, Boo! There's something going on downstairs! Quickly, come with me!' she whispered hoarsely.

Seconds later, Sextus appeared in his dressing gown armed with a torch in one hand and a poker from the fireplace in the other, he continued the whispered conversation:

'What is it, Boo? What's happening?'

'There's someone waving a torch around in one of the downstairs rooms, I'm not sure which room it is, and it's like...oh, I don't know...it's like...they're searching for something' she suddenly realised.

Before she'd finished, Sextus was off at a pace, his torch lighting the way down the main staircase. In the Hall, he stopped dead and turned to Boo to ask:

'...which direction do you think it was coming from?'

'I think, if I've got my bearings, it was one of the rooms near Dom Ambrose's study'

Turning back to walk on in that direction, Sextus caught his foot on an easel with a huge medieval portrait of St Thomas Aquinas, theologian and philosopher: the noise of it falling would have woken the saint himself.

'What the blazes...!' Sextus yelled.

The noise did not go unheard in the Abbot's study; its present visitor had only just managed to force open the locked drawer.

'Dammit!' was all he had time to say when he noticed that the blind had opened before switching the torch off and, close to panic, snatched the Rosary. Quickly assessing how far away the noise had come from; he reckoned that he had about thirty to forty seconds, no more, before whoever it was, arrived.

He rushed to the door. Seizing the door handle, he felt something brushed against his hand; the Abbot's spare habit.

Quickly pulling it on, he covered his face with the hood and threw open the door, running out into the corridor as lights began to go on all over the building.

Sextus and Boo turned into the corridor to catch sight of a monk's habit disappearing around a corner about thirty feet away.

'Hey, you there! Stop!' Sextus shouted.

But to no avail, the murderer was running as if the Old Nick himself had set the Hounds of Hell on him.

When Sextus and Boo reached the corner, they stopped for a moment to get their bearings only to see the cowled figure fleeing the building via the kitchen door.

With no-one else yet arrived on the scene to assist them, Sextus and Boo gallantly took up the chase afresh...but whoever it was, was too fast for them.

The quarry disappeared through another door on the other side of the quadrangle and by the time the two intrepid friends reached it, the habit-wearing fugitive had disappeared into thin air.

Forty

The cowled murderer did not stop until he'd entered the passageway in the Lumber Room where the battered body of Father Edward still lay huddled in the corner below the bloodied habit.

Careering up the staircase to the upper floor, the murderer pulled the handle releasing the catch on the fireplace: it was the room where he had murdered Monsignor Avrili. As an afterthought, he hung the Rosary on the handle before pushing the fireplace back into place.

'Just in case they do a body search on us' reasoned the murderer.

Standing in the middle of the room, he listened intently, hearing the noise of people beginning to rouse from their slumber.

On the spur of the moment, he removed the habit he'd stolen, rolled it into a ball and opening the window, threw it out as far as he could onto the driveway.

'That should throw them off'

Then, standing upright he took a couple of long slow gulps of air before putting an ear to the door.

His luck was in.

When he was sure that the coast was clear, he slipped carefully along the corridor, and had only just reached his bedroom door when two other doors flew open with their inhabitants in varying states of undress and calling out, asking what the dickens was going on.

He did a U-turn and joined in.

'What in the name of all that's holy was that noise?' Brother Joseph, the Bursar, called out angrily as he flicked the light switch on in the corridor.

'Yes, whatever was that awful racket?' Angus MacDorn-Smythe shouted standing by his door, hopping on one foot while pulling a shoe on the other.

'It sounded like a very loud clap of thunder except it came from downstairs,' Brother Fabian, one of the other residents of the corridor replied as he buckled his belt. 'I'll run on ahead to try to find out what's going on'

Brother Joseph and Angus MacDorn-Smythe swiftly followed on.

Forty One

Puffed out from their exertions, Boo and Sextus had stopped to catch their breath just as the first member of the household arrived; Father Ignatius.

'Miss Lavender, Mr Phipps, are you both alright? I heard the most almighty crash. What's going on?'

'Did you see anyone running in your direction, Father?' Boo asked breathlessly.

'No...no, I didn't'. The Prior's brow furrowed. 'Were you chasing someone?'

Neither of them could speak. Sextus just nodded.

'Who was it?'

'We didn't...'

Rushing feet were heard approaching.

It was Brother Fabian, the youngest and probably fittest member of the Order.

'Who's there? What's going on?' he cried.

The Prior stepped in and answered for them.

'Miss Lavender and Mr Phipps say they've been chasing someone. Did you see anyone on your way here, Brother?'

'Er...no, Father. I just heard a very loud bang and came down to see what the commotion was'

'Hmm, right' said the oldest member of the Community.

Suddenly, another voice called out which interrupted Miss Lavender's scrutiny of the first two people to arrive on the scene.

It was Dom Ambrose's commanding voice. He arrived at the same time as Brother Joseph and Angus MacDorn-Smythe. All were slightly breathless.

'Father Ignatius, what in the Good Lord's name has happened now? And what are you doing here, Brother?' the Abbot demanded from the first two arrivals.

Father Ignatius spoke up.

'As you know, Father, my room is closest to the main staircase and I suppose I would have been the first to hear that almighty crash. I quickly dressed and came down to find Miss Lavender and Mr Phipps here who say they've been chasing someone' He turned to Boo and Sextus and asked:

'Did you see where he went?'

'I don't recall saying it was a "he", Father' Boo said warily.

The Prior paused for a moment before exclaiming:

'A figure of speech, Miss Lavender, a figure of speech...nothing else' and then as an afterthought: 'My apologies'. But he was clearly irritated.

Nevertheless, Boo stored it away to be examined more closely later. Did the Prior know something? Did he know the murderer/thief was a man? Could it be he, himself?

There was a lull in the conversation and Brother Fabian saw his chance to speak.

'Father Ambrose, I was next on the scene and I suppose, like everybody else I was fast asleep and suddenly this almighty bang like thunder woke me up...'

'Me too' interjected Angus who was standing behind the Abbot.

'...and me' Brother Joseph agreed, standing beside him.

'I have to admit, it did me as well' the Abbot admitted grudgingly. 'But what was it? What's been happening?'

By then, Boo had regained some of her composure...and breath.

'I saw a torchlight flashing down here and I woke Mr Phipps. We both came down to investigate. What I can tell you is that whoever it was, was in your room, Father'

'My study?'

'Yes. However, the noise you all heard was Sextus tripping. Unfortunately, it also alerted our mystery burglar too. It was a large painting which fell over in the Hall that you all heard' she ended by way of explanation.

'Why on earth would someone be in my study at this time of...?' began the Abbot before it dawned on him '...the Rosary! Oh my God, I locked it in my desk. Oh, please...no!' he uttered despairingly.

The small group hurried back towards the study.

The Abbot flung open the door and saw at a glance that someone had rifled through the drawers.

It was gone.

Dom Ambrose collapsed into his chair.

'What am I going to do? What have we done to deserve this?'

The rest of the group stood in silence; there was nothing that any of them could say to ease his pain...or guilt.

Well, there was one...but he had other things on his mind.

Forty Two

A none too pleased Chief Superintendent arrived thirty minutes after the call was received from the Abbey.

His entrance was like that of a bad-tempered male member of the cattle family in a porcelain emporium. He was followed by three uniformed officers who appeared to be of a similar persuasion as their boss.

'Father...what's happened now?' Charlie asked, total disbelief in his voice.

'The Rosary's gone...it's been stolen...again' the monk replied matter-of-factly; he was too exhausted to elaborate.

'Again?' Charlie asked.

'I'm afraid so, Chief Superintendent. I had fully intended to give it into your hands for safekeeping but with so much on my mind...' The Abbot simply bowed his head. The combination of exhaustion and shame mingling together did not sit well on those shoulders. All of the feistiness appeared to have been sucked out of him.

'Well, at least no-one's been murdered...' thought Charlie '...or at least, so far'

But the question had to be asked.

'Is everyone accounted for?'

'Yes, Chief Superintendent. No-one else has disappeared' the Abbot answered catching Charlie's eye as if to say: "I know what you were meaning"

From behind his back, the Chief Superintendent pulled a small bundle.

'Does anyone know who this belongs to?'

The Abbot approached him and held out his hand to take hold of what everyone could see was a habit.

After a brief pause, Dom Ambrose said: 'Why, it's mine, Chief Superintendent...but what are you doing with it?'

'I found it in the driveway as we walked up'

'But...but it was...' the Abbot tried to recall the last time he'd seen it. 'It was hanging on the back of my study door. How on earth did it end up in the driveway?'

For a few moments, the place went silent, Charlie stood, waiting for some kind of answer.

'I think I may know' Boo volunteered.

'Yes, Miss Lavender?'

'I think the thief probably used it when they were making good their escape from Mr Phipps and myself and discarded it when they'd gotten away'

'Very good, she's clever that one!' the murderer thought with no change of expression on his face.

'But where would they be going?' the Abbot asked. 'There's nothing around here for miles'

'Perhaps they had a car parked outside the gates to make their getaway' postulated the Prior.

'I wouldn't have thought so' said Sextus doubtfully.

'...and we certainly didn't see anyone on the way here' the Chief Superintendent confirmed.

Silence fell on the group again. When nothing else was forthcoming, Charlie Chivers snarled:

'Right, men, I want this place searched top to bottom. Get on with it!'

They didn't need to be told twice.

Miss Lavender filled Charlie in on the circumstances surrounding the discovery that the Rosary was missing again. Within a couple of hours, the police had gone; it was nowhere to be found and unsurprisingly, no-one knew anything about it.

Well, except one...but he wasn't telling.

For the remaining few hours of darkness, the exhausted Community tried to get some sleep; one of their number in particular, slept like a baby.

Forty Three

By morning, a bleary-eyed Miss Lavender dragged her exhausted body from bed to wash quickly and dress for breakfast. Fortunately for her, the previous evening she had laid out her attire for the following day. Consisting of a full-length black woollen skirt, her white blouse and a deep green Cossack-style velvet jacket, the outfit was finished off with a rather smart black and yellow Prince of Wales check hat, designed by a well-known milliner who was a personal friend of Boo's bridge opponent, Kitty. Kitty had commissioned it to commemorate a "memorable" birthday of Boo's.

Tired though she may have felt, her sleepless night had produced results: she had worked out how Sir John had been poisoned...but not who had done it...yet.

By the time she had finished her ablutions, the tolling bell was calling the community from every part of the monastery's grounds for the first meal of the day.

When she entered the Refectory, the community of monks were standing behind their chairs, and as was their practice, maintaining what was referred to as the Grand Silence until the Abbot, who looked like he'd not slept very well himself, said grace.

In the first few days after Miss Lavender had arrived, the dining room would burst into loud talk and laughter as the chairs were dragged out from under the tables, but not today, and not for the last few days.

No more banter, no guffaws of delight at some comment made by one of their fellows, no, today the atmosphere in the community was one of immense sadness. A member of their community had disappeared, having allegedly admitted to stealing and, worse, two brutal murders. No, there was no reason for jollity today or for that matter any other day for a long time to come.

Miss Lavender tried to catch Sextus' eye but her well-rested friend was too intent on replenishing his own oversized personal food locker. She would have to hold her discovery a while longer.

'I wonder if he went to school with Billy Bunter?' she wondered irreverently.

Twenty minutes later, the breakfast dishes were being cleared away and the Refectory emptied as the community returned to its chores. Even those on retreat and visitors like Boo felt the oppressive atmosphere and quickly ate what was in front of them before shuffling off to do penance, pray or whatever it was they'd come there to do.

As usual, one of the last to leave, Sextus, was deliberately ambling slowly along the corridor from the Refectory, deep in thought, when he heard a 'Pssst' coming from a darkened doorway.

Immediately roused from his reverie, he turned to see Boo beckoning him to join her in, what turned out to be, a side entrance to one of the sitting rooms which was rarely used.

'Boo, I was just thinking about that poison administered to Sir John...' Sextus started to say.

'And that's what I wanted to talk to you about. Great minds!'

'You first' Sextus offered.

'I'd be happy to but I think it would be better if we wait for Charlie to arrive. He should be here...' she checked her watch '...in about ten minutes unless I'm mistaken'

Charlie's timekeeping was legendary; he was especially punctilious about punctuality. His subordinates learned to avoid him if he'd been held up or was late: fire-breathing dragon was a regular comparison.

'Boo, I know it's no good trying to prise it out of you but give me a clue' Sextus implored.

'Better still, why don't you tell me what you were thinking about' she countered.

'Well,' began her frustrated friend 'there's something I may have not mentioned at the time we discussed it. It seemed irrelevant'

'What, Sextus? Come on, man!' demanded Boo animatedly.

It was Sextus' turn to tease his friend.

'We...ll,' he began again slowly 'the thing about cyanide is that it can take several minutes to show any symptoms. I didn't bother to mention this before because it happened almost immediately after Johnnie sampled the wine'

'Sextus Phipps, you are a genius!' declared Boo. 'Now I think I know where we're going with this. Of course, it was staring us in the face. That's the second thing we got wrong'

'Boo, if you don't tell me, I think I may commit murder myself. And without revealing the name of the potential victim,' he paused '...let me put it this way, I may have to look for a new bridge partner' he declared, beside himself with curiosity.

'Let's go for a short stroll down to the gates to see if Charlie's arrived yet, shall we?' parried Boo.

'Boo Lavender, you really are the limit' averred her replete friend.

'Flattery gets you anywhere'

'I'm warning you, Boo'

'Oh look! Here comes Charlie now' Boo announced as they ambled slowly down the gravel driveway to the gate.

The Chief Superintendent's car pulled up outside the gates and the driver got out and held the door for his boss.

'Thank you, PC Evans' Charlie said as he emerged and saw the two friends waiting for him on the other side of the gate. 'They must be psychic'

'Saved in the nick of time' said Sextus' companion. It wouldn't be the last time that day that those words would be uttered but not necessarily by Boo Lavender.

'Good Morning, both' remarked the Chief Superintendent. 'Any news?'

'Indeed, Chief Superintendent, yes, indeed' Boo admitted.

'Excellent' was the reply. 'Shall we go inside and we can exchange our good news?'

'You have news as well?' she asked eagerly.

'Yes, yes, Miss Lavender'

Both Charlie and Sextus looked at the pained expression on Boo's face: now it was her turn.

'Ah ha, Boo! Now you know what it feels like' her bridge companion said, feeling smug.

Unbeknown to them, two pairs of eyes were watching them as they marched up the driveway. One pair was hidden behind a

160

curtain on the first floor, the other watched discreetly from a window on the ground floor.

Each observer had very similar thoughts:

'What the hell are those three up to?' and 'I don't like the look of this'

They were both right to be worried.

Forty Four

Their chairs were still where they left them the previous evening: around the desk in the Bibliotheca.

'So what's your news, Chief Superintendent?' Boo asked.

'Ladies first' countered Charlie.

'Fifteen love, I believe, to Charlie, Boo' laughed Sextus.

'Oh...very...well' said Boo admitting defeat. 'I didn't sleep last night but...it was worth it. I've worked out how Sir Johnnie was poisoned and thanks to Sextus here...' she flicked her head towards her friend '...I think I know who did it'

Stunned silence was accompanied by the usual dropping of jaws. Boo was supremely gratified.

'Con...con...tinue, please' the Chief Superintendent was all ears.

'Well, the way I look at things is this: if something is not right, it's wrong...and you have to go back to the beginning and start again. So,' she paused, knowing she had their full attention 'so, that is exactly what I did. Or to put it another way, solving a mystery, in this case a murder, is like mending a string of pearls. Each time a pearl or a clue is added, brings you closer to the end. When the last pearl is added to the necklace, you've completed the circle. With the mystery, when the last clue falls into place you've effectively completed the circle, there are no longer any missing pieces and the mystery's solved.

In Sir John's case, he died from cyanide poisoning, on that we are all agree. He sampled that very fine Margaux '26 before collapsing. After exhaustive tests by both Sextus and the police forensics team, the conclusion was reached that the poison was in the wine, which it was. And because the bottle hadn't been tampered with, we all assumed that it was the wine which poisoned him. The question is: how did the poison get in there? This was the conundrum.

We had what we thought were all the pieces to solve the mystery but we were wrong. The final part of the mystery was given to me, not ten minutes ago, by Sextus. There was something he hadn't mentioned at the time because it didn't seem relevant; that is, cyanide can take several minutes to take effect.

162

So, the answer, my friends, is...if it wasn't in there before, it must have been put in afterwards to distract our attention away from where the poison was administered to him in the first place.

Then I thought back to that night and I remembered that we'd had aperitifs just before we sat down to dinner... and that, gentlemen, is where and when the poison was administered' Boo concluded. 'I believe the glasses were deliberately smashed at the time to cover the murderer's tracks. If you remember, there was a bit of a scrum where everybody was trying to reach Sir John and during it, the table was cleared to lay Johnnie on it. All of the glasses, including the aperitif glass which Sir John had brought with him from the sitting room were knocked off the table'

'I remember!' Sextus said recalling that night. 'Someone cleared the table to lay poor Johnnie on it and the whole lot went flying. But no-one took any notice because we were all too concerned about what was happening to him. Didn't someone sweep it up? But I can't remember who, Boo'

'Oh, I remember who, Sextus, but the truth is, and I've just thought of this: there's something which doesn't quite fit. So, it's thinking caps time again'

'Well blow my socks off! Well done, Miss Lavender!' said Charlie, impressed with the Librarian's logic.

'Now, your news, please' demanded Boo.

'Nothing as good as yours, Miss, but all grist to the mill nevertheless. That candlestick I took away last night is covered in fingerprints. So, we'll have to set aside a room to take everyone's fingerprints. That should put the final nail in their coffin...whoever they are'

'Great news, Charlie' Boo stated reverting to first names when no-one else was around.

'Excellent' endorsed Sextus. 'Now what do we do?' he asked looking at them both.

'I think it's time to put the fox in the chicken coop and see whose feathers we ruffle' Boo suggested.

'Sounds good to me, Miss Lavender. What do you suggest we do and when should we do it?'

'I think you should arrive during lunch, Charlie, and announce to everyone that a habit has been found covered in bloodstains.

That should bring a few people out in a cold sweat, don't you think?'

'Fantastic, Boo!' agreed Sextus '...and make your entrance dramatic, Charlie'

'Oh, don't worry, Sir, I will' agreed the Chief Superintendent before a thought struck him. 'Here, Miss Lavender, you said you knew who murdered Sir John MacDorn-Smythe. Who is it?'

'Ah, I'm glad you asked, Charlie. I haven't quite worked it out yet because there's a piece of the jigsaw which doesn't completely fit. But I'm working on it'

'That's it?' queried Sextus.

'So far as I am able to confirm right at this moment, Sextus. Yes'

'Can we help?' Charlie asked frowning with frustration.

'Not at the moment, Charlie. I think the outcome this lunchtime will make things clearer' was Miss Lavender's last word on the subject.

'Now what about keeping an eye on the guest room where Monsignor Avrili was murdered? What's the best way to do it?' Sextus asked.

'To be honest, Sir, I'm a bit reluctant to let you and Miss Lavender here get involved in any kind of stakeout. We're dealing with a dangerous criminal and there's no telling what he or she might do'

'I agree, Charlie, but as we discussed last night, the first whiff of a uniform might send whoever it is running for cover...and we don't want that either, do we?' interjected Boo.

'You're probably right, Miss. So, any suggestions?'

'I think we should stick to what we said last night. You should have a couple of uniformed officers standing outside the lumber room which will look quite conspicuous while we secrete ourselves as close to the guest room upstairs without drawing any attention to see who takes the bait'

'...and I'll have a couple of uniforms hiding downstairs waiting for my whistle'

'Excellent idea'

'And then we nab the blighter!' chuckled Sextus who'd been in the armed services during the war and was quite capable of looking after himself.

A swift stern look from Boo brought an 'Oops, sorry Boo, thought I was back in mess room with the chaps'

'So we're agreed: immediately after lunch we'll meet in Sextus' room which is the closest to Monsignor Avrili's room. Yes?'

'Yes' her confederates chimed in unison.

'I don't think we should be seen together until this is over. Agreed?'

'Agreed'

Charlie went off to find a suitable room to set up for fingerprinting the entire occupants of the Abbey while Boo shooed Sextus away so that she could think about the anomaly she was faced with along the lines of:

'How could he have done that one but has a cast iron alibi for this one? Or is there really more than one murderer after all? Or are there two or more involved in the plot and if so, who murdered who?'

Frustrated with all the ideas floating around in her consciousness without any obvious answers, Miss Lavender decided to check out the lay of the land before this afternoon and made her way to the upper floor...to Monsignor Avrili's room.

It was only much, much later that it dawned on her how serendipitous it had been that she'd volunteered to pick up a small parcel for Miss Cosworthy of Chipping Campden from Jacksons the jewellers of Cheltenham.

Forty Five

Miss Lavender quietly made her way along the first floor corridor frequently checking the backward-looking mirrors in her spectacles. There was no-one around...so far as her all-seeing spectacles could establish.

Softly pressing on the handle of the door, she pushed it open only for her eyes to be drawn immediately to the monstrous dark stain in the rug: the only sign that violence had taken place in this otherwise peaceful setting.

Although tempted to open the entrance to the secret passage, she resisted. She stood there for a few moments, closing her eyes, soaking up the atmosphere. With a melancholic sigh, she opened them and was about to leave, having satisfied herself about the layout and potential dangers, when a movement outside the window caught her attention.

At first, not thinking anything about it, she turned back towards the door to leave, but then hesitated, her curiosity aroused, she walked back to the window to see who or what had caught her attention. If anyone had asked her later what made her turn back, she would struggle to answer: perhaps the famous "sixth sense" scientists talk about, she might hazard?

To her surprise, it was the person she believed to be the murderer. Or, as she would later think of him as, Number One Suspect.

'Hello, what's going on here then?'

He pulled the gate open and left it ajar before quickly walking to the far side of the telephone box where he would be hidden from the view of anyone leaving via the gates, or, at least, anyone he didn't want to be seen by. 'He seems to be waiting...' Miss Lavender thought '...but for whom?'

It wasn't long before that question was answered: one of the guests marched purposefully down the driveway towards the gates. Once outside, the guest halted. Looking left then right, a puzzled look spread across the guest's face Miss Lavender observed, before turning back to the right where the telephone box was located: Number One suspect had called out.

166

'I need to hear what they're saying' she thought anxiously.

Gently lifting the window a few inches, she tried but could hear nothing. Rummaging through her handbag looking for a small pair of opera glasses she kept there for exactly these sort of occasions, she came across the item she'd picked up for Miss Cosworthy from the jewellers: her hearing aid complete with new battery.

Without giving it a second thought, she inserted the earpiece into her ear and rested her hand with the small receiver in it on the window ledge pointing towards the two people standing by the telephone box.

Adjusting the volume setting, she sent a quick prayer up to the Almighty that it would work: it did. For a slightly deaf person, it would have improved the volume and quality of what they could hear. For Miss Lavender, whose hearing was perfectly normal, it enhanced what could be heard and more. She listened intently, holding her breath.

'...many times have I told you? Meeting like this could blow our cover' Number One Suspect said in a tone spiked with rancour.

'You know I'm within this much...' said the guest in a voice cracking with emotion, holding up thumb and finger less than half an inch apart '...of going to the police. You can't do this...it's complete madness!'

'Listen, you even think of doing that an' you'll be joining them!' Number One Suspect threatened. 'All this time I've been stuck in this place. My knees are black and blue with all this praying malarkey; bobbing up and down, genuflecting and all the other palaver. I had enough of that when I was forced to do it as a kid. No, I've not waited this long just to walk away from it...'

In her endeavour to hear everything that was being said, Miss Lavender leaned in slightly closer to the window and lost her balance; the hand holding the receiver pulled on the earpiece and it fell from her ear.

'Oh dear, oh dear' she muttered as she scrambled to retrieve the earpiece and replace it in her ear.

'...enough of the stuff left over from the old man...' In her panic, Miss Lavender hadn't fixed the earpiece properly into her ear and it fell out again.

167

'Oh my Lord, whatever is going on?' she thought frantically as, this time, she held the earpiece in place with her other hand.

'...the lot of them tonight. Then we'll get our hands on it at last. I'm sure Jack the Fence or Mickey the Schnozzle will help us break it up and sell it, no problem. But you, you need to keep in character. Remember, we're all holier than thou' Number One Suspect practically spat at the guest. 'Don't blow it or you'll answer to me. Got it?'

The guest nodded but from her vantage point Boo could see that the guest was scared.

'What did he mean: "...enough stuff left from the old man..."?' Boo struggled to fill in the blank spaces of the partial conversation she'd heard.

'Oh, come on Boo! What could he have said?' she whispered frustratedly.

Closing her eyes, she relaxed; she'd never get it if she strained or tried to force it.

"...the lot of them tonight..." came rushing back to her '...from the old man...'

Suddenly, she opened her eyes with a start; she'd been so busy trying to remember what he'd said that she missed what followed.

'...now don't speak to me again' and with that Number One Suspect looked around to see if there was anyone about before pushing past the startled guest back through the gates and up the gravel path.

Fortunately, he didn't look up otherwise he might have observed a dainty hand sticking out of a window on the first floor holding what looked like a miniature transmitter.

Boo quickly pulled her hand in after Number One had gone in and before the guest strode up the gravel driveway except this time, the guest did look up and saw her staring down and froze to the spot, panic clearly etched on that pale face.

Both looked at each other as time seemed to stand still and the moments that passed felt like minutes before Miss Lavender, taking control of her own fear, gave the guest a cheery wave. The guest, in return, did likewise but the maniacal smile on the guest's ashen countenance could not hide his tremendous apprehension.

'How long has she been there? Did she see the two of us outside the gate talking? Could she have heard anything?' the guest thought frantically. 'What should I do? Should I tell...?'

In the end, the guest was too scared to mention it and besides; hadn't Number One made it clear: "...keep away?"

'But what if she heard?' the guest reasoned approaching the portico. Then logic kicked in: she couldn't possibly have '...that window is too far away. No, she couldn't have heard anything' the relieved guest decided, who from now on would be referred to by Miss Lavender as Number Two Suspect.

Boo immediately went in search of Sextus: he had to find Charlie and bring him to the Bibliotheca immediately. Sextus heard the urgency in Boo's voice and didn't question the instruction: he located Charlie in the sitting room Boo and he had met in after breakfast, setting up tables and chairs for the fingerprinting.

'Can it wait, Mr Phipps?' he enquired as he instructed the two police constables how he wanted the room laid out.

'When she said "Immediately", Chief Superintendent, she left no margin for discretion. There is no question she has something of great importance to tell us'

'I'll come right away'

Forty Six

Number One Suspect lurked in the passageway close to the kitchens. What he was about to do was risky...but there was not a single scruple or hesitation in his mind: it would be done.

For what seemed like an age, he listened. The sound of pots and pans crashing and banging as they were emptied before being thrown in the sink made the murderer unwilling to enter the kitchen: when it was busy, like it clearly was now, the world and their brother knew that Brother Jerome, the cook, was almost always in a foul temper; no doubt, a throwback to his previous occupation as head chef at the Savoy hotel in London.

Number One Suspect moved closer to the door all the time listening to the raised voices.

'...can't you do anything right?' bawled the irritated cook '...if those vegetables end up like mush, they won't be the only ones' he threatened.

'Yes, Brother Jerome. Sorry, Brother Jerome. I just took my eye off them for a minute' confessed one of the kitchen assistants.

'If I'd done that when I was your age, my lad, my chef would have probably taken that eye out...Grrr!' he fumed.

'How can I find out what's for dinner tonight without attracting any attention?' wondered Number One.

His prayers were abruptly answered when he heard cook say:

'Do something useful, Tom, go and fetch me some potatoes from the storeroom...and make it quick!' he roared.

'Yes, Brother' replied the kitchen assistant scuttling towards the door.

The murderer withdrew from the doorway a few steps and pretended he was walking past.

The kitchen assistant, Tom Fairweather, from one of the nearby villages, came flying out of the door like a cat with its tail on fire.

''Allo, sounds like you might be in trouble?' said Number One jokingly.

'Oh, hello! Yes, Brother Jerome's in his usual good mood'

'I heard that!' came a bellow from the kitchen.

'Sorry, Brother' Tom cried out in a mockingly penitential voice as he stuck his tongue out and made a face.

'Listen,' began Number One 'what's on the menu tonight?'

'What? You haven't even had lunch yet' said Tom laughing. 'But if you must know, it's Brother Jerome's special: lamb stew'

'Yum, yum' declared Number One. 'You'd better get off and fetch those potatoes, otherwise you'll get a flea in your ear' he said walking off.

'...how did you know I'd been sent for pot...?' asked the puzzled kitchen assistant to the retreating back of Number One as he sped along the corridor.

'At least now I know. When it's quiet later, I'll deal with it then'

Number One's plan was now in place with one small detail required for it to be finalised.

Forty Seven

The normally calm Boo Lavender was in a considerable state of agitation, pacing up and down in front of the stain glass window of the Bibliotheca when the Chief Superintendent and Sextus arrived post haste; hysteria was far too strong a word to use of this lady but what she'd heard on Miss Cosworthy's hearing aid had sent the proverbial shivers on a marathon march up and down her spine.

'Miss Lavender, you look ill. Are you alright?' the Chief Superintendent asked anxiously. 'Would you like to sit down?'

'Er...thank you Charlie, that's very kind of you' replied Boo as he lifted over one of the chairs which were still positioned around the desk to the window where she had stopped pacing.

Both Sextus and Charlie were champing at the bit to know what she had discovered but, ever the country gentlemen that they were, they waited until Boo had recovered sufficiently before cross-examining her.

'A glass of water, if you please' requested the clearly shaken Librarian.

Sextus fetched a glass from the water decanter on the desk and brought it to his friend.

A few sips later, Boo was sufficiently recovered to begin her narrative.

With the exception of a couple of explosive "...he said what?" the men wisely kept their counsel until Boo finished.

A full minute of silence elapsed after she'd finished while the two men digested her reporting of the events and her interpretation of what it could mean.

'We weren't there, of course, Miss Lavender, but from what you've said...it's the only interpretation I can think of to give it' the Chief Superintendent concluded.

'Me too' agreed Sextus. 'So what should we do now?'

'Stick to our original plan' stated Boo decisively. 'Lunchtime has to be crunch time, I believe'

The silence fell for a second time as three formidable brains computed the consequences of those actions.

It was Charlie who broke the silence: 'Very well, Miss Lavender, we'll do as you suggest and see if we can flush these brutes out before they have time to fulfil their wicked plan'

The door to the Library creaked open and Brother Fabian entered.

'I thought I might find you here, Miss Lavender' he began embarrassedly. 'Oh, sorry...I didn't mean to interrupt...'

'That's alright, Brother, we were just about to leave' Sextus said. 'Miss Lavender has uncovered a fascinating book which she had to share with us on the subject of Chalfontbury Friary. Fascinating'

'Oh...right.' replied the young monk hesitantly: the blank expression on his face conveying his obvious unawareness of the book's, or indeed the name's, significance.

'The Abbot asked me to say when it's convenient; could he have a word with you in his office?'

'Yes, of course, Brother. I'll come along shortly and thank you, gentlemen, for allowing me to share my find with you' she concluded, nodding to Charlie and Sextus as they left with Brother Fabian.

The fact that that meeting took place almost resulted in the death of the Librarian.

Forty Eight

The present proprietor of the Charter happened to be passing along the corridor as Brother Fabian and Boo's confederates, Sextus and Charlie, were leaving the Library.

'Good Morning' the murderer announced chirpily as his breakfast heaved and nearly dropped into his socks.

'Good Morning' came back three replies in unison as they all went on their various ways.

Brother Fabian's task that day was to continue with the patching-up of the church roof's decaying fabric and so walked off in that direction. The Chief Superintendent made his way to the sitting room to continue setting up while Sextus, at a loose end, went off to the Chapel to pray for the soul of Father Edward, whom no-one apart from Boo, Sextus and Charlie and the present owner of the Charter, knew was lying dead behind the range in the Lumber room. However, that was all about to change at lunch.

'What were they up to?' the murderer fretted, his nerves already in shreds '...and in the Library? It can only mean one thing...that old bat's still poking her nose in where it doesn't belong! Something's going to have to be done about her'

Little did he know that someone else was thinking the same thing: his fellow treasure hunter who'd observed Boo, Sextus and the Chief Superintendent walking up the gravel driveway from the upstairs room the previous day while the possessor of the Charter had looked on from the downstairs window.

During the course of the morning, all of the protagonists did what had to be done.

Forty Nine

By the time Miss Lavender had regained her composure to make her way to meet the Abbot; the corridor outside the Bibliotheca was deserted.

Taking her time, she ambled along the corridors going over that conversation again in her head. The dark, musty corridors leading to the head of the Abbey's office were as silent as a graveyard until something wrenched Boo's thoughts back to the here and now: she had a sense that she was not alone. Even her mirrored glasses were unable to help her shake off the feeling. There appeared to be no-one following her...but the hairs on the back of her neck said differently.

Without warning, she stopped...and called out forcefully:

'Is there someone there?'

Number One Suspect slid silently around the corner ahead of where she was standing. A moment later the Charter-possessing murderer came out of one of the open doorways in the corridor behind her.

'Did I hear you call, Miss Lavender?' the man behind said in hushed tones unaware, because of the general dim lighting in the corridor, that they were not alone.

At the sound of the Charter-owner's voice, Number One Suspect slipped something back into his pocket, realising that he was not alone either with Miss Lavender.

'Can I help you, Miss Lavender?' he enquired in an obsequious tone.

Boo's head flicked from one to the other.

'Oh...I'm so sorry' she called out '...silly old me, I'm just very tired after last night'

The adversaries stood in passive silence at either end of the corridor eyeing each other up as Miss Lavender hurried on along the corridor passed Number One Suspect.

Little did she know how close she'd come to joining Johnnie and the others.

A question: has anyone ever been murdered twice?

Fifty

Unaware of exactly what had nearly happened, Boo approached the door to the Abbot's office. The telephone, the one which had been ripped from the wall, was ringing: the Post Office had obviously repaired it quickly.

Her hand rose to knock but for a moment she hesitated and in doing so, 'accidently' overheard the conversation, or at least the Abbot's side of it: it did not make pretty hearing.

'...yes I know it's overdue, Richard. I was working on it but, as you're probably aware from the national press, we've had two murders here at the Abbey...'

'No' Boo thought '...three'

The Abbot continued '... which have, if I'm being honest, diverted my attention from dealing with it'

Boo could hear the strain in his voice before he went silent and listened to whoever was at the other end of the telephone.

Boo couldn't hear what was being said at the other end but whoever was, was clearly angry: the exact words used were inaudible but what she could hear was a deep, muffled voice whose owner clearly wasn't mincing his words.

'Of course I'm well aware that being a parishioner of ours has put you in a difficult position and I do appreciate that your head office is putting pressure on you but what can I do? I simply can't give you what I haven't got'

Silence.

'Please, Richard, ask head office to bear with us for a little while longer and we will repay the loan. In fact, we are having the Library catalogued for our Anniversary and the lady Librarian from Cheltenham tells me that we have a number of First Editions which are worth quite a lot of money. While I'm loathed to part with our heritage, if I must I shall, and we will repay the loan. We just need a little more time'

The Abbot stopped talking but this time, the voice at the other end of the telephone seemed to have been mollified and softened its tone.

'Thank you, Richard. I appreciate that and God Bless you'

Boo heard the click as the Abbot hung up followed by a long, deep sigh. Still she waited.

Her maxim in situations like these was: when you think it's the right time, count to twenty and then proceed.

'Nineteen...twenty' and she knocked.

'Come in' was the weary reply.

'Father, you asked to see me?' said Boo, gently pushing the door open.

'Please sit down, Miss Lavender.' he offered. 'I'm afraid I'm guilty of the sinful act of procrastination, my dear. I've been putting it off but now needs must: we need to sell off those First Editions and we need to do so quickly' he stated honestly, exhaustion dripping off his every word.

'Father, my friend is on holiday in France at the moment but will be back in the next two or three days. Would that be soon enough?'

'That would be fine, Miss Lavender. We need to have them officially valued and put into auction as soon as possible'

'Ah, the church roof?' enquired Boo, casting her line into the water.

'If only, Miss Lavender. No, I'm afraid we were forced to take out rather a large loan after the storm of '52. It did a lot of damage which the insurance company didn't completely cover and now we're under pressure to pay it back. Fortunately, you came along and discovered our rare editions which might go some way to repaying it. I always say, the Good Lord provides and, in our case, he provided us with you'. With that, he let out an honest, genuine chuckle.

'Well, I'm sorry that it has come to that, Father. If there's anything I can do...' Boo's unfinished sentence was a genuinely open offer: she'd grown fond of the Abbot, realising that he was a decent man of integrity who cared not only for his community but for those less fortunate than himself.

'If you know any rich benefactors...' he began before breaking into laughter again. 'You know, Miss Lavender, you really are a tonic. Despite the terrible events we've experienced, you've managed to raise my spirits in a lot of different ways'

He started ticking them off on his fingers.

'You recognised our First Editions which could go a long way to helping us financially, you make me laugh and finally...and most importantly, you play bridge! And one day soon when things have calmed down a bit, I look forward to a good session with you and Sextus. What more could we wish for? How lucky were we to find you?' he beamed.

'Thank you for that, Father...and I hope I'm not finished yet' she added mysteriously.

By that point, her cryptic reply went sailing way over the troubled, tonsured head.

Dom Ambrose sank back in his chair and let out an almighty explosion of breath: it was a mixture of sheer tiredness and frustration.

'I have so many things in my head fighting for attention, Miss Lavender, and then suddenly one of them pushes to the front and says:

"Okay, I am the most important. I'm just about to tackle it when something else shoves it out of the way as if to say: "Hey, it's me, I'm the most important one! Deal with me first!"'

'I tell you Miss Lavender; it would try the patience of a saint'

'Well you have had a lot on your plate recently, Father; and now especially with the latest development concerning the disappearance of Father Edward'

'D'you know, Miss Lavender that is the strangest thing. I've known Father Edward for over twenty-five years and this is completely out of character for him. Yes, he's a bit of an old whinger sometimes...'

'...was' corrected Miss Lavender mentally.

'...but he's always been a solid, reliable pillar of our community. I just cannot conceive that he is a murderer or indeed a thief. The very idea of it is totally preposterous! But where can he have disappeared to? I mean, has he lost his mind?'

'No, his life' Boo wanted to say...but couldn't...not yet.

It was difficult for Miss Lavender to sit there, knowing what she knew and watching the desperation on this man of the cloth's face; now she understood how Sextus had felt. But she also knew that it could be dangerous to reveal what she was privy to: she bit her tongue.

'I really don't know, Father,' she lied 'but I'm sure we'll find out soon. Well,' she said after an awkward moment's silence when the Abbot looked straight into her eyes as if he could see that she did know something '...I'd better get on with the cataloguing and see what other treasures are lurking in your Library'

As she opened the door to leave, she turned to say goodbye when she caught the Abbot staring into space, a strange look in his eyes. What was he thinking about that could make him look so...aggressive?

'I can tell you, Miss Lavender, there is nothing I wouldn't do to save my community. Nothing in this world' he said with a ferocity Boo hadn't seen before: it frightened her.

'Did he mean what he just said about not knowing what has happened to Father Edward or...?'

Fifty One

Walking back along the winding corridors, doubts began to slither into Boo's consciousness: what did the Abbot mean? Had she misjudged him or was it simply the stress getting to him?

'I know good bridge players, and Dom Ambrose is definitely one of them, have a reputation for being utterly ruthless sometimes in their execution of...?' she shuddered at her choice of words. 'No, surely he couldn't...wouldn't...didn't...?'

Arriving at the door of the Library, she saw that the door was slightly ajar. In her mind's eye she rewound to thirty minutes earlier when she'd left for the Abbot's office. Yes, she recalled, she had closed the door properly so why was it not closed now? Had Charlie or Sextus come back?

The room was empty...except Miss Lavender knew someone had been there. There was just...something. Then it struck her. There was a smell, a smell which hadn't been there thirty minutes ago when she'd left; a smell which instantly took her back to the last time she'd played bridge. A smell which reminded her of Mildred.

Then the penny dropped: Professor Beech had been there.

As with Mildred, Miss Lavender realised that, in general, smokers' sense of smell was enormously diminished by their habit: so it would seem with Professor Beech. For not only did his suit reveal his habit by the burn marks in his waistcoat but also, the reek which emanated from the suit itself.

'Now what was he up to?' she wondered. 'I thought he wasn't interested? Or, is this what he meant when he said that he was "...checking out a few things"? Why so secretive but more to the point, what was he doing in here?'

After a cursory check around the place, Boo decided that nothing had been taken and decided that, at the present time, she had more important things to worry about and so the Professor was put on the back burner...for now.

But the thought stayed at the back of the queue for the rest of the morning as a very small part of her formidable brain engaged in dealing with the minutiae of archiving: the rest was dedicated to evaluating and re-evaluating the events, the scenarios, the conversations together with the various incidents viewed through her mirrored spectacles...but she kept coming back to her last conversation with the Abbot. Something wasn't right.

If it wasn't for the loud tick-tock of the clock she could have sworn that it had stopped: the hands on the dial seemed barely to move. More than once she uttered under her breath frustratedly:

'Ring, why don't you, ring' referring to the bell calling everyone to lunch.

About twenty minutes before lunch, Boo could stand it no more; she sat at her desk with a clean sheet of paper and drew a line down the middle of it.

On the left hand side at the top she wrote 'For' and at the top of the right hand column she wrote 'Against' and between these two words she wrote in capitals 'DA': Dom Ambrose.

Five minutes into her analysis, the bell tolled for lunch.

'Balderdash!' she thought irritably but really wanted to scream in frustration. 'Over the last two hours, the hands on that clock have moved at a snail's pace, now, when I need more time, it's like they're on wheels'

Looking at the sheet, she saw that the columns were more or less of equal length. 'That won't do. No, that won't do at all'

The most damning fact on the 'Against' column that she could see was that he was the only one who knew that the Abbey had previously been known as Chalfontbury Friary. So, did that mean that he also knew about the secret passages...and, if he did, what did that mean? Could he be the one using them? But why would he need to steal the Charter and Rosary? There were things which didn't add up.

Was he the missing link?

Fifty Two

By the time Miss Lavender had tidied up, she'd already decided to leave the sheet of paper with her thoughts on Dom Ambrose at the top of the pile turned over, and so mentally filed a note to herself: "to be continued". A quick glance at the clock showed that it was just a few minutes to one. Mindful that lunch was served promptly at that hour in the Abbey, she scuttled along the corridors as fast as her legs would carry her, keenly aware that time and the strict regime of this Abbey waited for no man or woman...visitor or not.

Finally, reaching the door to the Refectory, she stopped for a moment to catch her breath when a thought struck her:

'Really,' she thought, slightly winded by the rush 'this should have been such a straightforward assignment. When is it going to end and how many other bodies will be scattered along its path?' It did worry her immensely.

Steeling herself, she took a deep breath and pushed open the heavy door to be confronted by a sea of heads turning en masse to greet her with a silence so profound it felt menacing...and judging by some of the hostile glares she received, she wasn't wrong: not everyone in that room was pleased to see her.

Quietly and with dignity she made her way to the top table and joined the others, standing behind her chair waiting for the Abbot to say grace.

As the last word of prayer fell from the Abbot's lips, everyone muttered a subdued 'Amen' followed by a loud dragging of chairs from under tables.

Lunch began as it had since Miss Lavender arrived at the Abbey with a short reading from the New Testament followed by a reading from, as Miss Lavender had always thought of the author, "that boring man, Strachey". They were still being regaled, 'if that's the word' she thought resignedly, by the Cardinal Manning story. After a few days of this torture, Boo had enquired, slightly tongue in cheek, at the end of one lunchtime reading if they'd always had such interesting books. Dom Ambrose with a twinkle in his eye had replied: 'we've had worse', at which, the whole top table burst into uproarious laughter.

Apart from the clacking of cutlery on plates and the drone of the reader's voice, no other sound was heard...until the Refectory doors came crashing open. The brother who had been reading instantly fell silent while forks halted midway to mouths. Chief Superintendent Chivers, flanked by two uniformed policemen, strode into the tense silence. A bloodied habit hung over his outstretched arms like a limp body.

'This' he declared vehemently, 'has been found! Does it belong to anyone of you here?' he demanded, slowly turning from left to right, displaying the obscene article for all to see. He scrutinised the faces of the shocked diners, looking for signs of recognition.

Two seconds of silence passed before knives and forks clattered onto plates. Uproar followed.

Shouts of "Murder!" and "Outrage!" were heard as at least two of the monks called out Father Edward's name. The Refectory fell into total disarray.

'If anyone knows whose habit this is I need them to come forward...NOW!' roared the Chief Superintendent.

The Abbot, like most of the diners was on his feet. He called for silence: unusually, he had to call for it twice.

Slowly, a hush and some order came to the dining room.

'Chief Superintendent, would you be good enough to come with me to my office and we'll discuss this there?' There was no mistaking the firmness of the polite request by the Abbot.

'Certainly, Sir' responded the policeman who'd done what he'd come to do: provoke a reaction... 'and he got it in abundance' thought Miss Lavender, looking around the dining room at the scattered napkins and abandoned, half-eaten meals. She also noted that the shifting eyes had returned: 'Am I safe with you...or you...or you? Could I be the next victim?' the eyes seemed to ask as they scoured their neighbours' faces.

Fear was plain on every face...well almost.

In the chaos, Boo observed the clearly unnerved Number Two Suspect mouthing something to someone behind her. Checking in her mirrored spectacles, she observed Number One. He was shaking his head slowly at Number Two as if to say "Not here!" before jerking his head in the direction of the cloister.

Boo immediately checked her handbag to make sure she had the hearing aid to hand: praise the Lord, it was there.

Lady MacDorn-Smythe was the only one still sitting in her seat which was to the right of the Abbot's chair. To Boo's eyes, she was in shock but then her two children joined her, one either side, with Angus sitting on the Abbot's seat rubbing his mother's back and whispering in a comforting way while Gertie patting her mamma's hand in a reassuring way: both of them looked ashen. But Boo noticed that it didn't stop them from eyeing the Chief Superintendent's receding back closely as he followed the Abbot from the Refectory.

'They must be worried sick about their mother, poor lambs. What with their father murdered and now Father Edward. The whole community must be terrified that one of them will be the next target. How very sad'

But Boo knew she couldn't hang around; she had to find out what Suspects One and Two were up to.

'Maybe they're going to check the body: I'd better follow them. But what about Charlie? He's gone off to the Abbot's office...and where's Sextus?'

The light touch of a hand on her shoulder made her jump: it was Sextus.

'Quite a performance' he remarked.

'Sextus, quick, come with me. The suspects have just left and we have to follow them'

Sextus fell in as Boo led the way through the small groups huddled together postulating more and more outrageous theories.

'Quickly or we shall lose them, Sextus' Boo gasped frantically.

Once outside the Refectory doors, Boo looked left and right: nothing.

'Which way did they go?' she thought panicking.

Fortunately, the two policemen who had escorted the Chief Superintendent into the Refectory were standing guard one at either end of the corridor.

Trying to appear calm, something she felt anything but, Boo called out to one of them:

184

'Did you see anyone come out, constable?'

'Yes, ma'am. Two gentlemen. They went that way' said the young constable pointing to the cloisters.

'Thank you so much' replied Boo scooting along as fast as her short legs would carry her with Sextus following behind as best he could.

Fifty Three

Boo took the same route to the cloisters as Suspects One and Two had the night before, via the kitchens which had temporarily emptied when the chaos in the Refectory erupted. She halted by one of the open windows and was relieved to see the two of them sitting on the bench under the ancient oak tree.

She quickly removed the hearing aid from her handbag much to the surprise of Sextus.

'What are you doing, Boo?' he asked in a hoarse anxious whisper.

'Just be quiet for the moment and I'll tell you later, Sextus' she replied softly.

Pushing the hearing aid into her ear, she held the receiver on the window ledge and was immediately gratified to hear the amplified voices of the two men; clear as a church bell.

'...if anyone sees us and asks what we're doing here, we just say we've come out for some air, that we're in shock' began Suspect Number One.

'But I am in bloody shock!' retorted Number Two. 'Who's doing this? Do they know who we are? Are we next? I've had enough of this. Let's get out of here and get back to some honest thieving. You said this would be like taking sweets from a kid and all we've got so far is this pl...pla...ce' he stuttered '...filling up with dead bodies'

'And I've told you before; you'll be joining them if you don't play your part. How was I to know the old man was going to turn up? He recognised me. I know he did. And he would have spilt the beans that night if I hadn't done what I did and then we'd have been looking at a nice stretch at Her Majesty's pleasure. I didn't have a choice: it was him or us' he finished in a cold detached way.

'So it was them who killed Johnnie but clearly they have no idea who is responsible for killing the others: there is another murderer on the loose' Boo realised.

Sextus, who was watching Boo's face for any clues, saw the shock register on it. He began hopping from foot to foot impatiently.

'What are they saying, Boo? Can you hear everything?'

Boo put her finger up to her lips to silence Sextus while she listened to the rest of the conversation.

'Later' she mouthed.

'You know, thinking about it, you might be right about doing it tonight and then getting the hell out of here' said Number Two.

'I've already worked it out: I'm going to do it later when Brother Jerome and the rest of the kitchen staff are having their break before preparing for dinner'

'But who's killing all these people? It's like there's a madman on the loose in the place' said Number Two flipping his jacket collar up and hugging his thin jacket closer to his skinny body as the chill in the air made him shiver.

'I've no idea but after tonight it won't matter because...they'll all be dead! I'm not getting this close and giving up now' Suspect Number One barked.

'I'm really frightened' replied Number Two, looking around, still shivering despite his attempts to fend off the chill...or fear, in his bones.

'All you have to do is keep your nerve till tonight and then we'll be rich and free of this place'

'Oh, is that all?' Suspect Number Two asked sardonically.

'God it gives me the creeps this place. I'm supposed to be weeding the vegetable patch this afternoon so I'd better get on my way. But after tonight, the weeds can grow ten feet tall for all I care...but I'd better keep a low profile until then' thundered Suspect Number One as he rose from the bench. 'We'll talk later' and he skulked off.

'I do hope so' replied his accomplice, the mealy-mouthed Reverend Richmond.

Fifty Four

The Abbot held the door to his office open for the Chief
Superintendent who entered wordlessly and sat in the visitor's
chair across the desk from the Abbot.

As he walked slowly around the desk to his chair, Dom
Ambrose began:

'What was the meaning of that...outrage, Chief Superintendent?
There was no need for it. Our community is already living on a
knife edge: some of our guests were badly shaken by it. I really
must protest' he finished, the anger in his voice barely controlled.

'I'm sorry you feel that way, Father, but it's my job and I will
do whatever I deem necessary to flush out the perpetrator or
perpetrators of these vile crimes' offered the Chief
Superintendent in a placatory voice.

The Abbot flopped into his chair and with a loud sigh said:

'I suppose you're right, Chief Superintendent. I want these
people found as quickly as possible too, you know'

Both men then made eye contact with neither one prepared to
look away: first one to blink would be the loser.

Despite a lifetime of hearing confessions that could make a lay
person's toes curl and developing an ability to outmanoeuvre the
hierarchy of a Church steeped in strict protocol, Dom Ambrose
was no match for Charlie Chivers: that man had eyeballed more
villains than the Abbot had said Hail Marys.

The Abbot withdrew a large white handkerchief from his sleeve
and blew his nose very loudly to cover the fact that he had lost:
losing did not sit well, at all, with this competitive bridge-player.

Charlie just smiled and thought:

'In your dreams, Father' but said: 'Do you recognise the habit,
Father?' as he laid it across the desk...and waited.

The Abbot looked closely at the bloodied, tangled garment, his
face wrinkling up in distaste before saying:

'There should be a tag attached at the collar with a name on it'

'Then let's check, shall we?' and Charlie brought out the most
powerful weapon in his armoury; his trusty pencil.

188

Pulling the hood back from the body of the habit with the pencil revealed a tag sewn into the neck of the garment. But because of the proximity of the collar to the wound, a lot of blood had soaked in around the area of the collar where the small label was located.

They both bent over, the Abbot screwing up his eyes while the Chief Superintendent reaching into his pocket, removing his magnifying glass.

'I can't...quite make it out' admitted the Abbot.

'It looks like...like there's a "P" then an "A" then a "B" or "P" again but I can't make any of the rest of the letters out'

'PAB or PAP?' queried the Abbot 'Em...eh...are you sure the first letter is a "P"? Could it be an "F"?'

Charlie scrutinised the label again.

'You could be right, Father. Looking at it again,' and this time Charlie screwed up his own eyes as he tried to make out that first letter '...I think it is an "F"' he conceded.

'Then it belongs to Brother Fabian'

'Right, we'll need to speak to him as a matter of urgency. This can't wait'

'I hate to pour cold water on your theories or evidence, Chief Superintendent, but I'm afraid it'll do you no good' stated the Abbot laying the palms of his hands flat on the desk.

'Why is that, Father?'

'You see, we have two robes each and when we wear one habit, the other one is sent to be cleaned and when it's returned, it tends to just be hung on the back of the door, as mine did, and we forget all about it until it's time to change it again. So, he may not even be aware that it's missing'

'Is nothing straightforward in this investigation?' Charlie moaned internally.

'I'm sorry I couldn't have been more help, Chief Superintendent'

'So am I, Father. So am I' said Charlie crestfallen. 'Million things to do so I'd better crack on. But keep this to yourself, will you, Father? Probably better if you don't mention it to anyone'

Fifty Five

Boo managed to drag Sextus through the door from the kitchen just before Brother Jerome, the cook, returned. He stopped for a moment, gave them both a funny look but continued on into the kitchen and said nothing: had other things on his mind...probably, Boo didn't wonder.

'Boo, please tell me...what's happening?'

Boo gave him a quick précis including the confirmation she'd heard from the two suspects that there was, at least, one other murderer walking around the Abbey.

'We know about those two but who could the other one be?' asked her friend perplexedly.

'I hope you're right about it being only one other murderer, Sextus, I'm not sure we could cope with more' She heard a noise and turned. 'Ah...here comes Charlie. Any news?' she enquired, although she'd already noted the expression on his face as he turned the corner and walked slowly towards them.

It was not the look or the walk of a man close to solving a crime.

'Sadly, no, Miss Lavender. Apparently, they all have spare robes which could go missing and they wouldn't necessarily notice it'

'Well, we have a very important piece of information, Charlie'

'Good, I hope'

'I wouldn't say "good", Charlie, but it does help us'

Boo told him about the second murderer/ murderers.

'I hope we haven't missed them' said Charlie.

'Missed what?' Sextus asked

'Well, if it's not the other two who murdered Father Edward, we'd better get a move on to see if anyone's using the secret passage upstairs'

'Oh d...d...dear!' Boo stammered. 'I completely forgot about that. We were busy keeping an eye on the other two because we thought they were the murderers...which they are...but they're not responsible for all of them...' said Boo getting herself tied up into knots '...oh, you know what I mean' she finished exasperatedly.

'Let go' she said and without further ado, they hastily made their way up to Sextus' room.

As they mounted the stairs Sextus said:

'How will we know if they've been in there?'

'We won't, Sextus. We just have to hope and pray that they haven't had a chance to look yet with all the to-ing and fro-ing that's gone on. Given our present location, praying might not be such a bad idea'

'I'll offer up a quick one for us' proposed Sextus.

Nothing else was said until they were inside Sextus' room and the door closed.

'What next?' the room's temporary resident asked.

'To be honest, Sextus, we'll have to play this by ear. We don't know for sure if anyone has tried to enter by the secret passage in the guest room, so what I suggest is this: Charlie goes down to the lumber room and checks with the two constables he's posted there to see if anyone has been acting suspiciously around the area. If not, then I think we're in with a chance: the perpetrator won't have had a chance to check it out yet. Do you both agree?' she asked.

'We've got nothing to lose, Miss Lavender' Charlie said with a shrug of his shoulders 'We know what the scallywags are up to later...and we'll deal with that then. We could arrest them now but, and I think you'll agree with me here, if we do, it might frighten off whoever is responsible for the other murders. So, from that point of view, I agree with you; this could be our best chance to catch whoever else is in on it'

'Ditto' agreed Sextus.

'Very well, Charlie, Sextus and I will keep watch here while you go and check it out with the troops'

Charlie opened the door a crack to check for any movement. When he saw that there was none, he quickly opened the door and shut it rapidly and silently.

'Looks like he's done that before' Boo said to Sextus who laughed and said 'No more than hundreds of times, I shouldn't imagine'

'I suppose. Now what have we got that could wedge the door open a fraction, just enough to see if anyone goes by, Sextus?'

'What about this copy of the New Testament, Boo?' Sextus suggested picking up the copy which lay on the bedside cabinet.

'How very appropriate, Sextus. Well done'

Sextus jammed the thin volume under the door leaving it open a crack; no more than half an inch.

'Perfect' said Boo and she brought a chair over from the other side of the bed and sat down close to the door. From the crack in the door Boo was able to view the door to the guest room with the entrance to the secret passage.

No more than five minutes later Boo heard footsteps approaching.

Boo and Sextus exchanged looks nervously.

A light tap at the door made Sextus jump; he hadn't been expecting it.

'Psst, it's me, Charlie. Let me in'

Sextus removed the book and Charlie, after checking that no-one was watching, entered swiftly.

'Several people have sauntered past with one or two of them expressing surprise at the police presence'

'Blast and drat! So really, we're none the wiser. So, we'll just have to wait' concluded Boo.

'Agreed' was her companions' response.

And so they waited...and waited.

Fifty Six

They weren't the only ones waiting. The present owner of the Charter was in a state of high angst.

Pacing up and down his room, his mind in a whirl, for once, this supremely confident murderer was unsure what his next move should be...if any.

When the Chief Superintendent had produced that habit, he'd thought his number was up. How he managed not to give the game away, he just didn't know. His nerves were stretched to the point where one more incident, no matter how small, could find him collapsed in a heap, he thought. However, giving further thought to the situation convinced him that they were only on a fishing expedition and he relaxed somewhat. Ramming the proverbial rod into his mental spine, he made his decisions and how to carry them out.

That is until he made his way to the Lumber room only to be confronted by two policemen guarding the door: it threw him, he just wasn't expecting it. And his casual enquiry into their presence had been met with a perfunctory 'Sorry. Sir, we're just following orders'...which was no bloody use at all! What did that mean?

'Why have they got the Lumber Room under guard? Have they found the secret passage? Have they found the body? But if they'd found it, why didn't they come out and say they'd found it? Come to think of it, how did they get the habit? Surely they would have found the body at the same time? Or...' and here the doubt began to slowly trickle into this already troubled mind '...is that not where I left it? Aaah! What an utter disaster! Why did I ever start this?'

Five minutes later, he was back to frantic pacing, but at least the framework of a plan was beginning to form.

'For sure, if they haven't found the body yet I need to get there and get rid of that candlestick with my fingerprints all over it. But how can I find out if they've discovered the secret passage if I can't get into the Lumber Room? Hmmm...they almost certainly won't know about the secret passage connecting the Lumber

Room with the upstairs guest room. Maybe I could...maybe I could enter via the guest room to see if the body's been discovered yet. Good idea. All is not lost'

The murderer looked at the clock: almost three o'clock. 'With luck most of them will either be working, praying or having a nap. I'll do a recce first'

This clever, heartless murderer's plan was about to unravel like a ball of loose wool.

Because they did know...and more than he realised would be lost...but out of it, something good would come.

Fifty Seven

Lady MacDorn-Smythe sat on her side of the large double bed she and her husband had occupied every year, at this time, '...for over forty years' she recalled, at the invitation of the incumbent Abbot of the time, in gratitude for Sir John's grandfather's generous donation of the Abbey to their Order. Now, one half of that bed would remain cold and empty '...for the rest of my lifetime' she thought sadly. 'Why?' she asked herself for the thousandth time. 'Who would want to kill Johnnie? Oh, I know he could drive me to despair sometimes with his overgenerous ways: that's why we're in the position we're in now. He couldn't see someone in need without trying to help them, usually by dipping into his own shallow trouser pocket. Material things were never important to him...I suppose, that's what I loved about him' she sighed.

"Dottie, he used to say to me, you are my beautiful princess and I shall always love you but I was brought up to put others first. So, if you think I'm neglecting you sometimes, I'm not. It's just I have a duty to help others less fortunate than us in any way I can"

As these thoughts hurtled around in her head, her daughter, the Honourable Gertie, sat beside her mamma on the bed deep in thought.

'Should I or shouldn't I bring it up?' thought Gertie wrestling with her sense of decency. Finally, she decided that it needed to be dealt with. Now.

'Oh, mamma, what are we going to do now?' she began. 'I know that papa was going to speak with Dom Ambrose about our situation, but do you know if he did?' asked the sensible one in the family.

'I don't know darling. I think I'm going to have to broach the subject myself but I'll hate myself for doing it. I mean, the poor man has enough to deal with at the moment now that it looks like poor Father Edward didn't, in fact, run off but was...oh, I can't believe this is happening. It's all too much' blubbered Lady MacDorn-Smythe.

'And a fat lot of use Angus is, mamma. I thought he was lined up for a big important job in publishing? That could help'

'Oh, don't go on so, Gertie. Things will work out for us: they always do, darling. Now please don't say anything to Angus just now; he's wandering around in a daze: I think he's terribly overwrought about papa's death'

'...or another of his fancy ideas on how to get rich quick!' spat his sister.

'Well, yes, there is that. I mean, if it wasn't for the fact that papa had to pay those awful people who, Angus insists, cheated him...oh my poor darling!' and Lady Dottie burst into tears again.

Gertie wasn't sure if her mother's sympathy was aimed at her father or her brother but she let it pass: there was no point in stressing her any further.

A knock at the door halted Lady Dorothy's sniffling.

'Come in' she called out pulling herself together.

The Honourable Angus popped his head around the door.

''S'only me!' he said gaily.

'Huh!' was Gertie's huffy response.

'And hello to you too, sis' he said sarcastically.

'Oh, please you two. No bickering. Not now' Lady Dorothy said, intervening.

'Only came to see how you are, mamma?'

'Thank you darling, I'm alright' replied his mother as she dabbed the sides of her red-rimmed eyes with a handkerchief.

'Are you sure?'

'Yes, darling, I'm going to have a word with Dom Ambrose tonight after dinner...about you know what' she replied mysteriously.

'I wouldn't bother if I was you, mamma. He can hardly keep this place going from what...' Angus stopped mid-sentence. 'Anyway, must be off'

'Wait!' commanded Gertie. 'What did you mean? From what...to what?'

'Er...from what I've...er...heard. Look, I promised not to say anything but...' Angus looked both ways along the corridor and quickly entered the room and closed the door.

'...apparently, the Abbey has serious financial troubles. They can't go on much longer: they're jolly well skint; up to their necks in trouble. And the Abbot was pinning his hopes on raising funds from this Anniversary malarkey by getting people to leave legacies and donations etc. but with what's gone on, I don't think that's going to be happening now'

Both mother and daughter looked at each other, horrified.

'Oh no!' began Lady Dorothy 'but...but...' she was lost for words. Their last hope had just gone up in smoke.

'Well, that's just dandy!' said Gertie her temper rising. 'Always the bearer of bad news, eh, Angus?'

'I just didn't want mamma to be in the embarrassing position of asking only to be refused, that's all'

'Let's leave it there' commanded Lady Dorothy drawing on her faith. 'God will provide' she concluded.

'Oh look! A herd of pigs has just flown past the window. Anybody got a gun? I haven't been on a good shoot for ages!' was Angus' acerbic response.

'Oh, get out, you horrid man!' screamed his sister.

'Bye!' Angus called out as he flew to the door and closed it swiftly and loudly behind him: it wouldn't be the first time Gertie had thrown something. He waited for the crash...but nothing happened...this time.

'Ah well' he thought as he sauntered along the corridor.

Fifty Eight

Suspect Number One tentatively pushed the door open to the kitchen; there was no-one around.

'Good' thought the man who'd played his role to perfection.

How was he to know that the entire MacDorn-Smythe clan descended on the Abbey at the same time every year since before Sir John was married to his childhood sweetheart, Dorothy Peters?

Lady Dorothy's father had been the MacDorn-Smythe's broker since Sir John had been a boy. He and Dorothy had grown up together; both of their fathers, firm friends, were overjoyed when they found that the friendship of the families was to be cemented by the marriage of their children.

If only Sir John hadn't recognised him on that first night, things could have been so much different.

But then again, taking that waiter's job at Sir John's club in Pall Mall had, at the time, seemed a good idea. If only his fingers hadn't been caught as they were coming out of the till, then the baronet would probably never have remembered him.

It seemed like only yesterday that he was serving Sir John and his companion for the evening, Sir Reginald Grenville, permanent undersecretary at the Foreign Office, their favourite tipple of "large Scotch and water, please" when he overheard Sir John telling Sir Reginald the story of the 700th Anniversary of Brackenbury Abbey and the secret arrival of the priceless Charter and Rosary and the rumours of the fabled lost treasure attached to the Abbey.

Sir Reginald laughed as Suspect Number One served their drinks and said it reminded him of a story he'd read as a child: "King Solomon's Mines" by H. Rider Haggard.

'Hidden treasure, I love it!' replied Sir Reginald immediately transported back to his school days at Eton.

Later when Suspect Number One overheard the manager of the club in his office calling the police, he knew his number was up and legged it before he felt the hot sweaty mitt of a copper on his collar. And only just in time; another five minutes and he'd have been able to check out the improvements they'd made to Black Marias since he last rode in the back of one.

But then he had an idea: why not kill two birds with one stone? He could lie low from the cops at the monastery. With a bit of luck and a fair wind and if the story about the treasure was true, he might waken up to find that some of it had "accidentally" found its way into his constantly-haemorrhaging pocket.

He'd need a partner though and that's when he bumped into an old lag he'd met when he'd last received free board and lodging at Her Majesty's expense. Known to one and all in the clink as "Sticky-Fingered Fred", due to his penchant for pocketing anything which wasn't nailed down, Freddie Cornwall specialised in playing impecunious parsons and relieving elderly well-to-do widows of anything of theirs he could get his hands on.

So, Freddie Cornwall alias The Reverend James Richmond told the Abbot that although he was not of the faith, he had nevertheless heard good things of the Abbey and had decided to "refresh his soul" by doing a retreat there.

The Abbot swallowed both stories.

And that is how Suspect Number One ended up now in the kitchens of the Abbey about to commit an unthinkable crime.

His movements were smooth and silent as he neared the four large pots sitting on the cast iron Aga stove. He lifted each lid and sniffed.

'Heaven sent or heaven's scent?' he thought wickedly as he poured the liquid in equal measure into the four pots filled with stew. Picking up the spoon on the side, he gave them all a good stir.

'That should do it' he thought.

But would it?

Fifty Nine

The Honourable Gertie left her mother's room shortly after Angus had gone: his departure had left the two women in each other's arms consoling one another.

'He's such a beast, mamma!' exclaimed Gertie of her older sibling.

'Now, now, Gertie, hush' her mother replied, squeezing her daughter closer to her bosom.

'Don't deny it mamma. He's nothing but trouble. I don't think he's done one good thing in his entire life'

Once Gertie got onto the subject of her brother's antics, there was no stopping her.

And when Lady Dorothy saw that look in Gertie's eyes, she knew that even if one of the saints themselves walked through the door and asked her to stop, they'd have more luck squeezing a very large camel through the eye of a very small needle. So, she was required to tell a little white lie. Namely, that she had a migraine coming on and that '...mamma needs to rest, darling'

Still in a bit of a lather about her brother, Gertie closed the door none too quietly, regretting it afterward: it probably hadn't helped her mother's headache.

Ever since he was a child, Angus had been spoilt. As the male heir, he got his own way all the time: it drove Gertie mad. Why should he get his own way all of the time? But there you have it; such are the ways of the British gentry. One day it would change but for now...

For a moment she hesitated, unsure which direction to take before turning left toward the main staircase. Ahead of her in the corridor she saw one of the monks hurrying along head bowed. She called out:

'Hello, Brother! Sorry about the door banging; slipped out of my hand' she lied smoothly.

He halted, turning slowly and said:

'That's quite alright, my child. With everything that's going on, it is the least of my worries' he replied with more than the usual mournful timbre in his voice.

Something in that tone startled Gertie. She gazed at the monk whose habit had always hung loosely on his body as if it were made for someone three times his size.

'I suppose that's what helped him win the medal for the sprint at the Olympics' she thought '...all of the really fast runners are always thin'

Brother Joseph's cowl slipped from his head as he turned to go on his way, revealing the cadaverous face with its sunken cheeks and crooked smile which used to frighten her as a child but today, there was something else; the words 'haunted' and 'tortured' sprang to mind.

Brother Joseph moved off at a pace before stopping dead in his tracks and changing directions to head down the stairs towards the main hall.

Having more pressing matters to focus on, the Bursar's puzzling reply flew over the top of Gertie's head.

Sixty

With the door opened a crack, Boo was not only able to watch the guest room door, she also heard the altercation between the siblings further along the corridor.

'Raised voices? What's going on now?' she murmured.

She looked at Sextus and Charlie but they just shrugged their shoulders as if to say "has it got anything to do with what we're dealing with?"

Boo was on the verge of standing up to open the door to find out where it was coming from when she heard a more muffled conversation in the corridor this time.

She looked at her companions again and they repeated the shrug.

'That twitch you two have...is it contagious?' Boo whispered, annoyed by their seeming lack of interest about something which could be significant.

Suddenly, she heard footsteps approaching, stopping, starting hesitantly again...then stopping.

She held her breath: whoever it was, was only feet away from Sextus' door. Fortunately, the door opened the other way to the direction they were coming from so they couldn't see that the door was ajar.

Another few hesitant steps and the owner of the faltering walk came into view. Boo's eyes widened in disbelief.

'Surely not...!' she whispered.

The expression on her face caused confusion in the room. Sextus began to ask:

'Whatever is the...' but that's as far as he got before Boo finger rose to her lips to silence him.

'Wait' she mouthed: she knew something wasn't quite right.

The door to the guest room opened and closed. The next thing Boo knew Charlie and Sextus made their move.

'Right let's be having him!' announced Charlie grimly.

'No...no! There's something not right here. Please, Charlie, Sextus...we need to talk'

'Talk? Talk? It's too late for that Miss Lavender. Action is what's required to catch this villain. Action!'

With that, Charlie removed the New Testament from under the door and charged towards the guest room.

'Please, Chief Superintendent, wait!' implored Boo to no avail.

Sextus was right behind him, ready to do whatever was necessary to apprehend this monster.

Boo trailed behind them, knowing it was all wrong. It simply could not be...

But Charlie and Sextus were past hearing. As Miss Lavender used to say: "their ears were out of bounds".

'Please...!' she begged again grasping at Charlie's sleeve as he pulled his whistle from his pocket and put it between his lips before throwing open the door.

The whistle fell to the floor with a clatter.

'What the blazes...!' he spluttered 'who...what...?' He stopped, lost for words.

Sextus had a distinctly sheepish look about him and became enormously interested in the shine on his shoes while Charlie bent down to retrieve his whistle.

'Oh, hello Gertie, dear' interjected Miss Lavender taking charge of the situation. 'Sorry to interrupt but the Chief Superintendent wanted to see if revisiting this room could maybe bring something back I'd forgotten about. But how very inconsiderate of us: we've barge in on you. Are you all right, dear? Is there anything we can do for you?' she asked solicitously.

'No, thank you, Miss Lavender. I've just had a stinker of an argument with...' she hesitated but then continued, 'mamma... and I wanted to come in and have a look at the view to take my mind off it. When we were children, you know, this used to be our room and I especially remember this view. It holds a lot of happy memories for me here. It reminds me of when Papa...' Gertie's eyes brimmed over with tears as she choked up '...when he used to come up and read a bedtime story to us. I...I...do miss him so'. Wiping away a tear and blowing her nose, she said: 'But I'll get out of your way and let you get on with it, shall I?'

'That would be very much appreciated, Gertie. And just as I'm sure you miss your papa very much I'm equally sure that your mamma is grateful for all the support you are giving her at this very sad time'

At these words, unable to speak, Gertie fled along the corridor. A moment or two later, a door slammed shut.

'That was a close one' uttered Sextus.

'Why wouldn't you both listen? I told you something wasn't right. Now we have to hope that the real murderer hasn't been warned off by any of this' Boo said exasperatedly. Sometimes she could knock both their heads together.

'Apologies, Miss Lavender, I thought we had our man and I just wanted to...' The Chief Superintendent ran out of words again.

'Well, let's hope our murderer hasn't cottoned on that we're watching' Boo said.

'Can I ask a question?' said Sextus. 'Who says Gertie's not the murderer? I mean, you said yourself that poison was a woman's weapon, didn't you Boo?'

'He has a point, Miss Lavender' said Charlie in support.

'He does indeed, Charlie but it is a completely wrong one. Apart from her reaction when I mentioned her father, do you really think that girl could murder anyone? Why, she fainted at the sight of the body we found in this very room. Or am I the only one here who notices these things? And she has a rock solid alibi for at least one of the times the murders took place. But yes, they do say that poison is more of a woman's device'

'Sorry, forgot about her alibi' offered Charlie contritely.

'Don't you think we should get back to our stations?' said Boo sternly.

They all trotted out of the room, Charlie giving it the once over before closing the door and returned to Sextus' room and resumed their wait...in hope.

Sixty One

Dom Ambrose observed the figure of Brother Joseph, the Bursar, walking ahead of him, at speed, along the corridor, past the lumber room with the police guard outside, towards the Chapel.

'Isn't he supposed to be tending the vegetable garden with Brother Fabian?' he wondered, frowning.

Opening the door to the Chapel he saw the Bursar, already sitting in the monks' pew, his head bent over, seemingly, in prayer: he didn't appear to register the arrival of the Abbot.

With his own mind a maelstrom of problems and potential solutions, the Abbot approached the opposite end of the pew. The clip-clop of his sandals along with the rustling of his habit brought Brother Joseph out of his reverie with a start. A look of annoyance crossed his face at being disturbed; he rose immediately and with a brief nod of acknowledgement to the Abbot, left the Chapel in silence and in haste.

'He's only just arrived. Strange'

After a few seconds of reflection on his Bursar's behaviour, the Abbot carried on: genuflecting before falling with a grunt to his knees in the pew, he reflected on his options.

There really was only one.

He'd have to do what had to be done.

Sixty Two

The Charter-possessing murderer returned from his reconnaissance mission but by the time he was back in his room, The Honourable Gertrude MacDorn-Smythe had already had her little tete-a-tete with Boo and Co and had gone for a lie down, so he was none the wiser.

'If I could just get rid of that candlestick or at least wipe my fingerprints from it, there'd be nothing to tie me to the murders. I'd be as free as a bird and now, at least, I have the Rosary. But the truth is also: I have no choice. I have to do this. Now' thought the murderer steeling himself for his next challenge.

Like his efforts with the Charter, which lay hidden behind the chest of drawers, it would seem that the Fates were against him: his luck, or what was left of it, was on the point of leaving by the front door.

His hand reached for the door handle, without any warning he felt light-headed. His hand sought something to hold on to, to steady himself; the small chest of drawers was the nearest thing.

'For goodness sake, what's going on?' he thought as he made it to the bed and sat down until the dizzy spell passed. 'It's taken more out of me than I realised' he concluded. 'Just this last thing to do and it'll all be over'

He went to stand up but fell back on the bed again.

'I'd better lie down until it passes. Twenty minutes should do it'

Nearly two hours later and only half an hour before dinner, he woke up.

'Blast!' he swore, looking at his watch 'It's nearly dinner time. I need get this thing out of the way and finished once and for all' Sitting up on the edge of the bed, his head felt a bit fuzzy but '...I will do this' he determined.

This time, he stood up and after a moment reached for the door handle again: nothing was going to stop him this time.

With ears and eyes on even higher alert than they'd been on the day he'd waited for the arrival of "Senor Tartaglia", he slipped quietly along the corridor, stopping at each door along the way, pressing his ear to each, listening. At the first one, he heard a gentle snore. Moving along to the next one he heard a radio, turned low, with what sounded like the end of the afternoon play.

'Good so far' he decided.

By the time he got to the next room he concluded that, as he thought, everyone was engaged in other pursuits and he was in the clear to check out the secret passage between the guest room and the lumber room.

In the meantime, the gang of three in Sextus' room, who'd been taking turns at keeping watch at half hour intervals, were all a bit jumpy: they'd had two false alarms already.

Out of nowhere, the sky filled with dark and heavy rain clouds and the light quickly began to fade: sinister shapes began to form from the lengthening shadows.

'Whoever it is has either seen or heard us or they're not taking any chances' Charlie announced out of the blue. 'Another' he consulted his pocket watch '...twenty minutes and we'll have to call it a day. It's almost time for dinner'

Weariness and the fading light had definitely taken their toll on Boo's eyes and brain: they were in semi-trance mode. She almost missed the silent figure gliding passed in the gloom of the corridor. But what was it? A change in the air pressure? The odour of something or someone different? Whatever it was, it made her sit up. Fortunately, her unconscious mind must have taken over while her conscious mind was in relaxed mode. Whatever. Boo became aware of the figure of a man moving, '...no creeping...' she decided, towards the guest room. She could only see his back which she did not immediately recognise. But for a moment, he stopped; turning his head slowly as if he'd heard something: Boo recognised that profile. Her eyes widened in disbelief, stunned, she held up her hand to Charlie and Sextus not to move; the least sound at this point could have sent the murderer scurrying away.

'Best to let him get into the room and open the secret passage before we confront him...if it is him.' she thought, not wanting to believe it.

The Charter-possessing murderer's hand rested on the door handle of the guest room.

'Should I really be doing this? Or, should I wait to see what their next move is?' he thought worriedly.

On the verge of turning around and going back to his room, the sound of a door opening along the corridor settled it; his hand automatically pushed on the handle and a couple of seconds later he stood in the room where he'd done for the monsignor with the candlestick; the bloodstain on the carpet incontrovertible proof of what he'd done.

For a few moments, he stood in the silence, regretting his actions.

'Where has it got me?' he asked himself remorsefully.

But he was nothing if not practical and after a moment's regret, he moved towards the fireplace where he'd escaped that day.

At his touch, the whole thing fell forward and he entered the small dark passage with the downward leading staircase. Prior to descending, he retrieved the Rosary, which was still where he'd left it hanging, allowing it to run through his fingers for a few precious moments before pulling the lever and replacing the Rosary; the fireplace returned to its original position. No-one would ever know he'd been there.

Or so he thought.

Sixty Three

Meanwhile, Boo was having a job holding Charlie and Sextus back from rushing in to catch the killer in flagrante delicto.

'Wait! Wait!' Boo commanded forcefully. 'Remember what happened last time? What if he's not in the secret passage yet? If we burst in he could deny everything. He could say...anything! Come up with any number of excuses. No, we have to give him enough time...no...enough rope to hang himself' she heard herself say: an unfortunate turn of phrase.

'Oh, we'll save him the bother: we'll do that for him, never fear, Miss Lavender' Charlie said through gritted teeth.

'Hear, hear!' offered Sextus in support.

The grisly thought sent a cold shiver through Boo.

'D'you think we've given him enough time now?' Boo asked nervously.

'Let's get ourselves outside the door and have a listen, shall we?' said Charlie who fetched his whistle out of his jacket pocket: this time he meant to use it.

Boo looked at him in alarm thinking he was going to blow it too soon.

'Don't worry, Miss Lavender, the boys are standing by at the entrance; they'll be here in seconds when I give them two quick blows on this' he told a relieved Boo.

Charlie went first, pulling the book from under the door and tiptoeing the short distance along the corridor to the guest room door.

Putting his ear to the door, he listened for a moment before beckoning to Boo and Sextus to approach. Both of them followed Charlie's method and carefully tiptoed along to the door.

'Anything?' whispered Boo.

Charlie replied with a shake of the head.

'We'd better check then'

As quietly as he could, Charlie turned the handle and opened the door a fraction; nothing. All three entered to find the room deserted and the fireplace closed.

'He must be in there' Sextus whispered, pointing to the ornate inglenook.

Boo moved silently to the fireside and pressed her ear to it.

'I can't hear anything' she said.

'Well he's gone in and the only way out is this one unless he fancies his chances with the two constables standing guard outside the lumber room. Either way, we've got him' Charlie muttered with grim determination.

'I suggest that you stand back and let Mr Phipps and I deal with him until my boys get here, Miss Lavender'

'That makes eminent sense, Charlie' Boo conceded but nonetheless wanted to be there when the murderer emerged to gauge his reaction. For Boo, those first few moments were important ones; when a culprit finally realises that the game is up. For some of them, the admission of their guilt seems to come as a relief. But the truly hardened ones would try to brazen it out. Whichever category they fell into, it was their eyes she watched: they never lied.

'I shall be interested to see which one this murderer turns out to be' she thought reluctantly: she still couldn't believe who it was. But the truth was he'd disappeared into the secret passage and there was only one person who would do that: the murderer.

'I'll sit in this chair' said Boo indicating the winged chair where Monsignor Avrili had placed his hat and coat; it would give her a direct view of the murderer as he emerged from the secret passage.

'Mr Phipps, if you'd like to stand behind the curtain over there...' requested the Chief Superintendent, pointing to the other window '...and I'll wait here' Charlie stood three feet away from the fireplace where the wall dipped in. By the time the murderer saw Charlie it would be too late: the cuffs would be on him before he could draw his next breath.

'Now we'll wait' said Boo.

Not for long.

Sixty Four

The very first time he'd checked out the secret passage, the murderer had had the forethought to bring a candle with him which he'd wisely left there...just in case: this was the "just in case scenario". He struck a match now and lit it before descending the well-worn stone steps to the panel leading to the back of the fireplace in the lumber room.

With trepidation he began descending the steps, slowly, silently, wondering what he might find at the bottom.

When he reached the final step there was another lever to open the panel which slid back to allow entry to the tight space behind the fireplace.

The crumpled, dead body of Father Edward lay where he'd left it. The eyes of the murderer locked onto the dried blood spread over the elderly friar's contorted face. The mouth hung open with the few gnarled teeth bared. The staring eyes, glazed over with a watery film seemed, to the murderer, to be accusing him.

'I had to old man. I didn't have a choice. But I am truly sorry for what it's worth. It didn't even serve the purpose it was meant for'. That was his callous defence.

He waved the candle slowly around the narrow passage allowing its glow to penetrate the gloom.

'The candlestick! It's gone! Where is it?'

He had left it there: there was no question in his mind. So, where had it gone? His brain froze.

The realisation of what its disappearance could mean sent the eccrine glands in his armpits and hands into overdrive resulting in the candle almost slipping out of his hand. Hot candle wax dripped onto his bare skin scalding his hand and causing him to call out in pain.

The door to the lumber room flew open and one of the constables turned on the lights calling out:

'Who's there? Come out whoever you are' he shouted, a little too loudly: it was obviously giving him the heebee jeebees.

Silence.

The murderer stood stock still as small pinpricks of light filtered through the fireplace from the lumber room.

He could hear the two constables crashing around and talking loudly to one another as they went looking for whoever had made the noise: it almost made him laugh out loud with relief: it meant that they didn't know about the hidden passage behind the fireplace.

But where was the candlestick? Who else could have removed it if it wasn't the police?

When the two policemen were thoroughly convinced that the place was empty, they resumed their watch, turning off the lights as they left the room.

'Well, standing here isn't going to do me any good; I'd better get back and get ready for dinner'

The murderer was in a complete funk. The question buzzing around inside his head was not only "who" took the candlestick but "why"?

He trod very carefully up the stairs towards the guest room, aware that he wouldn't get away with making any noise a second time. With his mind focussed on being quiet and trying to figure out who could have taken the candlestick, he pulled the lever to open the fireplace, blew out the candle, and stepped out into the room absentmindedly before he became aware of a figure sitting in the chair by the window in the fading light.

It was only later that Charlie and Sextus explained to Boo why they didn't immediately reveal themselves and apprehend the murderer: they were the ones now in shock.

Not one to look a gift horse in any part of its anatomy, Boo took full advantage of the situation to see how the murderer would react.

'Hello, Angus' she said in a soft almost welcoming tone to her voice. 'What are you doing here?'

At that point, Charlie and Sextus caught each other's eye and signalled their decision to wait...to wait and see if this was indeed the murderer.

The Honourable Angus MacDorn-Smythe was as close to apoplexy as he could possibly get without physically falling over.

'I...I...I...but what are you doing here, Miss Lavender?' he asked regaining some of his composure, turning the question back on her to buy time.

'I was...just admiring the view from this window, Angus, something, I believe, you and your sister used to do as children?' offered Boo as she remembered what Gertie had said earlier.

Confrontation was not the way to go, Boo decided...not yet.

'Eh...yes, we often used to stand by this window and gaze out at the view'

A few awkward moments elapsed with Boo allowing it to linger as she watched him stand there like a naughty child caught in the act of doing something, having earlier been given strict instructions, not to do it.

Instinctively, Boo resolved to wrong foot him.

'Would you care to join me?' she said, indicating the chair opposite her own. This way, she could take her time in the knowledge that her trusty companions were not a million miles away if things got sticky.

Angus was more than happy to sit; his wits returned, he wanted to know how much she knew, if anything.

'Have you enjoyed your stay here, Miss Lavender?' he began.

'I don't think "enjoy" is the right word, Angus but...it certainly has been interesting. Oh, and may I say, I am so sorry for your loss. Your father seemed such a gentle soul'. The "gone fishing" sign had definitely been hung on the door.

'He was the gentlest and kindest of men but sadly...one of life's poorest too' said Angus sadly.

'Was he, Angus?'

It was like someone had just struck a match for Boo which she was about to use to walk down this dark tunnel of murder, mayhem and possibly, Boo thought, madness.

'Yes, he was not the best bookkeeper on the planet, a bit like Dom Amb...' he stopped.

'Like Dom Ambrose, Angus? Is that what you were going to say?'

Angus looked at her through the deepening gloom as what was left of the natural light quickly faded.

'Shall I put a light on?' he offered and began to rise from his seat.

'No, no, dear,' countered Boo quickly 'I like the peace and tranquillity that this light offers: it's very restful for the eyes...and the soul'. Boo Lavender knew exactly what she was saying and how she was saying it: 'let's see if he takes the bait' she thought.

Charlie and Sextus breathed a silent sigh, both of them thinking furiously:

'The game was nearly up then'

Angus slowly sat back in his chair, all the time thinking: 'Does she know?' That's all he wanted to know at this time and then...

'You said "like Dom Ambrose", Angus.' repeated Boo interrupting his thought. 'What exactly did you mean?'

She knew she needed to push him, keep him off balance.

'Well, I'm sure he won't mind me telling you that the Abbey is on its last legs: there is not a penny in the pot. It's all gone: like a puff of incense' and he cackled at his own joke.

'And how do you happen to know that?' she pushed.

'Oh, I happened to see it one day when I was in the Abbot's office' Angus replied sarcastically.

'What? The Abbot invited you to look at the finances of the Abbey?'

Angus, who thought he could enter a fishing competition with Miss Lavender and win it, decided that enough was enough, he needed to know what she knew: it was time for him to push.

'No, actually. It was lying open on his desk the day I ripped the phone wires from the wall' he said calmly, crossing his knees and smoothing out the creases in his trousers.

'Let's see how she reacts to that one!' he thought 'That should get things moving. Let's see if she's as naive as she appears to be'

'Oh, my dear Angus; are you telling me it was you who did that?' she asked slightly breathlessly.

'Precisely' was his succinct reply.

'Why?'

'I knew it would delay the arrival of the police' he replied candidly.

The time to pussyfoot around had gone: '...questions have to be answered now'. Miss Lavender decided.

'Then there's only one conclusion that can be drawn from that'. She paused. 'It was you who killed Monsignor Avrili'

At first, Angus didn't hear properly what she'd said.

'Wh...at?'

'Why else would you want to delay the police, Angus?'

'Why else would I rip the bloody thing out of the wall, you stupid old woman! Of course, I killed him! He had what I wanted, no...needed!'

Boo could see that the Chief Superintendent was about to put the whistle to his lips; in the fading light, she surreptitiously shook her head but Angus saw it and took it as a sign of her disapproval of his actions.

Now that she'd got him to admit to the first murder, Boo wanted to continue and get a second confession before finally extracting the reason.

'Then would it be fair to assume that it was you who killed Father Edward...' she continued matter-of-factly. '...but not your father?'

Again, there was a pause: Angus' brain was spinning like a planet out of orbit. Part of him was flattered; the other part of him was worried. If she knew so much, how many others knew?

But there was one thing The Honourable Angus did know: she'd be joining Monsignor Avrili and Father Edward...very soon.

The two other occupants of the room held their breath.

A calmness came over Angus: he was becoming quite used to cleaning up his own mess. One more, what difference?

After a long deep sigh, he answered: 'Yes...that was also me but not, as you say, my father. Such a tragic accident'

'That was no accident, Angus...but we can talk about that a little later'

Miss Lavender saw the look of surprise on Angus' face: it was genuine. So, he'd honestly thought that his father's death was a freak of nature, a fine bottle of wine gone wrong, and not manmade?'

Seeing him on the verge of questioning her about it, she knew she had to keep him focussed. She continued on:

215

'So tell me: why, Angus? You had a privileged upbringing; you still have a loving family. Why?'

Through the failing light, Boo watched his face and eyes intently.

When he began to speak, a driblet of saliva escaped from his lips trickling slowly down his chin as his eyes took on an iridescence which Boo had never noticed before but now recognised: there was madness behind those eyes.

'Why? Why?' he repeated. 'Money!' he shouted. 'The only thing in the world that matters. Money, of course!' and he began to laugh maniacally.

'But where was this money coming from?' Boo persisted.

'From that stupid old Charter which was supposed to have a hidden message about where the treasure was hidden: it turned out to be a fairytale'

'Tell me about it, Angus' replied Boo as she settled back in her chair as if she were his therapist.

That hesitation again.

'Why not? You do know that you're not going to get out of this room alive, don't you?' said Angus.

Boo was shocked at the directness of his threat but she knew if she showed it, she'd never get to the truth. She did not respond: she waited.

At the same time, the Chief Superintendent knew he ought to blow his whistle, they'd heard enough but he also knew that Miss Lavender wanted to know why three people had to die. So did he. His hand with the whistle dropped to his side. He'd wait.

When Boo showed no reaction, Angus launched into his tale of misery.

'Where to begin? When I was sent up to university, I studied History. For my Masters, my thesis was on the Reformation and with my connections...' and here he smiled '...I was able to gain entry to the Vatican Library, studying some of the most wonderful books of antiquity. That's when I came across the Charter and Rosary of Queen Eleanor. The only trouble was; no-one was allowed to touch it; it could only be viewed in its glass case. I didn't think any more of it until this priest, who was helping me with my research at the Library, showed me the diary

216

of the Abbot at the time the Charter and Rosary were smuggled out of England'. Angus stopped. 'Are you truly interested in this?'

'Fascinated' was Boo's one-word reply: she would have preferred to say nothing. She was scared if she interrupted him, he would stop.

'Very well. In the diary, he spoke about the fabulous wealth of the Abbey and how he had managed to stop the King's men from getting their hands on it by hiding it. That was all the diary entry mentioned. I was hooked. The thought of that treasure has haunted me since: it took over my life. I became obsessed with it.

When I came back, I began to look for anything and everything connected with Chalfontbury Friary: that was the original name for the Abbey. Again, with my family's connections to Brackenbury, I discovered a later diary note from one of the monks who had helped to hide it. In there, he hinted that the location of the treasure was hidden in a message. That message, according to his diary, was contained within the Charter.

And that's when I began to plot to arrange to have the Charter brought over to the Abbey on the pretext of the 700th Anniversary. I persuaded Papa...' he cleared his throat. In the gloom, Boo saw a solitary tear rolling down his cheek '...and he in turn suggested it to the Abbot who grasped it with both hands. I didn't realise it then but the timing was perfect: the Abbey was in desperate need of funds.

It took two years of negotiating with Rome to finally get agreement to bring it over here. It was the only way I could get my hands on it to have a proper look at the damn thing, don't you see?'

'Yes, of course, Angus' If he'd said the only way to get his hands on it was to dance a highland fling on the top of Ben Nevis 'don't you see' she would have agreed: she wanted to keep him talking.

He continued: 'The rest you pretty well know. I dressed in a habit to lure the courier...'

'Monsignor Avrili?' interrupted Boo.

'Yes, him. It really went very well except before I could silence him he let out a cry; almost perfect but not quite. I only just managed to get the entrance to the secret passage closed before everybody arrived.

But I thought it was rather clever of me to use the staircase and come out downstairs. I joined you, Miss Lavender, and we both came upstairs together'

She remembered now; that was what had been playing on her mind about the murder of Monsignor Avrili.

When the Prior was walking up the driveway from the phone box after calling the police, he'd called out to her when he saw her watching him from the window of the guest room. He'd called out but she hadn't been able to hear him because of the distance between them and the thickness of the old walls. Yet, when she'd met Angus, he said he'd heard the scream from the cloister gardens. Well, of course, he couldn't have. So, she should have known then that he was lying.

'I knew there was something not quite right...' she thought.

It was a matter of seconds to process that thought before she continued:

'But why kill Father Edward? He wasn't involved in any way with your plans, was he?

As she was asking the question, the thought occurred to her that maybe, just maybe, Father Edward had been involved in the conspiracy with Angus. Had they fallen out?

'What? That old man? No, not at all. He was meant to be a distraction for the police while I went looking for this non-existent treasure. He was a miserable old so-and-so anyway' declared Angus offhand.

'But he didn't deserve to die, Angus' contended Boo heatedly. 'Some of us, when we get older, may get set in our ways or want things done in a certain way or may not even be as much fun as we were when we were in the first flush of youth...it doesn't mean that we should forfeit our lives'

'Don't lecture me, you old bat!' said Angus furiously. Once a spoilt brat...

Boo had let her sense of justice override her sense of preservation. She had most of what she needed, it was time.

She sat back and calmly announced unexpectedly:

218

'Would you kindly call your men, please, Chief Superintendent?'

Two short blows on the whistle from Charlie and footsteps were heard rushing up the stairs.

Angus' initial response was one of sheer disbelief. Without warning he lunged out of his chair at Boo...but not before the man behind the curtain and the Chief Superintendent were on him. They caught hold of him just as his hands were reaching for Boo's throat.

'I knew I should have dealt with you before! You're nothing but an interfering old troublemaker!' he screamed at Boo.

Sextus and Charlie, standing either side of Angus, holding an arm each, looked at one another: did they just hear right?

Without any warning, Angus collapsed in a heap, sobbing.

'Now then, my lad, let's not be having any more trouble from you' said Charlie to the crumpled figure as he handcuffed him and stood him up.

Miss Lavender remained seated throughout.

Putting a restraining hand on Angus' arm as they held him, Boo said in a voice laden with sympathy:

'Angus...what about your poor mother...and Gertie? I mean, you're supposed to be the breadwinner now that your father has died. What will they do?'

'Why do you think I became obsessed with the treasure? It was my way of providing for us all. I was just trying to do something right for once. My sister thinks I'm a no-good wastrel and I wanted to prove that I was able to make a positive contribution to my family. Now I've messed everything up'

Two young police constables rushed through the door, truncheons drawn, only to be greeted by darkness.

'Put the lights on, will you, please, PC Greene?' requested the Chief Superintendent.

The PC's hand scrabbled for the light switch and the room suddenly became illuminated. All around the room, hands flew to eyes, shielding them from the glare.

Seeing the handcuffs on the Honourable Angus MacDorn-Smythe's wrists, PC Greene's colleague said:

'What do you want us to do with him, Sir?'

'Take him downstairs and hold him in the sitting room while I decide what's the best way to proceed' said his boss.

As they marched Angus away, he stopped by the doorway, turning his head back into the room, he said:

'Chief Superintendent, I know I don't deserve this but could I ask you something?'

The Chief Superintendent was in no mood for granting favours to someone who had just admitted to committing two murders, but he nodded.

'What is it?'

'My mother and sister have been through a lot lately as you know. Please, and I ask this for their sake, not mine, if I give you my word that I'll not try to escape, will you allow me to join them for dinner one more time to explain things and then I'll do whatever you say?'

'And you give me your word?' asked the policeman who'd caught and prosecuted enough criminals to know when he was being lied to.

'My word of honour' promised Angus sincerely.

'And will you also bring the Charter and the Rosary, Angus?' interjected Boo.

'Yes, of course' he answered.

'Very well then. Uncuff him, Greene. You have until after dinner and then you'll be taken into custody'

There were a number of reasons why the Chief Superintendent permitted Angus these last few hours of freedom, the most important of them being that he knew Angus' type: if he tried to escape, he wouldn't get past the front door before he was caught. Whereas some of the hardened criminals he'd dealt with in the past, give them two minutes to go to the lavatory uncuffed and you'd never see them again in this lifetime. Not this one: he was going nowhere.

'Thank you, Chief Superintendent. And...' Angus struggled to speak but pulling himself upright he said: '...please accept my apologies, Miss Lavender; I don't know what came over me. This...blackness seems to descend over me and...' he was clearly very upset but continued: '...the fact is...I haven't been feeling well for a long...long time' and he left before Boo could answer.

'Now for the next lot' said the Chief Superintendent resolutely.

Sextus and Boo looked at each other: they'd never seen Charlie look so grim.

But then it's not every day someone was about to attempt the murder of an entire monastery full of people...in full view of a Chief Superintendent, late of the Metropolitan Police.

'Greene!' the Chief Superintendent called out, beckoning him over after they'd released Angus and sent him on his way. 'I want every exit from the Refectory covered once everyone has entered...but not before. Got it?'

'Got it, Sir' he repeated it back to his superior. 'Once everyone has arrived we cover the exits and make sure no-one leaves' He finished and saluted before moving off to carry out his orders.

Charlie turned to Boo and Sextus and said:

'You'd better make your way to the Refectory' and then to Boo: 'Make sure no-one touches it!'

Sixty Five

Making their way rapidly down the main staircase, Sextus spoke sotto voce to Boo:

'I can't believe it. Is it true? Is it really their intention to...?'

'Shht' whispered Boo.

Lady MacDorn-Smythe was following them down the stairs accompanied by The Honourable Gertie.

'Good evening, Miss Lavender, Mr Phipps'

'Good evening Lady Dorothy, Gertie' they both said.

Gertie just nodded. There was a sadness about them both which would not be improved by the end of the evening.

The two ladies strolled past them walking towards the sitting room where Angus was supposed to have been held. Old habits die hard: the pre-dinner aperitif.

'How awful for them' Sextus said, watching them bear their suffering with the dignified composure of true aristocrats as they disappear through the door to the sitting room.

'Bad enough to have lost a husband and a father: now it's a son and brother. Terrible' agreed Boo shaking her head.

They walked on along the corridor towards the Refectory, Boo glanced at her watch: 5.45, just then the bell began to toll alerting everyone that they had fifteen minutes before dinner started.

'Are you sure you're up to this, Boo? I mean, your life has just been threatened...' began Sextus.

'These two are common criminals, Sextus. Speaking with Angus just now I really believe he thought he was doing it for the good of his family. Sounds like he's been a bit of a rotten apple most of his life and this was his way to try to make up for it. Of course, in no way does it justify the murder of two totally innocent bystanders but I think by then, his mind had gone. He is unbalanced. Would you agree?'

'I don't think there's any doubt about that, Boo. And I do see where you're coming from, but he has to pay the price'

'And no doubt, he will'

Sixty Six

By five to six, everyone was standing behind their chairs waiting for the Abbot to say Grace. The talk was, as it had been for the past few days, desultory. Most had nothing to say.

Both Boo and Sextus noted that Angus had arrived with the case containing the Charter under his arm. His mood appeared to be one of quiet reflection, not making eye contact with anyone. His mother spoke softly to him, but whatever it was Boo didn't hear and, in reply, Angus just shook his head.

Boo would never know what made her do it but she walked over to Angus and touched his arm. He jumped.

'Angus,' she said 'I just want you to know that I forgive you for what you said to me. I know you've been under a terrible strain especially after the sudden death of your father' Boo saw the small tear trickle down his cheek before he wiped it away with a handkerchief pulled from his top pocket. 'I see that you have the Charter with you as we requested, but may I ask, is the Rosary with it?'

Angus shook his head. 'No, Miss Lavender, it's hidden...it's back in the passage behind the fireplace in the guest room. I thought it might be safer there as only you and I know of the passage's existence'

'Probably very wise, Angus. I hope things go well for you when you speak to your mamma'

Boo returned to her place feeling strangely sorry for the boy who could do no right.

In other circumstances, Boo and Sextus would have been excited at the thought of the return of the Charter and the Rosary, but with three tragic deaths since their arrival under the Abbey's roof, it had lost its allure for them.

At six o'clock, Dom Ambrose intoned the prayer and everyone pulled their seats out to begin dinner; one, that none of them would ever forget.

Any minute now, things were about to get worse, much worse.

From her position at the top table, Boo was able to keep a very close watch on the two criminals. Both, sitting at different tables, were acting with extraordinary coolness: almost as if butter...or in a few moments, lamb stew...wouldn't melt in their mouths.

The kitchen staff brought in the four large pots, steam rising from them. Usually they would place them beside the head of each table to dish up but as they'd been instructed, they placed them on the top table in front of the Abbot.

Striding in closely behind them came the Chief Superintendent, Charles Chivers and four PCs who closed the doors before standing to attention.

Boo and Sextus exchanged nervous glances: this was it.

'Good evening all' he announced.

'Oh, what now?' Boo heard the Abbot mutter under his breath.

'I have it on good authority that Brother Jerome, the Abbey's cook, makes a wonderful lamb stew. From what I've heard, it was his signature dish when he was head chef at one of the swankier hotels in London'

'The Savoy, actually' Brother Jerome muttered sniffily under his breath in his broad Scottish accent.

'Please bear with me for I want you to see just how good it really is. I would like to call for two volunteers to sample the stew tonight and give us their opinion before the rest of you tuck in. Would anyone care to volunteer?'

'Really, Chief Superintendent, I must protest' declared Dom Ambrose. 'We have all had a very stressful time over the past week and I don't think anyone is interested in playing your games'

'Oh, this is not a game, Father. Bear with me for just a few moments longer' was the Chief Superintendent's enigmatic reply. Earlier in the day, weighing up the pros and cons of playing out this charade, Charlie had had serious doubts; a lot of things could go wrong. But now, he knew. He knew it was the only way to do it. The only way to flush out these unprincipled, callous brutes.

'What? No volunteers?' he called out looking around the room.

Boo watched the two murderers with keen interest; they were looking a little less cool by this point.

'I wonder what their reaction is going to be?' thought the woman who knew what was coming.

224

'Then perhaps I can choose two'. Charlie's eyes seemed to wander aimlessly around the room, stopping at the fake vicar. 'What about you, Reverend Richmond?' said Charlie pointing to the vicar who went as white as a ghost. '...and...' here, the Chief Superintendent's eyes roamed around the Refectory again, seemingly unable to make up his mind, until he pointed at Brother Fabian '...and you Brother? Will you both join me?'

Brother Fabian glared at the Chief Superintendent and then at the Reverend Richmond.

'If looks could kill, they wouldn't have had to bother with concocting this stew' she observed as the sham monk, Brother Fabian, continued to look daggers at the Chief Superintendent before turning his black looks on Miss Lavender herself.

'Oooh!' thought Boo giving a little shiver. 'It's like someone just tiptoed over my grave'. Brother Fabian's penetrating stare remained on Boo.

Finally, and with great reluctance, the two 'volunteers' rose from their seats to make their way to the top table where the Chief Superintendent was standing with a plate in one hand and a ladle in the other.

'Now then, who would like to go first?' said the Chief Superintendent nastily.

'Really, Chief Superintendent, I must protest in the strongest terms!' insisted the Abbot rising from his seat. 'Brother Fabian is a member of our Community and the Reverend Richmond is a guest under our roof. Can you please explain what is going on?'

The Chief Superintendent did not answer but ladled a portion of the stew onto a plate and held it out to the phony vicar who happened to be nearest to him.

The look of horror on the Reverend Richmond's face said it all: he knew what was in it. He started to back away.

'No...no...!' he whined, shaking his head, his eyes opened wide in terror.

'Then what about you Brother Fabian...or should I say Frankie...as in Frankie Benson, the jewel thief?'

The entire room filled with raised voices. People were standing up protesting. Chaos enveloped the room. What was going on?

'Quiet, please' the Chief Superintendent called out, placing the plate on the table behind him and using both hands in an up and down motion to get everyone to return to their seats.

The PCs stepped in and helped to get everyone back into their seats.

Everyone that is except Freddie Cornwall, aka the Reverend Richmond, and the figure of his criminal partner whose habit he stood cowering behind. Not so, Frankie; he didn't cower for nobody.

He stood there eyeballing the Chief Superintendent, all pretence gone, the arrogance, hidden and controlled these last few months, returned; he was as cool as a cucumber fresh out of the fridge.

Frankie Benson had poisoned Sir John MacDorn-Smythe because he'd been recognised by him on that first night, no other reason. Ruthless, like all of his sort, he'd set out, this afternoon, to poison everyone sitting in that room with the remains of the cyanide he'd used on Sir John. Retrieving it from the vegetable patch where he'd hidden it from the prying eyes of the police, he'd fed it into the lamb stew which the Chief Superintendent was now inviting him to sample.

He was prepared to kill all of those people for a pie in the sky treasure map; a map already found to be less than useless by a young man with a tortured mind; but Frankie wasn't to know that.

'Don't mind if I do' quipped the fearless criminal.

A gasp rose from those who knew what the stew contained.

'Give it 'ere' said the one-time jewel thief, losing his 'h's' now that he had no more need for pretence.

Charlie Chivers gave as good as he got in the eyeballing game and, not for one second, did he take his eyes off this rotten apple. 'He's a bad 'un, right enough' thought the Chief Superintendent.

Charlie picked up the plate, keeping his eyes firmly on his quarry; Frankie reached out slowly to take it. At the last moment, he gave the plate a backhander and sent it flying across the room. Simultaneously, he reached in and pulled a revolver from the deep right-hand pocket of his habit. Charlie Chivers froze; he knew Frankie had killed Sir John MacDorn-Smythe and would have no compunction in shooting him...or anyone else in the room. But he'd wait...his moment would come.

'You'll never get away with this, Frankie' said Charlie whose eyes had dropped to the gun.

'Oh no, copper? Let's see!' he said putting his finger to his lips and feigning an air of puzzlement. 'Who's got the shooter? You or me?' He paused then went on: 'I 'aint got no beef with you apart from the fact that you're a copper; not my favourite drinking companion, I'm sure you'll understand. But you, you old troublemaker...!' Frankie slowly swivelled the gun towards Boo, who had remained seated next to the Abbot. The whole room held its collective breath.

'You couldn't keep your nose out of things, could you? He...' Frankie pointed the gun back at Charlie '... is only doing his job. You are nothing but...'

The Abbot stood up at this point, presuming that "Brother Fabian" was about to blaspheme, he called out:

'Enough, Brother! That will do!' he commanded.

'I'm pleased to say I 'aint your "Bruvver" anymore, Father. I resign' and he sniggered.

Sextus went to stand up but the movement caught the eye of the Reverend Richmond who pulled out a small calibre pistol and yelled fiercely: 'Sit down or you'll be the first to get it!'

Reluctantly, Sextus lowered himself back into the chair, eyeing the cutlery as he did so. His old army days came back to him as if they'd never been away: he waited until their attention was focussed elsewhere before slipping the sharp-looking knife from his place setting up his sleeve.

'All I'll need is that split moment of distraction just like that time in Libya at Tobruk...poor fellow never knew what happened to him' he thought as he worked on a plan on how to separate them. Their sort was always easier to deal with when they were on their own with no backup: they weren't quite so brave then.

'If we can get them separated it won't take two seconds to disarm them' the old soldier in Sextus decided.

While all this was going on, Lady MacDorn-Smythe had been sitting in stunned silence. If any eyes had been on her at that time they would have seen that her mind was elsewhere: she was working things out.

In the few moments of uneasy quiet which followed Frankie's resignation speech, Lady Dorothy finally got it.

'Was it you then who killed my husband?' she whispered into the silence.

Frankie grimaced.

'Yeah, well sorry about that, m'lady but he had to go. He'd recognised me and was gonna blow my cover. Nice old geezer but he was a goner once I realised that he'd sussed me'

'But why? What harm could he do to you?' she asked wanting to know why her precious Johnnie had been taken from her; there was no anger in her now, just emptiness.

The Chief Superintendent could see that Frankie was getting twitchy with all these questions and the number of people he was having to watch. 'Does he think he'll be able to keep us all under control?' he thought as he himself tried to work out the best way to end this without any bloodshed.

Almost as if he'd read the Chief Superintendent's mind, the Reverend Richmond suddenly turned so that his back was almost touching Frankie's, giving them 360 degree coverage of the Refectory.

Knowing he had nothing to lose, Frankie answered Lady Dorothy's question.

'He would have exposed my past little indiscretions and the months I'd spent in this dump would have all been for nothing'

'Look, what is it you want, man?' asked the Abbot anxious to get rid of these evil men from this place of sanctity which felt defiled with their presence.

'Two things' replied Frankie. 'One, to find this bleedin' Charter that everyone's been talking about. I want that treasure! And two, I want the cop's guarantee that me and my mate here...' he said waving the gun at the Reverend Richmond '...will be given a fair start. Otherwise, we'll have to think about everybody sampling the good Brother's stew'

'You know I can't do that, Frankie' replied the Chief Superintendent honestly.

'Well then, we've got a problem, 'aint we?' snarled Frankie.

Whilst everyone was digesting this latest threat to the community's safety, Angus stood up and announced:

'Perhaps I can help you with the first part of your requirement. I have the Charter here'

Frankie's face took on a nasty sneer, he said:

'Give it here boy!'

'I will if you promise to let these innocent people go: they hold no interest for you nor them in you' responded Angus calmly.

'I make the decisions 'round here. Now give it here...unless you want to be the first one to get it!' threatened Frankie.

'You killed my father, do you really think your threats will work on me?' responded Angus in an almost resigned manner.

Boo, Sextus and the Chief Superintendent exchanged glances: they had all noticed the change in Angus: it was as if he was accepting of his fate but was trying to make amends for his misdeeds.

Boo worried about Angus' state of mind; to her, he appeared to be coming apart at the seams.

'Please, stay back, Angus' Boo called out in warning. 'Whatever you're thinking: he's dangerous'

All at once, the dynamics in the room changed.

The Reverend Richmond began waving his gun around, almost as if he expected some of the diners to rush them.

'Stand back, I'm warning you...!' he yelled menacingly.

Then Frankie made what would prove to be his undoing: he turned the gun back on Miss Lavender.

'I'm warning you, old woman, if one more word comes out of that mouth of yours, I guarantee it'll be the last one'

Despite Boo's warning, Angus stood up and left his seat walking towards Frankie with the case containing the Charter dangling from his left hand by its straps.

'Point the gun away from her: she's done nothing wrong' Angus called out in a commanding tone.

'Forgotten already, son? I'm the one with the gun and I give the orders, not you'

To make sure his message got through, Frankie pulled back the trigger and aimed it towards Angus.

'You really don't frighten me, you know' Angus uttered calmly.

As he walked slowly towards Frankie, Angus was assessing the situation and realised that with the gun now pointed at him, the only safe way to avoid anyone from being hit was to strike the gun from beneath; to hit it left or right would endanger others including his mother and sister.

'Mea culpa, mea culpa, mea maxima culpa' he uttered with passion under his breath beating his breast with his free hand three times as he said it. He was only a few steps away from Frankie.

In a flash, Angus gripped the leather straps of the Charter case and lashed out, aiming to catch the gun beneath its short barrel. The explosion, when it came, sounded much louder within the enclosed space of the Refectory; the smoke and smell of graphite pervading the entire room.

But he'd only managed to catch it a glancing blow and the gun swiftly discharged its deadly contents: the bullet's trajectory, unhampered, hit Angus and passed straight through his heart. He was dead before his body hit the floor.

Lady Dorothy fell into a faint but in doing so, distracted the two villains' attention long enough for Sextus to get around the table. Whipping the knife from his sleeve, he grabbed hold of the Reverend Richmond from behind by the neck with the knife pressing gently on his jugular. Considerably larger than he was when he fought at Tobruk, Sextus could still move rapidly when the occasion demanded. But the Reverend Richmond wasn't for giving in without a fight. He tried to wriggle free of Sextus' grip. In the ensuing struggle, the Reverend Richmond pulled back the trigger of the weapon he clung ferociously to, ready to shoot Sextus when he got the chance. But in the scuffle, the knife slipped across the villain's jugular vein and blood gushed out staining the dog collar he'd feloniously taken to wearing, a bright crimson.

Frankie, though in shock at how quickly events had turned around, hastily weighed up how things stood: 'Not good' was his assessment. With eyes darting all over the place, he retreated towards the Refectory door.

'Out of my way coppers...otherwise you'll get what he got!' he rasped pointing the gun at Angus' lifeless body.

Armed with only wooden truncheons, the PCs reluctantly opened up their ranks for the double murderer.

He opened and slammed the door, grabbing a chair from the corridor and ramming it under the handle.

'That should 'old them for a few minutes and give me a chance' he thought trying feverishly to work out an escape route.

The Chief Superintendent was a brave man, not in the least frightened of the likes of Frankie and his accomplice Freddie Cornwall, but like his men, faced with guns, he felt powerless. Once Frankie was out the door, he picked up Frankie's fatally wounded partner's gun and shouted out:

'Get that bloody door open! Now! One of you check him' he commanded indicating the inert body of the Reverend Richmond which was leaking blood like Brother Jerome's colander.

The PCs rushed to the doors, finding it jammed from the other side they put their not inconsiderable broad shoulders to good use; the ancient oak frame of the door did its best but with age comes a certain fragility and in the end, gave way ungraciously, splintering into clouds of dust and small shards of rotting timbers.

Frankie was nowhere to be seen.

Sixty Seven

'Okay, everyone' the Chief Superintendent called out to his men 'spread out. You, Sergeant Butters take two PCs and check the upper floor, the rest of you come with me'

While they went off looking for Frankie, the rest of the community had remained in the Refectory, most of them in shock.

'Are you all right, Sextus?' Boo asked sympathetically, using her napkin to dab away the blood which had splattered his clothes.

'I'm fine, Boo. But how is Her Ladyship? Dear God! What is the world coming to? How can such a thing happen in a place like this?'

'Greed' was Boo's one-word response.

'But according to what Angus said; this mythical treasure doesn't exist. If it had surely it would have been found by now?'

'Haven't you heard of El Dorado, Sextus? There are people, even now, looking for it. There is no time limit on or evidence required for greed; only possibility, that is sufficient'

'I suppose you're right' he answered '...but here, of all places! And the body count! How many are there now?'

'It doesn't look like an ambulance will get here on time for the Reverend Richmond, so if we include him, that'll be five. Poor Angus! Looks like he tried to do the right thing but, in the end, he got it wrong again'

'Yes, Boo, but please don't forget what he did do'

An old army man, Sextus was a staunch member of the black and white brigade: "Right is right and wrong is wrong". "Everything in life has a price and, eventually, it has to be paid...one way or another" he would regularly think to himself when he read of certain events or people getting their comeuppance.

'Yes, I agree, Sextus, but what about the people that are left behind?'

'Meaning?'

'Meaning, Sextus, what about Lady Dorothy, who's lost a husband and now a son? And Gertie. I know they had their differences but at the end of the day, he was her brother. And remember, they don't know what he'd been up to. As far as they're concerned, he's a hero. He did try to stop Brother Fabian from shooting me, Sextus. I will always remember that'

'I suppose when you put it like that...' replied Sextus hesitantly, not a hundred per cent convinced.

Dom Ambrose took control in the Refectory ordering one of the novices to run to fetch his holy oils to give Angus and the Reverend Richmond the last rites. Dom Ignatius, the sub Abbot, oversaw the disposal of the poisoned stew.

'Careful, Brother!' he called out to an older member of the Community who was carrying one of the pots of poisoned stew when he almost skidded on the mess strewn across the floor by Frankie.

Gertie's shoulder was, once again, in use as a support for her mother who was crying piteously for the loss of her husband...and now her only son.

'I can't begin to imagine...' Boo said to Sextus as they observed the mother and daughter.

'Neither can I, Boo. It must be terrible'

Looking at Lady Dorothy and seeing her pain and suffering galvanised Boo.

'We need to get out there and find this fake Brother Fabian but we also need to be careful, especially you, Sextus; you killed his partner'

'I didn't do it intentionally, Boo. He struggled, the knife slipped and that was it: he was past tense. His own fault really'

'Well, I'm not sure the fake Brother Fabian will see it like that'

As they passed through what was left of the Refectory door, Boo and Sextus stopped for a moment, observing Dom Ambrose kneeling over the lifeless body of Angus. He began the ritual by kissing the small purple stole which he'd unravelled before putting it around his neck and then intoning the opening words of extreme unction: 'Per istam sanctam unctionem...' while anointing the forehead of the young man's lifeless body with holy oil.

233

Both Boo and Sextus were terribly moved by the tenderness shown by the Abbot.

They left in silence out of respect for the dead.

Sixty Eight

As it turned out, Boo was right.

Not only had Frankie lost the Charter but his partner-in-crime had gone to the Old Lag's Hangout in the Sky...and he wanted revenge. Not just for Freddie but for the time '...I've wasted bowing and scraping in this God forsaken place'

He laughed out loud, forcing him to cover his mouth with his hand.

'I like that' he thought. 'This God forsaken place being the one place where God's not supposed to forsake: it being a monastery'

But the laughter was momentary as he heard running footsteps in the cloister again and he ducked instinctively, even though there was no need to; they were never going to think of looking for him where he was.

In an effort to flee, Frankie had ended up in the cloisters, running this way and that in an effort to avoid the cops who were coming at him from all directions. In the end, he hid in the only place he thought they'd never think of: underneath their noses. Or to be exact, just above their noses. With the echo of gumshoes and voices in the cloisters, and not sure which direction they were coming from, he quickly shinned it up the old oak tree in the middle of the cloister gardens.

Hidden by the branches which, thankfully, were filling out with leaves, he watched as they raced around the quadrangle, through the kitchens and back out again: the trail had gone cold.

'Well, can you believe it!' he heard PC Greene say as he stopped to catch his breath. 'I thought we had him there, Sir' he said addressing his Chief Superintendent 'I saw him disappear around a corner in the corridors and I thought:

'Got you now, you bugger...only to find he'd disappeared. And he would have been my first collar!'

'Don't worry, son, there'll be plenty more of them to come' the Chief Superintendent insisted matter-of-factly. 'He may have gone to ground in one of the secret passages here in the Abbey, Greene. But don't worry, we'll flush him out'

'No luck then?' Sextus asked as he and Boo emerged from the kitchens.

'Not yet, Mr Phipps, but we'll get him. No fear of that, we will'

'Not if I can help it, copper' thought Frankie glowering as he looked down on the small crowd gathered by the archway into the gardens.

'Miss Lavender, where's that book with the whereabouts of the secret passages? There is a possibility that he's hiding in one of those. We need to check them all' the Chief Superintendent said.

'In the Bibliotheca, on the top of my desk, would you like me to come with you and show you?'

'There's no need and anyway I have to check on what's happening with the other search team. I'll be back in two shakes of a lamb's tail'

'You can't miss it' Miss Lavender called after the Chief Superintendent's retreating back.

'PC Greene, you and the others keep checking the grounds and use your whistle if you find anything' were his instructions to the young PC.

The Chief Superintendent went off to fetch the book and check on the others who were engaged in the room by room search upstairs.

Despite the chill in the air, Boo and Sextus decided to wait there for the Chief Superintendent and made their way through the portico into the garden and sat on the bench behind which young Angus had hidden on the night he'd heard the other two murderers plotting. It also happened to be, at that precise moment in time, where one Frankie Benson aka Brother Fabian, jewel thief and Charter hunter, was perched on a bough...above their heads.

Sixty Nine

In the course of all of this going on, Dom Ambrose had retrieved the Charter and taken it for safe keeping to his office.

In a moment of silent contemplation, with the Charter still in its case, lying on his desk, the Abbot hesitated: the temptation to look at this thing which had caused so much loss of life was overwhelming. His hand hovered over the leather carrier but duty took over: he really had more urgent things that needed attending to. So, without even having a quick peek, he locked the office and made his way back to the Refectory where everything seemed to be getting back to normal '...if there will ever be such a thing again within these hallowed walls' he sighed.

Before the painful task of removing the bodies had been undertaken, Lady Dorothy had been helped to her room where she had been sedated; young Gertie was in attendance by her bedside.

A little later, the bodies were removed and temporarily placed in one of the sitting rooms: both had been wrapped in bed sheets, awaiting transport to the mortuary.

'Those poor women' thought the Abbot compassionately. 'Haven't they been through enough? To lose a husband and a father and now to lose a son and a brother so soon? My Father...' he began praying, paraphrasing a passage from the Gospel of Matthew '...if it is possible, let this chalice pass from them. Amen'

The prayer for the living over, the Abbot ran through a mental list of what had still to be done; checking his watch he saw that it was nearly time for Compline.

Father Ignatius, clearly exhausted, entered the Refectory and said:

'We've disposed of the poisoned food safely, Father. Is there anything else you need me to do?'

'Yes, Father Ignatius. It is incumbent on all of us to pray for the souls of the departed. So, with that in mind, would you please arrange for the bell to be rung, summoning our Community to chapel for night prayers? We should all of us join in praying for their immortal souls'

Father Ignatius wavered; it was on the tip of his tongue to say:

'Haven't we been through enough tonight, Father? Couldn't we miss it just this once?' But he thought better of it: his vow of obedience forbade him to question the Abbot's authority.

The bell was dutifully rung and the Community responded; there were no absentees.

Seventy

Boo and Sextus sat in the quietude of the gardens, the sounds of the search a distant muted background noise, like an aeroplane floating in a cloudless blue sky on a summer's day.

'It was very comforting' Sextus announced out of the blue.

'Pardon, Sextus?' Boo, whose train of thought was elsewhere, asked.

'What Dom Ambrose did when he performed the last rites. Just to know that those prayers have been said over Angus will bring enormous solace to Lady Dorothy and Gertie. And although I wouldn't say it to anyone else: I think poor Lady Dorothy has lost a good husband but a bad son. Whether, of course, the Reverend Richmond...I can't get used to calling him...what was it Charlie said his name was...Freddie Cornwall...deserved to be anointed or not, I'm not so sure'

'Well, my dear Sextus...' began Boo '...in the Good Lord's eyes, we are all his children, wayward or not, and equal in his eyes...'

Suddenly from above their heads a shout erupted.

'And who the hell are you to judge, eh? What do you two know? You do-gooders: you make me sick!'

It was the voice of Frankie Benson alias Brother Fabian.

'Don't move, either of you. I have a bullet with your name on it Mr Bloody Phipps! And I'm sure Freddie is looking forward to meeting up with you on the other side. But for the moment, I've got my gun trained on your nosey companion. I know she's the one who's caused all this trouble. One false move and she gets it'

Sextus knew that they were at a disadvantage, they couldn't see Frankie; they could only hear his voice. Worst of all, what he was saying about the gun trained on Boo was probably true. If it were up to Sextus, he would have taken his chances but he couldn't, nay, wouldn't risk Boo's life. He'd have to wait.

'Where do we go from here, Mr Benson?' Boo asked as if she were enquiring about one of her reader's requirements. He wouldn't be the first one to make the mistake of seeing what appeared to the naked, untrained eye: a gentle, fuddy-duddy disposition. But ask any of her bridge opponents; she may not be the most physically robust but mentally, Boo Lavender was one of the toughest, most resilient and ruthless players you would ever want not to meet.

Mr Benson would have been better keeping schtum; but that, in bridge terms, was not his best suit.

Frankie slowly climbed down the trunk of the tree, all the time pointing the gun firmly at Boo.

'You two are going to 'elp me get out of this place. Move!' he commanded flipping the gun at Sextus and then back to Boo. When Sextus stood his ground, Frankie pulled the trigger back and aimed it at Boo's heart. 'I said move.' he said it so softly but with such venom in his voice that Sextus reluctantly accepted that he didn't have a choice.

'Where do you want us to go?' Sextus finally asked

'Walk slowly in front of me towards where the cars are parked in the driveway. I need to borrow one of the copper's vehicles. And don't try any funny business, Mr Phipps; otherwise your lady friend here gets it'

Sextus had the feeling that Frankie almost wanted him to try something. The only reason Boo was still alive was because Frankie needed to use her to keep the men in check. He knew that if he killed Miss Lavender, the men were more likely to have a go.

But once he got the key in the ignition of the police car...it would be a different story.

What Frankie didn't know was that the Chief Superintendent had heard the raised voices when he was rummaging around the desk which Boo used. It didn't take two seconds for him to suss out what was going on. He moved to the window and what he saw confirmed what he'd heard: Frankie was holding the two friends at gunpoint.

'Damn and blast!' he swore.

Rushing out the door of the Bibliotheca, he called to Sergeant Butters and the two PCs with him.

At the best of times not a man to waste words or time, he said tersely:

'Frankie Benson is walking through the ground floor towards the entrance with Miss Lavender and Mr Phipps. He's threatened to kill Miss Lavender and make no mistake...he means it and will do it. So...' Charlie was thinking on his toes '...right...got it! Okay, here's what we do'

And he explained exactly what he was going to do.

Seventy One

Frankie followed Boo and Sextus closely, the gun held tightly in his hand aimed at Miss Lavender's back.

By the time they reached the main entrance where Angus had waited for Senor Tartaglia on that fateful morning, the stage was set with everyone in their places.

Unaware of the police presence hidden around the vicinity of the hall area, Frankie began to think he could actually get away with it. For a few moments, his attention was diverted as he attempted to get a better view of where the police cars were parked. He could see two of them off to the right of the entrance.

However, while Frankie's attention was wavering, Miss Lavender's was most definitely not. She, of the mirrored glasses, had seen Charlie hovering nearby who raised his finger to his lips to warn her not to give the game away. As soon as Charlie saw Frankie's attention focussing over to the right, he signalled her to move quickly to the left.

Boo didn't need telling twice. In one swift movement, Boo veered off a couple of feet to the left...and that's what saved her.

Frankie kept walking forward, unaware that his hostage was no longer in front of him. Now, the gun was pointing at...nothing: there was only emptiness in front of him.

Timing was crucial: it was too tight for the Chief Superintendent to shout a warning. He raised the Reverend Richmond's gun with both hands. Sighting Frankie carefully down the barrel, he fired.

Frankie fell to the floor screaming; the bullet hit him in the shoulder. His gun went off with a loud bang: Frankie had been holding that trigger too tightly. Fortunately, no-one was injured.

'Right decision' thought the Chief Superintendent, pleased with his judgement call.

Miss Lavender adjusted her hat gave a little cough brought on by the smoke from Frankie's gun and said in a rather nonchalant way:

'Thank you for that, Chief Superintendent, very kind of you, I'm sure. Oooh, I do fancy a cup of tea, Sextus! What about you?'

One very tough cookie, Hilary B Lavender.

Boo marched off in the direction of the kitchen while the menfolk stood and gawped.

Regaining his composure, Sextus called out:

'Wait for me, Boo. Come to think of it, I haven't eaten yet and I'm jolly hungry'

'...and, no doubt, not a little grumpy!' retorted Boo merrily. She was not going to let a wretched creature like Frankie Benson win.

As he walked past the pathetic, writhing creature who had dared to pull a gun on his friend, Sextus accidentally gave him a good kick.

He bent over and whispered softly:

'And that's for Angus'

'Watch yourself there, Mr Phipps, you nearly tripped!' the Chief Superintendent called out, knowing full well that it may not have been an accident.

'Thank you, Chief Superintendent. These flagstones are dreadfully uneven don't you think?'

'You take care, Sir'

Loud voices accompanied by the pitter-patter of sandals on flagstones could be heard racing along the corridor.

'What's happened now?' exclaimed the Abbot who was the first to arrive. 'Did I hear gunshots?'

'You did' confirmed Boo '...but the police have it all under control now. Is there any chance of a cuppa, Father, and perhaps a morsel to eat? My friend here...' she said indicating Sextus '...is wasting away in front of my eyes!'

'Oh, I wouldn't go so far as to necessarily say that, Boo' Sextus said a little embarrassed.

'How long have I known you, Sextus Phipps?' Dom Ambrose asked in what could have been construed as a slightly sarcastic tone.

'Oh, well...I mean...' stuttered Sextus and the three of them burst out laughing

'Come on' said the Abbot. 'I'm sure Brother Jerome can rustle something up for you'

'Well, if you're sure, Father. I mean, I don't want to put anyone to any trouble' said the teller of little white lies with false modesty...but there was nothing false about his relief.

'Oh yes, you do' Boo said, bursting out laughing again: the levity, albeit false, was definitely helping to relieve the tension.

As the three of them walked back towards the kitchens, Dom Ambrose turned back to see the person he'd thought of as Brother Fabian being helped up by Sergeant Butters and his PCs.

He looked very ashen and subdued.

'I do hope he's all right' Dom Ambrose said.

'I am at a loss as to why they would bother patching him up' responded Sextus candidly.

'What a terrible thing to say, Sextus Phipps' declared Miss Lavender surprised by her friend's seemingly callous attitude.

'Yes, I agree' the Abbot concurred, mystified by his friend's outburst.

'No...well...what I mean is: they're only going to hang him so why go to all the bother of nursing him back to health, sending him for trial where he'll be found guilty only to kill him...because he will surely hang!'

His two companions said nothing but kept their own counsel as they continued on their way to the kitchens: part of them agreed with Sextus' assessment of the situation but somehow it felt wrong.

What will be, will be.

Seventy Two

While Sextus filled his boots, Boo and the Abbot shared a pot of tea.

'I'm glad you weren't hungry' said Boo in a mocking tone as she watched her friend demolish everything in front of him.

'He hasn't changed, Miss Lavender' laughed the Abbot.

'You're ever so funny, you two' retorted Sextus who didn't give a fig. 'Sticks and stones and all that' he thought as he munched his way through the plate of sandwiches prepared by Brother Jerome.

Charlie Chivers walked into the Refectory and flopped down next to them, removing his hat and throwing it on the chair beside him.

'Something the matter, Charlie?' asked Sextus in between mouthfuls.

'Any tea in the pot?' the Chief Superintendent replied fending off Sextus' question.

'Certainly' said Boo pouring a nice, strong, dark cup of tea. 'At least they're still using loose tea and not these new-fangled tea bag things' Boo thought gratefully.

'Fancy a sandwich?' Sextus offered.

'Don't mind if I do'

All three pairs of eyes keenly watched and waited while Charlie took a long, slow swig of tea. Leaning over the plate, he bit off nearly half the sandwich, then began chewing and pondering... before stopping mid-chomp...only to recommence his chewing and pondering again but this time with greater gusto: there was definitely something troubling him.

Letting out a long baleful sigh he finally announced:

'Frankie Benson's just died: we couldn't stop the bleeding. I cannot believe what's happened. What a mess!' he finished, shaking his head.

There was a moment of stunned silence, each of them contemplating the events of the evening.

'Que sera, sera' uttered Sextus eventually, conscious of his tirade in the corridor not ten minutes hence.

The Abbot sighed. 'Perhaps it's all for the best. The Lord works in mysterious ways and then he added: 'Eternal rest grant unto him, O Lord, and let perpetual light shine upon him: may he rest in peace. May his soul and the souls of all the faithful departed through the mercy of God, rest in peace. Amen'

The others bowed their heads and said: 'Amen'

No-one ate or spoke very much after that: even Sextus went off his food.

Seventy Three

As the police enquiries continued, Boo and Sextus suddenly felt overwhelmed by the events of the day: it's not every day that your life is threatened, you take someone's life and you're present when three people die violently.

'No, not one of my better days' Boo concluded wearily in one of her quieter moments.

Feeling as though they'd done a double shift at the coal face, the pair decided to retire for the night, making their way to their respective rooms in the hope that sleep would come quickly and resuscitate their exhausted bodies while restoring some semblance of normality to their lives. However, there are times when hope is not enough and with that in mind, Sextus turned to his brandy flask while Boo counted Cotswold sheep or, as they are also known, "Cotswold Lions".

Neither was successful.

Much tossing and turning and creaking of bedsprings could be heard that night throughout the Abbey as sleep eluded most of the residents; collectively, not more than a couple of hours' sleep was shared by the entire community.

At least Miss Lavender had the satisfaction of having worked out the who-did-whats which she promised herself she would share with the boys in the morning.

'Perhaps I can go back to cataloguing my Library now that it's all over' she thought when her eyelids finally fluttered closed just as the sun was beginning to peep over the horizon.

Old King Priam comes to mind yet again.

Seventy Four

Boo did not attend church the following morning. As it was, she could barely keep her eyes open; an affliction most of the community seemed to be suffering from, judging from what she saw when she walked through the gap where the door to the Refectory used to be, for breakfast.

Approaching Sextus, she greeted him with a chirpy 'Good Morning', which she wasn't exactly feeling and to which the barely audible reply was: 'And...good morning...to you.' His reply was a little difficult to decipher given that there were at least two yawns in the middle of his attempted salutation.

'Good sleep?' she enquired.

'Not a wink'

'Me too. So, what are you doing today, Sextus, now that it's all over?' Second time she'd made that mistake.

'I think I'll just say my farewells to Dom Ambrose and head back to Bishop's Cleeve. To be honest, I'm looking forward to some peace and quiet after the last few hectic days'

'I know what you mean. It'll take me at least another two days before I can go home. I'm really missing Hamish, you know. Bless his little cotton socks! But before you go, I'd like to have one more meeting with you and Charlie to dot i's and cross t's if you know what I mean'

Sextus' head suddenly jerked up and he looked straight into her eyes.

'You've worked it all out, haven't you?' he said with a small smile on his lips.

'Yes, I have, Sextus and I feel that I owe it to you and Charlie to shed some light on the events of the past week or so before we all go our separate ways'

'Well I for one am looking forward to it'

'I also have a suggestion to make which you and Charlie may not agree with and although it would mean bending the truth slightly, it would be a decent, kind thing to do'

Sextus noted the emphasis on the word 'slightly' but decided to hear Boo out with an open mind before making a decision.

'Can't wait to hear it' said Sextus 'But where is Dom Ambrose? My tum thinks I've fallen out with it' he said, irritation creeping into his voice.

Boo had been aware of a rumbling emanating from nearby but had politely ignored it.

About five minutes later, Dom Ambrose entered the Refectory looking more than a little grey, nodding to this one and that one as he made his way to his seat at the top table.

Unsurprisingly, Lady Dorothy and Gertie's seats remained empty: a grim reminder of what had occurred there the previous evening.

The Abbot immediately said Grace and everyone sat down. Again, the loudest sound heard was the scratch, scratch, scratch of cutlery on plates with only the occasional remark passed on the weather outside which had turned warmer: almost as if God had finally decided to turn up the thermostat.

With no-one in the mood for conversation, breakfast drew to a speedy conclusion, each one going their separate ways in silence.

For the first time since they'd arrived, Sextus vacated the breakfast table before Boo that morning.

Soon after, Miss Lavender rose to leave when Dom Ambrose's hand landed on her shoulder.

'What will happen now, may I ask, Miss Lavender?' he enquired.

'Well, with your permission, Father, I would like to resume cataloguing the Library; another two days should see it finished'

'And what of Sextus? What are his plans?'

'I believe he intends to bid you farewell today and set off home'

'I see. Shame. We never did get to cross swords, did we?' he said, referring to the bridge game that never was. 'Perhaps before he leaves us you would both like to come along and view the Charter? We at least owe you that'

'That would be very much appreciated, Father. I'll let Sextus know' responded Boo gratefully. 'What time would be convenient for you?'

The Abbot hesitated, thinking of what work he had to do that day: despite what had happened, he was determined that the Abbey should adhere to its routine.

'Er...around ten forty-five in my office, if that suits you both?'

'I'm sure that will be fine, Father. May we bring Chief Superintendent Chivers along as well?'

'By all means, I think he too deserves our thanks...and our prayers' he said with conviction.

Boo thanked the Abbot and left the Refectory to find Sextus waiting outside for her.

'Is everything all right, Boo?'

'Very much so, Sextus. Dom Ambrose has invited us to view the Charter this morning at ten forty-five, just before elevenses, in his office. It's funny, he didn't mention the...oh my goodness, Sextus!' she said excitedly.

'What, Boo? What is it?'

'With everything that's gone on, it completely slipped my mind about the Rosary! It'll still be where Angus left it...behind the entrance to the secret passage in the guest room. Quick, we must go and retrieve it!'

Suddenly, lethargy leapt out of the window and they both felt energised.

Seventy Five

Sweeping along the corridor as fast as her short stubby legs would carry her, Boo reached the bottom of the stairs and halted for a moment to catch her breath.

As she was leaning on the railing, Sextus arrived; if the occasion did not demand it, he could be less than fast.

'Boo, I've been thinking about it: should we fetch Charlie to come with us? Come to think of it; where is he anyway?'

'I could answer that, Sextus,' began Boo 'but I'll let him tell you himself because here he comes'

Boo had just spotted Charlie in her mirrored glasses marching along the corridor towards them purposefully.

'Wh...at?' spluttered her confused friend.

'Ah, Mr Phipps, Miss Lavender. I've just seen the Abbot and he tells me we're invited to see the Charter later this morning. Is that right?'

'Yes, Charlie, it is. But we'll have something for him to view too'

A quizzical expression appeared on the Chief Superintendent's face.

'The Rosary, Charlie. I forgot about it. Angus told me where he'd hidden it...it's behind the fireplace in the guest room. We're just on our way to retrieve it. Will you join us?'

'Wouldn't miss it for anything. Lead on. Oh by the way,' Charlie continued 'I heard this morning that there'll be an inquiry into the three deaths last night but the outcome's pretty much a forgone conclusion; murder, in the case of Angus and self-defence in the other two.'

'Isn't it strange?' Miss Lavender opined. 'I've just realised: three innocents murdered and then the three murderers suffer the same fate. It's like a quid pro quo'

The other two digested this thought in silenced. As they approached the door to the guest room, Miss Lavender's tummy felt a bit queasy.

'What if we can't find it? What if Angus just said he'd put it there but he didn't? What if... oh dash it all, Boo Lavender...' she admonished herself '...I'm sure it'll be there. So, shush!'

Leading the procession all the way to the door, Boo halted so suddenly that Charlie went into the back of Sextus.

'Ooops, sorry' they said simultaneously.

Boo's hand reached for the door handle just as the doubts began to surface again.

'Oh dear, I really must stop being silly'

'Right,' she said out loud 'let's do it'

The room looked exactly the same; the bloodstained carpet still lying where it had soaked up the prelate's blood.

'Really, why hasn't someone attempted to clean it up?' Boo wondered before remembering that other events had occurred in the interim. She moved over to the fireplace. Rubbing her hand over the surface of the stonework, she sought the cherub, which when turned, would open the secret passage.

Several carved cherubs and a couple of nerve-tingling minutes later she located the correct one. With one quick twist, the fireplace swung open to loud gasps from the three of them.

Even then, Boo hesitated.

'Would you like me to go in first, Miss Lavender?' Charlie offered, sensing her reluctance.

'No thank you, Charlie. This is something I want to do...for Angus' sake'

The two men looked at each other, baffled at her reason, but said nothing.

Boo noticed the candle sitting on a ledge just inside the narrow corridor.

'Does anyone have a match?'

'I've got a box' said Charlie.

Boo took the box and shook it; the rattle reassuring her that there were plenty in there. Striking a match, she lit the wick of the candle and an eerie, smoky glow spread throughout the confined space behind the fireplace.

But there it was, as Angus had said, draped over the handle which closed the fireplace back to its locked position. The jewels

252

glittered in the candlelight, producing a warm twinkling glow, like fairy lights at Christmas.

Boo picked up the Rosary, almost letting it slip out of her hand, before marvelling at its ornate beauty.

'May I, Miss Lavender?' asked Charlie, holding out his hand. He seemed mesmerised by it.

He turned it slowly in his hand, his eyes totally absorbed by the allure of this holy object which had caused so many senseless deaths.

'I can see why men would fall under its spell' Boo remarked.

'Yes, so can I' said Sextus, gently removing it from Charlie's hand before holding the precious item in his own hands, allowing the beads to run through his fingers as if in prayer.

Boo was fascinated by her friends' reaction to it. Both men were highly intelligent: Sextus didn't talk about it, but she knew he'd been invited to join the High IQ Society, Mensa, when it first began in 1946. Yet here they were, like a couple of schoolchildren who'd found a mysterious object on the beach: they were enthralled.

To break the spell, Boo said: 'What is the time, please?'

That seemed to bring them back from the brink...but only momentarily.

Sextus pulled a fob watch from his top pocket, opened it and said:

'It's...a little after ten thirty', before his eyes returned to the Rosary.

'It's a little early but shouldn't we be making our way to the Abbot's office?' Boo continued trying to prise their eyes from this object of wonder.

'Er...yes, I suppose we should' said Charlie with a hint of reluctance, his eyes never leaving the Rosary.

'Then, let's go!' Boo announced with gusto, hoping to release them from the Rosary's irresistible enchantment.

With great reluctance, Sextus handed the Rosary to Boo who placed it in her handbag.

'My goodness,' thought Boo 'such a powerful reaction to an inanimate object. I wonder if it will have the same effect on the Abbot?'

The three of them took their time walking along the corridors towards the Abbot's small office.

'Are you two all right now?' she asked.

'What do you mean, Boo?' said Sextus.

'Well, I was fascinated by both of your reactions to the Rosary. Never have I seen grown men so...so smitten by a thing!' she declared.

'I suppose I was fascinated by it' admitted the Chief Superintendent.

'Suppose?' repeated Boo. 'You were absolutely mesmerised'

Sextus gave her a sideways glance.

'Don't look at me like that Sextus Phipps. You were just as bad' piped up Boo.

'What...?' said Sextus completely flabbergasted: this was a conversation he was never going to win.

Before Boo could get started, they arrived at the door to the Abbot's office which was slightly ajar.

'Hel...lo?' Boo called out.

No response.

This time Charlie called out in a louder voice...but still no reply.

Boo gently pushed the door open; no-one was there.

The three of them decided to wait inside for the Abbot.

Minimally decorated, the office held few distractions while they waited. Apart that is, from the leather case lying on the Abbot's desk which they all knew contained the Charter: Sextus and Charlie were again completely enraptured.

Restless with anticipation, Sextus shifted his position in the armchair, crossing his legs one way, then the other, looking at the case the way a child does at a present sitting under the Christmas tree, impatient for Christmas morning to arrive but, in the meantime, trying to guess from the shape of it what it was.

Finally, unable to contain his curiosity any longer, he blurted:

'Shall we open it...just to make sure it's there?'

Boo couldn't believe her friend's limp excuse to get a quick look before the Abbot arrived.

'Sextus Phipps, honestly! I'll bet as a child you ripped open all your Christmas presents in seconds'

'Doesn't everyone?' asked Sextus who obviously still did it and was surprised that his friend even asked.

'Doesn't everyone? You mean you still do it?' asked Boo incredulously. 'By the way, Charlie, before I forget, I have something I want to talk to you and Sextus about'

Before he could ask what it concerned, the Abbot pushed open the door and hesitated, taken slightly aback.

'Oh, hello everyone. Sorry, I completely forgot about you coming. I've been trying to get back into our routine. It's very important for us to maintain our discipline. Now then,' he said placing some official-looking papers on the desk and picking up the case '...let's have a look at what's been the cause of all this trouble and grief, eh?'

All three friends rose from their chairs and leant over the desk anxious to view the famous historical document. Boo's request for a chat with Sextus and Charlie went completely out of the window.

The Abbot removed and unravelled the Charter with its magnificent illuminated script from its case for his guests and that was when Boo remembered the Rosary in her handbag.

'Oh, Father, I must give you this' she said reaching in and gently removing the glittering object as the occupants of the room fell silent and gazed at it in awe.

'It's good to have it back where it belongs' said the Abbot with a tremor in his voice.

'Indeed, Father' added the Chief Superintendent. 'I suggest you put it somewhere safe for the moment while we look over the Charter'

The Abbot placed the Rosary in his desk drawer before unfolding the fragile document to a collective intake of breath.

'Wow!' was the Chief Superintendent's one-word reaction.

Sextus managed a little more in the way of response: 'Wow, indeed!'

'Amazing!' said Boo reverting back to the one-word response as she studied the beautiful hand-painted parchment.

Five minutes of silence followed as they each, in turn, used the magnifying glass which the Abbot retrieved from his desk drawer, to inspect the vibrant blues, reds, greens and yellow in the Charter.

Boo paid particular attention to the magnificent historiated initials used by the monks at the beginning of each of the paragraphs. Because of its importance, Boo assumed, all of the historiated initials in the Charter had been encapsulated in gold leaf.

Finally, Miss Lavender quizzed them: 'Well, did anyone notice anything?'

Three frowns and shakes of the head later, she gave them a one word clue.

'Smell' she offered.

Sextus was the first to get it.

'Lemon. Yes, I can definitely smell lemon, now that you mention it, Boo'

'Oh yes, so you can' agreed the Abbot.

The Chief Superintendent stood back rubbing his chin.

'So what is the significance of that, Miss Lavender?' he asked.

'Well, I'm guessing, of course, but I think...' it was on the tip of her tongue to use Angus' name but at the last minute she stopped herself and continued '...someone's been using heat...look, you can see slight scorch marks,' she said, pointing out the singe marks. 'Obviously, they were trying to see if there were any hidden messages in amongst the lettering, but clearly, without success. But isn't it odd that there is a clear smell of lemon, which would suggest some kind of subterfuge, but for there to be no writing appear at all?'

'Yes, funny that' the Chief Superintendent agreed.

'It's almost as if it's cursed' the Abbot said grimacing.

'No, Father, this is an innocent, inanimate object; it's the human factor which is the problem' corrected Boo.

'So many lives lost over an old wives' tale' remarked Sextus with a shake of the head.

'What do you mean?' the Chief Superintendent asked; he'd forgotten with everything that had gone on about the conversation Miss Lavender had had with the Abbot which she'd relayed to him and Sextus.

The Abbot dutifully repeated the story.

256

'According to folklore, it was believed that the Charter contained a hidden message about the whereabouts of a secret treasure trove'

Charlie remembered then and said: '...and so that's why all of these people had to die?'

'Exactly' confirmed Boo.

'If only it had been true' Dom Ambrose posited.

'Why do you say that, Father?' enquired Sextus.

The Abbot's eyes slipped to the papers on his desk.

'Well, to be honest, the Abbey's finances are not in the best of health'

'I'm sorry about that, Father. Is there anything I can do?' asked Sextus.

'Thank you, my friend, but, as I mentioned to Miss Lavender, unless you know of a wealthy benefactor who is looking to support a worthy cause to the tune of...oh, oh, forgive me, I'm becoming boring' and the Abbot stopped speaking.

Both Boo and Sextus had pretty much the same thought:

'Apart from the fact that Dom Ambrose is a decent human being, it would've been nice to help, considering what the Community has had to go through recently'

'I hope you found it interesting' asked the Abbot.

'Fascinating!' was the consensus.

'I'm so glad' said the Abbot with a touch of sadness in his voice. The signs of stress were still clearly etched on his face: the pallor of his skin together with the appearance of bags under his eyes, which Miss Lavender remembered as having a sparkling quality to them when she first arrived, now seemed to have aged him twenty years.

The Abbot began to carefully roll the parchment when Sextus noticed something. Something that looked like small black spots on the back of the parchment in the top left hand corner...then he saw that there were more.

'Hold on,' he cried, 'whatever is that?'

'Are they dots or...' Sextus stopped.

Boo quickly scooped up the magnifying glass.

'It...it looks like...Hmm, it's very small... but it's...its writing. But I can't quite make it out. Could you lay it out on the desk again, please, Father?'

The atmosphere in the room became charged.

The Abbot, his hands shaking, gently laid the Charter on its face.

'Look!' exclaimed Sextus 'All that writing. What does it mean?'

'I can tell you one thing, Sextus' said Boo.

'What's that?'

'It's obvious it didn't occur to the person who used the heat of a candle on it to check the back of the Charter. Look, it's definitely the heat which has brought out the writing'

Charlie Chivers was as excited as they were but he was also keenly aware that there was a backlog of work still to be taken care of. Torn between the two, he knew he had to prioritise and in the end, his sense of duty won out.

'I wish you all luck but I really must get back to work. Please keep me informed'

'As soon as we know, you'll know Charlie. That's a promise' declared Miss Lavender.

The Chief Superintendent reluctantly left the three of them to get on with it. But for the rest of that day, his brain kept returning to that first time he saw the mysterious, black dots. What did they mean? Did they amount to anything? Is there really hidden treasure? Does it contain directions to it?

A million other questions popped into his head throughout the day, refusing to go away.

Seventy Six

The door had just closed behind the Chief Superintendent's back when the bell on the telephone rang, making the three of them jump.

The Abbot picked up the telephone to hear the one voice he did not want to hear: the dulcet tones of his Bishop. His eyes rose heavenwards when he looked at his two companions. Dom Ambrose knew what old dulcet tones was calling about; the bank loan. There were times when he got the impression that the Bishop would like to close down the Abbey all together; the monks were far too independent for his liking. And now with the loan coming due, Dom Ambrose got the distinct feeling that the Bishop was going to try to use it to put pressure on them if they couldn't pay it.

'Excuse me, Your Grace,' he interrupted dulcet tones in full flow 'but I have someone with me at the moment. Would you mind holding on a minute?' He waited for the reply before saying 'Thank you'

Putting his hand over the mouthpiece, he said:

'I wonder if we could continue our deliberations in say...thirty minutes?'

The two friends nodded their acquiescence and left the room. Even as they walked along the corridor in the direction of the Refectory, they could hear the Abbot's raised voice pleading for more time.

No words were spoken between them but the exchanged looks expressed their sympathy for the distraught cleric.

Boo decided to lighten the sombre mood which had descended upon them.

'I suppose you're going upstairs to pack now, are you, Sextus?' Miss Lavender teased her friend.

'What'd you mean, Boo?' he asked, baffled.

'Well, I thought you were looking forward to returning to the peace and tranquillity of Bishop's Cleeve?'

'Now, Boo, don't you be so wicked. You know you'll need my help. And anyway, who was it that spotted the secret writing?' he replied with an air of superiority.

'Oh, I suppose I'll give you that' Boo conceded.

'How very kind. But seriously, Boo, wouldn't it be truly amazing if it turns out to be the treasure map that everyone's been looking for?' he said excitedly.

'Now don't go raising your hopes...or anyone else's, for that matter, Sextus' Boo said with that stern schoolmistress voice she used sometimes when he'd overplayed a hand. 'It could turn out to be a load of old gobbledygook'

'I know but...it appears to be in some kind of code...surely that's a good sign?'

'It's a sign all right but I don't know what of, Sextus' Boo declared passionately '...and what if we can't break the code? What then?'

'We will, Boo, we will' Sextus replied resolvedly.

'I wish I had your confidence, Sextus'

'Oh, ye of little faith!'

'Let's grab a cup of tea before we make our way back to the Abbot's office'

'That's the most sensible thing you've said today, Boo Lavender...and perhaps a little something to keep the wolves from one's front door till lunchtime perhaps?'

'Sextus Phipps, you are a gannet!' There were times when Boo did not mince her words with her friend.

'Have I ever denied it, my little cockatoo? But then I don't suppose you'll be having any ginger nuts?' he retorted. It was his turn to tease.

'Good Lord, is it eleven o'clock already?' Boo said looking at her wristwatch 'Well...well, I suppose...' It was yet another one of those occasions, which had occurred more frequently recently, where the lady Librarian was unable to find a suitable rejoinder.

'Feeling guilty? Cat got one's tongue, perhaps? Hmm?' Sextus was positively wallowing in it; it was nice to turn the tables sometimes.

Twenty minutes later, Boo had been to Heaven and returned to earth while Sextus had found something for the abyss which needed filling.

Boo checked her wristwatch again.

'Time to head back'

The two of them ambled along the corridor chatting away about what the secret writing might mean and how they could work it out.

Seventy Seven

Arriving at the door to the Abbot's office, Boo knocked and entered before being invited. Dom Ambrose sat there, head in his hands looking very forlorn.

'Father, are you all right?' she asked.

'Oh...er...yes, Miss Lavender' he replied looking up, his tired eyes now full of sadness. 'Shall we continue?'

'Only if you feel up to it, Father' she answered, concerned.

'To be honest, Miss Lavender, I don't but it'll probably do me good to take my mind off other things' was the rather despondent reply.

'But Father what if...' began Sextus.

The jerk of Boo's head together with the singular raised eyebrow in his direction was enough to silence Sextus.

No false hopes was what had been said.

'Now, where were we?' began the Abbot as he carefully stretched out the Charter so that they all could see it.

Before them the Charter lay face down with the cryptic writing facing upwards: they concentrated on the tiny writing in the top left-hand corner which read:

Forty Seven
S Fifty Five
D Seventy Nine
D One hundred and twenty six
S Fifty Seven
S Thirty Four
D Forty Eight
D Twenty Three
S Forty One
D Twenty Six
S Eight

Mental sleeves were rolled up as Boo suggested:

'A pen and paper, if you please, Father'

'Good idea, Miss Lavender. I think we should all write down our thoughts on what it could mean and then compare? What do you think?'

'Agreed' said Boo and Sextus.

For the next hour the only sound in the office was the occasional mumbled comment or the sound of a pen scratching through another theory as its owner discarded it and took up the magnifying glass to revisit the mystery letters and numbers.

Occasionally, one of them would think they'd found something and say:

'Ah! What about...' before coming to the conclusion that their theory was a load of old bunkum before they'd reached the end of the sentence.

They say time flies when you're having fun; but as the three of them also found out, the hands seem to whirl around the face of the clock when you're deeply absorbed in something.

The bell for lunch tolled.

'Good Lord, is it that time already?' exclaimed Dom Ambrose whose brain had been busily working on several levels simultaneously.

Miss Lavender let out a long low sigh. 'Phew, I'm jolly glad it's lunchtime. My head is spinning. Your thoughts, gentlemen?'

'I seem to be going around in circles, Boo. I start with one thing, go off at a tangent and before I know it, I'm back at the beginning again. I've just done a complete circle yet again' admitted Sextus frustratedly.

'I've been having the same problem' agreed the Abbot. 'One thinks one is getting somewhere and then...poof, it's gone. It's so complicated'. He sounded very deflated.

'Then we're all in the same boat. I think it'll be a good idea to have a break for lunch and then afterwards we could start again'

'Sounds about right, Boo' Sextus agreed.

The Abbot painstakingly rolled up the Charter and placed it back in its case before the three of them strolled at a leisurely pace to the Refectory.

Walking through the gaping hole where the doors used to be, Boo and Sextus both observed the melancholic expression which descended on the Abbot's face as he stopped to inspect it. He picked up a splinter which had been missed in the clear-up and regarding it as if it were the Holy Grail which someone had found and accidentally dropped; that's how much the Abbey and its contents meant to the Abbot.

During a brief respite from the code-breaking in his study, Dom Ambrose had informed them that the Refectory doors were quite ancient, dating back almost four hundred years.

Firmly in the hope that he would be able to have them restored to their former magnificent, imposing state, he moved on without dwelling on it any further. 'God's Will be done' he decided and besides, he had much more urgent matters to deal with.

Lady Dorothy and Gertie were keeping to their rooms: no need to impose their grief on others, they would suffer alone and in silence. With two empty spaces at the top table, the Abbot insisted that Sextus should join himself and Boo. Despite Sextus' protestations, Dom Ambrose shooed him along to Lady Dorothy's seat.

When the readings were finished, all three began speaking at once; they couldn't wait to offer up their own theories on the Charter.

'Well, I think it's some kind of co-ordinates' suggested Sextus.

'I thought that at first...' agreed the Abbot '...but did they have such things then as ordinance maps? I'm not sure' he concluded.

'To be honest, I immediately excluded that from my calculations for that very reason. Then, I wondered if it had something to do with nearby places like local villages or towns but then apart from the top one, they all begin with 'D' or an 'S' followed by a number and there aren't very many places around here which begin with those letters...and anyway what's the significance of the number? It surely must have some relevance? Perhaps...' Sextus hesitated '...no, I'm sure houses didn't have numbers in those days'

Boo decided to hold fire on her own thoughts and concentrate on what the two others had come up with.

All three of them lapsed into silence, each of them thinking about the others' contribution to see if they could find something which would fit.

'What about place name changes? I mean, I'm sure there must have been hamlets which have been incorporated into nearby villages since this secret map was fabricated or...' the Abbot brain was mashing permutations like a milk churn '...maybe...' he stopped, shook his head and said despairingly: '...I'm just clutching at straws' and shut up.

Boo leaned back and quickly looked over at Sextus behind the Abbot's back, expecting him to say something inappropriate again. But he was beginning to learn, this time he returned her look and just shook his own head sadly.

'What a to-do' thought Miss Lavender. 'I came here, with reservations, to catalogue a library and end up chasing a mythical treasure. Who would have believed it? Whatever will happen next?'

It was only when that thought occurred to her that she realised that there was a hush hanging over the other tables; everyone had finished lunch and were looking to the Abbot to ring his bell so that they could get back to their work. By the looks on most of the faces around the Refectory, they were mightily glad that their routine was getting back to normal.

Boo surreptitiously nudged the Abbot.

'Wha...t? Have you come up with something, Miss Lavender?' asked the man deep in thought.

'I think you'll find that everyone else is finished and waiting to get back to work, Father' Boo pointed out.

'Oh...oh...sorry! Of course' and he reached for the small hand bell which was sitting by his left hand and gave it a short, sharp ring.

Immediately, the whole Community rose and stood behind their chairs for the Abbot to intone the prayer of thanks.

Observant as always, Boo noted that one or two of the monks were chatting about everyday events ("I've moved all of my ewes and lambs into the lambing jugs and we've only lost two so far") as they left the Refectory. On the surface, the monastery's routine was returning, albeit slowly.

She overheard another one of them commenting: "It's such a relief now that things are getting back to normal again"

'Maybe not for much longer' thought Boo, knowing the trouble the Abbot was having with the Bishop and the bank.

'If only...' she began to daydream before pulling herself up. 'You've just rebuked Sextus for doing that. Stop it!' she chided herself.

'Shall we get started again?' said the Abbot with false joviality in his voice.

Seventy Eight

Removing the Charter from its case, the three of them sat down for another brainstorming session, discarding theories with a "tsk, tsk" and the inevitable shake of their head as soon as they thought of them.

Dom Ambrose began to speak, almost as if to himself.

'The monks, in those days, really weren't that sophisticated. There were the learned ones, of course, who could read and write and who'd spend hours in the Scriptorium producing the wonderful works we admire today. But the others were very often uneducated men of the land, peasants; no disrespect to them but most of them couldn't even write their own names let alone produce a complex set of cryptic instructions. At the end of the day, whoever produced this map wouldn't have known who was going to find it either. So, what I'm trying to say in a roundabout way is: are we trying too hard? Is it much simpler than we think? Are we over-thinking it?'

'You have a point there, Father. Hmm' the frustrated Librarian replied.

That got the three of them thinking at a different pace, a different level.

'Maybe we are looking for problems where there are none' admitted Sextus.

That was when it happened. That totally serendipitous event that changes everything like the time Miss Lavender's car wouldn't start and she had to take the bus: the lights went out.

'Oh bother!' cried the Abbot frustratedly as he reached for a candle in his drawer and lit it. 'Sorry about this' he said holding up the candle to let the wick fully catch the flame before setting it into a holder lying on the desk.

'Oh, don't worry, Ambrose. It's still a regular occurrence where we live' admitted Sextus.

Miss Lavender smiled in the gloom as she recalled her own experience of blackouts during war time.

'You know I can remember during the war we always had a supply of candles to hand because you never knew when a power cut would occur' chuckled Boo. 'In fact I can still tell you the number of steps required from anywhere in our house to anywhere else in the house...in total darkness! I would memorise the number of steps in case I was nowhere near a candle when the world suddenly went black. So often when the air raid sirens would go off, the curtains would have to be closed immediately and the electric lights turned off and then there'd be a scramble to find a candle. So, memorising where all the furniture was, I knew, for example, that it was a total of 32 steps from the pantry door to the drawing room. It worked out at: 11 steps to the door leading into the hallway, then a further 8 across the hall to the door of the drawing room...and if you were lucky there'd be the stub of a candle in its holder on the mantelpiece. Going upstairs you had to be careful...lose your count and you'd be sure to trip up! Yes, I remember there were 12 steps up to the first landing...' Miss Lavender closed her eyes; the two men could see from her eye movement that it was as if she was walking up those stairs again '...followed by another 8 steps to the bathroom and oh, let me think and...16 steps to the side of my bed. Goodness, I can't believe I can still remember all those numbers after all this time' she declared.

'Amazing!' Dom Ambrose concurred, fumbling around in his desk drawer for a couple more stumps to light.

Suddenly, in the faint glow of the single candle, all three froze and looked from one to the other, eyes opened wide in surprise.

'Boo, I think you've hit it on the head: that could be it!'

'Oh, what have I just said?' exclaimed Boo half questioning, half in realisation as her hand flew to her mouth.

'If you'll pardon the pun, Miss Lavender; that puts it in a completely different light' said the Abbot, his spirits suddenly lifted.

'Indeed' Sextus agreed.

'Let's not jump to conclusions, gentlemen' Miss Lavender cautioned.

'More light, that's what we need' said Sextus exasperatedly.

As if 'He' was listening, the lights came on and all three blinked at the sudden brightness, shading their eyes from the glare.

'Oooh, they might have given us some warning' complained Sextus squinting.

'Never mind that, Sextus; let's have a closer look at this blessed Charter' Dom Ambrose said excitedly.

For the next ten minutes, the sound of pen furiously scratched across paper was the only sound to be heard. Thoughts were zooming along their mental pathways faster than a prize-winning greyhound chasing an electric bunny.

Finally, it was Boo who spoke:

'Conclusions, gentlemen?'

Silence.

'Oh, come along, don't be shy' Boo said trying, in a light-hearted way, to lift the spirits of the others in the room.

'Well...' began Sextus before stopping and looking at Dom Ambrose for support but the Abbot just shrugged his shoulders, leaned his head to the side, pursing his lips and raised his eyebrows in resignation.

'Hmm...' began Miss Lavender '...it is...possible...' she conceded '...that the numbers refer to steps. That I grant you. But where is one supposed to start and what do these blessed 'Ds' and 'Ss' stand for? How significant are they? And why does the first one not have a letter? Did whoever write the code forget to give it one...or was it deliberate? And what do they refer to? A place, a...' She ran out of ideas and steam. A very loud whoosh of expelled air followed as she blew out her lips.

'What next?' she asked finally.

'We need to distract ourselves from it and not think about it at all. If it comes into your mind just shoo it away. Eventually, as often happens when I do the Times cryptic...'

'You still do it, Sextus?' Dom Ambrose interrupted, surprised that his friend still did it after all these years.

'Course, I do: couldn't start the day properly without it. So, as I was saying...put it out of your mind like I do with the crossword and when you go back and look at it again, why the answer will literally jump out at you and you'll hear yourself say: "It was so obvious!"' declared Sextus forcefully.

Two very doubting Thomases, called Boo and Ambrose, regarded Sextus as if he were mad but, out of politeness...and nothing else, declined to call his sanity into question...out loud.

'If you say so' Boo said finally.

'I do' Sextus replied emphatically.

'Very well. What time shall we meet back here?' she asked.

'After tea?' replied the man whose life-clock revolved around the partaking of sustenance.

'After tea it is then. I do hope you're right, Sextus'

'Hasn't failed yet!' replied the confident one.

'There's always a first...' began Dom Ambrose.

'Don't say it' Sextus said holding up his hand to stop the Abbot.

Without very much more ado, the three of them went their separate ways.

Seventy Nine

Miss Lavender found it wasn't easy to switch her mind off from the Charter and its hidden message; she wondered if Sextus and the Abbot were having the same trouble.

But the more she tried not to think about it, the more the idea of the steps seemed to make sense.

'If that is the case then there are two mysteries we have to solve: One: where is the starting point? And two: what is the significance of the letters 'D' and 'S'? And should we attach any significance to that first number which doesn't have any letter? I can't see any point in continuing with the steps theory until these mysterious letters give up their secrets.' she concluded before returning to the stack of books she'd just lifted on to her desk in the Library.

Flicking through them, she let out a little 'Oooh!' as she caught sight of another little beauty: this time, a 1770 edition of "Systema Naturae" by Carl Linnaeus, the Swedish scholar.

'Worth a pretty penny, I shouldn't wonder' she thought. 'When I think about it, if all of the volumes I spoke to Dom Ambrose about went to auction, I think it would go a long way to alleviating the Abbey's problems...but, of course, it is up to him' she decided, knowing and understanding the Abbot's reluctance to let the Abbey's heritage go.

Sitting down for a few moments to take stock of what still needed to be done before her assignment there was finished, she paused as a germ of an idea floated across her consciousness.

'I wonder...' she thought wistfully '...that's definitely a possibility to bring up with the boys.' referring to her friend, the highly-thought of member of Mensa and his friend, the spiritual leader of the esteemed establishment where she was presently residing. The Boys indeed!

One or two further small 'oohs!' and even an 'aah!' brought her to teatime.

'Wonder if the boys have come up with anything?'

Eighty

Needless to say, Sextus was already there.

'Why, what a surprise, Mr Phipps...you're here already' Boo said, feigning astonishment.

'I've only just arrived, Boo...' Sextus confessed sheepishly as he took the time to interrupt the flow of food.

'Sextus, if the Good Lord ever gets spectacles you'd better watch out! His aim with those lightning bolts will be much improved'

'Oh, Boo, you know me. I can't help it. I love food!'

'I'm only teasing, you old rascal. Had any thoughts?'. Dipping her head in closer to Sextus, he whispered:

'I thought we agreed that we weren't going to think about it until we met again?'

'Sextus, I just couldn't stop thinking about it'

'Ah, here comes Ambrose' Sextus said catching sight of the Abbot rushing through the doors of the Refectory.

Before either Boo or Sextus could say anything, the Abbot blurted out:

'I couldn't stop thinking about it! It's driving me mad. Either of you two had any luck because I haven't' he reported honestly.

'I haven't thought about it actually' Sextus said sniffily.

'Well, I have...and I think I might have something. But I need you boys' help'

Dom Ambrose and Sextus looked at one another; it'd been a long time since either one of them had been referred to as a 'boy'. But they let it pass.

'Come on then, Boo, spill the beans!' her bridge partner demanded.

'Yes, do put us 'boys' out of our misery' the Abbot chuckled as he absentmindedly picked up a scone dripping with butter and jam from Sextus' plate, much to Sextus' horror. Boo just smiled a little knowing smile at Sextus.

'Shall we have tea first...' she ventured '...and then continue in your study, Father?'

Boo Lavender knew how to keep an audience interested.

Tongues were bitten and tea somehow taken...but in silence...with the degree of civility marginally above freezing.

As the three of them strolled back to the Abbot's office, they spotted Lady Dorothy and Gertie sitting in the gardens under the oak tree conversing in a quiet, gentle and caring way; they were obviously a source of great consolation to each other.

Dom Ambrose was about to split off from the others to speak to them when Boo caught his arm saying:

'They seem to be coping, Father. Maybe it'd be better to leave them to grieve in peace for the moment but, I'm sure, there will come a time when your services will be required.'

'You may be right, Miss Lavender' Dom Ambrose concluded softly and moved on, leading the way to his office '...and I shall be there. Oh, yes...I shall be there'

Seeing them reminded Boo that she'd not had her conversation with Sextus and Charlie yet.

Eighty One

Settling down in the Abbot's office, the two 'boys' got comfortable and looked expectantly at Boo.

Returning their stares with a 'Yes? What is it?' sort of look, Boo was squeezing all the teasing out of the situation.

Finally, succumbing to those expectant stares which were beginning to morph into pathetic, pleading gawps, Boo relented and said:

'All right' to two rather large sighs of relief. 'Tell me, Father, what was the language used at the time this would have been written?'

Suddenly, two light bulbs went on in the boys' heads.

'Of course, it was always Latin for anything written' the Abbot confirmed what Boo had assumed.

'O...kay' Boo said. 'So, you two need to get your thinking caps on and think what the letters 'D' and 'S' could stand for in Latin'

'You are a clever one, Miss Lavender' the Abbot beamed.

'Yes, but I was the one who saw the writing first' complained Sextus who felt he wasn't getting enough of the credit.

'Oh, don't be such an old fuss pot, Sextus. Can't you see we're getting closer to solving the mystery of the Charter? Come on, man! Thinking caps on, please' Boo instructed like an invigilator at a university entrance exam.

'And think about why the first number doesn't have a letter. Mistake or deliberate?'

For the next hour and a half, those three powerful brains sat and dissected the potential meanings...again and again.

Finally, it was Sextus who shouted 'Eureka!' punching the air.

'What? What is it, Sextus? Have you unlocked the key to the code?'

'I believe I have, Boo' he said rather smugly.

'Get on with it then, man' she uttered frustratedly.

'Well...' Sextus settled down comfortably in his chair '...as you know...'

'I apologise for teasing you earlier, Sextus. Now spit...it...out' declared the woman about to go mad with exasperation.

'All of my life I've worked with Latin in my job as a chemist. And for the most part, we would use abbreviations when writing anything down. A quick example would be when writing the word "grain" it would be abbreviated down to "gr": not to be confused with the letter "g" which represents "gram" or "grams". Saves getting writer's cramp. Now I've wracked my brain for what the 'D' and 'S' could stand for and based on Boo's theory that the number represents steps, I believe the 'D' stands for 'Dexter' and the 'S' for 'Sinister''

With that, Sextus sat back with a "cat that got the cream" self-indulgent look.

''And?' Boo pressed when no further explanation was forthcoming.

'What Sextus is trying to say, Miss Lavender, and I believe he's got it, is that the 'D' represents the Latin word 'Dexter' which in English means 'Right' and the 'S' stands for 'Sinister' which is 'Left' in English'

'Ah ha!' the lady librarian broke in. 'Now we are getting somewhere! So now all we have to do is work out the starting point and why the first number has no accompanying letter'

Three frowning faces looked at the clock as the bell began to ring for supper.

'Looks like we've hit the next brick wall' Dom Ambrose conceded.

'Oh, come on Father, we're a lot closer than we were this morning' offered an equally frustrated Librarian.

'Yes, and don't forget I was the one who saw the writing first' Sextus remarked defending his right to recognition.

'For two pennies...!' began Boo, raising her hands towards Sextus' throat.

'Miss Lavender!' the Abbot exclaimed, shocked.

'You're only pretending to be shocked, Father, because you'd love to do it yourself but your innate goodness prevents you. I am not tethered by such restrictions!' laughed Boo.

'Well, yes, there is that, I suppose' said the Abbot.

'Nevertheless, we are no further forward' added Sextus the sensible one.

'True' admitted the Abbot. 'I shall pray for guidance from the Good Lord'

A fairly subdued supper was over quickly with Compline following at nine o'clock. This was followed by lights out where most of the Community, glad to return to their normal routine, slept as sound as a baby on a full tummy...except for a certain three residents.

It would prove to be a long and fruitless night...for all three.

Eighty Two

The following morning, a bleary-eyed Boo arrived for Matins as the monks of Brackenbury Abbey filed into Chapel in silence: the Grand Silence was still in operation until breakfast. Boo slid into the pew beside Sextus.

The dull droning of the monks' voices reciting the Holy Office caused Boo's head to slump forward intermittently with the result that twice she nearly fell out of the pew into the aisle; Sextus, sitting next to her wasn't in much better shape.

'It'll be better when we've solved the mystery of the Charter...' Boo promised herself '...the big question is: will we? But the even bigger question is: when?'

After what felt like one of those weeks at work which never seem to end, the prayers finally did and everyone made their way to the Refectory to break their fast.

Grace said, a very tired looking Abbot asked Boo and Sextus before they'd even dragged their chairs from under the table, 'Any luck?'

Both shook their heads before the Abbot continued with: 'Me neither. What's to be done?'

'I have a suggestion' Boo put forward.

'Yes?' the Abbot perked up.

'Is the Chief Superintendent around today, does anyone know?' she asked, turning to each in turn. Sextus shrugged his shoulders while the Abbot replied:

'I believe they've pretty much finished their investigation here now but I think I heard him say that he was going to be here today'. He continued 'One hears so many snippets of information during the course of one's day that unless it's got a "you must not forget me" note attached to it, I'm afraid it flies off into the blue yonder'

'Yes, Father I know what you mean; there are so many "things" vying for our attention these days. Whoever invents a way of expanding our memories to retain all of them will make a fortune. But to get back to the point in hand, if the Chief Superintendent is around today, I proposal that we bring him into the group; new eyes etc'

Although they could see the sense in it, the two men were obviously disappointed. They simply could not believe that the considerable brainpower shared by the three of them could not solve what they all now believed to be a relatively simple code.

'I suppose it might help' Sextus replied doubtfully.

'Well, I think we've all gotten too close to it and it's the old story of not seeing the forest for the trees: we need a fresh pair of eyes to look at what we've already garnered i.e. the trees and see if there is a way through those trees to the forest' Boo finished obliquely.

'Miss Lavender, I think you've confused me more than ever' the Abbot admitted.

'Thinking about it, Father, I'm not sure what I meant myself' confessed Boo.

'I think I know what you meant and you're right, Boo' piped up Sextus. 'A fresh set of eyes, eyes which are used to being presented with what seem like unrelated clues and making sense of them could definitely help. And let's face it; he's been solving crimes for a very long time'

'Thank you, Sextus. That is what I was trying to say. With his vast experience, I think we're going to solve it...this time'

'Alleluia!' Dom Ambrose responded joyfully 'Hope at last!'

The Abbot hurriedly left the Refectory with a spring in his step and a beaming smile on his tired countenance to deal with the business of the day for the Abbey.

Boo and Sextus tarried; Sextus to butter a leftover piece of cold toast while Boo wanted to talk to her friend before she got to work on the final bits and bobs of tidying up the Library.

'May I just say something, Boo?' Sextus asked as he followed the most important rule of life his mother ever instilled into him, namely, "Waste not, want not"

'Yes, Sextus?' after a few seconds when nothing else was forth coming.

'Er...I thought we weren't going to raise any false hope for anyone?' he observed with his eyes followed the path which Dom Ambrose had recently taken.

Boo contemplated what Sextus had said for a moment before admitting contritely: 'You're quite right, Sextus. I shouldn't have been quite so emphatic that with Charlie's assistance we'd solve the mystery of the Charter'

'But the truth is, Boo, even if we do solve it, there's no guarantee that we'll find anything'

'True also, Sextus. There may be nothing to find or it may already have been found'

With that, both of them sank into silence before going their separate ways: their thoughts too deep and depressing to share.

Miss Lavender quickly marched along the corridor to the Library and found a sheet of paper, scribbled a note requesting Charlie to "pop in and see me when you have a moment in the Library" before attaching it to the front door in the main hall: he wouldn't be able to miss it there.

Then she waited.

About an hour later, Boo, deeply engrossed in putting the finishing touches to the cataloguing of the Abbey's precious archive, failed to hear the door of the Library opening; someone had oiled the squeak.

'Miss Lavender, you wanted to see me?' It was Charlie.

'Goodness gracious, you gave me quite a scare, Charlie! I wish they'd let me know that they'd oiled the hinges.' Drawing a deep breath, she continued 'Yes, Charlie, we have need of your services'

'Oh, yes?' his interested heightened.

'Yes, we've hit a bit of a wall with the Charter. We think we've worked out that the numbers which appear on it represent steps and Sextus, very cleverly, worked out that the letters are from the Latin for 'Left' and 'Right' but that's where the wheels come off; we can't seem to get any further and we were wondering...' Miss Lavender's voice trailed off.

Charlie picked up where she left off.

'...if a gentleman on the right side of the law who's used to piecing bits and scraps together and coming up with solutions and who happens to have a bit of spare time on his hands, could help possibly? Was that what your little group was wondering, perhaps?'

'Perhaps' a little voice answered.

'I'm sorry, I couldn't hear you' teased Charlie.

'Oh, all right then, Charlie. Yes, it is what we happened to be wondering!'

'Then I'd be more than happy to oblige, Miss. Now, what have you got? We're all but finished here and I'd rather spend a bit of time with you solving this mysterious Charter thingy than stuck behind a desk at headquarters. So, let's have a look at it'

'I've got about an hour's worth of work to do here and then I'll be finished, Charlie. What about if we say after lunch? We can meet in the Abbot's office and take it from there? Would that be all right?'

'Suits me. I can tie up the loose ends here and then I'll be clear. Yes, let's say after lunch'

Charlie left, but his arrival had taught Miss Lavender a very important lesson: when her back was to the door she'd keep half an eye on the internal mirrors of her spectacles. She would not be caught out again.

A lesson well learnt because not thirty minutes late, the door opened a tad as if the person opening it was trying to have a sneaky look in without being seen.

'Come in!' Miss Lavender bellowed in her most commanding voice.

The door began to close but not before Miss Lavender bellowed again:

'I said "Come in". Now do please come in'

A rather timid-looking Professor Beech popped his bespectacled head around the doorframe and squeaked:

'Sorry to disturb you, Miss Lavender, I'm leaving today and I just wanted to see how the cataloguing was getting on'

'Oh no, you didn't' she thought 'You're after something...but what is it?'

After all that had happened, Miss Lavender decided that the time for pussyfooting around was long gone. The bespectacled head became an entire body as the elderly scholar slowly did as he was commanded and crossed the threshold.

'Now, Professor Beech,' she addressed the Professor in her most stern schoolmarm's voice 'you've been in here several times when I've not been here'. The professorial head began to shake and the lips shaped up to form a denial but Miss Lavender persisted. 'I know you have' she ventured, not entirely sure of her theory. 'Why? What is it that you want? Maybe I can help'

'I...I mean...I...'

'Come on, Professor Beech, you've been on retreat to cleanse the soul. Now's your chance to get whatever it is off your chest' she stated firmly but encouragingly.

A very long sigh followed before the Professor nodded.

'I...I...had heard that the Abbey has the most wonderful collection of first editions and...I suffer from that most deadly of the deadly sin...covetousness. I came here to repent my sins...and to see the collection for myself. There, I've said it'. So great was his relief that he seemed to deflate. The words came out so fast it was like an express train coming out of a tunnel: it took Boo's breath away.

For a few moments Boo digested what the Professor's had said, realising with relief that she was not dealing with another murderer or thief. She enquired kindly:

'And what was it you were hoping for, Professor?'

'To be honest, Miss Lavender, I have never stolen anything in my life but...I just want to hold them...to feel them...to read them...to...' as he said this, his fingers began to caress the imaginary books.

'Yes, Professor, I think I get where you're coming from' Boo butted in.

'Can one ever be forgiven, do you think?' he pleaded in a whinny voice.

'Oh my God...it's a confessional this man needs' she thought alarmed.

I'm...I'm sure the Good Lord will forgive anything when a person truly repents' offered the Reverend H B Lavender.

'Oh I do, Miss Lavender. Honestly, I do!'

'Then come and let me show you what I have discovered since I've been here and then you won't need to think anymore about it'

For the rest of that morning, the Professor thought he had indeed died and gone to the Great Library in the Sky.

Eighty Three

As the bell tolled calling the community to lunch, Boo let out a sigh. 'Just nice time' she thought, feeling a warm glow of satisfaction as she gave a slow sweeping scan of the rows of books sitting neatly on their shelves; the Professor had left not fifteen minutes before, thanking Miss Lavender profusely...over and over...and over and etc.

'He's not such an old curmudgeon after all. In fact, once you get past that old grump on the outside, he's not so bad' the kindly Librarian thought. 'Anyway, I wonder if this will last them until their next anniversary?' she giggled to herself but then remembering the financial plight the Abbey was in, brought her back to earth with a bump and her smile slowly waned.

The half eye she had kept on the miniature mirrors nestled in her spectacles caught a movement behind her: the door opened, followed by the cheery face of Sextus.

'Come to escort me for the last time to lunch, have you Sextus?' she announced without turning around.

'Great Scott, Boo, I keep forgetting about those "eyes" you have in the back of your head' he declared.

'You and Charlie are the only ones who know about them, Sextus; no-one else does. And as you know, they have proved their usefulness on many an occasion'

'As I recall, they've actually saved lives...as well as help you catch the lighter-fingered members of your readers'

'Indeed, my old friend. In fact, just before I came here, there was one of those situations with one of my elderly gentleman readers. But a little diplomacy and tact and another international incident was averted'

They both hooted with laughter.

'You know, Sextus, after what's transpired here, I think we both need a jolly good laugh to get rid of all the angst that's built up over the last few weeks. It was only this morning that I realised the toll the last few weeks have taken'

Sextus inclined his head in agreement.

'What say you to a trip to The Gaumont when things get back to normal? I had call to drive passed there recently and it looks like they've got some marvellous acts billed for their forthcoming variety shows'

'Marvellous idea, Boo. What about inviting the terrible twins, Kitty and Mildred?'

'Smashing idea, Sextus...maybe we could make a night of it and take in dinner too?'

'We could book The Regent'

'I say, steady on, Sextus. Remember Mildred will probably still turn up in her Railway uniform...with a hint of ''Eau de Fumee'''

'Oh, I forgot about that. Hmm, then maybe we'd better stick to the Bluebell cafe'

'Now, Sextus, don't be awful. I refuse to get dressed up to eat in a greasy spoon' declared Boo to much guffawing from Sextus.

'Well, what about Giovanni's?'

'Lovely! I think we all like Italian food and Mr Rossi, the owner, is such an attentive host: he makes everyone so welcome' The conversation at that point stopped dead which caused Sextus to regard Boo who seemed to have come over all peculiar.

'You all right, Boo?' he asked, concerned.

'Er...er...I was just reminiscing about my last visit to...that restaurant; such a lovely night'

Sextus did not miss the blush slowly rising up his friend's throat as she spoke. It was perfectly obvious: Miss cool-as-a-cucumber Lavender had fallen for the charms of the suave Italian!

Sextus decided to keep that bit of information for teasing until a more 'advantageous' time arose.

'Right!' said Boo, pulling herself together and completely unaware that Sextus had spotted her little weakness.

Standing in the doorway she took one last look at her handiwork and silently closed the door; a most unusual adventure, albeit sad, and not at all what she had expected.

Eighty Four

There were three people dining in the Refectory that lunchtime for whom Mr Strachey's narrative could not come to an end quick enough.

And if the Community were surprised by the brevity of the reading, no-one showed it: chatter was back to the pre-Johnnie MacDorn-Smythe's murder levels.

While the rest of the Community's conversation focussed around their work within the Abbey, the leader of their Community could think of one thing and one thing only: the discovery of treasure...and lots of it.

'Did you speak with the Chief Superintendent, Miss Lavender?' he enquired in an offhand sort of way; he wasn't fooling anybody.

'Yes, I did, as a matter of fact, Father. He'll be joining us after lunch in your study, if that's convenient?'

'Perfectly. Had any further thoughts on it yourself?' he probed tentatively.

'Oh dear...' Miss Lavender thought '...I really have raised your hopes' but she said 'To tell you the truth, Father, I haven't'. It was on the tip of her tongue to say: '...but I have high hopes when Charlie has a look' Just in time, she managed to stop herself.

The Abbot then turned to Sextus, on the other side of him and said in that "I'm just asking to pass the time" sort of casual way: 'What about you, old chum? Any thoughts?'

'Yes, lots' began Sextus a bit grumpily '...but none of them about the Charter'

That stopped that conversation in its tracks.

'Lovely weather we've been having' interjected Boo in a feeble attempt to head off a minor World War.

'Er...quite' was Dom Ambrose's stunned reply.

'I don't think anyone's spoken to him like that for many a long year' Boo decided tucking into her pudding. 'It seems to have taken the wind out of his sails'

She was so wrong.

In the world of thick skins, it is generally the rhinoceros which is regarded as having the thickest of skins. However, in this case, not even a cuddly rhinoceros could compare with this particular Dominican Abbot who'd gotten the bit between his teeth. Nothing was going to stop him charging into the fray, it seemed.

'Right, well if we're all finished, I'll say Grace and we can get on with it' the head of the Abbey announced.

A large dollop of bread pudding delicately balanced on Sextus' spoon was midway to his open mouth when the sharp tinkle of the bell rang out.

If looks could kill...

At the final 'Amen', the rest of the community proceeded in an orderly manner to vacate the Refectory and return to their duties while the Abbot rubbed his hands together and boldly declared: 'Let's go treasure hunting!'

Boo's look of concern was not lost on Sextus; this was turning out to be a bit of a rum do.

Sextus' attempt to rein him in fell on deaf ears.

'We don't know if there is any, Ambrose. Don't raise your hopes only for them to be dashed'

But the Abbot was having none of it.

''Course we'll find it. With us three and the Chief Superintendent's help, we can't fail'

Reluctantly and with not a little regret, Boo and Sextus followed Dom Ambrose as he practically skipped along the corridors to his study.

Eighty Five

As they walked along the corridor towards the Abbot's office, the telephone could be heard ringing inside.

Dom Ambrose unlocked the door and the three of them entered while the telephone's strident tone continued; whoever it was, was not giving in. 'I'll bet it's the Bishop. Well I'm not here, so there!' the Abbot called out and blew a raspberry.

'Most unbecoming behaviour for a man of the cloth' Boo reflected but she was beginning to understand the pressure he must be feeling. 'I suppose he's not used to it, having been cocooned within the walls of this Abbey for so long'

The three of them sat down to wait for Charlie; they didn't have long to wait. Two minutes after they'd arrived, a knock at the door brought the Abbot to his feet and calling out:

'Come in, Chief Superintendent, do come in'

Charlie opened the door, surprise written all over his face at the exuberance of the welcome.

'Er...hello, Father. Miss Lavender thought...oh, you're here, Miss' he said catching sight of her sitting by the desk. 'I was saying, Miss Lavender here thought I might be able to help with unravelling this mysterious message on the Charter'

'Absolutely, my dear Chief Superintendent'

Charlie caught the look of consternation on the other two occupants' faces.

'Well let's see, shall we, Father?' he replied cautiously.

The Abbot retrieved the case with the Charter in it and rolled it out flat onto the desk, gently flattening it out with the heel of his hand.

Charlie pulled out his hankie and wiped the lenses of his spectacles before donning them to have a look at the Charter with the minute writing which, in case anyone had forgotten, Sextus had spotted on the back of the Charter.

'Can I borrow a magnifying glass, Father? I've left mine back at the station'

'Of course, of course, Chief Superintendent, help yourself'

Charlie leaned in closer to take a look at the coded writing.

While he was examining the secret code, Boo made an observation: 'I can only conclude from the precision engaged in the production of this very exacting task that whoever copied this must have been young. Only the sharp eyes and steady hand of youth could have produced something so meticulous'

'I agree, Boo' Sextus said.

Dom Ambrose nodded. 'I do too. The concentration it must have taken would have been exhausting. There was a time when I would have been able to do something like this...but not now' he admitted.

Charlie, used to doing two things at the same time, listened to this background conversation while his eyes and brain were taking in the code and running through possibilities.

'Has anyone added up these numbers to see if there's any significance in the total?'

All three answered simultaneously: '542'

The speed at which all three responded took Charlie aback. 'All right, all right, I only asked'

The others laughed; amazed that they all had had the same thought of combining the numbers as Charlie had now. But they had failed to see any significance in that final number: would Charlie?

Charlie continued: 'So let me get this straight,' he continued to sweep the glass over the tiny letters and figures 'you've dismissed the possibility that these letters and numbers represent any town or village or hamlet in the vicinity of the Abbey? And you don't think they could be referring to a landmark or...monument nearby?'

Boo and Sextus both shook their heads while the Abbot sat behind his desk gnawing on a thumbnail; clear evidence of his stress levels on the rise.

Charlie continued: 'I see what you mean, Miss, that the numbers could represent steps; that would seem to make sense. And Mr Phipps, you say that these letters could be the Latin words for left and right?'

Sextus nodded.

'Okay. Then what seems to be the problem?'

'Well,' Boo began uncertainly '...we're not sure why the first number has no letter beside it and, also, we have no idea how we are supposed to work out where the starting point is'

'Yes...well...mmm...at least now I know where you're stuck'. Charlie looked around the faces around the desk. 'Mind if I sit down, Father? I've been on my feet all morning'

'Not a problem Chief Superintendent' the Abbot removed his thumb to answer.

Charlie lifted a chair over from the far corner of the room and joined the others.

'Anyone object if I light my pipe? It helps me to concentrate'

'Please do.' the Abbot offered.

The others watched as Charlie pulled a well-worn briar from the left-hand pocket of his jacket and his pouch from the other before carefully packing the tobacco into the bowl and lighting it. Slowly, a sweet-smelling hazy cloud of smoke began to rise over the desk where they were all seated.

'Hmmm' he sighed, clenching the pipe between his teeth.

The others exchanged glances but said nothing as new thoughts began to swirl around inside their brains like the pipe smoke above their heads.

'Em...what about...?' Sextus let out before shaking his head despondently. The others who'd stopped mid-thought, returned to them.

'Well, perhaps...?' the Abbot uttered quietly before falling silent.

This went on for about forty-five minutes until Miss Lavender came up with something she thought might work.

'What if the first number doesn't have a letter because the number represents the number of steps you're supposed to take in a straight line from the start point before you begin to turn left or right? Eh?'

'Good, Miss Lavender, yes, very good. I like the sound of that' the Abbot said perking up.

'Excellent, Boo. Sounds like you could be onto something' encouraged Sextus.

'Well, if that is the case...' the Chief Superintendent put in '...all we have to do is work out the starting point and we're there'

An ominous silence fell on the group again.

Charlie's words simply confirmed what the problem was. The realisation that what would have been the starting point several hundred years ago would, almost definitely, have been destroyed or obliterated or covered over or moved or...the possibilities were endless...and they all knew it.

Unknowingly, as the silence and the area covered by Charlie's pipe smoke grew, each of them developed a kind of tic. When he wasn't inhaling, Charlie was tapping the stem of his pipe on his teeth: Father Ambrose was back to gnawing on the same thumbnail: Sextus crossed and uncrossed his legs every few minutes while Miss Lavender pushing out her bottom lip and pouted as she looked off into the distance. So absorbed were they with their own thoughts on solving the mystery of the starting point that none of them even noticed the others' foibles.

'I can't see how we're going to work this out' the leg crosser concluded frustratedly.

'That's what I was thinking...' agreed the Abbot who'd begun to sink again after perking up at Miss Lavender's breakthrough.

'There's only one thing for it...' Miss Lavender said.

'Yes?' pressed Charlie.

'...we'll have to make a list of all the 'points of interest' we can think of. Then we'll have to try our theories out on each of them'

'But there'll be hundreds!' protested Sextus.

'Anyone have a better suggestion?' she asked.

The sudden return to silence was her response.

'Exactly! Now where do we begin?'

'It's back to the old pen and paper, I'm afraid. I have my own pen but do you have some spare paper, Father?' the Chief Superintendent requested as he unscrewed the cap of his fountain pen.

Resignedly, the Abbot rose and fetched a bundle of paper for each of them. The long process of adding and eliminating potential starting points to the list began.

It looked like it was going to be a long day.

Eighty Six

It turned out to be an even longer and more exhausting day than any of them had imagined and it ended with them getting no further: the starting point remained elusive.

An uneventful supper and Compline arrived and departed.

'I'm looking forward to a jolly good night's sleep' Sextus said to Boo as they sipped a lovely hot cup of Ovaltine.

'Me too' agreed Boo in between yawns.

But sleep she did not. Her brain was spinning faster than the Earth on its axis.

'There must be some way of working out the starting point. Surely there must be a clue in the Charter or...or...'

There had to be an alternative way to finding the place to begin.

'What about looking at it from a different angle? Or have we overcomplicated it again? Is the answer quite simple? If the starting point isn't mentioned in the Charter then...then...why not? Why put all these directions in code and then not mention or give a clue as to where to start from? Is it something or somewhere which doesn't need to be described or something which would be instantly known by one of the people this monk expected to find the coded message? Now what about that? Does that work?' she thought feverishly. 'Maybe the monk who wrote down these instructions assumed that whoever found the directions would understand or know where the start point would be. So, does that mean it could be somewhere in the Abbey? Now that would make sense. I think that's it. But where? The starting point is somewhere in the Abbey because the person who was supposed to find the instructions would know where the starting point is. Yes! So, what I need to do is, firstly, get some sleep. Then, in the morning, I'll speak to Dom Ambrose and ask him: if he wrote this coded message for one of the monks without mentioning a starting point, where in the Abbey, would the monk assume the starting point was? I'm getting warmer' she decided. 'Now get some sleep, Boo Lavender. That's an order!'

The sun was, once again, starting its ascent as Boo's eyelids were beginning to close.

'Oh, please, let me have a teensy-weensy bit of sleep. Please' she implored the Somnus, the Roman god of sleep.

She nodded off and was abruptly woken by the bell calling the Community to breakfast.

'Oh, Good Lord, I was out for the count. Better get a move on and have that conversation with the Abbot'

By the time she'd washed and dressed, breakfast had already started. But being Boo Lavender, she couldn't just rush off; she had to make sure that everything she was wearing that day would complement her Prince of Wales accessory. Today, it was her very flamboyant black and white Prince of Wales check bonnet finished off with a magnificent eagle's feather. As a result, the rest of the outfit had to be black, apart from her white starched high-collared blouse.

One final look in the mirror and she decided that she could face the world and whatever it threw at her today.

'...and with a bit of luck, we shall find the answer to our conundrum today. Whitwoo!'

Hope and positivity cohabited in Boo Lavender's life.

Three minutes later she stood outside of what was left of the Refectory doors and adjusted her bonnet before entering.

Eighty Seven

'Good Morning, Miss Lavender. Sleep well?' the Abbot enquired when Boo sat next to him.

'Yes, good morning, Boo,' added Sextus cheerily 'solved the riddle yet?'

Sarcasm she could do without so early in the morning when she'd had hardly any sleep.

'Good morning, Father. And good morning to you, Sextus, and for your information, yes, I believe I may have cracked it'

The Abbot sat bolt upright. 'Truly, Miss Lavender?'

'I think so, Father. I need to ask you something but would you mind if we have breakfast first and then retire to your office?'

'Of course, enjoy your breakfast, Miss Lavender' offered the man who was so close to being at his wits end...but who just now heard that there might be a glimmer at the end of his very long, personal tunnel.

Boo was getting vibrations from the two gentlemen to her right; they were desperate to know what she'd worked out. 'Well, they'll just have to wait'

The Abbot did all but drum his fingers on the table as he waited on tenterhooks to find out what Miss Lavender had worked out during the night hours.

Finally, after her second cup of tea, she indicated to the Abbot that she was finished. The prayer of thanksgiving duly said, the Community returned to their duties as the Abbot, Sextus and Boo made their way to his office; it would be a little while before Charlie arrived.

Two expectant faces met Boo's gaze as she took her place around the desk.

'Father, I need to ask you a question'

'Yes, Miss Lavender, what is it?'

'If you were to have written this coded message for someone in the Community and the starting point was omitted, where would they assume the starting point was? Let me clarify: I believe that the starting point is here in the Abbey and that whoever wrote this message assumed that the person finding it would know where to start from'

She sat back and waited.

'That's it?' complained Sextus 'Nothing else?'

'Oh, Sextus, just hold your horses. I think Miss Lavender is onto something here'

'You see, Father, I think we've all set hurdles where there might not be any. I mean, there's no mention, in code or otherwise, of a start point in the Charter. Why is that? I think it's because anyone in the Community, at that time, who found this message, would have known where to start. Hence, my question to you'

'So, you're thinking somewhere like...the front door or the hall or one of the rooms like the Infirmary or the Almoner's office. Somewhere like that, do you mean?'

'Precisely, Father'

'Then the question also arises: have any of them been altered or changed or moved?' Sextus put forward getting into the spirit of things.

'We'd need to check what plans we have of the Abbey as it was then. And if you still have that copy of the book on Chalfontbury Friary, Miss Lavender, that might have a layout of how the Abbey used to be. What else could help us?' The Abbot sensed they were getting nearer.

'I think that will do for a start, Father' Boo said.

About thirty minutes later, the three of them were still chatting about other possible avenues of research when Charlie arrived.

'Any luck?'

'Miss Lavender has come up with a possible solution' the Abbot announced.

'Well, if anyone was going to solve it, I knew it would be her'

'Oh, please, Chief Superintendent' said Boo blushing.

'Come along, Miss Lavender, no need to be modest. Mr Phipps and I have been around the block with you too many times. I've been there when, out of the blue, you've solved a mystery which would have kept Scotland Yard running around in circles for years' the Chief Superintendent admitted honestly.

'It's true, Boo' Sextus said with conviction.

'So, Miss Lavender' the Abbot said '...no time for false modesty. Let's get to it'

The four of them left the Abbot's office and made for the Library where Miss Lavender had left the book. But as they travelled along the corridors, Miss Lavender had an uncomfortable feeling.

'What is it?' she thought There was a niggle somewhere at the back of her mind and no matter how she tried to push it, shove it or drag it to the forefront of her mind, it wouldn't budge.

She brooded. 'Blast! I'm sure it was important. What was it?'

But it wouldn't come.

If only the Abbot had focussed on her question instead of going off at a tangent.

Eighty Eight

As it turned out, the book was of little use; the chapters which might have been helpful had all but disintegrated through centuries of damp and mould.

'It's at times like this I wish I were a lay person' the Abbot said frustratedly.

'Why?' Sextus asked, flummoxed.

'...I could utter a jolly good curse, get it out of my system, put a sixpence in the Poor's' box, be forgiven and forget all about it!' was Dom Ambrose's response.

'Father!' retorted Miss Lavender, feigning shock.

'Well, there you have it, Miss Lavender. I confess I'm not perfect' he admitted candidly.

'I can see that, Father. Nevertheless, we must pull ourselves together. Otherwise, we'll never find the starting point. Now, where were we?'

'No further forward' Sextus confirmed.

As he said it, the niggle returned.

'What is it?' she asked herself again. 'It wouldn't keep coming back if it wasn't important'

But still it refused to surface.

Before she could give it any more attention, the Chief Superintendent asked:

'Then where do we start? I've got a couple of lads with me and we've brought along a couple of shovels just in case...' He stopped.

'Let's not waste time' the Abbot proposed getting all excited '...let's get cracking'

'Then where do we start?'

'Let's use the front door as the starting point' Sextus suggested.

This time the niggle dropped very suddenly to Miss Lavender's tummy.

'There's something I'm missing here...and I can't think what it is' she admitted.

'Better to do something than nothing' It was the Abbot who spoke; desperation in his voice.

'Very well, then' Charlie said '...the front door it is'

The three men marched off in the direction of the front door with Miss Lavender trailing along slowly behind.

'What is it?' she reflected for the nth time.

But it wouldn't come.

Meanwhile, Charlie had gathered his men, armed with shovels, and joined the Abbot and Sextus outside the front door. Miss Lavender remained on the inside gazing out of that window at the five men setting off as if they were on an Enid Blyton adventure.

'Boys!' she grumbled, but inside she knew they were wrong. She didn't know why...but that niggle she had, meant that they were on the wrong track.

Eighty Nine

Forty minutes later, Miss Lavender went out in search of the 'Boys'. She found them whooping and hollering as they watched the two young constables who had begun to dig in a part of the grounds at the back of the Abbey which had been a huge, unruly mass of brambles before they'd cleared it away and got started.

'Come on, chaps, put your backs into it!' the Abbot called out in encouragement.

'Ah, here comes, Miss Lavender' Charlie announced to the other two as she sauntered down the path towards them.

'What's happening?' she asked.

'Well, we've followed the instructions to the letter and it's led us here to a part of the Abbey which fell into disuse long before I arrived here, Miss Lavender' the Abbot confirmed.

The young men were certainly putting their backs into it; shoving away the dirt and occasionally hitting what they all hoped would be some kind of treasure chest only for it to be another massive discarded stone.

Once they'd reached a depth of about three feet and nothing to show for it, the Abbot's regular companion for what seemed like a long time, despair, began to hover over the entire group.

'Hmm, maybe not' Sextus concluded as he peered into the hole. 'Are you sure we followed the instructions correctly? And Chief Superintendent, you took the steps. Maybe your legs are too long or are they too short? We never thought about that. I mean, how long a stride should we be taking? Come to think of it: how long is a stride?'

'I see what you mean, Sextus. And indeed, thinking about it,' said the man clearly clutching at straws 'how tall or short were men in those days? I seem to recall reading somewhere that we, as a nation, have grown several inches since then. So, are our strides too long, perhaps? Maybe next time, I should do the steps and see how that works out'

But Miss Lavender wasn't convinced.

'Don't you think before you go rushing off again, you should take stock of what's happened and what your next step should be?'

'Oh, very good, Boo' Sextus said. 'Very droll. Our next step. Very funny indeed'

'You know very well what I mean, Sextus Phipps' Miss Lavender said, getting annoyed at her friend's flippant remark.

'What are we supposed to do, Boo? We don't know where the starting point is, so we're improvising'

Boo did sympathise but at the same time realised that there was no point in just rushing into it like a blind chicken or whatever the metaphor she was looking for, said.

'Right, we need to try somewhere else' the Abbot, whose blood pressure seemed to be rising by the minute, suggested.

'Try what somewhere else?' a voice enquired from the footpath Boo had just walked down: it was the bishop.

'Oh, Bishop Newman, what a surprise' Dom Ambrose spoke, almost choking on the words; the last person in the world he needed to see right now.

'You know what they say, Ambrose: "If Mohammed won't come to the telephone, then, the mountain has to pop around to see him" or words to that effect.'

Boo took an instant dislike to the man; remote, full of airs and graces; she could have gone on but decided it would serve no useful purpose.

'No, not someone I could warm to at all. Unlike like Dom Ambrose whose humanity shines out of him: a caring man, able to laugh at himself and everything the world throws at him. I'll bet he's in for it now' she surmised.

'Might I have a word in private, Ambrose?' the bishop requested, a sneering tone in his voice: it was not a request.

Boo felt that what the Abbot really wanted to say was: 'No you can't, just go away!' but instead he hung his head and joined the bishop while the others stood in silence watching them walk away up the path.

'I won't be long' he called back to his helpers.

Sextus was the first to speak. 'He's not very well liked in the diocese, Bishop Newman. Seems to have lost his humility somewhere along the way'

'You don't say!' Boo observed sarcastically.

That broke the tension; they all laughed.

'Now we have to find this treasure to help poor Father Ambrose' said Sextus who knew the reason for the bishop's trip.

'I agree, Sextus, if it exists, but instead of charging in, let's take a moment to reflect and see if we can come up with something a bit more concrete than just digging up the entire abbey's grounds'

'I can't argue with you there, Miss Lavender and, I'm sure, neither would my lads.' said Charlie Chivers, referring to the young constables who were happy to help out '...but there is a limit' one of them thought, not unreasonably.

The constables filled in the hole they'd created and awaited further instructions from their boss.

'Shall we move back inside the front hall?' suggested Sextus who, although it was a fine Spring day, felt it was a little 'parky' to be standing around waiting outside.

Fifteen minutes later, they were standing waiting in the hall when the bishop emerged from the corridor leading to the Abbot's study, his gait and face a picture of grandiose pomposity.

'Will someone fetch my car? I'm ready to leave'

Sextus went outside and beckoned to the chauffeur to bring the car up to the door; it was parked not fifty yards away.

'Well, goodbye everyone' and he held his hand out to Boo who shook it. Sextus, knowing the protocol, knelt and kissed his ring: Charlie shook the hand firmly when proffered and added in something which the bishop would not have noticed: a Masonic handshake.

After he'd gone Boo asked Sextus '...what was that all about?'

'Oh, it's the done thing with our lot' he said. 'Whenever a bishop or someone further up the chain offers you their hand; you're supposed to kiss his ring'

'I'm glad I'm CofE' asserted Boo.

'Me too' concurred Charlie.

'To be honest, sometimes, I wish I was' It was the Abbot. No-one had heard him approach as they watched the bishop depart.

'Not a very good meeting' he announced.

By that, they all assumed it was a terrible one.

'Need to find anything, Father?' asked Sextus, attempting to lift his friend's spirits.

'In the next 24 hours, if that's not too much to ask'

Dom Ambrose looked them all in the eye and burst out laughing and was joined by the others.

'Seriously, he's given me 24 hours to repay the Abbey's loan otherwise the diocese will step in and that, my friends will be the end of that'

He didn't elaborate; he didn't need to. They knew trouble when they saw it.

'But what the Good Lord means to happen will happen, even though we may not understand it' he concluded resignedly.

'And that's exactly what I meant about you, Father' Boo thought. 'You don't become bitter about the cards you've been dealt; you accept them and get on with it...like the good bridge player you are'

Finally, at that point, Miss Lavender's considerable brainpower grappled with the niggle and won; she remembered what it was she had forgotten.

'Father!' exclaimed Boo loudly, making them all jump 'I've remembered what it is I wanted to ask'

'Alleluia, praise the Good Lord' interjected Sextus.

'Earlier, I asked you a question but we digressed and, for whatever reason, it was never answered. So, let me ask it again' she paused, realising the importance of the answer to this question.

'If you had written that coded message for anyone in this Community to find, where would they assume the starting point was, Father? Before you answer, let me explain: I believe that your Community, in many ways, does not differ from your fellow Dominicans of hundreds of years ago in that you both follow the same way of life. So, the things which were important then are still at the heart of your Community now. Am I correct in thinking that?'

'You are indeed, Miss Lavender. Our way of life has hardly altered since our Community was founded by St Dominic de

Guzman in the thirteenth century but you're right, we did get off the subject, didn't we? Now then, let me think'

Boo held her breath: she knew this was make or break.

'Really there is only...one place...it's at the centre of our lives now and has been...of course...why didn't I think of that before?' The Abbot slapped his forehead and broke into the widest of grins.

Boo wanted to shout out: 'Well, out with it, man' but didn't want to break his train of thought.

Unable to contain himself, it was Sextus who cried out: 'Come on Ambrose. Put us out of our misery'

The Abbot composed himself and in a more controlled tone said:

'The High altar. That is probably the only part of the Abbey which has never been altered or changed or indeed moved, in any way. In fact, it has probably looked like that since the Abbey was built. That's our starting point' he announced to the delight of his companions.

The four of them plus the two young constables, who by now had caught the treasure-hunting bug, went off towards the Chapel. On entering, the Abbot and Sextus both dipped their fingers in holy water from the font and made the sign of the cross as they genuflected towards the tabernacle where the Host was kept.

'Now then,' began the Abbot 'let's see if I'm right'

The Chief Superintendent handed the Abbot the piece of paper with the code written on it.

Walking from the altar towards the main door of the Chapel, he passed through the altar rails counting out loud as his enthusiastic entourage followed on.

'It begins with the number 47. So...' the Abbot began pacing '...one, two, three...'

'Cor...' said the younger of the two constables excitedly to his colleague '...this is better than pounding the beat'

'Well, don't get too used to it, m'lad,' interjected the Chief Superintendent 'this is most definitely a one-off. But an experience, I don't think, you'll ever forget'

'Too true' replied the older of the two.

301

'Forty-five, forty-six, forty-seven. Perfect!' said the Abbot animatedly. 'From the altar to the door is exactly forty-seven steps. I think we're onto a winner'

'Not yet, Father, but it does look promising' allowed Miss Lavender.

'Now then, "S Fifty-five" which means fifty-five steps to the left'

They all followed in his trail as the Abbot painstakingly counted the fifty-five steps.

'Look,' he declared 'it's taken us to the end of the corridor. This has got to be it'

Sextus looked at Boo. He smiled cautiously at her: "could this be it?" the smile asked.

Boo leaned her head to one side with her eyebrows raised urging circumspection. Nevertheless, the niggle she'd had in her tummy was now replaced by a collection of butterflies floating gently around. 'This really could be it, but please, whoever it is up there; don't let the Abbot down...he doesn't deserve it' she prayed.

'Now according to the code, we turn right here for seventy-nine steps.' and off he went again with the rest of them following.

The mood in the small group was intensifying; the steps seemed to be accurate...so far.

It took them to the front door.

'D126' the Abbot announced with barely concealed excitement.

And that's when they hit a brick wall...literally.

The Abbot was so intent on measuring and counting his steps that he almost walked into the wall of the outhouse.

'Fifty-eight...ouch!' the Abbot called out, stubbing his toe on the wall.

'Can I help you, Father Abbot?' said the head which popped out of the door at the side of the outhouse. 'I heard a sound and wondered what it was' announced Brother Robert, the head gardener.

'We were...' began the Abbot, hesitating because he didn't want one of the Community to think their Abbot was losing his marbles.

'...we were ...just measuring out for a marquee which the Abbot was thinking of erecting for the celebrations, Brother' Sextus quipped, quick as a flash.

'Oh, right' said Brother Robert. Boo could tell that he was not entirely convinced but he returned to his work inside the outhouse saying: 'I'd better let you get on with it then'

They all stood in silence. What to do now?

'That outhouse was built over a hundred years ago, if I remember correctly' said the Abbot. 'How do we get around that?'

'We'll have to guess the approximate depth of the building and work out how many steps it represents and carry on from there' suggested the Chief Superintendent.

'Excellent idea, if I may say' said the Abbot.

The Chief Superintendent sent his constables off to check the width of the building while the others waited for them to come back with the information.

'It's about twenty-five feet deep' the younger one informed them.

'Right,' said Charlie 'and how long do you reckon your stride is, Father?'

'About three feet, I would guess'

'So, that would be just over eight steps? Would you agree?' said Charlie turning to Boo and Sextus who nodded.

'So add that onto...was it fifty-eight, Father?'

Dom Ambrose nodded.

'I make that sixty-six. Yes?' Everyone agreed. 'So let's get to the other side and continue'

Charlie was in no mood for beating around the bush, so to speak, nor indeed, a hundred year old shed.

'Father, can I just ask' Boo enquired, 'how many more instructions are there?'

The Abbot counted and replied: 'Six'

'Let's get on' said Charlie impatiently.

'Agreed' Sextus responded.

Boo bided her time.

When they reached one hundred and twenty-six steps they halted. Dom Ambrose looked at the instructions and announced: 'S57'

'Why so many steps? At this rate we'll be over the wall and far away' she said jokingly. 'I realised that the starting point had to be an obvious one to a member of the Community but why are there so many instructions?'

Then it dawned on her.

'Of course, it was to put off anyone who was not supposed to find the code. I'll bet it's taking us around on a bit of a wild goose chase so that it would put anyone off the scent who was not meant to find the spot'

They continued on and, sure enough, Miss Lavender was right. Within ten minutes they'd arrived back within the confines of the Abbey and found themselves in the cloisters surrounding the inner gardens where Angus had hidden the night he heard the other two murderers conferring.

'I'm beginning to lose hope' the Abbot admitted.

'That's what was meant to happen, Father. They didn't want the wrong people finding it and so they've been leading us around in circles, hoping that it'll put us off. Do not despair, we are close...very close' predicted Boo.

Unwittingly, they'd entered the gardens before the Abbot announced: 'This is where it stops'

They were under the oak tree where Angus and Frankie Benson had hidden and Lady MacDorn-Smythe and Gertie had comforted each other...and, unbeknown to them all, where Angus had first hatched the plan to bring the Charter to the Abbey.

'We'll I'll be...' the Chief Superintendent proclaimed scratching his head.

Ninety

Sensing they'd reached the exact spot, the Chief Superintendent issued his instructions: 'Right, lads, get digging'

The two of them stripped their jackets off and began digging while the others stood around in the area of the oak tree.

'I can't believe this is happening' exclaimed the Abbot. 'Could this really be the resting place of the abbey's ancient treasure? All these years it's been under our noses and if it weren't for Angus...' he stopped there: the memories of recent terrible events still raw in his mind.

It provoked a different thought for Miss Lavender: "Every cloud has a silver lining" and '...I'm hoping for a lot more than just silver'

The lads worked up a sweat and after twenty minutes, they both leant on their shovels and puffed.

'Sloth, as the good Father will tell you, is one of the seven deadly sins. Now get your backs into it, you lazy...!' Charlie didn't get the chance to complete his gentle exhortations.

The Abbot called out: 'Please, Chief Superintendent! These young men are doing a marvellous job. Maybe we should call a halt to the proceeding and have some refreshments?'

'What time is it, please?' asked Boo.

'Twenty past eleven' Charlie answered consulting his wristwatch.

Boo's eyes bulged in surprise but she made no sound. She'd been so wrapped up in the treasure hunt that she'd forgotten about her elevenses: her ginger nuts, more precious to her than all the gold in Christendom.

Gulping, she finally managed to say: 'What a good idea'

Sextus could hardly contain himself; he was well acquainted with Boo's small Achilles' heel.

'How very abstemious of you, Boo' he declared mischievously.

'And I suppose you don't happen to be feeling peckish?' was the barbed reply.

'Touché' was his white flag of surrender.

'What's that all about?' the Abbot asked.

'Oh, just one of the games we play, Ambrose' Sextus replied vaguely.

By then, the two young constables had stepped out of the hole they'd dug, wiped their hands and were looking forward to some sustenance to help replace the energy they'd burned off.

As they approached the entrance to the Refectory, the hum of conversation was louder than normal.

'What is going on?' was the thought shared by several of the group as they entered.

It was as if someone had turned off a buzz saw when they appeared in the doorway, all eyes turned to the doorway and conversation ceased.

'Good Morning again, everyone,' announced the Abbot, 'is everything alright?' he asked, curious about the sudden silence during what was usually a companionable time of the day.

Father Ignatius spoke up.

'We couldn't help notice you all walking around the grounds before descending on the gardens and beginning to dig, Father. Are you digging for bodies? Have there been more murders?'

A murmur of agreement went around the room.

The Abbot laughed. It didn't take long in an enclosed community for rumours to get started and flourish out of control like a forest fire.

'Of course not, Father, but...' and here he looked around the room at all of his monks standing there '... can I ask you all to bear with me for just a little longer? I think what's happening will be good news for the whole of our Community but before I say what it is; will you give me till suppertime this evening, please?'

A general murmur of 'Of course, Father' went around the Community of monks in the room.

'Thank you' said the Abbot humbly, almost reduced to tears by the trust they showed in him.

Everyone drifted back into small groups and began chatting again about the more usual topics of rain, aches and pains.

As the visitors got stuck into their mid-morning snacks, Father Ignatius pulled Dom Ambrose to the side.

'Father, Lady Dorothy asked me to ask if it would be possible to have a word with you? So, I took the liberty of checking your diary and saw that you had nothing booked in for this morning and I said after the mid-morning break might be good but I'd check with you first. Would that be in order? And shall I say in your office, Father?'

The Abbot wanted to say: 'Absolutely not, I'm on a treasure hunting expedition!' but instead said: 'Please tell Lady Dorothy that that would be fine. I'll be there in about ten minutes once I've had something to eat'

Father Ignatius left immediately to tell Lady Dorothy who was still keeping to her room.

''Damn, damn, damn!' Dom Ambrose swore inwardly and immediately regretted it and asked for forgiveness from the Almighty. 'That poor woman. What she's gone through...and poor Gertie too. Bless them. I must remember to say a Mass for all of the family. What a tragedy for them. And I must try to be more patient' he chastised himself. 'I will be more patient' he decided.

In the meantime, he was lucky to find any food left at all; between mouthfuls, Sextus was busy keeping a close eye on the competition, the young constables, who were gobbling up the food almost as fast as he was.

Cheeky young monkeys!

Boo, as always, munching on her three ginger nuts, was far, far away; where, exactly, no-one was sure but she looked beatific.

Finally, the time came to get on with the work at hand but Dom Ambrose, without any explanation, asked his visitors if they also would bear with him for a short while before the excavation began again.

'Of course, Father' said Charlie. 'How long will you need?'

'Could we continue after lunch, do you think?' the Abbot asked.

Gobsmacked was not a word which Miss Lavender had ever used but, for the first time in her life, she experienced what it felt like.

When the Abbot left the Refectory, they all hummed and hawed and looked at their feet until finally Boo said: 'I wonder what's happened? He seemed so keen'

'Boo,' said Sextus between mouthfuls of food 'you have to understand; it could be something which he's not able to speak about. A priest's work very often involves situations or events which he cannot reveal because of the seal of confession'

The conversation ended there with nods of understanding from the group.

'So,' said Charlie, all business-like 'shall we meet after lunch under the old oak tree?'

Nodding, they all went off to fill in the time till lunchtime before resuming the search.

Ninety One

Miss Lavender and Sextus sauntered along to the Bibliotheca where Boo had offered to show Sextus some other treasures she'd come across during the final stage of the cataloguing.

Whilst drawing his attention to some of the more esoteric volumes, she explained to Sextus what she'd found out about Professor Beech: that although she'd never considered him to be a suspect in the murders, his actions and demeanour had led Boo to take both eyes off the ball, albeit briefly. But the reality was that the man was a troubled soul: that was it, nothing else.

'So, his only interest was in these magnificent tomes then, Boo?' her friend asked.

'Entirely, Sextus. There was a point where I almost suggested that he be added to our pot of suspects but something about him reminded me of one of my readers...for the life of me, I can't remember which one or why. However, my instincts told me that he wasn't the murdering type and so, although I didn't know which box he belonged in, I discounted him and moved on and I'm glad I did...turned out, I'd have been wrong anyway'

'Well done Boo. But you know these are truly amazing' Sextus remarked excitedly after she'd finished clearing the air about the sad little man whose only crime was being an inveterate bibliophile. 'The sheer number of first editions would make any of the large institutions like the British Library or the Bodleian fall over each other to add these to their collections'

'I know, Sextus, and I have spoken to Dom Ambrose about putting them into auction. I think if push comes to shove, he will, but I understand his reluctance, after all he is the keeper of the Abbey's heritage. But then again, none of the Community has been in the Bibliotheca for years according to the Abbot. Don't you think it's a shame that such important historic volumes such as these go unread and unloved and indeed unseen? I, for one, do'

'I can see it from both sides, Boo, but hopefully he won't have to sell them if we can find that blessed treasure. It would certainly solve a lot of the Abbey's problems'

'Sextus,' said Boo sternly 'I know we're in the process of digging up the gardens but it doesn't mean that we'll find something. For goodness sake, let's be practical. There is no guarantee that there's anything to find. How many times does it have to be said?'

A crestfallen Sextus replied in a subdued tone:

'All I ask, Boo, is: let us have a little hope...please'

'Sextus, I want to find it as much as you do but we have to take the sensible approach'. Boo paused for a moment and then said in her best devil-may-care voice: 'Oh, whatever, Sextus! Let's hope for today and see what it brings. Tomorrow will be time enough to be practical, I suppose'

'That's more like it, Boo. Let's up and at 'em!' whooped Sextus, the eternal optimist.

For the next hour or so, the two friends spent time leafing through the treasures which Boo had dug up in the Library of the Abbey.

Both friends, for that day at least, hoped to dig up another trove of treasures: but this time, one which had been unseen for hundreds of years.

Ninety Two

While Boo and Sextus were pottering about in the Bibliotheca, Dom Ambrose was sitting listening to the widow of Sir John MacDorn-Smythe; it did not make for happy hearing.

Lady Dorothy ended with:

'...and so that's where we are at the moment, Ambrose'

'Oh, Dorothy, I'm so sorry. What has happened to you over the last week, words cannot describe. But now to hear this, it really is too much'

But she was a tough old bird, Lady Dorothy.

'We still have friends, Ambrose, and I know that if they can, they will help'

'But you shouldn't be in this situation now, Dorothy. I've known Johnnie for so long and I always knew he was a soft touch but really...tut, tut, so sad. But, there may be a solution. I can't say too much in case it doesn't come to anything but can you leave this with me and whatever happens, I, personally guarantee, that things will be sorted out. Leave it with me until tonight, will you?'

'Certainly, Ambrose, and trust me when I say I am so sorry to bring this to your door: you have had more than enough to deal with especially with these events of the past few days. As you know, I have found it very difficult to come to terms with them but...Gertie's been a real tower of strength'. Lady Dorothy's eyes filled up. 'I don't know how I would have survived these past few days without her'

'Then bless her and bless you too' said Dom Ambrose with feeling as he made the sign of the cross over Lady Dorothy. Receiving the blessing seemed to bring to her feelings of peace and solace.

'Thank you, Father' she said as the deep sadness etched in her ashen face seemed to ease a little.

Having known the family for so long, Dom Ambrose felt like one of them and Lady Dorothy and Gertie's loss was his loss too: Johnnie was one of his oldest and dearest friends and although he hadn't christened young Angus, he was like the godson Ambrose had never had.

Lady Dorothy withdrew her handkerchief and dabbed away the tears which had gathered in the corner of her eyes.

'I knew if anyone would understand it would be you'

'Never fear, my dear, the Good Lord will provide' the Abbot said...and meant it.

Lady Dorothy stood up and hugged the Abbot before leaving; something she'd never done in all the years he'd known her.

Left alone, the Abbot sat and pondered what his friend, Lady Dorothy, had just revealed to him: basically, the family was broke. No other way to put it. Johnnie for all his wonderful charm and kindness had practically bankrupted the family giving to charity especially to those who came to him with a sob story.

'No doubt some of them were confidence tricksters' the Abbot thought angrily 'but Johnnie wasn't a man to walk past on the other side of the street and ignore someone in need, if he thought he could help'

He and the Abbot had discussed how lucky Johnnie felt about his life on many occasions; not only to have a wife whom he adored but to have the two wonderful children he and Dorothy had been blessed with. But he wasn't blinkered; Johnnie knew that Angus could get in with the wrong crowd and had had, on more than one occasion, to bail him out. But, Johnnie's answer to those who would raise the subject with him was always the same: "Let he who is without sin...". Gertie, of course, was a gem: the apple of her father's eye. She must be missing her papa.

Johnnie MacDorn-Smythe, in the Abbot's opinion, epitomised the definition of a truly decent human being and a true English gentleman.

There and then, the Abbot made the decision that if they didn't find this fabled treasure, he would sell the book collection, as Miss Lavender had suggested, and whatever funds it raised would go to pay off the Abbey's loan and provide a sizeable annuity to support Lady Dorothy and Gertie. It was the very least his Order could do for the family who had given the Abbey and its grounds to it.

Ninety Three

Lunch: normally a leisurely affair at Brackenbury Abbey enjoyed by residents and visitors alike, in the middle of their day.

Not today however. As a rule, the reading lasted until the end of the main course. Ha! By the time the tureens of meat and vegetables for the main course had been dished out onto plates, the Abbot was ringing the bell signalling the end of the reading and for conversation to begin...which it did at an ear-splitting level.

'My, my, the atmosphere is certainly charged today.' Boo burst out. 'Any particular reason, do you think, Father?'

'I can't imagine, Miss Lavender' replied the Abbot full of high spirits and hope himself.

To say the Abbot gobbled his meal down would be an unkind thing to say...but how else do you say it? He attacked his victuals like a man who'd been on a fast for a week.

'In a hurry, are you, Ambrose?' Sextus said, astonished when he caught sight of the Abbot's empty plate.

'Oh, you know, Sextus,' replied the Abbot with a twinkle in his eye 'places to go, people to see, treasure-hunting to be continued...that sort of thing'

The air of the place was filled with the kind of merry banter that generally occurred on feast days like St Dominic's on the Eighth of August when everyone in the Abbey rested from their usual daily chores and conviviality was the order of the day.

Boo noticed that Charlie and the two young constables had been invited for lunch and were seated at the end of a table near the shattered entrance to the Refectory.

'Could be a bit draughty sitting so close to that large gaping hole' she thought 'but I suppose those boys are used to pounding the beat in all kinds of weather and standing on windy corners keeping the general public safe. The little darlings'. However, if it was a bit parky, she noted, it didn't seem to interfere with their appetites.

The Abbot interrupted her thoughts.

'Looking forward to solving the mystery, Miss Lavender?'

'Well, I hope for all concerned it will turn out to be worthwhile, Father' she replied evasively.

'We seem to be on the right track though, don't you think, Boo?' Sextus chimed in.

'It would seem to be the case, Sextus' she said hesitantly.

The truth was: a different sort of niggle had settled into Miss Lavender's stomach.

'What if it's all pie in the sky? Who's to say that it hasn't been discovered before? Has it lain dormant for the last few hundred years with no-one breaking or finding the code?'

These and many more questions contributed to make up this niggle she had floating around in that area which acted as her barometer for unresolved situations: her tummy. However, on the other hand, she thought wistfully '...if the code hasn't been broken and if the fabled wealth is still buried there...how wonderful! But...'

Caution: one of Miss Lavender's by-words.

'Is everyone finished?' enquired Dom Ambrose impatiently looking left and right along the length of the top table.

Now if there is one part of a meal that Sextus really enjoys, it's his pudding. And today's offering of spotted dick and custard came very close to the top of his list of favourites.

'Give us a chance, will you Ambrose? I've only just started' Sextus said in a half-joking way: Boo knew better, of course.

Being rushed at the dinner table should, in Sextus' opinion, be added to the list of the Seven Deadly Sins and bring its total to eight.

A thought which would regularly occur to Sextus on those sorts of occasions was: "I wonder what would have happened throughout the ages if...and he knew it was an enormous if...instead of interrupting lunch or dinner, all of the great military commanders had finished their meals before deciding how to proceed into battle?"

That thought would often conclude with what he considered to be a perfect example of the kind of change of outcome he was thinking of: The Charge of the Light Brigade.

On reflection then, people might, perhaps, think twice about interrupting one of man's greatest pleasures in life: the consumption of food.

But back in the Refectory Sextus felt the pressure to rush. As he watched Dom Ambrose out of the corner of his eye, he observed the man forming a cat's cradle with his fingers while his thumbs began twirling busily around each other. 'Patience. Where has it gone in today's world?' Sextus wondered.

Three minutes later, as Sextus, his appetite sated, temporarily, of course, laid his spoon in the empty bowl, the Abbot rang the bell signalling the end of lunch.

Charlie and his boys joined Boo, Sextus and the Abbot at the top table after the thanksgiving prayer while the rest of the Community left the Refectory.

'Thank you for inviting us to lunch, Father. That was very kind of you and I speak for the three of us when I say that it was very enjoyable' said Charlie patting his stomach.

'Most welcome, Chief Superintendent. Shall we adjourn to the garden?'

'Yes please, Father. We're all curious to know what we're going to find...if anything' he quipped.

The Abbot's face changed: the thought of there being no treasure was too much for him to bear and sent his brain scurrying back into a dark place.

All six exited the Refectory and made their way along the corridors towards the outside.

This was it.

Ninety Four

The shovels were still standing upright in the soil under the shade of the old oak where the young constables had left them. The air in the garden was cool but warm enough for them to remove their uniform jackets again.

'Right, lads, sleeves up and let's get to it' the Chief Superintendent ordered. 'The quicker we find it, the quicker we'll be away'

With that, the young men put their backs into it, shovelling great clods of earth out of the hole onto the side and at the same time, building up a great lather of sweat. The higher the mounds became, the more the two young men came to resemble a couple of gravediggers...or was it grave robbers, Miss Lavender reflected?

In their enthusiasm, some of the earth splattered the shoes of the non-shovellers.

'Oi, careful you lot!' Charlie called out as his immaculately polished brogues were at the receiving end of some of it. When he was sure than no-one was looking, he rubbed them on the back of his trousers. What would his subordinates think?

'I'm getting nervous now' the Abbot admitted 'but I can't decide if it's with excitement or worry'

'I feel the same' confessed Sextus dodging some of the muck which was flying out of the deepening hole.

Just as doubt began to seep into the whole group, out of the blue, they all heard a distinct clang as one of the shovels hit...something.

'Aye, aye' the Chief Superintendent called out '...what have we here?'

The four non-shovellers moved closer to the edge of the hole and peered in.

'What've you got there, Jenkins?' he asked to the younger of the two constables.

'Seems to be some kind of box, Sir'

316

'Right, well gently ease the shovel around the edges of it and see if there's a handle or grip to pull it out...and remember it's four or five hundred years old. So, careful does it'

They all waited, teetering on the edge, as the two diggers slowly attempted to prise the box from its resting place.

'Come on then' their boss admonished them.

It took Sextus back to pudding time in the Refectory that afternoon. 'Patience. Has the world supply of it run out? Or is it in short supply like butter?'

After much pulling and wiggling, the damp earth finally relinquished its long held secret.

With one final grunt the two diggers lifted the box onto the side.

'So...o...o,' said Charlie 'let's see what we've got here'

The small rectangular box measured eighteen inches by ten inches and had about one foot of depth to it. It wasn't heavy and had more of the look of a lady's jewel case than a treasure chest.

'Hmm, not the coffer I'd imagined' he admitted.

'Nor me. I expected it to be massive' Sextus replied.

The Abbot and Boo said nothing. The leader of the Community, drained by the events of the recent past, hoped. Hoped that the Good Lord had finally allowed 'it' to be found and that inside there might be something so valuable, it could solve the Abbey's problems.

Cleaning away the muck around the hinged lock, Charlie could see that it would have to be forced open – a situation that he was not totally unfamiliar with.

'Jenkins, give me that shovel, will you?'

He laid the box with the lock pointing upwards, jamming the edge of the shovel just under the hinge. Holding it in position with his foot, he gave the shovel a quick yank upwards and the ancient rusting metal hinge flew off with a dull clanking sound.

'The moment of truth' announced Charlie like a town crier.

Breaths were held as three pairs of eyes, whose owners teetered on the edge of the precipice, locked onto the box as Charlie forced open the lid. The two young policemen, remaining at eye level with the box, stood in the hole they'd created, gawping.

However, those breaths were rapidly released as Charlie revealed its contents. On the inside of the lid there was a slightly

317

mottled mirror, no doubt caused by its exposure over time to the moisture in the soil. Apart from that there was nothing.

Charlie held the box upside down like a magician showing that there was nothing inside when a small fragment of folded parchment fluttered out to land on a heap of earth.

Boo turned to the Abbot who'd gone ashen and looked like he was having a turn.

'Are you all right, Father?'

'If you don't mind, all, I think I need to sit down' and he tumbled onto the bench under the oak. This was not what he'd hoped for.

'Dear Lord,' he prayed silently 'thy will be done. But...' words failed him; he bowed his head, overcome with emotion.

Sextus retrieved the piece of parchment and unfolded it. It was fragile, very brittle, with just a few words of writing that had almost disappeared with time.

'Chief Superintendent, do you happen to have your magnifying glass with you?'

Charlie retrieved it from his pocket and handed it to Sextus.

'It's written in Latin' he said squinting at it through the lens. 'It says...er...er... 'Quid tu...em...vides?" Yes, that's it. "Quid tu vides?' which translates as: "what can you see?"'

'What can you see?' Charlie repeated, clearly puzzled.

'Yes,' Sextus responded 'obviously some kind of riddle'

'Oh, for heaven's sake!' the Abbot cried out. 'I do not need a riddle at this point in time. Not now!' He thumped the seat with the flat of his hand.

As Boo looked at him, astonished at his outburst, she thought he seemed to shrivel within his habit. This happy, handsome man had suddenly aged. 'Stress...really can destroy people. Poor man. He really doesn't need this' she thought.

'All it means is, we're not quite there yet. But never fear, Father, we'll get there' Charlie declared emphatically.

'Absolutely, Chief Superintendent' Boo agreed. She was determined to see it through and help this man who had shown her nothing but kindness.

318

'You're all very kind' the Abbot said in a voice tinged with sadness. 'But unless we can solve this by tomorrow, the Abbey is lost'

'Plenty of time' Boo proposed with more bravado than she really felt.

'Back to the drawing board...or at least to the desk in the Bibliotheca' Sextus exhorted.

With heavy hearts, Sextus, Boo, Charlie and the Abbot dragged themselves to the Library.

Ninety Five

Sextus pulled an extra chair to the desk they'd kind of made their HQ to accommodate the Abbot, who seemed very distracted.

'So,' began Charlie 'what do we actually have?'

'We have a riddle, set, no doubt, by the monks to keep the wrong people from finding the monastery's wealth' Boo turned to the Abbot. 'Will you be able to help us with this one, Father? Anything in the history of the Order which might give us a clue or perhaps it's some kind of code which has been used by members of the Order in the past?' she asked.

'Er...er...I can't think at the moment but perhaps if you good people wouldn't mind talking amongst yourselves, something might stir in this old brain of mine'

'Of course, Father' Sextus put in. 'So...any suggestions?' He looked from Boo to Charlie and was greeted with blank stares.

After a minute, Boo broke the silence.

'It's a funny thing to say: "What can you see?". I mean, what could you see? There was the oak tree and the flower beds, the bench, the cloisters, the beautifully manicured lawn...the building surrounding the garden. What else? Anyone think of anything?'

The others remained silent.

'This simply won't do. We can't just sit here looking at the ceiling and contemplating our navels' Boo thought getting really annoyed. 'So, what else could it possibly mean?'

For an hour, the four of them sat, mostly in silence, before Boo came to a conclusion.

'I'm going out to the garden again. Charlie, where is the box?' she asked.

'It's here' he said lifting it up from the side of his chair.

'Anyone else coming?' ...but they all sat there. They couldn't see how standing in the garden could help. This was a cerebral matter.

'I won't be long'

She was right.

Ninety Six

It was still early Spring and the days were drawing in early, so the light was starting to fade as she stood by the mound of earth left by the young constables.

She stood there looking down into the freshly dug hole before her eyes flickered upwards, scanning the entire area of her vision in front of her, looking to see what there was to see. There was nothing to add to the list she'd already put together.

'There's only one thing for it, just like when Sir John was poisoned; if your thinking or theories don't produce a solution, start again'

'So, the answer is in the clue: "what can you see?"'

For a few moments more she looked...and looked, trying to keep her mind free from any preconceived notions or thoughts. Nothing jumped in to replace them.

Still standing in front of the hole, she opened the box she'd brought from the Library, held it up and looked inside. As she did so, she caught the mottled reflection of her own face looking back at her from the lid.

A thought occurred to her.

'Why place a mirror in the box, why not just a plain box? If the riddle setter put a mirror in the box, then it can mean only one thing – it has to be involved with the solution'

She lifted the mirror up and looked again at her face only this time, she noticed something else – what she could see behind her: the background.

'Of course, how stupid! "What do you see?" applies to not only what you can see in front of you but what you can see when you look in the mirror. I should have known that especially with my mirrored spectacles. What a chump you are sometimes, Boo Lavender! Now then...'

Boo turned around and began looking closely at what lay behind her but within a minute she'd decided that eight eyes would be better than two, albeit, observant ones, and so she retraced her steps back to the Library.

The Three Wise Men were sitting where she'd left them, no further forward.

'We are getting there, Boo. Never fear' was Sextus' not overly confident reply when she opened the door.

'I think I may have something' she announced sotto voce.

That made them jump.

'You have?' Charlie asked excitedly.

'What is it, Miss Lavender?' the Abbot practically pleaded.

'The answer was in the riddle: "What do you see?". When someone reads that message, the natural thing to do would be to look up, straight ahead. And that's what the setter of the riddle intended. But then I got thinking.

Why would they put a mirror in the box? If the box's only purpose was to carry a piece of manuscript, why would it require a mirror? And that's when I decided that the mirror had to play a part in the solving of mystery.

As you look in the box, the first thing you see is the mirror and, in it, you cannot only see your reflection but what is behind you. That, gentlemen, is where you come in. I need your help. I think whatever it was that was hidden from the King's men is in the area behind where we were all standing earlier. Any volunteers?' she asked mischievously.

Now, if you've ever been in a classroom when the bell rings for the end of class and witnessed the scrum which followed, then you'll know immediately how the "volunteers" behaved.

'Me first!' was one of the unseemly cries as three grown men dashed to the doorway and tried to squeeze through an opening which was made to accommodate one...at a time.

'No, me!' another voice shouted.

'Gentlemen, can we have a little decorum, please?' insisted Miss Lavender.

That brought them to a halt.

Ties and waistcoats, as well as some clerical attire, were adjusted. A considerable amount of clearing of throats with absolutely no eye contact, followed.

'Quite' was the one-word reproof from Miss Lavender. 'Now, please follow me'

Ninety Seven

All four of them stood with their backs to the hole but this time they surveyed the area between the oak and the cloister at the back as Miss Lavender had suggested.

'What sort of thing are we looking for, Boo?' Sextus probed.

'I'm not sure, to be honest, Sextus, but whatever it is, I'm sure it's here'

Miss Lavender stood quietly for a moment, recalling part of the history she'd read about the origins of the Abbey:

Back in the thirteenth century, before the first Abbot of Chalfontbury Friary took Orders, he'd fought in the Crusades. He returned to England a changed man. The horrors he'd experienced in The Holy Land abhorred and repulsed him so much that he decided to take Holy Orders and dedicate his life to preserving life instead of taking it.

On his way back to England he travelled extensively in Europe and visited an abbey in Germany called Kloster Ebenbach, which had been built about a hundred years earlier.

Shortly after that, thanks to the generous endowment of a benefactor, he was able to build one of the first Dominican monasteries in England: the design of it based on his memories of Kloster Ebenbach.

The walls surrounding the garden were about four feet in height and two feet in depth, topped by sturdy columns supporting the upper floor.

It was within the confines of these walls that the four of them began their search.

'Nothing, nothing and still nothing!' the Abbot shouted after a few minutes of thrusting one of the shovels methodically into the earth around the area between the hole and the wall.

'I can't find anything either' Charlie reported.

Sextus, who was poking around in the flower beds just looked at Boo and shook his head silently.

Just then, Dom Ambrose's shovel hit something. Heads lifted from what they were doing and they all rushed over. The Abbot dug the spade into the damp earth and shovelled frantically, lifting out a few clumps of earth and tossing them aside: it was a boulder.

The Abbot almost wailed. He was sinking fast in front of their eyes.

'What are we doing wrong?' Boo asked herself. 'Have I got it wrong? There's only one thing for it' she decided

'Back to basics' she decided, walking over to the hole, she picked up the box. The others joined her. Boo opened the lid again to see if she was missing something. Staring at the mirror she saw the wall, the pillars, the...

'Wait a minute!' she thought excitedly '...what I can't see is the ground and that's where they've all been looking. So...what does that mean?'

'Boo...' Sextus began.

'Shh, Sextus, I've nearly got it, I think' Boo hissed.

'Sorry' he whispered.

Her brain was doing somersaults trying to understand what it meant.

'The clue is "what can you see?". Well, I saw the wall, the pillars, the empty space behind...then that means...it means...it has to be in the wall or the pillars because that's what I can see when I look in the mirror. Not the earth or the bushes or the flowerbeds...the wall and pillars!'

Boo gently closed the box and turned, the others looked on expectantly.

'Boo, are you all right? You look as though you've seen a ghost' Sextus said worriedly.

'I might very well have, Sextus; the ghost of times gone by'

Sextus looked at his friend strangely.

'Has she lost the plot or found the answer?' he wondered uneasily.

'...because this time, I think we may have it, my friends' Boo concluded.

'Yes?' they were all a little more than agog.

'The treasure left by those monks...is...in...the...wall!' she said pointing to the wall she'd seen in the mirror.

'It's what?' exclaimed the Abbot.

'The only thing I can think is that they must have pulled the wall down and rebuilt it and hidden the treasure inside. Now who would have thought of that, I ask you?'

'So, we'll have to break the wall down because you think it's hollow and that's where the treasure is?' Charlie asked who was as astounded as the rest of the group.

'Yes' she replied simply.

'Well, we'll need more than these shovels. Brother Robert, our Gardener, will have a pick or something we can use to break it down' the Abbot suggested. 'Chief Superintendent, would you mind asking one of your young men to go and ask Brother Robert for an implement to break into the wall?'

'Well, jump to it, Jenkins! You heard the good Father!'

'Yessir!' the young constable shouted, saluted and was gone.

The whole group exploded with excitement as they gathered around the wall, each postulating their theories about what could be inside the wall.

If Miss Lavender's hunch was correct, they'd have solved a mystery which had baffled many a fine mind for centuries.

While they waited, Sextus, Boo and Charlie poked at the wall, half-expecting the treasure to fall out from between the limestone mortar and bricks of the age-old wall; the Abbot simply prayed a silent prayer.

After what seemed like a very long time, but in fact was only ten minutes, young Jenkins returned with a pick and a large hammer.

'Who wants to strike the first blow?' Charlie called out.

'Don't you think it should be Miss Lavender?' Dom Ambrose suggested.

Boo was taken aback. She really wasn't a physical sort of person – more the cerebral variety.

'That's very kind of you Father but I'll pass, if...if...if you don't mind' she stuttered.

'Shall we toss a coin then, Father?' asked Charlie.

Boo wanted to scream. Boys!

'Who cares who lands the first blow? Let's see if my theory's correct' she wanted to yell...but prudently resisted.

Charlie pulled a half crown from his pocket.

'Heads or tails, Father?'

'Tails' the Abbot called gleefully getting into the spirit of it.

Charlie looked crestfallen, it was tails.

'Okay, Mr Phipps, it's between you and the Father. Heads or tails?'

'I'll say...tails' Sextus said.

'Tails it is' declared Charlie and handed Sextus the hammer.

Sextus lifted the large wide-headed hammer and swung it at the wall.

Crash! The sound was deafening!

But not even a chip flew off the wall.

'I think we'd better leave it to the youngsters, Father' proposed Charlie. 'Stand well back now...' he said, ushering the small group away from the wall and out of reach of the swinging hammer...and you two be careful' he warned.

The two young policemen attacked the wall with gusto, taking alternate swings at a central part of the wall.

'Just a small section in case our theories are wrong' the Abbot called out hesitantly, a little worried...and just a little too late.

After five or six swings each the wall began to disintegrate...and objects of varying shapes and sizes wrapped in cloth could be seen through the debris and dust.

'Hurrah! We've done it...we've saved the Abbey!' the Abbot shouted at the top of his voice.

By now, faces, some with puzzlement, others with wonderment, were beginning to appear at windows around the quad. Others, who were working nearby, came and stood watching in bemused silence as the wall tumbled down.

'Stop, stop!' the Chief Superintendent cried. 'Let's see what we've got before we go any further'

He, Boo, Sextus and Dom Ambrose approached the, as yet, unidentifiable objects through showers of white dust from the ancient limestone mortar which slowly floated through the air clinging to their clothes and faces and nasal passages, causing one or two Atishoo's.

Out of deference, the others waited while the Abbot moved to unwrap the first item.

His hand wavered wondering which item to choose first. He decided on a small bundle and removed the cover. A wondrous gold chalice inlaid with precious gems appeared from under the first piece of cloth.

Without a word, the Abbot lifted it heavenwards in thanks and, almost as if to show His approval, for a few moments, the sun burst through the clouds and shards of golden light twinkled around the gardens from the precious artefact.

There was a collective intake of breath from members of the Community and visitors alike.

'Well, if that's the start, I can't wait!' Dom Ambrose declared eagerly already looking twenty years younger now that it was clear the Abbey was saved; repairs that were years overdue would now be able to be done properly instead of being patched up and Lady Dorothy and Gertie would be saved from penury. 'All in all, a good day's work...' he concluded '...and all thanks to Miss Lavender. How can we, as a Community, ever repay her?'

Within the hour, all of the precious artefacts had been retrieved and carefully stored in boxes brought to the gardens by the monks, all of whom, with the permission of the Abbot, had abandoned their work for that day.

As the light began to fade, they all realised that it was long passed afternoon teatime...even Sextus.

Fortunately, Brother Jerome, the cook, was at hand and rustled up heaped plates of sandwiches from bread he'd made at the beginning of the day. This was accompanied by two plates of assorted biscuits normally reserved for special occasions and feast days...and the Abbot had ordained that that this was indeed 'a very special occasion'.

If the memory of Sir John wasn't still so painful, Dom Ambrose would have opened some of their vintage bottles of wine. After all, this was a time to celebrate.

By then, Lady Dorothy and Gertie had joined them in the gardens. It would have been difficult for them not to have heard the cheering and general high spirits taking place there. Their curiosity aroused, they'd come in search of the reason.

Miss Lavender observed when Lady Dorothy and Gertie arrived, the Abbot took the widow to one side and had a lengthy whispered conversation during which, Boo observed Lady Dorothy's eyebrows twitching skywards, several times, in disbelief. Nevertheless, the general impression Boo was left with, from her radiant smile, was that she was very pleased with what Dom Ambrose had imparted.

Boo could not have known that the good Lady's standing and dignity had been saved that day too as well as the future of the Abbey.

...and the day wasn't over yet.

Ninety Eight

The rest of what was left of the fading daylight was put to good use transporting the boxes of antiquities to the Father Abbot's room for safekeeping. 'If there are any others, they can wait.' thought Dom Ambrose. They'd lain in their walled tomb for nearly four hundred years; another few days wouldn't make any difference.

It would take a number of scholars and antiquities experts several months to work out the value of the treasure which had been uncovered in that small section of wall.

Mindful of how close the Abbey had come to ruin, Dom Ambrose made the phone call he had, earlier, been dreading but was now very much looking forward to placing: the call to the bank manager, Richard Morris, when he informed him of their discovery.

In the event, it turned out that not only was Mr Morris delighted but he immediately offered to extend the Abbey's loan indefinitely. The Abbot thanked him for his kind offer but explained that that would not be necessary...now.

His next call was to the man in charge of the diocese, Bishop Newman. He felt certain that the bishop would be equally pleased when he passed on the good news: politics and a certain smugness were not the exclusive reserve of the laity.

And if Miss Lavender thought she'd uncovered some masterpieces during her travels in the Bibliotheca, they were nothing compared to what had been found in the gardens.

By then, stomachs and boxes were replete and the bell for Vespers began to ring out.

Much as she was excited at the find, Boo thought about joining them but decided to skip it; the day had been quite exhausting enough. When she was sure everyone had assembled for prayer, she returned to the garden, carefully edging around the hole that had been left there, and sat on the bench beneath the oak, contemplating the events of the day. And what a day it had turned out to be!

As the temperature dropped and with a light wind adding to the chill in the air, Miss Lavender pulled up her jacket collar. A shiver sprinted down her spine, all the way to her well-shod feet, reminding her that '...winter has not departed these shores for far off climes quite yet' she thought bleakly.

While those and other thoughts drifted lazily on, the sound of male voices singing drifted towards her from the direction of the chapel. The hymn was one she didn't recognise, '...not one of ours' she thought but, as she listened, the swell of the voices grew louder; it was a happy sound.

Probably, she guessed, one of thanksgiving.

With the arrival of twilight and the light almost gone, Miss Lavender's eyes drifted leisurely around the garden noting the mounds of earth, the broken brickwork, the...

That train of thought was interrupted by another, crossing over it like a train line.

'...Is it possible that there could be more treasure buried within those walls?' she wondered.

The thought made her look up and squint at the wall as if trying to see through it and what lay behind the undamaged brickwork.

'I dare say the Nationals will have a field day' she reckoned animatedly. 'I can see it now: "Buried Treasure Discovered in Walls of Ancient Abbey" or some such lurid headline' It tickled her.

Lying beside her on the bench was the box which had started it all. For no reason, Boo picked it up and returned to the spot where she'd first worked out the meaning of the riddle. Facing the oak as she did that first time, she opened the box. She could barely make out her own reflection, it had grown so dark. Smiling at the memory, she started to close the lid when something twinkled in the corner of the mirror: a brief flash like a shooting star passing across the heavens.

'What on earth...!' she thought curiously.

She turned to see what it was. Was it someone approaching with a torch? Is that what the mirror had caught? A torchlight moving around? Nothing. She gingerly stepped around the mounds of earth and looked over the wall to see if someone was there. Still nothing.

'What was it?'

She was about to return to the spot and look through the mirror again to see if she could spot it again; something had definitely glinted and caught her eye. That's when she spotted the "something": a small chip had come out of the plasterwork of one of the pillars where the wall had taken a pounding and...Miss Lavender looked closer at the cracked plaster.

'What is that?' she wondered poking her finger into the small break in the plaster.

'Drat! I'll have to get a torch to have a look'

She decided to take a shortcut through the kitchens.

Brother Jerome was there; he'd left the service early to begin preparations for the evening meal.

'Miss Lavender, I thought you'd be at Vespers' he said turning to greet her while ladling fat over a tray of big fat potatoes which were '...browning just nicely' Boo noted.

'Oh, Brother, I need a torch. Do you have one here?'

'Not looking for more buried treasure, are we, Miss Lavender?' he joked while pulling out the next tray of potatoes and making sure each of them had a generous covering of hot spluttering fat.

'Not at all, Brother, just wanted to have a look at something'

He eyed her charily. 'Are you sure, Miss Lavender?', his thick Scottish accent laden with suspicion.

Boo laughed. 'What a suspicious mind you have, Brother'

'I wonder why?' he answered, all prim and proper as he closed the oven door and fetched a torchlight hanging from a row of hooks beside some kitchen implements.

'Thank you, Brother. By the way, supper not only looks wonderful but it smells divine'

'The Good Lord always provides, Miss Lavender' laughed Brother Jerome. 'He just leaves the preparation to the rest of us!'

Boo left the gregarious monk humming merrily away to himself while he juggled the preparation, cooking and timing of the evening meal. It was a feat which still left Boo in awe. Getting everything prepared to serve to so many at the same time? Amazing.

But by the time the door closed behind her she'd already forgotten what would be served up for supper that night. She was itching to find out what it was behind the plaster in the pillar...because there was something there. No doubt.

Manoeuvring around the obstacles in the garden, but this time with the aid of the torch, she arrived at the spot where the small piece of plaster had come away from the pillar.

'They must have given the wall some serious whacking for the plaster to fall off this pillar' she presumed as she examined it excitedly.

Trying to hold her eagerness in check, she shone the light on the pillar. She saw that the crack went all the way up to the top of the column.

'Wait a minute,' she mumbled. 'what is that?'

Wiggling her finger into the small aperture she managed to pull a bit more of the plaster away.

What she saw took her breath away.

'No...it can't be!' she uttered incredulously. 'Surely not?'

...but it was.

Boo rushed out of the garden, through the kitchen where Brother Jerome turned again to greet her as she sped past him.

'Miss Lavender, whatever is the matter?' he called to her back as she raced out into the corridor. 'Women, I've never understood them' he remarked shaking his head and turning back to his pots and pans.

Miss Lavender was walking at a fast rate, too fast really, for she almost tripped up a couple of times...but what she had to tell them just couldn't wait another minute.

'Oh dear, oh dear' she repeated over and over to herself as she moved closer to the Chapel.

Reaching the intricately-carved door to the Chapel she opened it just in time to hear the congregation say its final 'Amen'. The service had just finished.

'Thank goodness' she sighed. The thought of interrupting the proceedings worried her greatly but she would not have to do that now.

Nevertheless, she had to get their attention.

'Father Ambrose! Father Ambrose!' she called out. 'Please!' But the realisation of what she'd found together with the effort to get to the Chapel took its toll, she collapsed onto one of the pew seats, clutching her chest.

Sextus was the first to reach her. 'Boo, what's happened? Are you all right?' he asked alarmed at her pallor which had turned a nasty shade of pale grey. 'Has she had a heart attack or maybe a stroke?' was his first thought.

'I've never been more all right in my life, Sextus Phipps, thank you very much! But may I have a glass of water, please? I'm a little winded, that's all'

One of the young novices fetched a tumbler of water and her colour quickly returned to normal.

Everyone gathered around, concerned that the hero of the hour was suddenly taken unwell.

'Just give me a moment to catch my breath and then I want you all to come with me. I can't believe it. I simply can't believe it'

'Can't believe what, Miss Lavender?' Dom Ambrose asked, his brow furrowed with more than a hint of curiosity in his voice.

'I need to show you' was her frustrating answer.

And so, everyone waited while Miss Lavender gathered herself together before they all followed her out of the Chapel.

At a more leisurely pace this time, Miss Lavender led the entire congregation, including Lady Dorothy and The Honourable Gertie, back to the garden.

On the way, she suggested that they picked up all the torches they could find. If Miss Lavender's assessment was correct, they were going to need them.

Marching along the outside of the building with torches blazing, it reminded Miss Lavender of one of those midnight processions on Guy Fawkes Night...and it was only the beginning of March.

When they reached the arched entrance to the garden, the Community of monks stood aside and let the main protagonists enter while they waited outside.

Miss Lavender led followed by Dom Ambrose, Sextus, Lady Dorothy and Gertie...but no Chief Superintendent Chivers who, by then, was on his way back to Cheltenham police headquarters.

'So what is it that you've found this time, Miss Lavender, that brings us all out on this chilly Spring evening?' Dom Ambrose asked while shivering in the cold air.

'This, Father' Boo answered simply as she pointed to the small hole in the cracked plaster.

The Abbot and Sextus drew closer, pointing the beam from their torches at the break in the plaster of the pillar.

'I can't see...' Dom Ambrose said squinting at the small break in the plaster before exploding. '...Good God! Oh, I do beg your pardon, ladies and gentlemen! Miss Lavender, is that what I think it is?'

'What do you think it is, Father?'

While they were talking, Sextus bent closer before suddenly standing upright, eyes wide in shock. He stood rooted to the spot trying to speak. Finally he spluttered, 'It...it can't be, Boo'

'I think you'll find you're wrong, Sextus...I believe it is!' Boo said full of the joys of Spring.

'But it looks like...like...'

'Come on then, say it, man' Boo hollered at her friend.

'...like gold! I mean, if this whole pillar is gold inside that plaster, why...it would be worth a fortune!' and Sextus fell into silence again, stunned by the magnitude of the find.

'Am I understanding you correctly, Miss Lavender, are you saying that this whole pillar behind the plaster is solid gold?' a completely baffled Lady Dorothy asked.

'That is exactly what I think, Lady Dorothy' Boo replied in a more measured tone now that the shock of her find had subsided. 'Obviously, it will have to be tested to confirm that. But, at first glance, it does appear to be...solid gold'

Everyone in the garden fell silent before the Abbot blurted:

'Miss Lavender, if this is...gold' he struggled to say the word 'you will have secured the Abbey's future for the next hundred years'

'Is that all, Father?' Boo joked.

Those within the Community with better hearing had by now heard what was being said and were relaying it to the older, hard of hearing, members.

Gasps and cheers were erupting once again. A find like the one in the afternoon comes once in a lifetime but now this find; the whole Community couldn't believe their luck.

Pulling himself together, with enormous difficulty, the Abbot asked Father Ignatius to call police HQ and request that the Chief Superintendent perform a U-turn, with his two constables in tow.

'We'll need someone to stand guard over this latest find until...' he was suddenly lost for words '...until we can get it to a place of safety' he finally managed to get out.

What next everyone wondered...not least Miss Lavender.

Ninety Nine

Charlie Chivers was regaling his two younger colleagues with stories of his exploits at Scotland Yard when the call to return to the Abbey came over the radio. The controller could not give an explanation as to why they were needed but when duty called: Charlie Chivers was always ready to answer.

Eighteen and one half minutes after turning on the Winkworth Gongs, the squad car pulled up outside the rusting gates of the Abbey.

'Please do not tell me that there's been another murder' the Chief Superintendent prayed silently.

Charlie and the two young constables marched up the gravel path to the front door to be greeted by Father Ignatius, who'd been looking out for them.

'Good evening Chief Superintendent. Thank you for coming. I think I'd better let Father Abbot explain everything to you. Let me lead the way'

'Something's not right here' Charlie thought. 'Father Ignatius is smiling! All the time I've been here and I've never seen his lips move in an upward direction. No, something's not right'

Unable to work out what it was, Charlie followed the cleric along the corridors towards...

'Isn't his office that way, Father?' Charlie enquired pointing to another corridor.

'Father Abbot's not there' the monk replied mysteriously as he kept walking without turning around.

They lapsed into silence as Charlie and the two constables were led outside.

'Now I really am confused'

As they approached the garden, they could see torchlight beams crisscrossing the whole area.

'What's going on here, Father?'

'Oh, you'll see' was all that was said in reply.

At the archway, Dom Ambrose was giving instructions to members of the Community when he saw Charlie.

'Ah, Chief Superintendent, good of you to come' he called out.

'What is it, Father? Please don't tell me you've found something untoward?'

That took the wind out of the Abbot's sails for a moment but he recovered saying:

'No, Chief Superintendent. But come and have a look at what our clever Miss Lavender has found now'

Charlie squeezed passed the monks who were milling around in the garden, approaching the place where the treasure had been discovered.

'Charlie,' Miss Lavender called out, forgetting that she only called him that out of earshot of the general public, when she saw him approach 'lovely to see you again so soon'

'So what've you been up to now, Miss Lavender?'

'Have a look for yourself'

Boo handed him her torch and Charlie flashed the light at the area she pointed at.

'Bloody hell!' he exclaimed.

The expletive was out of his mouth before his hand could reach his mouth to hold it in.

'Please excuse me everyone, it's been a long day' he whispered to Boo: 'You might have warned me, Miss Lavender! How did you...I mean, is it really...'

'Charlie, if you'd like to complete a question I might be able to answer you' she replied cheekily.

'I'm stumped, Miss' he finally got out.

Boo took pity on him and retold the story of her latest discovery.

'Unbelievable' was all he could say.

'I've been thinking about it, Charlie,' Miss Lavender began hesitantly 'I can only assume that the monks at that time must have been trying to melt down as much of their gold wares like their chalices and ostensoria or monstrances, as I think they were called, before the King's men arrived to plunder the place and then plastered around it. Anything that they couldn't melt down, they simply wrapped up and hid within the built-up wall. Amazing really. And then to leave that riddle! Genius!'

Dom Ambrose approached them and addressed Charlie.

'Do you think your men would be able to stand guard until we can remove it to a place of safety, Chief Superintendent?'

'I don't think there'll be any problem, Father. I'll just have to clear it with HQ'

'Please use the telephone in my study'

Charlie instructed his men to stand guard while he called in and arranged for another couple of constables to come out to act as relief for his men.

When he returned, Boo took him and Sextus aside and said:

'Could I have that word with you both now? It's been so busy recently we haven't had a chance and this thing is beginning to play on my mind'

They both agreed and all three of them went off to find a quiet spot.

Boo poked her head around the door of the Bibliotheca; it was empty. Everyone was in the garden trying to make things as secure as possible before supper.

'Now then, gentlemen,' Boo opened as they took their seats 'I have a very big favour to ask of you both and you, in particular, Charlie'

'How can we refuse the heroine of the hour, Boo? Ask away' declared Sextus who was still flying high.

'Yes, Miss Lavender, what is it you want from us?' the Chief Superintendent asked a caution in his voice.

'It's...it's...' It was Boo's turn to be tongue-tied. 'What I want to ask you is...' she began again '...is: would you consider leaving Angus out of your report, Charlie, and for you Sextus to keep quiet about his role in the whole affair and letting the other two "take the rap" as I believe our American friends call it? And before either of you reach a decision, let me explain'

The two men settled down into their seats to hear Miss Lavender's reasons for this most unusual request.

'It's been playing on my mind about young Angus...'

Charlie interrupted. 'He was a murderer and a thief, Miss, let's not forget that'

'Charlie, I know, and what he did was unforgivable but he did pay the ultimate price for his crimes. However, when he explained why he did it, I could understand it ...to a point...'

338

Charlie opened his mouth to speak.

'Please, Charlie, let me finish and, at the end of it, if you feel for whatever reason, that you can't keep his name out of it, then I will accept your decision'

'As long as we are in agreement on that, then please continue' Charlie agreed, mollified.

'Phew, it's been quite a day' Boo confessed, gathering her thoughts. 'Anyway, where was I? Oh yes, there are a number of reasons why I think it would not be unreasonable to do it. One, he saved my life; there is no doubt about that. Then, he lost his own life trying, I believe, to save others who were present. Also, he was traumatised by the murder of his father which again, I believe, affected the balance of his mind. But my main reason for asking you is for the sake of Lady Dorothy and Gertie. They are the innocent parties in all of this. At this point in time, they think their son and brother is a hero, sacrificing his own life for the sake of others. They have also lost a husband and a father who was entirely without blame. For them to have lost Angus only to find out later that he was a thief and a murderer, well, I think they've been through enough and, frankly, don't deserve it. They've got enough to bear on their fragile shoulders. And let's be honest, gentlemen, the other two were thoroughly bad pennies with long criminal records. What difference would it make to the outcome, Charlie, if in the end a little more of the...' Boo thought about the word she was searching for '...responsibility was attributed to them? Would it harm anyone? Would it change the outcome?'

Boo stopped. She'd said her piece. Now she waited for Charlie and Sextus to speak.

The two of them sat, Sextus folding his hands in his lap, and considered the arguments put to them by Boo.

Each of them had their own thoughts on crime, justice and punishment.

But equally, they were also thoroughly decent men who had a sense of fairness and without consulting one another, they both came to same conclusion: the only ones who would suffer now would be the innocent: in this case, Lady Dorothy and The Honourable Gertie.

Angus MacDorn-Smythe, Frankie Benson and Freddie Cornwall had escaped justice in this world; whatever they were facing in the next was neither Sextus nor Charlie's concern.

After spending some minutes weighing up the pros and cons, they eyed each other up and nodded. Instinctively, they knew that they were in agreement. What Miss Lavender had proposed made sense for the living...and the dead.

'Very well, Miss Lavender, we agree' Charlie announced eventually.

'Thank the Good Lord for that!' Boo cried out. 'Now can we please celebrate?'

Before they rose from their chairs, there was a knock at the door and Lady Dorothy entered. Sextus and the Chief Superintendent stood up.

'Good evening all' she remarked. 'I thought I could hear voices. My, my...what an exciting day...and all thanks to you, Miss Lavender. And' she said casting a look around the room 'may I say the Library is looking rather splendid. What a wonderful job you've made of it. Would you mind if I join you?' asked the lady who had been the topic of discussion not two minutes earlier.

'Thank you for your kind words, Lady Dorothy' Boo replied slightly disconcerted. 'But we were just about to join the others for supper. Would you care to walk along with us?'

'I would love to. I was going to freshen up but I don't think anyone will mind tonight, do you?' Her mood appeared to have lightened. Maybe the Abbey's good luck had taken her mind off things.

Although slightly dishevelled himself from his toils in the garden Sextus piped up: 'Not at all, Lady Dorothy, you look absolutely fine'

All four toddled along to the Refectory where the noise emanating from it was like the monkey enclosure in London Zoo at feeding time.

'All in all, a good day's work' the saviour of the Abbey thought.

One Hundred

By way of a thank you to the Chief Superintendent, Dom Ambrose invited him to join the top table: an honour indeed.

In the end, the Abbot did decide to open a case of 1928 Chateau Margaux, a bottle of which was placed on each of the tables. Hence, Boo supposed, the uproar and racket like the chimps' tea party. The monks clearly did not indulge in "the hard stuff" very often.

Father Ignatius, Boo noticed, looked like he was three sheets to the wind, giggling like a schoolgirl while he ladled big fluffy roast potatoes onto each of the plates.

At last, feeling that the crises were finally over, Boo was pleased that she had brought some cheer to the Abbey and its residents after the events of the last few weeks. After a glass of the fine, earthy wine, she felt a little tipsy herself.

'Good stuff' her frazzled brain thought.

'Fancy a game tonight, Sextus?' Dom Ambrose asked over Lady Dorothy's shoulder. Both she and Gertie had resumed eating in the Refectory.

'I'm game if you are Boo. Are you up for it?' enquired her jovial bridge partner.

'I'd love to have a game but I'm not sure I'd be able to recognise the dots on the cards' and then hiccupped. 'Oh, I do beg your pardon!' she apologised.

The entire top table erupted into raucous laughter.

Boo blushed.

'Perhaps another small glass, Miss Lavender?' the Abbot asked of his heroine, tipping a little into her glass before she could answer.

'Oh, go on then, Father, you're only young once' she mumbled fuzzily.

Sextus observed his friend of long-standing. It'd been a long time since he'd seen her so relaxed.

'What an amazing woman! She's catalogued the Abbey's library, found the most extraordinary first editions, solved three murders...and now ends up saving the Abbey from ruin. Hats off to you, Boo' he ended as he caught her eye and toasted her.

Dom Ambrose who was feeling the effects of the heady Merlot himself saw what Sextus did and, on an impulse, picked up his hand bell and rung it for silence. It took a little longer than normal but tonight he was prepared to make allowances.

'Please, everyone, I'd like to propose a toast to our saviour, the genius that is our own Miss Lavender, not only for putting our Library back into some kind of order...'

There were a couple of 'Here, here's!'

'...but for saving this, our little oasis of tranquillity in this troubled world we live in today'

Everyone rose from their seats and raised their glasses.

'To Miss Lavender, a brave and courageous spirit!' the Abbot toasted.

'Miss Lavender!' they all toasted and cheered, then began to applaud.

In the meantime, Miss Lavender sat, her colour rising, basking in the standing ovation in her honour.

The Abbot reached out, took her hand and encouraged her to stand, which she did, a little giddily.

The applause increased and Boo bowed, very humbly, acknowledging the respect they had accorded her. Brother Jerome, the cook, gave a loud wolf whistle which quickly drew a very strong disapproving look from his Superior. He removed his fingers from his lips, remembering, a little too late, that he was not on the football terraces now.

That night, not a few heavy snores could be heard along the corridors of the sleeping quarters of the Abbey...and that included the visitors' rooms as well.

Meanwhile, the two young police constables, armed with flasks of good hearty soup, sandwiches and tea provided by Brother Jerome stood guard over Miss Lavender's latest find: the solid gold pillar.

Life would never be the same...for any of them.

One Hundred and One

The following morning, Boo and Sextus attended church for the last time where special prayers were offered up for the dearly departed. Miss Lavender's name was also given a special mention, although the lady herself did not fully appreciate it as she was feeling a little the worse for wear. A drinker's life was not for Miss Lavender.

After breakfast, Sextus and Boo packed their cases. Before departing, they decided they wanted to have one final look at the gold pillar in daylight. As it had been for the last few days, the temperature was still on the fresh side. Nevertheless, the sun glinted off the stripped down pillar sending colourful flashes of light to all corners of the garden while trying to coax the trees into full blossom but without too much success.

They arrived at the entrance to the garden where two fresh-faced young probationers were standing to attention as if they were on guard duty at Buckingham Palace.

'Good morning, Ma'am. Good morning, Sir' they both responded to Boo and Sextus' greeting.

'We've come to have one more look at the pillar, if we may, before we leave'

'Right you are, Ma'am' they said, saluting.

In the sunlight, the pillar, with its plaster chipped away, looked almost unreal. 'How much gold is in this?' Boo wondered not for the first time. Sextus was thinking the exact same thing.

They both stood in front of it, in silence, both gently stroking the surface of the gold as if it were a favourite pet's coat.

'Amazing, isn't it, Boo? It's been covered up, holding up this building for over four hundred years and it took you, my friend...' Boo looked at him, embarrassed by her friend's praise '...yes, my astute friend's sharpness of wit to work out that it was here. I'm honoured to call you my friend, Boo Lavender'

'Thank you, Sextus, but I couldn't have done it without you and Charlie. It was a team effort' Boo replied self-deprecatingly.

'I suppose we all added our bit' Sextus said thoughtfully. 'Well, best be off'

Despite the horrors which had occurred since she'd arrived there, Boo had grown attached to this place, even more so, now that a sense of peace and tranquillity had returned and was to be found once again within its gates.

With a last glance back, Boo and Sextus walked with heavy feet to their cars.

The entire Community came out to wave them off including Gertie and Lady Dorothy who would not now have to face a life of poverty with her only surviving family member...but only Dom Ambrose and Lady Dorothy would ever know that.

Boo followed Sextus along the quiet country roads back to their own corner of the wonderful Gloucestershire countryside. She couldn't wait to see little Hamish; how she'd missed him! And, it would be nice to get back to her routine: driving her trusty library bus, Old Blunder, around the countryside: her readers: the gossip (she had a lot to catch up with!): a decent game of bridge...even the bickering between Sextus and Mildred would be welcome.

'Oooh, the list is getting longer by the minute' she thought. The left-hand indicator popped out of the side of her little Austin as she turned off onto the Cheltenham Road and left Sextus to continue on to Bishops Cleeve. With one final beep-beep of farewell, she would be home well before Sextus.

One Hundred and Two

The following day, things returned to normal, almost as if Miss Lavender had never been away.

Five minutes before the alarm clock was due to go off, Hamish leapt onto his mistress' bed and stood next to the head poking out of the covers, watching for the first sign of her eyes being opened.

At the first flutter, he was on her, tail wagging, tongue licking and generally jumping around like the wild animal he was!

'Oh, it's so lovely to be home, Hamish' she yawned in delight as she tentatively stretched her arms out from under the blankets, checking the level of chill in the air. 'To sleep in one's own bed and be woken by my boy: what more could anyone want?'

A short while later, Miss Lavender, dressed and with walking stick in hand put young Mr Hamish on the lead before setting off for her morning constitutional.

By eight o'clock, she'd set off for the Library and parked up beside Old Blunder who, very kindly, started up first time with a roar and belch of thick black smoke.

'That's my girl!' Boo declared, laughing. 'It's good to be back'

With a chill still persisting in the bright Spring air, Boo ran the engine and turned the heater on full blast to heat the interior.

'Can't have my readers catching a chill' she concluded as she strolled along the aisle, eyes on high alert for any miscreant volumes.

When everything seemed to be shipshape, Miss Lavender popped into the Library to catch up on her paperwork and pick up the latest additions for the mobile library.

'Quite a few interesting ones here this time' she observed as she flipped through the fiction first before checking the non-fiction offerings '...now who was it that wanted the latest Miss Marple mystery? Was it Rosemary? Hmm, I'm not sure but it is her kind of thing. Anyway...'

Shortly afterwards, she was on her way to the first stop of the day: Upper Slaughter.

As the week progressed, it didn't take her long to catch up with all the gossip she'd missed while she was away. Not only was the gossip go-round still alive and kicking, it was positively blooming like the rest of Nature by then.

The prize for the most interesting titbit, Miss Lavender decided, went to the Bibury branch, where, apparently the Misses Whittam had had a spectacular falling out with Colonel Forbes over his Springer spaniel Roddie's continual use of their magnificent Weigela shrubs as a place to leave small deposits. Miss Lavender was very glad that she didn't live in Bibury; Mr Hamish was none too particular where he left his "little messages".

When the time came for Chipping Campden to receive its visit from Old Blunder, Miss Lavender remembered to put the item Miss Cosworthy had asked her to pick up from the jewellers in Cheltenham in her handbag.

'I wonder how things would have wound up without it?'

One of Miss Cosworthy's neighbours, Mr Witherspoon, a retired gardener, was trimming her hedges when Miss Lavender arrived and called out a greeting to her.

'How is she?' Miss Lavender asked in a loud whisper. It was only afterwards that Miss Lavender remembered that she could have hollered it at the top of her voice and Miss Cosworthy wouldn't have heard it but, no matter, Mr Witherspoon's reply was a sad shake of the head and his thumb making a downward motion.

'Oh dear, I do hope she's all right'

Even though she wouldn't be able to hear, out of courtesy, Miss Lavender knocked at the door of the cottage before turning the key in the lock and letting herself in. As her infirmity had worsened, Miss Cosworthy depended on neighbours for shopping and company and the simplest way to let them in was to leave the key in the door: it's what country people do.

To make sure she didn't go without over the weekend, the local headmaster would send one of the older children over, after school on a Friday, to ask if there was anything she needed from the corner shop which doubled up as the village Post Office.

But Miss Cosworthy's most welcome, and favourite, visitor was always Miss Lavender. Not only because she brought with her a wonderfully diverse collection of books which allowed Miss Cosworthy's mind and soul, if not her body, to fly free from the confines of her comfortable prison; but gossip, the darling of the chattering classes, to be readily exchanged and updated.

Miss Lavender quietly opened the door to the sitting room and poked her head around the door to see her friend sitting dozing on her favourite chair, a faded dark green velvet winged-chair. Quickly surveying the room, it was clear that a duster hadn't been flicked over its surfaces for some time, and that, together with a number of half-empty cups of unfinished tea dotted around, caused Miss Lavender some concern. Her friend was a stickler for tidiness and order. And it was quite clear from the state of the room that something was amiss. But what was it? The opening of the door probably caused a change in the air pressure in the room and Miss Cosworthy stirred.

'Wha...t...?' she uttered, a little confused.

'Hello, Miss Cosworthy, it's Hilary...Hilary Lavender. How are you?' the kindly Librarian said in a loud voice.

'Oh, Miss Lavender, how lovely to see you' she said brightening up 'I have missed you'

'Well I'm back into my routine now and I must say I've missed you. But how are you? Has anything happened?'

As always with Boo Lavender, she stopped there. She'd said what she needed to say and would now allow the other person a chance to answer. In this case: as long as she needed.

'Oh, Miss Lavender, where do I start? The gentleman who took over when you were away was very nice and polite but...I don't mean to be rude when I say this but he hadn't a clue!' The last few words came out in a rush as her voice quickly rose in pitch.

Boo frowned and inclined her head as if to say: 'How so?' Miss Cosworthy continued:

'The books he brought...cookery books...gardening books...books for old ladies! Bah! Nothing like what you bring me. When I read one of your selections, I am transported. From the time I open it, I am in that place described in the book whether it's a murder mystery or one of those wonderful travel books you give me from time to time. One of my all-time favourites was Gerald Durrell's "My Family and Other Animals". There were times when I was walking with him on that island in Greece. Corfu, I think it was. Can you believe it? Marvellous'. As

347

she spoke, she became more and more animated. She stopped for a moment to catch her breath; Miss Lavender could see that Miss Cosworthy had transported herself back to one of the scenes in the book as she was speaking.

'She's probably strolling with Mr Durrell right now' Miss Lavender decided.

Boo left her to her reverie. How could she not? Miss Cosworthy's face was glowing with sheer pleasure. She was definitely somewhere else. 'And why not?' thought Boo 'That's what books are for: to take us out of ourselves, forget our problems for a little while and hopefully when we come back, we'll feel just a tiny bit better because we've given ourselves a break from it'

Miss Cosworthy came out of her dream and continued:

'I mean, I'm sure he meant well but he just didn't know me like you do, Miss Lavender'

'Well, in fairness, Miss Cosworthy, I have been supplying you with reading material for...a very long time'

'I've...missed you' Miss Cosworthy announced forlornly.

'Have you, dear?' and Boo again let the question hang in the ether. 'It's not only good to take up reading to help us forget our problems for a while: it's also good to share them'

'Yes I have' she said nodding her head, looking into the distance.

Boo waited and was rewarded with the reason why Miss Cosworthy appeared to be going downhill.

'I've missed you, Miss Lavender and I've come to realise that as I have become less and less mobile I have to depend on others...something I've never been good at. But with you, I get the whole package: good reads, catching up on the latest news and over the last few weeks when you've been away...I've been feeling low'

'Ah ha! Now we're getting to it'

'But now you're back...' she hesitated and then her eyes opened in surprise. 'But how rude am I? I haven't even offered you a cup of tea' and suddenly, she was up and shuffling off in the direction of the kitchen.

'Do you need any help?' Boo called out.

No response.

'Deaf as a doorpost' Boo thought shaking her head.

Minutes later, Miss Cosworthy appeared with a tea tray and a plate of ginger nuts.

'How kind' Miss Lavender thought.

As she went to sit down, Miss Cosworthy noticed, as if for the first time, the half-empty cups of tea strewn around the room.

'Please leave the tea to mash for a couple of minutes, Miss Lavender, while I tidy away these cups. And look at the dust on this table. What have I been thinking about? Tsk, tsk'

Five minutes of brisk polishing brought the shine back to the furniture in the room, with Miss Cosworthy's circular rosewood dining table reflecting the brilliant sunlight into every corner of the room.

Disappearing for a few minutes, Miss Cosworthy re-entered with combs in her hair and her appearance freshened up.

'That's more like it, dear' Boo thought. 'A visit from an old friend can make a big difference. Shall I be mother?'

'Yes, please, Miss Lavender. And do tell me everything, and I do mean everything, about what happened in that Abbey. Brackenbury, wasn't it?'

'Not lost all of your marbles yet, have you, Enid?' Boo concluded as she poured.

'Yes, it was' she answered. 'Well, let me begin by saying: would you believe it if I told you that, if it weren't for you, Miss Cosworthy, myself and most of the inhabitants of the Abbey would be dead by now?'

'Never!' Miss Cosworthy said almost dropping her ginger nut into her teacup in the excitement of it all.

'It's the truth' began Miss Lavender and for the next half an hour Miss Cosworthy was spellbound by the blow-by-blow account of what went on at the Abbey.

When she'd finished, Miss Cosworthy said:

'So you were able to hear that scoundrel plotting to kill everybody with the help of my little hearing aid?'

'Exactly' Miss Lavender agreed emphatically.

'Well, I can't believe it' Miss Cosworthy declared.

349

But Miss Lavender could see a complete change in her friend's demeanour and mental alertness from when she'd arrived.

'I'd better not leave it so long next time. A bit of female company and a little gossip to keep the mind sharp and Miss Cosworthy will be with us for a long time yet'

When all the gossip had been caught up with, Miss Lavender took her leave and promised to bring a fresh batch of reads for her friend the following week.

One Hundred and Three

The following Tuesday evening found Boo attending Mildred's for the bridge evening... alas, it was her turn...again.

She'd made her 'special' rock cakes which, historically, even Sextus struggled with.

'Fill your boots, ladies and gentleman!' she announced as she brought the plate of steaming hot burnt offerings to the table.

The others looked on with a little less than relish. But Sextus had a cunning plan.

'D'you know,' he began in an absent-minded sort of way 'I forgot what day of the week it was and I ate before I came out. I shall have one of these little blighters, Mildred,' reaching for the smallest one '...but I shall have to be abstemious for the rest of the evening'. Sextus was not the best of liars. They all knew that when push came to shove, Sextus could eat for England. Boo and Kitty drew him a filthy look; they'd have to eat (or hide) more of them. Mildred was completely oblivious. 'Ah well, more for the girls to feast on!' she declared through the haze of smoking emanating from her side of the table.

Another round of filthy looks directed at Sextus.

When Mildred went out to refill the teapot, Kitty whispered viciously under her breath:

'I'll make you pay, Sextus Phipps, if it's the last thing I do! You see if I don't.' Poor Kitty! She had the appetite of a sparrow and, by the end of the evening, a handbag bulging at the seams. Well, they had to be eaten (or at least appear to have been).

Sextus simply smiled serenely but he knew he couldn't use that excuse too often for even the seemingly oblivious Mildred would begin to suspect.

During their respite from the fray, Boo and Sextus were questioned by Mildred and Kitty who'd read every single lurid detail of their sojourn at Brackenbury Abbey.

'...I couldn't believe it when I read it, Boo. A member of the aristocracy poisoned by ne'er-do-wells...and in a monastery. What is this country coming to? And it was you, wasn't it, who found an entire wall of solid gold hidden for centuries behind another secret wall?' Mildred asked, repeating almost word for word what she'd read.

'I wouldn't believe everything you read, Mildred dear' Boo said patiently. 'It was a pillar of gold not a wall but the wall did happen to be filled with precious artefacts. Of course, I couldn't have done it without the help of Sextus'

'And to think we said that nothing exciting would happen when you went there' exclaimed Kitty in amazement.

'In some ways it was very gratifying, but in others, it was terribly sad. A total of six people lost their lives...and all over money. Tragic. But, at least, the money raised from the find will help to secure the Abbey's future. So, I suppose, in some ways, good can come out of bad'. As she spoke, Boo bowed her head as a picture of The Honourable Angus' inert body lying in the Refectory came to mind followed by memories of the short time she'd spent in the company of Johnnie MacDorn-Smythe.

Oblivious to the sudden stillness which had settled over her friend, Mildred turned to Sextus and said:

'And you, Sextus, I read that one of the villains was going to shoot the lot of you but you saved the day'

Sextus decided that there was a long and a short version of what had happened that night. In the end, he just agreed with Mildred's version and left it there. He was quite a modest sort of chap.

'Well, yes, Mildred, I suppose I did' he concurred.

'Without Sextus' intervention, I don't know what would have happened. We'd probably all have been murdered!' Boo averred, returning from the dark place she'd visited and threw her hands in the air in mock horror to inject a bit of spice into it for the girls.

'I forgive you' Kitty whispered out of the side of her mouth, glancing sideways at Sextus while clenching her jewelled cigarette holder between her teeth.

Sextus understood exactly what Kitty meant but Mildred was confused.

'What for?' she asked, taken aback.

'Oh, just something' was Kitty's mysterious response.

'No wonder I prefer trains' concluded Mildred. 'They're dependable, run on time and what you see is what you get. Whereas...'

'Yes, thank you, Mildred' Boo intervened before Mildred got into the whole thing. 'Now where were we? Oh yes, one spade': Boo's opening bid. The evening ended with a resounding...draw. A long time since that had happened.

'Well, thank you, Mildred, for a lovely evening' Sextus said as the three visitors donned their coats to face the chilly evening journey home. But being Sextus, he couldn't resist having the last word.

'And I'm so sorry I couldn't indulge in your rock cakes tonight, Mildred...'

Before he could say anymore, Mildred interrupted saying:

'Don't worry, Sextus. Next time I'll put a few extra in for you to take home. You won't go without when you come to your Auntie Mildred's, no fear'

The enigmatic look on Boo and Kitty's faces, which some might have mistaken for smirks, would have put the Mona Lisa's to shame.

A thought came to Kitty:

'Revenge is a dish...of Mildred's rock cakes made especially for you, Sextus Phipps, you fiend'

'That's very thoughtful of you, Mildred' Kitty offered who couldn't resist it.

'Yes, indeed, Mildred, very thoughtful' agreed Boo, rubbing a little more salt into Sextus' wounds. 'You'll look forward to that, won't you, Sextus?'

'Why can't I learn to keep my mouth closed when I'm winning?' he realised despairingly.

'...er, yes. Lovely' was the less than enthusiastic response.

'Serves you right, you horror! Boo thought mischievously.

'Oh, and before I forget, is everyone up for a night out at the theatre and dinner afterwards?' Sextus enquired.

'Boo mentioned it and I'm game' was Kitty's reply.

'Me too, count me in' Mildred agreed excitedly.

'Excellent.' Sextus said. 'I'll check what's on and book it'

A few minutes later, an aerial view of the Gloucester countryside around Mildred's cottage would have shown three sets of headlights heading in different directions.

One Hundred and Four

'It always happens when you least expect it' Boo's mamma used to say.

And in this case, it could not have been truer.

It occurred one Saturday morning, a couple of months after Boo's exploits at Brackenbury Abbey.

The postman delivered the post: gas and electricity bills ('Why do they always have to come together?' grumbled Boo) but tucked in alongside them was a letter written, Miss Lavender noted, in the most beautiful, flowing handwriting.

'Has to be a scholar' she decided after studying the perfectly-formed, fluid letters for a few moments.

The address read: Miss H B Lavender, Daffodil Cottage, off Shurdington Road, Cheltenham

Upon opening the fine quality vellum envelope, an invitation on stiff hand-cut card, edged in gold and written in the style of an illuminated manuscript with blues and golds, reds and greens, was inside from the Abbot, Dom Ambrose. It requested the presence of Miss Hilary B Lavender at the official opening of the exhibition to celebrate the 700th Anniversary of Brackenbury Abbey on 15th June.

His Eminence, Cardinal Xavier Alexander Davy, the most senior Catholic cleric in England, would be opening the exhibition which would be preceded by a sung High Mass. In conversation with Sextus since their visit, Boo found out that the Abbey choir had the reputation of being able to knock out a good tune. Or put it another way, their "Credo" would '...bring a tear to the most atheist of ears' or so Sextus' mixed metaphor claimed.

'High Mass, eh? Hmm. All that incense, Gregorian chant and Latin? What to do?'. There was a lot for Boo to take in.

She had her doubts. But after what they'd all been through, she came to the conclusion that it was incumbent upon her to attend.

'I'd better get myself off to Cheltenham to get "kitty-ed out"' she was considering when the telephone began to ring.

'Cheltenham 624, Hilary Lavender speaking'

'Hello, Boo. Sextus here. How are you?'

'I was just thinking about ringing you'

'Ha! Beat you to it' he laughed. 'You've just received your invitation as well, I presume?'

'Of course, and you have too' she now understood why he'd called.

'Full sung High Mass. What d'you think of that, my fine Anglican friend?'

'Well...' began Boo hesitantly.

'You'll be fine, Boo, and besides, you love classical music. It's just you won't know the words to sing along to'

'Sextus don't be so frivolous. You make it sound like a knees-up in a public house!'

'It's probably the equivalent of one of them in the Middle Ages'

'Sextus, you obviously are not worried about the day you have to take that long walk up to those Pearly Gates. There's a man there who might want to have a word with you about your flippant blasphemy!'

'Oh, if only that was all I had to worry about, Boo, I'd be fine. No, I think I'll be trying to sneak in the back door using dodgy ration coupons!' and he hooted.

'Sextus Phipps, if you were a member of our congregation you'd be thrown out. However, I know where you're coming from and hope that the Good Lord takes pity on you'

'Amen to that. Now down to practicalities; shall I drive that day or you? There's no point in wasting petrol. I can't believe it's still on ration. I noticed in The Telegraph the other day that nearly every other European country has done away with rationing and yet we still have it...and all those other countries are much cheaper. The other day I was charged six shillings in Cheltenham: six shillings for one gallon. Can you believe it?'

The chatter then descended into chit-chat about the price of this and that and how in the "good old days...." etc.

But Boo's mind was made up: she would attend the opening.

One Hundred and Five

On the morning of 15th June, the sun was high in the sky and not a cloud was to be seen. Everywhere the birds twittered from trees whose branches, thick with leaves, swayed gently in the warm summer breeze. Honey bees made their way hither and thither busily collecting pollen from Miss Lavender's neatly laid out garden; they were showing particularly interested at the moment in her geraniums and roses.

'Maybe He does look after his own' Boo decided, looking up at the cloudless sky out of her bedroom window before donning the new outfit she'd purchased from Kitty's emporium the previous week. It was only thanks to Kitty's generous 'friend's' discount together with the income from bequests left to her by a number of well-to-do spinster aunts that allowed Boo to shop at Kitty's exclusive ladies' boutique. Her own modest Librarian's salary would have precluded her from ever crossing the threshold.

The very fetching navy two-piece, finely edged in cream, was hanging on the side of her wardrobe, complimented by a pale blue, high-necked blouse with a small motif of abstract pattern and topped off with the, de rigueur, item of Prince of Wales pattern; this one, in the form of a cloche hat matching the cream piping of her suit. Her shoes and bag matched, of course, and were of a light cream colour. They were designed by one of a new batch of designers to emerge from post-war Paris and a firm favourite of Kitty's, Hubert de Givenchy. To complete her outfit, Boo slipped her hands into the final item of her wardrobe; lovely new soft white cotton gloves. On grand occasions like these, a lady always wore gloves.

As she took a quick twirl in front of the mirror, a car horn beeped; it was, of course, Sextus.

Earlier, after her morning constitutional, she'd dropped Hamish off at Dumpty's, so with one final check to see that the gas was out and the lights were off, she closed the door and placed the key under the mat before walking out to be greeted by a waft of sun-warmed air.

She paused for a moment, eyes closed appreciating the surroundings of her beloved Daffodil Cottage; sniffing and identifying the myriad floral scents; listening to the chatter of the birds before lifting her face towards the warmth given out by the fiery globe in a sky of endless blue.

'Come on, old girl! Better get a move on' Sextus called out from the window he'd wound down.

One deep breath later, she opened her eyes and marched over to the passenger door to be driven to...well, something she was not expecting...at all.

One Hundred and Six

Fortunately, Sextus had allowed plenty of time to reach their destination. With the roads regularly blocked by tractors now that summer had arrived, he was wise not to take any chances but as luck would have it, they had a clear run, with only one minor delay.

What else? Sheep!

'How do they always manage to get out?' Boo wondered as Sextus shooed it back into the field.

As they approached the Abbey, Boo gave out a little gasp, not for the last time that day; gone were the rusty old gates to be replaced by shiny, newly painted black ones.

On duty at the gates was Brother Augustus: not a squeak was heard as he swung them open.

'Welcome, welcome!' he cried in delight, so happy to see the saviours of the Abbey again.

Sextus rolled down the window and the plump friar motioned to a space in front of the main building saying:

'Good morning, Mr Phipps, Miss Lavender, would you mind parking by the black Daimler, please?'

Sextus recognised the Primate of all England's chauffeur-driven motor, a black Vanden Plas, and mentioned it to Boo.

'...and jolly posh it is too' she remarked, admiring the immaculately polished limousine.

Sextus' little red Austin A40 looked rather insignificant beside it.

'I'd rather have parked somewhere else, Boo'

'Don't be so silly, Sextus. Your car is perfectly nice...and more than adequate for your needs'

'I suppose' he replied, still feeling a little overwhelmed.

As they got out of the car, Dom Ambrose approached grinning from ear to ear.

'Welcome back!' the Abbot called out, moving to the passenger side and offering his hand to Miss Lavender who accepted graciously.

'And how have our heroes been keeping?' he gushed merrily.

'Oh, Father, it was nothing' was Boo's response, blushing at a term she had only heard used for men who'd fought at the Front or a person who'd rescued someone from a blazing building.

''Nothing? Well, it's nothing if you don't count the rather large surplus residing in the Abbey's accounts at this moment. No, it's right that we should acknowledge your contribution to the Abbey's future. And to that end, we have a surprise for you'

'May one enquire what it is?' the lady Librarian asked.

'Not yet, my dear lady, but all will become clear very soon. But please, your timing is perfect. The Cardinal would like to meet you both'

'Timing?' queried Sextus.

'Elevenses, Sextus' Boo said almost in disbelief at Sextus' naiveté, before the Abbot could answer. 'Fortunately, I remembered to pack my ginger nuts'

'As if you'd forget, Boo' retorted her friend.

'Come' insisted Dom Ambrose. 'He's waiting in the Refectory'

Entering through the main door, memories began to stir for the friends: some good, some bad. Boo shivered.

'You alright, Boo?' Sextus enquired concernedly.

'Yes, thank you, Sextus, Monsignor Avrili just popped into my mind'

'Poor man'

'Yes, such an unnecessary death'. She sighed.

The rest of the winding corridors they walked along in silence with their own thoughts for company.

'Well, here we are' announced the Abbot.

'New gates, Ambrose and now new doors' enthused Sextus.

'Yes, Sextus, it was a bit parky without them' confided the Abbot about the replacement doors which bore a remarkable resemblance to the old ones. 'We were fortunate in that one of our parishioners was able to acquire them for us for a modest sum'

Had they known the cost, Boo and Sextus might have been tempted to disagree; antique doors of the quality of those lost when the police had to break them down in pursuit of Frankie Benson did not come cheap...nor would the pair have considered them to be in the "modest" bracket.

The Abbot pushed the doors open to be greeted by what Boo imagined the noise level would be like on the day of a Football Cup Final: deafening.

'My goodness!' Boo declared throwing up her gloved hands to cover her ears.

For Sextus, standing behind them, it brought back memories of the officers' mess as he broke into a grin at some of the more vivid ones.

'Loud, isn't it?' shouted the Abbot.

'I beg your pardon, Father?' Boo said.

'I said it's loud!' he repeated even louder.

'Er...yes' was Boo's response, not knowing what else to say.

'Let me introduce you to His Eminence' Dom Ambrose offered as he led them through the throng of visitors.

Here and there as he passed through the crowd, the Abbot nodded and occasionally shook a hand before they reached a small group standing by the top table.

Surrounded by a circle of local VIPs, some adorned with gold chains of office, the Cardinal turned and smiled as the Abbot approached. Old sourpuss, Bishop Newman, was standing by his side with what Boo initially regarded as a fixed "grin" but on second thoughts decided it was more like a "grimace". 'Not at all a very nice man', she decided. Dom Ambrose bent over close to the Cardinal's ear, cupped his hand and shouted:

'Your Eminence, let me introduce Miss Hilary Lavender and Mr Sextus Phipps. Miss Lavender is the Librarian who, not only catalogued our Library for the Anniversary celebrations, but discovered many fine First Editions in the course of doing so and it was she who was also responsible for finding the treasure which will secure our Abbey for many decades to come. Mr Phipps is her close friend who ably aided her in her search for the treasure'

He omitted to mention that she had almost single-handedly solved the murders which had taken place at that time; this was to be a time of celebration, not a time for raking over unfortunate events of the past. He then turned to Boo and Sextus and said:

'Miss Lavender, Mr Phipps, His Eminence, Cardinal Davy'

Boo was never one to be overawed by someone's position in society but, not being of the Faith, she was unsure how to address this dignitary. It didn't, however, stop Boo from noting the fine handmade black mohair suit with the black material surrounding the dog collar edged in red. Around his neck hung a gold chain with a crucifix, adorned with precious stones and, she noted, on his wedding finger, an intricately-wrought gold ring. The man himself, to Boo's trained eye, was of medium height, about seventy with a slight stoop and on top of a magnificent mop of snowy white hair sat a skullcap of, Boo guessed, red silk. An easy, gentle smile gave him an aura of quiet warmth, Boo concluded.

Sextus sensed his friend's unease and stepped forward to take the lead.

'Your Eminence' Sextus said a little in awe as he knelt to kiss the Cardinal's ring.

'Thank you, Mr Phipps, for your help in saving this very important part of our heritage' the Cardinal declared while he held onto Sextus' hand for a long moment.

'It was an honour, Your Eminence' the retired chemist beamed at the praise heaped upon him by someone he held in high esteem.

'And you, Miss Lavender!' Here the Cardinal turned to the Abbot 'Is this the lady after whom...' but before he could finish, the Abbot interrupted him.

'Yes, it is, Your Eminence, but...not yet'

'Oh, I see' the Cardinal replied mysteriously and smiled. Boo, however, didn't.

The Cardinal turned back to Boo and said:

'Very pleased indeed to make your acquaintance, Miss Lavender. I've heard all about what you did' he said, looking straight into her eyes.

She returned it knowing that he'd heard "all" of what she'd done; she was certain of that.

'And it's very nice to meet you, Sir' Boo replied shaking his hand firmly.

'Ah, I believe you are not of our faith, Miss Lavender?' the Cardinal enquired gently.

'No, Sir, I'm Church of England myself' Boo answered confidently.

'I know Archbishop Jeffries well. We often meet and dine together. It's so refreshing to hear another point of view...and we share a passion for jazz' he said, revealing a common interest.

Boo was well aware that Archbishop Jeffries as the Archbishop of Canterbury was Head of the Anglican Communion, but was surprised to hear that he met his opposite number of the Roman Faith on a regular basis socially.

All around them, people were eavesdropping, listening for titbits which they could share with friends: just as Miss Lavender did with Miss Cosworthy. A little bit of gossip goes a long way...in the countryside.

Within a few minutes, Boo was chatting to the Cardinal like an old friend. Whether it was down to him or her didn't matter. Because of their jobs, each of them could feel completely at ease in new company and both were quite used to breaking down social barriers.

Of course, it didn't take long for Sextus and Boo to find out that the Cardinal was fond of a game of bridge: although modest about his abilities, Boo could tell that he would be a formidable opponent. And so, it was arranged that later, in the privacy of the Abbot's office, the Abbot would partner the Cardinal for a rubber or two against Boo and Sextus before dinner.

'Boo Lavender,' Sextus later declared when they'd moved off to have some refreshment before High Mass at twelve o'clock 'I can't believe how clever you are. You've actually arranged to have a game with the Primate of All England. We'll have to let him win, of course'

'No chance, Sextus. No prisoners taken! Just imagine when you look at the Cardinal that you see Mildred. Then see if you're prepared to let him win'

'Well, put like that, Boo, His Eminence doesn't stand a chance. But what a nice surprise. It's going to be an interesting day'

More than either of them expected.

One Hundred and Seven

By five to twelve, the Chapel was bursting at the seams with guests. However, it turned out that Boo and Sextus had seats reserved in the front pew. As they waited for the service to begin, Boo donned her mantilla just as Lady Dorothy and The Honourable Gertie rolled up to join them.

'Lady Dorothy, how lovely to see you' exclaimed Boo '...and you Gertie. How are you both?'

'We're a lot better, Miss Lavender, thank you for asking. And how are you yourself?' Lady Dorothy answered sweetly; the dark rings under her eyes had all but faded but Boo could see that there was still a touch of sadness in her demeanour. Gertie just smiled but said nothing.

'I'm well, thank you, Lady Dorothy. Back into the old routine' she replied, thinking: 'I'll bet you'd give anything to be back to yours with your Johnnie and Angus; it must be hard'

'We must catch up over lunch' Lady Dorothy continued in a low whisper; talking in Church was frowned upon by Catholics, Boo remembered hearing.

The monks of the Abbey were, as always, sitting in the side pews which, for centuries, had kept them apart from the laity. The air was filled with incense wafting around the place '...like Old Blunder when she's on form' Boo thought cheekily but, truth be known, it was growing on her. A bit like her first encounter with blue cheese: once she overcame her initial suspicions, she had become rather partial to it.

Boo was fascinated by the swirling smoke dancing in the sunlight flooding through the stained glass windows of the Chapel onto the High Altar which was festooned with blazing candles and gloriously wild blooms from Brother Robert's garden; it was captivating. The shafts of coloured sunlight lit up the sanctuary through the haze of smoke creating an image which Boo would never forget.

'This is the first time I've seen the pomp and ceremony of a Roman Catholic service and I can see the attraction of it;

although, for myself, I still prefer the simplicity of Low Church' she decided at length.

The organ struck up a voluntary and the whole congregation stood.

Father Ignatius, at the head of the procession, walked slowly down the aisle bearing a tall brass cross in front of him; the monks who followed were dressed in albs and chasubles. They, in turn, were followed by the Abbot, hands joined in prayer, then the Bishop, who preceded the Cardinal, resplendent in a magnificent cope of gold thread with matching mitre.

As he moved slowly along the nave, the Cardinal turned from side to side blessing the congregation, leaning on the ornate crosier in his other hand.

After the Cardinal had changed into a chasuble at the altar, the service began.

The whole spectacle mesmerised Boo; she had never seen anything like it; for her it was like being a spectator at the Games in Ancient Rome.

Sextus had been right; the Gregorian chant was simply divine. It was not something Boo had listened to before but the haunting quality of the plain chant kept her captivated.

The service lasted one and a half hours but for Boo it could have gone on: it was almost too beautiful to stop.

But stop it did and shortly afterwards, lunch was served with Brother Jerome producing a lunch worthy of his old stomping ground, the Savoy.

Boo was seated between Dom Ambrose and Lady Dorothy: Sextus' lunch companions were the Cardinal and Gertie and a jolly time was had by one and all.

The bell rang to end the meal and after the prayer of thanksgiving, the Abbot announced that there would be a short break before the inauguration of the new Library by the Cardinal.

Boo was slightly taken aback: there hadn't been any mention of it before.

One Hundred and Eight

Boo and Sextus took a turn in the gardens before the inauguration.

'...it's funny, don't you think, Sextus, that Dom Ambrose never mentioned it before about the Library? I wonder what it is they've done?'

'Haven't a clue, Boo' was her friend's reply.

Except there was something in Sextus' tone which made Boo turn to look sharply at him: for sure, Boo decided, the rascal did have a clue...but was not telling. They continued on their promenade around the gardens soaking up the lush bouquet of the mishmash of wild and cultivated flowers as the bees went about zealously collecting their quotas of pollen. All around, the birds twittered and sang cheerily from the branches of every tree, adding to the peace and serenity of this place which had come to mean so much to Boo.

But that tone she'd heard in Sextus' voice; she was having difficulty putting her mental finger on what it meant.

'I mean, Sextus,' she continued 'I haven't been in contact with the Abbot since we left but I would have thought he'd have mentioned it to you at some point. You have spoken to him, haven't you?'

'Er...er...no...well actually, ye...s I have, but I can't recall...' stammered the man who seemed to have developed a convenient case of amnesia '...no...I can't recall...isn't that a beautiful hydrangea?' he suddenly blurted out, changing the subject completely.

Neither subtlety nor feigned innocence was Sextus' strong suit but then it dawned on Boo what had been bugging her: it wasn't amnesia he was suffering from; it was a severe case of shiftiness. He most certainly did remember; he chose not to disclose the content of that conversation, Boo concluded.

'Now I know you know something, Sextus Phipps' Boo had decided. She hadn't spent the best part of twenty-five years trying to read his bridge bidding without knowing when he was telling a great big fib.

'Do not!' was the vehement response.

'Do too!' came back the sharp riposte.

Fortunately for Sextus, the bell calling everyone to the ceremony saved him. The two friends walked back together enjoying the warm sunshine while Boo tried to work out what was going on...unsuccessfully.

One Hundred and Nine

As they neared the corridor leading to the Library, Boo was once again confronted by a near deafening noise; the football crowd were out in force again.

There must have been over a hundred and fifty people crowded into the small corridor leading to the Library...and all of them were conversing as if the person they were speaking to was on the other side of the room instead of inches away!

Boo could see that the entrance to the Library had been covered over by a large set of drapes.

'Whatever is going on, Sextus?' she asked, baffled.

But this time, Sextus was a little more forthcoming. 'Wait and see, Boo, it'll all be worth it. Trust me'

Out of the crowds of people milling around in the corridor, a diminutive figure in the form of Professor Beech, wobbly glass of bubbly in one hand and the obligatory Capstan in the other, held high in the air, in what had become the latest fashion with thespians, emerged. Clearly, it wasn't his first glass of fizz judging by his exuberant greeting.

'Miss Lavender, Mr Phipps, how lovely to see you both' the elderly bibliophile gushed 'How can we ever thank you, Miss Lavender? I mean what a marvellous idea! Was it yours?'

Before Boo could question the overexcited man of letters, he disappeared back into the crowd greeting other guests like long lost friends.

Puzzled, Boo turned to her friend to ask what the Professor had meant, but just as she opened her mouth the Abbot called everyone to order.

'Quiet please, everyone. Cardinal Davy would like to say a few words. And please, could you make way for our honoured guests'

The Abbot gently elbowed his way through the crowd to where Boo and Sextus were standing and much to Boo's surprise whispered:

'Please come and join us Miss Lavender...and you too, Sextus' and he led them back through the crowds.

The Cardinal was beaming.

'Ladies and gentlemen and honoured guests...' he began, nodding to Miss Lavender and Sextus '...it gives me great pleasure to announce today that Father Ambrose, the Abbot of Brackenbury Abbey has agreed to open the Abbey's Library of rare First Editions to scholars and to those members of the general public who have a particular interest in the subjects covered in these books'

An outburst of applause was followed by the Cardinal waving his hands around for hush.

The penny dropped for Boo: now she knew what the Professor had been talking about.

'...and...' he continued melodramatically '...I have great pleasure in opening the newly refurbished Library which has been renamed...'

Here he pulled a cord at the side of the drapes which slowly began to open.

'...the Hilary B Lavender Bibliotheca!'

Boo was absolutely stunned. She turned to look at Sextus who was grinning like a Cheshire cat.

'Did...did you know about this, Sextus?' she finally managed to say above the applause.

'I did, Boo' he acknowledged beaming and nodding at the shock on his dear friend's face.

'How...wonderful' was all she could manage.

Sextus drew Boo's attention to the large gold lettered plinth over the doorway of the Bibliotheca, it read:

"The Hilary B Lavender Bibliotheca' opened on 15th June by His Eminence, Cardinal Davy in celebration of the 700th Anniversary of Brackenbury Abbey in the year of Our Lord One Thousand Nine Hundred and Fifty Six AD"

The Cardinal shooed Boo in first.

'Go, go, go!' he urged.

Boo pushed the door open and her mouth fell open in silent delight.

There were newly constructed bookcases filled to bursting with the tomes she had catalogued.

She wandered around for the next few minutes pushing the odd wayward book back into its place; it made it easier for the eye to find things.

The rest of the invitees slowly filed in to view the Abbey's valuable collection. Some of the faces Boo knew and recognised; they all queued up to congratulate her.

'Sextus, I am flabbergasted. I had no idea, no inkling!' Boo admitted, beaming brighter than the summer sun outside.

'No more than you deserve, Boo. Honestly, what you've done for the Abbey, you can't begin to imagine. Ambrose told me that he's a changed man. No more stress and sleepless nights worrying about the Abbey's finances. You truly deserve this'

By about four o'clock, almost all of the invited guests had said their goodbyes.

Dom Ambrose caught Boo's eye and nodded towards his office: the time had come.

As they walked along the corridor, Boo felt the time was right to tell the Abbot about something which had been playing on her mind.

'You know, Father,' she confessed 'at one point, I believed you might be the suspect'

'Me...me, Miss Lavender?' the Abbot asked, taken back by her revelation.

'Yes, Father. There were a couple of times, when I saw a look in your eyes and then there one or two things which you said. To be honest, I did wonder' she answered forthrightly.

The Abbot laughed and replied:

'Well,' he said 'if we're being honest, I thought at one point that it was Brother Joseph. He'd been acting strangely and, oh I don't know, sort of doing things in a distracted sort of way which were totally out of character for him. When we eventually got back to normal, I challenged him about his behaviour. It turns out that his sister had been very poorly and he'd been worried about her. But I'm pleased to say the lady has turned the corner and is now back on the road to a full recovery. It just goes to show you...you think you know people...but do we ever truly know them?'

'You have a point, Father'

By that time, they'd arrived at the door of the Abbot's office. Dom Ambrose opened the door to find the Cardinal already sitting, waiting, in his stockinged feet, chatting to Sextus, whom Boo had failed to notice, had gone walkabouts.

'Ah ha, Miss Lavender. I've been looking forward to this' the Cardinal declared.

'Please, Father, call me Boo.' she answered.

'Then you must call me Xavier. It's so nice to be able to let one's hair down occasionally, don't you think?'

'Absolutely...Xavier' Boo felt a little strange using the Cardinal's first name '...but I warn you, Sextus and I take no prisoners' she laughed.

'That's fine by me, my dear. Let battle commence!' the less than formal prelate challenged.

For about three blissful hours, the four companions fought tooth and nail trying to gain the upper hand. In the end, the final rubber was to be the decider; up until then the teams had won three rubbers each, neither giving an inch away to the other.

It came down to the final hand and it was the Cardinal's turn to deal, Boo cut the cards.

Sextus pre-empted with Three Hearts, Dom Ambrose passed. With the scores 70 to the Cardinal and the Abbot and Boo and Sextus on 60, Boo passed. She had more than enough to put Sextus to Four Hearts but there was no need...they'd romp home...which they duly did.

With final farewells made, the Cardinal demanded a replay...and soon.

'When you're ready, Xavier, we're just a phone call away' Boo offered and the two friends drove off with the inhabitants of the Abbey giving them a cheery send off.

'I can't begin to tell you how I feel, Sextus' Boo began snuggling into her seat for the journey.

'Oh I think I can imagine'

'For once, Sextus I don't think anyone can. This has been the most amazing day of my life'

The two friends drove off to the sound of wild cheering into the beautiful Gloucestershire countryside, both of them looking forward to a long and peaceful summer.